RAGING SOUL

RAGING SOUL

A decade of murder, a lifetime of redemption

Amy Mayhew

ARCHWAY PUBLISHING

Archway Publishing books may be ordered through booksellers or by contacting:

Archway Publishing
1663 Liberty Drive
Bloomington, IN 47403
www.archwaypublishing.com
1 (888) 242-5904

Cover designed by Jeremiah Brown, jbCreative, LLC,
Warren, MI, jbcr8tv@gmail.com

ISBN: 978-1-4808-5102-3 (sc)
ISBN: 978-1-4808-5103-0 (hc)
ISBN: 978-1-4808-5101-6 (e)

Library of Congress Control Number: 2017912312

Print information available on the last page.

Archway Publishing rev. date: 8/25/2017

Acknowledgement

Having had so many family members, friends and colleagues support me throughout the long process of writing this book, it's impossible to personally acknowledge everyone. However, if I had to pick the top two people who have been instrumental in helping me to pursue my dream, it would be my husband, Tony, and my dear friend, Carrie Woodzell. Thank you both for never letting me give up, and for helping with the endless brainstorm sessions, the enduring rewrites, and the mind-bending plot adjustments. I simply could not have done it without either of you, and I love you both with all of my heart.

1

On October 4, 1966, Jasper Deerfield stood in the warm kitchen of his farmhouse, filling a Thermos of coffee to take back into the field.

"Can I make you an afternoon snack?" Meryl asked, running her hand across her husband's broad back.

"Nah, coffee's good," Jasper said. Looking down into the face of his mischievous six-year-old, he mussed her mousey brown hair with his rugged hand.

"Didn't you tell your mama 'bout our deal, Shawnie? You know— about how you promised to make my favorite cookies in return for a ride on the tractor later?"

"Can we, Mom?" Shawn whined.

"Yeah, we can probably do that. If we hurry, maybe we can have them in time for when your sister gets home from school."

Jasper leaned forward to kiss his wife's cheek. "You know where to find me. If the rain holds off, I should be able to finish harvesting the corn by nightfall." Aiming a wink at Shawn, he added, "Don't give your ma any trouble."

Shawn stood on a kitchen chair and watched her dad begin walking to the barn before snatching the canister of sugar off the counter top. "C'mon Ma, let's make sugar cookies."

Practically all of Jasper's life had been spent working his family's farmstead. As he made the short walk to the barn, his mind flooded with fond memories of time spent with his father, and many of life's ups and downs he and his wife had managed to tackle over the years.

It hadn't been easy, especially when it came to starting a family. Having experienced the heartbreak of a stillborn son in 1949, the couple continued to battle fertility problems until Beverly was born in May of 1954. At seven pounds three ounces, the doctors called her a miracle, and she filled the Deerfields' lives with joy.

When Bev turned six, Meryl became unexpectedly pregnant again. At the age of thirty-four, and after a troubled pregnancy, she remarkably delivered another perfect baby girl—Shawn.

Unlike Bev's placid debut, Shawn Evelyn Deerfield came into the world kicking and screaming. A colicky baby, Shawn was a complete opposite of Bev, challenging Meryl and Jasper's parenting in just about every way.

Jasper thought about his beloved wife and daughters as he climbed up on his old tractor and started the engine. The work wasn't easy, but for Jasper, his family and the love they shared made it all worthwhile.

By the time Bev Deerfield walked through the front door of the old family farmhouse a couple of hours later, the house was flooded with the aroma of fresh-baked cookies.

Throwing her school books down on the sofa, Bev squirmed out of her jacket and hung it on the coat rack.

"What's going on in here?" Bev came up behind her little sister and hugged her.

"We're making cookies for Dad," Shawn said as she ran her small hands through some flour on the countertop.

"It looks like you're making more of a mess." Bev smiled at her mom, who stood rinsing a pan in the sink.

"How was your day, hon?"

"It was OK. I have a lot of homework tonight—I have a math test tomorrow."

As a seventh grader at Lakeview Middle School, Bev did well in her classes, and was a popular student both among her peers and her teachers. Meryl and Jasper took great pride in her accomplishments, and marveled at her maturity.

Bev helped herself to a glass of milk before plopping down at the kitchen table in front of a plate of warm cookies.

"Mmm, my favorite." Bev took a big bite into a cookie, and savored the warm, sugary goodness.

"Hey! Those cookies are for Dad!" Shawn rushed toward the table and reached for the plate.

"There are plenty for everyone," Meryl said, turning toward her daughters. "Shawn Evelyn Deerfield, what have I told you about washing your hands before eating?"

Shawn scampered out of the kitchen to wash her hands as Bev took a sip of cold milk.

"Why are you baking cookies so late? Supper is at five, isn't it?" Bev asked.

"Your dad thinks he'll be done harvesting the corn by nightfall, so we're probably going to eat a little later tonight. He really wants to get this done before it rains."

"It's so cold out, it might just snow." Bev looked out the window into the field.

"Let's hope not. I don't think I'm quite ready for winter just yet," Meryl said.

"Your dad was out there all morning and finished the front forty around noon. He started the back field around one o'clock. He really should be done by four or four thirty."

Bev stood up to get a better look out the window. "Then why's his tractor stalled out there?" Bev pointed to the field far behind the barn. "Shouldn't he be further along than that? If he's been working since then, we shouldn't even be able to see him."

Meryl came to the window and looked out. "Hmm. I don't know, unless he's having trouble with the tractor engine again. Why don't you run out there and see if he needs any tools?"

Bev shoved the last bit of cookie into her mouth before getting up from the table. "I'll grab the small toolbox out of the barn on my way out—he probably needs it."

After putting on her jacket, Bev exited through the back door of the kitchen and ran to the barn. With no toolbox in sight there, she shrugged and figured her dad was probably already working on the problem. Bev put her hands in her coat pockets. The vividly colored trees stood out against a gray October sky as she made her way down the path to the cornfield.

By the time she reached the edge of the field, Bev knew something wasn't right. Fifty yards into the cornstalks, she could hear the tractor's engine running, yet the tractor wasn't moving.

Picking up the pace, Bev trotted down the row toward the tractor. "Daddy? Dad?"

As she approached the tractor, Bev saw what appeared to be her father's left leg stretched out behind the corn picker.

"Daddy, Daddy!" she yelled frantically as she began running and stumbling toward the machinery.

Barely able to raise his head and weak from loss of blood, Jasper heard the cries of his daughter and turned to look.

"Oh, my God—Daddy! Daddy, what happened? Oh, my God!"

Jasper's blood-spattered face was drained of all color, and his respiration was shallow.

"Turn off the tractor," he mouthed to his daughter.

Bev scrambled up onto the old Allis Chalmers and turned the

key with trembling hands. Jumping off the seat, she knelt at her father's side.

Bev could see bare bone where Jasper's arm had become caught in the corn picker. Pulled in up to his shoulder, sheer determination and strength were all that stood between Jasper's torso and the blades of the picker.

"What do you want me to do?" Bev cried. Tears streamed down her cheeks as she stared at his blood-soaked jacket.

"Nothing to do," Jasper whispered. "I'm dying…too much blood."

"No, no! You can't give up!" Bev cried. "I'll go get help. Just hang on!" She began to turn away.

"Beverly Jane—listen to your father," Jasper said, summoning all the energy he had. "Come here. I need to talk to you."

Bev continued crying and held her father's left hand.

"I was hurrying to finish before the rain—my fault—my fault," he said, wincing in pain. "Now it's too late."

Jasper's head slumped forward.

"Daddy—Daddy, please don't die …let me get some help," Bev pleaded. "I love you, Daddy. You can't die! We need you."

Jasper looked into his daughter's beautiful eyes. "I need you to keep a secret for me—somebody needs to know before I die."

While Bev was only twelve years old, she had a maturity about her that made everyone forget she was still a child.

"Can you do that for me?" he asked.

Bev nodded, choking back the tears.

"You have an older brother living somewhere in the Upper Peninsula."

Bev's eyes widened as she wiped her nose.

"I ain't proud of it," Jasper said, tears blurring the blood spatters on his face. "Happened on a hunting trip. Your ma doesn't know. I never could tell her—woulda broke her heart since we had so much trouble having you and Shawnie." His breath was fading.

"I—I just wanted someone to know before I leave this Earth," Jasper said, as he slumped forward. "Don't tell your mama. Promise me."

Clenching his blood-spattered left hand, Bev promised. "I won't, Daddy. It's our blood secret."

Jasper managed one final smile before closing his eyes and mouthing the words "I love you."

"Daddy? Daddy?" Bev screamed.

Dropping his lifeless hand, Bev turned and ran for help.

2

Within a few hours, word of Jasper's farming accident had spread throughout the small farming community. Friends and relatives descended on the Deerfield's home, providing support to Meryl and her two girls, and depositing casseroles, sandwiches and other comfort foods in the small country kitchen.

"Now you be sure to let me know if you need something tonight," Pastor Brown said to Meryl as he got up from the living room sofa. "I'm only a phone call away."

Fumbling with the buttons on his woolen jacket, Pastor Brown struggled to find the right words.

"Bev, I know it's a bitter pill to swallow," he said patting her on the shoulder. "You did all you could—there wasn't anything anyone could have done—he just lost too much blood."

Still in shock, Meryl stared at her daughters. How would she raise them alone? What was she going to do about the farm? How could she possibly make ends meet without Jasper?

"I'll be by around ten o'clock tomorrow to pick you up," Pastor Brown said, turning toward the door. "Oscar Logan is expecting us then. I'll help you make the funeral arrangements."

"Where's Daddy?" Shawn whimpered. "Why isn't Daddy here?"

Meryl leaned down and strained to pick up her young daughter. "I just … can't believe …" she said, choking back a sob.

"I know. I know. The Lord works in mysterious ways. We just have to trust that He knows what He's doing."

Meryl tried to nod.

"Beverly, remember what I told you," he said, before stepping outside into the cold fall air. "I mean it—it wasn't your fault."

When the door closed behind the pastor, Shawn's tiny arms wrapped around her mother's neck and she nuzzled her head into the nook of Meryl's shoulder.

Several of Meryl's friends from church stood in the living room, overwhelmed with the tragic circumstances, and struggling with what they could do to help.

"I'll help with the kids if you just want to go to bed," Sue Daniels said. Sue and her husband George were close friends of the Deerfields, both through farming and church.

"It's been a long day, and tomorrow isn't going to be any easier." Sue leaned forward and hugged Meryl and Shawn. "Let me take Shawn."

"No, that's OK—Shawn and I are going to sleep in the guest room down here tonight, Meryl said.

"Are you alright? Meryl asked, turning her attention to Bev. "I'm not sure there's room for three in the guest room, but we can try."

Bev wiped her face with her sleeve. "No. I'll be OK in my room," she said.

"Sweetie …there was nothing any of us could do," Meryl said. "Try to get some rest. We'll talk more in the morning."

"I'm just so sorry, Mom," Beverly wrapped her arms around her mother's waist. "We'll get through this, right?"

Emotion gripped Meryl's throat, making it impossible for her to respond. Sympathetically, she gazed into her eldest daughter's eyes and nodded.

An awkward silence hung in the air as the group listened to Bev climb the small wooden staircase to her bedroom alone.

"We'll just clean things up around here and lock up when we're done," Sue said. "You two try to get some sleep tonight—George and I are so sorry for your loss."

From her bedroom, Bev could still hear Shawn's faint whines from below as she flopped down onto her bed. Staring up at the ceiling, images of her father's lifeless gaze as emergency workers attempted to pull him from the machinery still played out in her head.

"Stop thinking about it," she said aloud, as she sat up on her bedside. Looking at her hands, Bev saw a smudge of her father's dried blood and remembered her promise. Bev stood up from her bed, opened the door to her closet, and pulled a small throw rug from the floor. Beneath the rug, Bev quietly removed a flooring slat that concealed the diaries she'd been keeping over the last two years.

Removing the 1966 volume from her hidey-hole, she sat back down on her bed, grabbed a pen off her nightstand, and flipped to the first available page.

> *Tuesday, October 4, 1966*
> *Dear Diary:*
>> *My dad died today and it's all my fault. Why didn't I run for help? Now Daddy is gone forever. I'm so scared of what our family will do. Just before he died, my dad told me that I have a brother in the Upper Peninsula. I still don't understand what he meant. How can this be? He made me promise not to tell Mom and I won't—EVER. I told him it's our secret, and it ALLWAYS will be.*

Bev drew the shape of a heart at the bottom of the page, and scrawled "Daddy" in the middle of it. Moistening a remaining blood spatter on her hand with saliva, she left a brownish-red smudge on top of the heart before closing the diary and returning it to its hiding place. Covering the floorboard with the rug, she closed the closet door and got ready for bed.

3

John Hanson read the names carved in the knotty pine paneling as he relieved himself in the trough urinal. The stench of urine, cigarette smoke, and beer permeated the room. Zipping his fly, he turned to wash his hands at a grimy, rust-stained sink. A clouded mirror hung on the wall directly in front of him. John stared at his face, tanned and several days past a shave. With no paper towels to be found, he wiped his hands on his jeans and limped back to his seat at the bar.

The brilliant sunshine of a late August day went virtually unnoticed in the dark confines of the rural bar. Sunlight streamed in through small windows, casting smoky beams of light across the room.

A half glass of warm beer sat in front of John as he removed a cigarette from a crushed Marlboro pack in his shirt pocket.

"You want another one?" asked the bartender.

"Yeah, why not," responded John as he lit the cigarette.

The bartender lumbered away and returned with a Pabst Blue Ribbon draft. "This one's cold. You wanna run a tab?"

"Yeah, whatever," John said, exhaling smoke as he answered.

Having bought the bar in 1952, Chuck Preston had spent the last two decades getting to know his customers. Not recognizing John, Chuck found himself wondering where he came from. Still, something about him told Chuck to mind his own business. If John wanted to chat, Chuck would certainly listen.

The creak and slamming of the rear screen door rose above the country music twanging from the jukebox. A waitress appeared around the corner, looking hurried and out of breath.

"It's about damn time, Des," the bartender barked at the young brunette.

"I ain't on the clock 'til seven, Chuck—don't start that shit already," she rebutted as she stashed her bag behind the bar. John acted as though he wasn't listening.

"Kate, when does Bev come in?" Chuck shouted to the bleached blonde in the back, tending the grill.

"Jesus God, Chuck. Can't you keep track of nothin'?" Kate said, poking her head through the service window. "She comes in any minute now."

A couple of locals were perched at the bar chatting. "Hey ya, Kate. Chuck's got you makin' burgers again, eh?" Des winked and flashed a devilish smile.

"Shit, Chuck's got me doin' everything as usual," Kate said in a huff. Can you take their order over there?" Kate asked, gesturing to a booth across the room.

"Sure thing." Des finished tying her apron around her waist, grabbed her order pad, and headed for the booth.

"Hi Des," came another voice around the corner. Blonde and well rounded, John noticed.

"Glad to see you show up tonight, Bev," Chuck said, looking up from washing beer mugs.

"Was there ever any question?" she asked as she breezed by Chuck, casually touching his shoulder, and smiling at John.

"You gotta lighten up, Chuck," Bev said as she tied an apron around her waist, covering the front of her cut-offs. Taking a tube of lip gloss from the pocket of her shorts, Bev transformed her lips from pink to rusty red as John watched.

"When do you go back to school?" Chuck asked.

"Um…after Labor Day," Bev said, stashing the lip gloss in her apron pocket. "I told Kate that next Friday, the first, that's my last day workin' here."

"Are you shittin' me?" Chuck hand-dried a mug as strings of his comb-over fell over his brow. "Labor Day weekend is always crazy in here. Honey, we're gonna need you to work."

"I can't, Chuck. I have stuff to wrap up on the farm for my mom that weekend, and I told my little sister we'd hang out before I go to East Lansing."

"Don't worry 'bout it, hon," came Kate's smoky voice through the service window. "Chuck, lay off. I told you I'd handle it. She needs to be with her family then." Kate smiled at Bev. "Oh, and by the way, happy eighteenth birthday."

"Thanks, Kate. It isn't until tomorrow, but thanks just the same."

"Can I get you another one of these?" Bev asked John as she cleared away his two empty mugs.

"Sure," John said.

"Draw me another Pabst, Chuck. This handsome fellow is about to die of thirst," she said, delivering a beautiful smile in John's direction. "You gotta be pretty direct with Chuck here," she told John as she placed the cold beer in front of him. John fidgeted with a wet cocktail napkin and looked away.

Bev lingered for a moment before going to the opposite end of the bar to wrap silverware, obviously smitten with the handsome stranger.

"So you're eighteen tomorrow, huh?" Chuck asked as he wiped down the bar.

"That's what they tell me," Bev said.

"Well, remind me later, and Kate and I'll buy you your first legal drink—how'd that be?"

Bev nodded and continued to wrap silverware as she kept an eye on John.

"He's a little old for ya, don't you think?" Des whispered in Bev's ear. "I know you like older men, but that guy has to be thirty at least."

"Yeah, but isn't he cute?" Bev gushed. Des laughed as she placed an order on the service window. "Order in, Kate."

The fact was, John was thirty-two. Standing six feet tall, he had an athletic build, and looked younger than his years. Had it not been for John's fine features, his dark wavy hair and deeply tanned skin would make people wonder if he was an Indian.

The tavern began to fill with locals as the evening closed in on eight o'clock. John continued to sit at the bar and drink, leaving his spot only when nature called.

"The band starts at nine," Bev said to John as she automatically brought him another beer. "That's why it's gettin' so busy."

John crushed out another cigarette in an ashtray. "Hon, after this beer, can I get a shot of JD?"

"'Course you can," said Bev, flipping her blonde hair back over her shoulder.

Both waitresses raced from table to table, constantly delivering food and drinks, taking orders, and cashing people out. Whatever Chuck paid them probably wasn't enough.

"Where the hell is Big Lou?" Chuck asked Kate, who had come out of the small kitchen to get some air and have a cigarette break. "He shoulda' been here an hour ago."

"Beats the hell outta me," Kate said, exhaling smoke and putting an ice-cold mug of beer to her lips. "I told ya you shoulda' fired him long ago. He's way too unreliable, and on a Friday like tonight, we really need him." She took another long drag on her cigarette.

"Well, if he don't show up, we'll just have to make do for tonight," Chuck said shaking his head. "I'll fire the fucker tomorrow."

The noise level of the tavern was rising by the moment. The band had arrived and was doing sound checks from the stage at the opposite end of the tavern. Booths and dark-wooded tables surrounded the small dance floor.

By nine-fifteen, the amateur country band was well into their first set. The tavern hadn't completely filled, but people continued to stream in. Normally, Big Lou the bouncer checked IDs, but he had failed to show up for work. That was Big Lou's way. If something better came up, he'd ditch work without so much as a phone call.

John had been drinking steadily all night and was already on his third shot of JD. Returning from the bathroom to his barstool, he found another beer waiting for him. "I didn't order this," he said, lighting a cigarette.

"I know it," Bev said. "You just looked like you could use one. It's on me," she flirted. "Hey, what did you do to your leg? I noticed you limping."

John took a long swig of the beer and glanced at Bev, then away. "It's a long story," he said, flicking an ash into the ashtray.

"Well, I got all night," she said, leaning forward, showing a little cleavage.

John shifted in his seat. It was usually he who made the moves. "Really—it's none of your concern." John looked away, in the direction of the band.

"Well sorry," Bev said, more than likely thinking John was just another drunken asshole.

"Bev! Order up," Kate shouted from the kitchen. Bev turned away and hurried down to the window for her order.

John watched Bev scurry away. She looked pretty good from

behind. He knew he'd pissed her off, but it wasn't up to her to call the shots. After all, girls that came onto men were nothing more than whores. Still, he found himself attracted to her. Maybe it was just the drinks.

As the band wound up their second set, John looked at his watch. It was nearly ten-thirty. He'd been drinking all night, but didn't feel drunk.

"Hey, Chuck, you got any cigs for sale? I'm just about out," John said, reaching for his wallet. Chuck pointed past the end of the bar. "There's a cigarette machine out there by the back door. It takes quarters."

John stood up and tossed a dollar onto the bar. "Can ya change that for me?" Chuck snatched up the money, rang the cash register, and returned with a handful of quarters.

"There ya go," he said, slamming the coins down on the bar. John grabbed the change and limped down past the other barflies, around the corner to the cigarette machine.

"Stop it! You're hurting me!"

John looked down the hallway and saw an overweight drunk pinning Bev up against the paneled wall. His pudgy hands were making their way all over Bev's white tank top.

"You heard the lady, asshole," John said, grabbing the drunk by his arm.

"Mind your own fuckin' business," the drunk slurred as he took a swing at John.

Within seconds, John had ducked the punch and delivered one of his own to the letch's left eye.

"You fucker," the drunk yelled as he wiped blood off his cheek. He lunged toward John. John threw two more punches to the midsection and sent one more crashing against the side of the drunk's head. Down he went with a loud thud.

Chuck rounded the corner carrying a baseball bat. "What the hell's goin' on?" he yelled.

"This drunk was hurting your waitress, here. I knocked some sense into the son of a bitch," John said, dragging the guy toward the screen door. "Think you can help me?" he said glaring at Chuck. "He weighs a ton."

Chuck dropped his bat, and the two of them dragged the drunken patron out the door and propped him up against the siding.

"Fuckin' lard-ass had his hands all over your waitress," John said as he tucked in his shirt.

"Can't you never learn?" Chuck asked the drunk. "This here's Kelly Chapman," Chuck explained. "He's had the hots for Bev ever since I can remember. And the drunker he gets, the hornier and meaner he gets."

The screen door opened and two rednecks stepped out. "Who the fuck did this to Kelly?" asked one of them. "I did," John said, getting in his face. "Your friend here was hurting one of the waitresses."

Looking at each other, both men backed away. There was a certain air about John. People knew when he was serious. "You better load up his sorry ass and get 'im outta here," Chuck said. "I don't wanna have to call the cops on you guys. You'll probably get a DUI, and I'm sure Bev would want to have a word with the cops about what happened here tonight."

The two men strained to help Kelly to his feet. "Sorry, man," one of them said to Chuck. "We don't want no trouble. We'll leave."

"Best you had," Chuck said as he turned to open the screen door. "Get the hell outta here, and when Kelly wakes up, you tell 'im he ain't ever welcome in here again."

Chuck turned to Beverly. "You OK?"

Bev's eyes were swollen from crying as Des patted her on the back.

"I told you about that damn bouncer," Kate said as she stood smoking in the hallway. "He's as useful as tits on a boar hog. Thank God this man was here," she said, gesturing to John.

"I …I don't know …what I would have …" Bev began crying again. "I don't know what I would have done if you hadn't been there," she said, trying to stop sobbing.

John handed her his hankie. "It's over. He won't hurt you again," he said turning away.

"Thanks, buddy," Chuck said to John. "Forget about paying your tab tonight. Everything's on the house for ya." John said nothing and made his way to the cigarette machine.

"OK, everybody back to work," Chuck said as he trundled back behind the bar.

"Are you OK to stay on tonight?" Kate asked Bev.

"Yeah, I just need to freshen up, and I'll get back at it." Bev walked down the hallway to the women's restroom.

Bev touched up her eyeliner and lip gloss in the chipped bathroom mirror. "What happened to you?" asked a patron as she exited a stall.

"Some drunk was trying to play grab-ass with me."

"Around this place, that must happen a lot, huh?"

"Usually we have a bouncer, but he didn't show up tonight. Another guy who's been up at the bar all night saw what was happening and stepped in to help me."

"Not that looker at the end of the bar!" the woman slurred.

"Oh, did you notice him, too?" Bev said, slightly smiling.

"Who the hell hasn't, honey? Did you see his ass in them jeans? Lord have mercy!" They both laughed as they exited the small restroom.

The band was in full swing in their third set. It was nearly midnight. The crowd had thinned considerably, leaving the hardcore partiers behind to dance and drink the night away.

Bev pulled a cold mug of beer and delivered it to John. Placing it in front of him, she touched his hand and thanked him again.

John's face flushed. "Glad I was there," he responded as he pulled his hand away and reached for his lighter. "Assholes like that don't belong in public."

"Well, I was really scared, and I just appreciate you coming in and saving the day like you did. What's your name, anyway?" Bev asked.

"John. John Hanson," he replied, lighting a cigarette.

"Well, John Hanson, you'll always be a hero in my book. I'm Bev Deerfield."

As she turned to walk away, John spoke up. "I—I was wounded in 'Nam."

"What?" Bev said hesitating, and turning to look at John.

"My limp...I was wounded in 'Nam four years ago." John nervously flicked an ash into the ashtray, being careful to avoid eye contact with Bev.

"Oh God. I'm sorry," Bev said, placing her tray on the bar. "I can't imagine what it must have been like over there for you. I'm against the war. I think we need to get the hell out of there, but I still support our guys who are there ... and the ones who have come back, like you."

"I'm sorry I was such a jerk to you earlier," John said. "I'm just shy around girls, especially pretty ones like you—and Happy Birthday," he stammered.

Bev could feel herself blush and unconsciously began to twiddle a long lock of hair.

"After it calms down, would you join me for your first birthday drink?" John asked shyly.

"Yeah, I don't think Chuck would mind if I knock off a little early tonight. It's been a helluva night, and he owes both of us."

Another forty-five minutes passed before Bev finished for the night. Perched on the tall barstool next to John, Bev watched as Chuck brought her a mug of beer, and replaced John's half-drunk warm brew with a new one.

"Happy Birthday, hon," Chuck said, winking as he moved away. "Enjoy."

John nodded to Chuck and raised his mug in the air. "To a very Happy Birthday," he said, turning to Bev. "Thanks," Bev replied, clinking her mug with his.

"So, do you live around here?" Bev asked as she took a dainty sip.

"Nah, not really. I'm originally from the Upper Peninsula, up there near Newberry. You've probably never heard of it. It's a little town called Germfask," he said, lighting a new cigarette.

"Germfask…no, I guess I don't know where it is. We took a trip to the U.P. once when my dad was alive."

"Your dad's gone?"

Bev looked down into her mug. "Yeah, he died six years ago in a farming accident."

"That's rough. I never knew my old man. I guess he just blew through town, had a one-nighter with my ma, and never came back again." He took a drag on his cigarette. "Mama died when I was eighteen. Some kind of cancer, I guess."

"Brothers or sisters?" Bev asked.

"Yeah, I have a little sister. I pretty much raised her after my mom passed. She's all grown up now."

"The U.P. is a long way from Mulliken." Bev set her mug down on the bar.

"Yeah, it sure is. I just kinda find work wherever I go. Right now, I'm working up in Lansing. I've never been one for staying in one place too long."

"How the heck did you find this place?" Bev chuckled. "I mean, let's face it. There are probably better places in Lansing."

"Yeah, probably, but I like country bars. I like watching people." His lips curved into a slight smile.

"Well, I'm glad you came here tonight." Bev took another sip from her beer. Raising her eyebrows, she added, "I'm going to be leaving for school up in East Lansing."

"Is that right? At Michigan State?"

"Yep, I'm studying to be an elementary school teacher. I just love kids," she said twiddling a thread on her apron. "It will be my first year. It's been tough, what with my mom trying to make ends meet. But I got a scholarship, I work summers here, and plan on getting a job somewhere up there during the school year."

"You sound like a hard worker," John said.

"That she is," said Kate as she came by to place a shot of JD in front of the John. "Bev is one of the best waitresses we've ever had. I don't know what we'd do without her." Kate smiled at John. "You really saved our ass tonight, and we just want to thank you."

"Just glad I could help. Bev here's a beautiful girl," John said, gazing at Bev's fresh complexion. "Wouldn't want nothing bad to happen to her, now would we?"

Bev cheeks reddened by John's apparent interest.

"Well, you two enjoy. Thanks again." Kate turned back to the few remaining people at the bar.

"So you're living out here with your mom, but are headed to East Lansing pretty soon, huh?" John sipped on his JD.

"Yeah, I help out at the farm, and I spend time with my little sister. She's twelve and is a real handful for my mom."

"Yeah, I bet. What about your mama? Does she work the farm alone?"

"She hires help to come in and works up at Logan Funeral Home part time," she said, gesturing westward.

"Sounds like your mama's pretty busy," said John sympathetically.

"I'm telling you, there isn't anyone like my mom. She's so dedicated. When Daddy died, I got so scared. I really didn't think my mom would pull out of it. I mean, it was tough, She'd lie around in bed all day. I looked after my kid sister because I didn't know what else to do. The farm just went to hell that first six months or so. Finally, Mr. Logan from the funeral home stepped in and helped my mom pull things together."

John listened intently.

"He helped us all through the funeral, and even gave Mom a part-time job to help pay some of the bills."

"How'd your daddy die, again?"

"Farming accident—his arm got caught in a corn picker. It was awful."

"Must've been pretty hard, alright," John said taking a drag off his cigarette.

"It was." In a more upbeat tone, she added, "But things are better now. What about you and Vietnam?"

"There really ain't much to tell," John began. I signed on in '65 when I was twenty-eight years old. I wasn't doing shit with my life … always in trouble, so I decided it would be the noble thing to do to fight for my country." He took another hit off his cigarette.

"I wasn't married, didn't have kids, so I thought, what the hell, y'know?" he said, flicking an ash in the tray.

"I was a private in Company B, first battalion of the fifth marines. For three years, I did pretty good at not getting my ass shot off." A smile flickered. "But in '68, we'd spent a few days in the countryside out on some damn rice patty in the Quang Nam province. Our work was pretty much done there, and I guess we were—I don't know—we just put our guard down for a minute." He paused to toke his cigarette. "I was ridin' on top of a M111—an APC— that's what we called 'em anyway. It stands for armored personnel carrier."

Bev watched John's every move. She was entranced by his story.

"Those things were made out of pretty light metal, y'know? They needed to fly 'em all the way the hell over there, so they couldn't be real heavy," he said, scrubbing the butt of his cigarette in the ashtray and exhaling smoke toward the ceiling.

"Well, that day, like I said, I was ridin' along on top, keepin' a good lookout, or at least I thought, and outta nowhere came a missile. Just like that," he said snapping his fingers. Bev's eyes widened "Well, I guess I was the lucky one. That missile blew me clean off the APC. All I got was a big old chunk of aluminum in my ass, hip, and leg. So, that's why I walk funny," he said, trying to lighten the mood.

Bev reached for his hand. "But you lived."

"Yeah, I lived alright. But every single last one of my buddies died right then and there." He reached for his drink, not noticing his other hand in hers. "Every single one of them bastards burnt up like pieces of bacon in a frying pan."

Bev dabbed her eyes and moved closer to John. "I'm so sorry," she said.

"It ain't your fault, honey," John said as he edged away.

"No, I mean, I'm sorry you lost your buddies and had to go through that," she clarified.

"Well, there's just things that happen in this world that nobody can understand, I guess." John continued to inch away from Bev. "I mean, why the hell wasn't it me? You know? I ask myself that every fuckin' day—why them and not me?" he said, shaking his head.

"God had something else in mind for you, John," Bev said kindly.

"Oh, is *that* what it was? I just thought it was a big joke on me, you know?"

Bev sat back and stared at John.

"What's the matter?" John taunted. "Is this discussion getting too disturbing for you?"

"I better get going." Bev hopped off her stool. "Thanks for helping me out tonight."

"No, just wait a minute. This is why I hate talking about 'Nam. It gets me all riled," he said, running his big hand through his wavy hair. "I get a little carried away. Look, I'm sorry. Sit back down here." He patted her barstool. "I'm sorry—c'mon, I'll order us another round," he said, flashing a handsome smile for Bev.

"I don't need another drink, I'm still working on this beer," Bev said defiantly.

"Sweet pea, just sit down. Let's talk about happier things and we won't have a problem. OK?"

Bev cocked her head and considered a moment before taking her seat on the barstool. Once she was seated, John walked down to retrieve another cold mug of beer for himself.

"What time is it, anyway?" Bev asked as he returned. "Looks like it's about one-thirty," he said, taking his seat and placing the beer down in front of himself.

"You smell like a fresh-baked apple pie," he said, trying to make up for his temper. "Has anyone ever told you that?"

Bev blushed again. "It's probably just my cinnamon lip gloss." She sipped at her beer, looking around the virtually empty bar. "Chuck will be closing up in a few minutes."

"Let's finish these. Then I'll give you a ride home, if you're OK with that," John said in a gentlemanly fashion.

"Usually Chuck and Kate drop me off ...but I suppose they would like the night off for a change." Bev said.

"You got it." John lit up another cigarette. "So, you're working here for another week or so, then you're off to East Lansing to start college, is that right?"

"Yeah, that's right." Bev took a swig of beer. "My mom has some things she needs help with at the farm before I leave, and I told my little sister we'd spend some time together."

"Well, you're a good daughter and sister to do all that. Shit, when I was your age, my mom had just died, and I didn't do much for anybody. I just managed to get into plenty of trouble—that's about all," he said, exhaling slowly.

"Do you regret it now?"

"Yeah, I suppose I do." John shifted on his stool. "There are plenty of things I've done in this life that I regret, but I can't do nothin' about 'em now 'cept move on, I guess."

Bev smiled. "I suppose I've done my share of stupid things, too," Bev said as she picked up her mug.

"Stupid?" John looked blankly at Bev. "I didn't say I done anything stupid—I said I've done things I *regret*. Doesn't make 'em stupid," John said angrily.

"No, no, I didn't mean that," Bev backpedaled. "I mean, I've done things that I regret, too—you know?"

"Yeah, I guess," John said, chugging the last mug of beer. "So, are you ready?"

"Yeah, just let me tell Chuck that I'm leaving and won't need a ride home tonight."

Bev went to the kitchen area, where Kate was busy cleaning the grill. "I'm leaving, if that's OK with you and Chuck."

"Well, Chuck's off taking a dump and I'm workin' my ass off as usual—I don't think it will be a problem." Kate wiped a sweaty strand of hair from her eyes. "Don't you need a ride, though?"

"No, John's going to drop me off."

"You sure that's a good idea? I mean you just met him tonight, and he is a lot older than you."

"Yeah, I know, but the guy saved my ass this evening. John Hanson is a good guy and isn't anything to worry about, Besides, I'm just up the road, you know?"

Kate went back to cleaning. "Well, if you're sure, honey, that's fine. You're an adult now anyway, right?"

Bev beamed. "Yep, I'm legal!"

"Then I guess we'll see you tomorrow night?" Kate said gently.

"Yeah, absolutely," Bev said as she stashed her apron behind the bar. "And we'll have a bouncer here, right?"

"Yes we'll have a bouncer," Kate said from the kitchen. "If Chuck don't fire his ass tomorrow, I will." She popped her head through the service window. "And I'll have Chuck's son come in and bounce if we have to."

"Oh God, I don't know what's worse, Big Lou or Chucky Junior," Bev said smiling. They both laughed.

"See ya tomorrow, Kate," Bev called over her shoulder.

"OK, hon. Have a good one, and Happy Birthday!"

5

The wooden screen door slammed as John and Bev walked to his awaiting car.

"This must be yours, hey?" Bev gazed at John's pristine '68 Dodge Dart. "You sure keep it nice and clean," she said, sliding onto the front vinyl seat.

"Yeah, I like to keep my stuff in order." He slammed her door and walked to the driver's side. "I got it when I got out of the service."

Bev peered through the windshield at a clear sky and full moon. The temperature had cooled to a chilly sixty degrees or so, but the evening was one of the best Bev could remember in quite some time.

It was nearly two in the morning, and John had been drinking for just about nine hours straight. John opened the driver's side door and got in.

"Are you OK to drive?" Bev asked as he made his third attempt to fit the key into the ignition.

"Yes, I'm fine," John said sternly.

"OK, OK, just checkin'."

John started the car, then leaned in Bev's direction and opened the glove compartment, exposing a small flask.

Bev stared as John quickly unthreaded the top and took a swig, but shrank back and stayed quiet. Evidently, Bev's glare was well noticed.

"What? Now you're my mother?"

"You know what? Maybe this isn't a good idea after all." Bev began to unbuckle her seat belt.

John slammed the car into drive and stepped on the gas. The gravel under his tires pierced the silent air and filled it with a dusty cloud.

"John, c'mon. Slow down—*please!*"

John didn't say anything.

"So when you come out of the lot here, take a right. My mom's farm is just east of Mulliken off this road, M-43." She watched him take another swallow.

John turned right and quickly picked up speed along the highway. The glow of the dashboard lights reflected on the silver flask.

"We're only up here about three miles or so." Bev felt like she was talking to herself. "What's wrong, John?" she said, placing her hand on his forearm.

John glanced at her hand, returned his eyes to the road, and drank another swig of whiskey. "Nothin's wrong."

"OK—just up here past this barn—that's my house," she said, pointing off to the right. John didn't slow down. "Take a right here! Or you're gonna miss it!" John sped by.

"John, you need to turn around, you missed it!"

"I know I did, sis. I just thought it's a beautiful night for a drive, don't you think?" He looked over at Bev and winked.

"Yeah, I guess …but it's really late, John. If I'm not home by two-thirty, my mom will really be worried."

John's mood was doing the same thing it had at the bar, flip-flopping from highs to lows.

"OK, John …just for ten minutes, but then I gotta go home, OK?"

"OK, baby, sure. We'll just go down one of these dirt roads and find a good place for us to pull over and look at the stars," he said, glancing at her innocent face.

"Why don't we just go back to my house? We can sit on our porch and look at the moon, the stars, everything."

John turned north and traveled down a long, paved road, bordered by farmland.

"We're gonna be in the middle of fucking nowhere if you go down here, John!"

"Ain't that the idea?" he said, grabbing her crotch with his right hand. Bev squirmed and pushed his hand away.

"John! We just met tonight—I mean, c'mon," she said, almost pleading.

As they continued down the road, Bev saw nothing but farmland and woods. "There isn't anything back here, John. Let's just turn around and go back to my house," she begged.

"Honey, you've been askin' for it all night, and I'm gonna give it to ya." John returned to his flask.

"I haven't been asking for anything. You saved my ass tonight from that pig at the bar and I am thankful for that. But I don't want anything else from you!"

John continued to watch the road. "I just felt sorry for you," Bev blurted.

"Sorry for me?" John glowered at Bev.

"Well, you know what I mean …all that stuff about Vietnam and your limp…you know," Bev stammered.

"I'll show you 'limp,'" he said grabbing her hand and pressing it against himself.

Bev began to sob. "Don't do this, John …you're a better man than this."

The road dead-ended at desolate dirt road, and John turned left.

Just up on the right, John saw a clearing near an expansive wooded area, apparently, a parking area for hunters. He turned off his lights and pulled in. Bev scrambled to open the door.

The next thing Bev felt was John's huge hand around her neck and the weight of his body against hers in the front seat. "It doesn't have to be like this," John whispered into her ear as he used his other hand to unbuckle his pants.

Bev's muffled, wheezing sobs continued as his grip tightened on her windpipe. In a last-ditch effort, Bev jerked her right knee upward, striking John in the groin.

John grunted as he let go of Bev's neck and grabbed his crotch. Bev, hardly able to breathe, fumbled with the door latch, but managed to break free.

Falling out of the car onto the hardened earth, Bev heard John yell. "You bitch—you fuckin' bitch!"

John struggled to exit the vehicle while clutching his nuts. Quickly, he grabbed a tire iron from beneath the passenger seat.

Bev rolled away, managed to get to her feet, and slammed the car door on John's huge hand.

"Jeeeeesus Christ!" John roared as the door struck his hand. Blood dripped from his knuckles. "Now you'll pay!" John called into the darkness.

Bev ran into the woods, stumbling through the pucker brush and low-hanging branches, scratching her flawless face.

She tried to scream, but the crushing influence of John's hand had rendered her vocal cords useless. Gasping for breath, she wheezed loudly as she tried to gulp air.

The canopy of trees made it nearly impossible for moonlight to penetrate the woods. Bev's white tank top was easily spotted in the darkness. Her legs, face, and arms were deeply scratched, her knees bloodied from where she had crawled away from the car.

Bev could hear John's drunken voice from the clearing. "I'm comin' after ya, you hear me?" he shouted into the darkness. "I've crawled through worse places than this."

A deserted deer hunting ground blind lay some fifty yards ahead of Bev. Crying and nearly hyperventilating, she hurried to the crude structure. Bev crawled behind its branches, and curled into a fetal position.

As Bev lay in the dirt and leaves, images of her short life flooded through her mind. She imagined her baby sister Shawn, as she lay sleeping in her bassinette. Memories of her dad wiping sweat from his brow after plowing the back forty; her mother's gentle smile, Kate's smoky laugh—the images all swirled together into one single moment.

John staggered from the clearing under the trees. "You can run, but you can't hide—I was in 'Nam, remember?" he said, tramping through the leaf litter. "I used to chase after gooks through worse shit than this, and when I found them, I killed them just like I'm gonna kill you." He halted, listening for any sound.

"There you are—I see ya," he said, lurching forward. Bev scrambled from behind the blind and continued to run, branches and raspberry bushes scratching her entire body. John was within ten feet of her, but struggled to keep up with his bad leg.

Bev scurried through the woods and began thinking that she might actually be able to outrun him. Looking over her right shoulder, she never saw the branch that would then become her biggest mistake. A thick and rotting branch had tripped Bev up, sending her head-long into a thorny thicket of darkness.

"Oh my God," Bev gasped as she struggled to free herself. Her ankle was broken, while hordes of two-inch thorns pierced and tore her skin. "Please! Just leave me here! Leave me alone. I'll never tell anyone what happened," Bev pleaded aloud as she heard John's footsteps draw nearer. "Please—I'll do anything—just don't kill me," she sobbed.

"Well, well, well—didn't you get yourself into a big mess here?" John said tossing the tire iron to the ground, wading through the thorns, and grabbing Bev by the wrist.

"Let go of me, you son of a bitch," Bev screamed, her voice hoarse and scratchy. Bev thrashed in the thorns like a wounded deer making a last-ditch effort to get away.

"C'mon bitch," John said, yanking her from the thorn patch. Bev screeched in agony as she staggered to her feet, putting weight on her crumpled ankle.

John used his good hand to grab Bev's long hair from the back, yanking it backward and violently forcing her chin upward. Bev whimpered and fought to stay standing.

"Please—please," Bev pleaded in a hoarse whisper. "Just leave me here …I'll never tell them who did this to me." Blood and dirt-stained tears poured down her scratched cheeks.

"Who did this to you? Who did this to *you*? You done this to yourself, don't you remember?" he asked, shoving her forward, and causing her to fall to her knees.

John placed his boot between Bev's two shoulder blades and pushed her forward again, thrusting her face first into the leaves and debris. Using the same boot, he wedged his toe under her shoulder, and rolled her over onto her back.

"Now I'm gonna give you what I promised I'd give ya."

John stood over her, unbuckling his pants. Without thinking, Bev thrust her unbroken leg upward, once again delivering a crippling blow to John's balls.

"You little bitch!" John growled, falling to his knees and clenching his crotch. Bev clawed her way backward, throwing up leaves and dirt as she attempted to get away from the monster that moaned in front of her.

"Now you're dead," John hissed as he staggered forward on his knees. John propelled himself forward, gripping Bev's thin neck with both hands and staring down at Bev's bulging eyes. Gurgling sounds came from her throat as she struggled for air.

Thrashing in the leaves, Bev's unblinking eyes locked on John's. With his heavy weight bearing down on her, Bev felt John stifle all attempts she made to free herself. Soon she was gone, leaving Earth on the same day she had joined it eighteen years earlier.

John carried Bev's lifeless body further into the woods, up and down several challenging hills before stopping at the foot of a ravine near the marshy perimeter of a swamp. Nobody would ever find Bev now.

Having made a make-shift sling out of his shirt, John weighted it with heavy stones and tied it securely to Bev's thin body. Wading out as far as he could into the muck, he heaved her body into the water. She sank below the scummy surface in no time.

Not only was the swamp remote, but he knew the snapping turtles and other scavenging wildlife would make short work of any mess that might remain.

As the alcohol dissipated from John's system, his head and hand began throbbing threefold. Teeth chattering, he turned back and began walking toward the clearing.

Within 30 minutes, he was back at his car. The driver's side door remained ajar, and the dome light still flickered with the power of the battery.

John slid onto the front seat, picked up his awaiting flask from the floor, and took a long pull of whiskey. Turning the key in the ignition, he snapped on the lights, backed out onto the road, and began traveling south back to M-43.

It was almost four-thirty. The sun would be coming up soon, and people would be looking for Bev.

"They'll never find her," John told himself. Within a couple of minutes, he had already concocted a plan in his head. He'd get rid of his soiled clothing in a Lansing supermarket dumpster. The only incriminating evidence on the car was John's blood on the doorjamb, and even that didn't point to Bev. Nope. All he had to do is stay cool and calm if anyone managed to track him down.

John turned east onto M-43. The rural highway was deserted and dark, and the crystal-clear evening had given way to a blanket of clouds that had moved in.

"A little rain wouldn't be all bad," he thought as his determined face transformed to an evil sneer. He had gotten away with yet another murder. Saving Bev from that drunk at the bar couldn't have worked out any better. From the first punch he delivered on her behalf, he had won Bev's trust. Hell, he'd won the trust of the barkeeper and his girlfriend, too. It had all been so easy.

John soon realized that the half-pack of Marlboros in his shirt pocket was undoubtedly at the bottom of the swamp along with his victim. As he drove along M-43, he leaned over to the glove box and rummaged through its contents, hoping to produce a cigarette. "Goddamn it," John bellowed in frustration, flinging his registration and other documents to the floor of his car. "There has to be one fuckin' cigarette in here."

John glanced up from the glove box in time to see a deer streaking out in front of his car. Traveling seventy miles per hour, he swerved toward the shoulder of the highway, slamming on the brakes and throwing his vehicle out of control.

Hitting the doe head on, the hood of John's car flipped backward, sending his unbelted bulk slamming into the steering wheel and dashboard. The Dodge Dart careened off the road, rolling over two times before smashing into a huge oak tree that bordered a farmer's field.

John was unconscious when his car burst into flames. As it had been for Bev earlier that evening, in an instant it was all over for him, too.

With very few people traveling the road on an early Saturday morning, it was 6 o'clock before the first passerby saw the wreckage. By then, there wasn't much left of John—just a crispy body and the burned-out shell of a Dodge Dart.

The ringing phone on the nightstand startled Kate. Leaning over Chuck and squinting to read the clock radio, she picked up the phone.

"Hello?"

"Kate? Oh, thank God," Meryl Deerfield blurted. "Is Bev there with you? I woke up around four-fifteen and got up to make sure Bev had come home, and she isn't here. Is she there with you? I'm worried sick."

"Meryl? No, darlin', she ain't here," Kate said, crawling further over Chuck.

"What's wrong? What the hell's goin' on?" Chuck moaned. Kate gave Chuck a hard "shush" and snapped on the light.

"What time did you drop her off last night? She was at work, wasn't she?" Meryl said, her voice cracking.

"Settle down, hon, settle down. I'm sure there's a reasonable explanation," Kate said, trying to gather her thoughts.

"Actually, Chuck and me—we, uh ...we didn't drop her off last night," Kate said. "It's a long story, but this real nice gentleman ...John ...John something-or-other. Well, he and Bev really hit it off chattin',' and he volunteered to give her a ride home at the end of her shift," she said, pressing the heel of her hand to her forehead.

"Oh, God! How could you and Chuck let her ride home with a stranger?" Meryl began to cry.

"Calm down, hon—calm down. That John fellow, he seemed like an A-1 guy, nothing but a gentleman. They're probably still off talking somewhere."

"Do you think I should call the police?" Meryl said, beginning to take comfort in Kate's words.

"Well, now that's up to you, but I really think she'll be along. It's her eighteenth birthday. She's probably just out havin' a little fun before she has to leave for school, don't you think?"

"You're probably right," Meryl sighed. "I'll give it another hour or so—she'll probably want to sneak in before I get up."

"Yeah, I'm sure. It's just your normal college kid stuff, but call me the minute she gets home, though, will ya?" Kate asked.

Kate had raised two girls of her own, and ever since Jasper's death, Meryl appreciated her insights.

"I will. Thanks for talking me down, Kate. You're always right about stuff like this." The line went silent as Meryl hung up.

Leaning back over Chuck, Kate hung up the phone and hesitated in thought.

"What happened?" Chuck asked. "Bev didn't go home last night?"

"Looks like she and that John feller hit it off better than we thought," she said, snapping off the light and returning to her side of the bed.

"Yep—kids! When they hit that eighteenth birthday, they think they own the world," Chuck said, rolling back over on his side.

"Ain't that the truth?" Kate said closing her eyes.

Meryl's next phone call came at six-forty-five. This time Chuck answered.

"So what is her excuse this time," Chuck said, assuming it was Meryl reporting that Bev had come home.

"Oh Chuck—I'm so worried. She still isn't home." Meryl was sobbing.

"Hang on—hang on, Meryl. Let me put Kate on the phone." Kate was already out of bed and waiting for Chuck to transfer the phone to her.

"Meryl? Now what's going on? She ain't home yet?" Kate said in a concerned tone.

"No, she still isn't home," Meryl said. "This isn't like her. Something's wrong, I just know it," Meryl said, choking back another sob.

"OK. Let's hang up, and you call the sheriff," Kate said. "They can help. Give 'em my phone number, and Chuck and me can talk to them about everything that happened last night, and give 'em anything else they might need." Kate reached for her pack of cigarettes on the nightstand.

"It really just isn't like Bev. Usually she's so—so responsible," Meryl stammered. "I can't believe you'd let her ride home with a stranger!" she said again.

"Meryl, listen to me: Just call the sheriff. It don't matter how it happened. They might already know something, if they got into an accident or something."

The line was silent except for the slight whimpering Kate could hear at the other end.

"Honey, I'm sure she's fine; just call the sheriff. Do you want me to call him?" Kate asked sympathetically.

"No, no. I'm OK. I'm fine. I'll call him right now." Meryl said calmly. "I'm just letting my mind run away with things. I'll make the call and call you back when I know anything."

"We're getting up now, and we'll be over to your place in two shakes," Kate said.

"OK—I'll see you in a few minutes."

"C'mon in, it's open," Meryl shouted from the kitchen. Shawn sat wrapped in a blanket at the kitchen table. It was late summer, but nervous energy caused the twelve-year-old to shiver.

"What a rainy miserable morning, huh?" Chuck said, as he helped himself to a cup of coffee. Kate sat down at the table with Shawn while Meryl was on the telephone with the sheriff.

"No, she's usually home by two-thirty," Meryl said calmly into the phone. "She works up there in Mulliken at the Sportsman's Tavern."

Kate reached into her purse and produced a pack of Virginia Slims. "Will your mom mind if I light up?" she asked Shawn.

Meryl waved the "go ahead" sign to Kate. Shawn got up and retrieved an ashtray from the cupboard. Nobody used the ashtray anymore after her dad died.

Chuck joined them at the kitchen table and brought a hot cup of coffee to Kate. "You want anything, darlin'?" he asked Shawn.

"No, thanks," Shawn said, eyes brimming with tears.

Kate reached over and rubbed Shawn's arm. "Oh, honey, don't you worry. Your big sister will be coming through that door any minute. I'm sure there's a reasonable explanation."

"When? Where?" Meryl said, looking alarmed.

"What? What's going on, Meryl?" Chuck barked from the table.

"Jesus God, Chuck, can you just shut up for a minute? Can't you see she's busy?" Kate said flicking an ash into the awaiting tray.

"Just a minute, they're here, I'll ask," Meryl said, cupping the receiver with her left palm. "Do either of you know what kind of a vehicle that John fella drove?" Meryl said choking back tears. "Do you even know his last name?"

"Hmm, let's see," Chuck said, swiping at his comb-over. "It was John—oh, what was it? I heard Bev say it last night …John Hanson? Was that it, Kate?"

"I don't know. I was back busting my hump in the grill area most of the night."

"Yeah, it was Hanson, 'cause I remember wondering if he was related to any of the Hansons around here. Yeah, that's right, it was John Hanson for sure."

"OK," Meryl said. "But do you know what kind of car he drove?"

Kate shook her head. "I have no idea—Chuck did you see it when you and John tossed that loser out last night?"

"Shit, Kate, we was packed last night. There was tons of cars in the parking lot by then."

Meryl looked annoyed. "No. The only thing they can tell me is that his last name is Hanson—they think—but they have no clue on what he was driving."

After a pause, Meryl asked, "Right now?" Her long fingers nervously twiddled with her long graying hair.

The three stared at Meryl in complete silence.

"We'll be here, then. Is something wrong?" Meryl asked. "Oh, OK. Yeah, then we'll be here," she said. "Yeah, thanks. Bye."

Meryl hung up the phone and looked at the woeful trio in her kitchen. "That was strange," Meryl said, turning to pour another cup of coffee.

"What?" Kate asked, exhaling smoke.

"As soon as I mentioned the guy's last name, the sheriff—he just seemed flustered and said he was coming over," Meryl said. "I mean until I said the name, he said there wasn't anything he could do, because she's not been missing for over 24-hours," Meryl said. "Isn't that a little strange?"

Hands shaking, Meryl set a steaming cup of coffee down on the table and sat down. She reached and began to stroke Shawn's tangled hair. Shawn leaned toward her mother, nuzzling her rough hand.

"We'll find her, hon," Kate said reaching over and patting Shawn's blanketed knee.

The grandfather clock in the Deerfield's den chimed nine times as Meryl watched the sheriff's car make its way up her long muddy driveway. Oscar Logan had joined the group of worried family and friends as they awaited his visit.

Meryl had secured a job at Logan Funeral Home in Mulliken following the sudden death of her husband six years prior. As an undertaker and owner of the small funeral home, Oscar was a rock for Meryl.

"Just stay calm until we hear what he has to say," Oscar said quietly to Meryl. "Everything is going to be fine." Meryl nervously pushed her hair behind her ears as she opened the screen door.

"Morning," said the officer as he approached the front stoop. Rain dripped from his hat and ran down the broad shoulders of his raincoat.

"C'mon in outta the rain. Thanks for coming," Oscar said, helping Meryl open the door.

"I'm Sheriff Hoffmann, out of the Eaton County Sheriff's Department," he said, holding out his hand. "You must be Mrs. Deerfield?"

"Yes," she replied. Shaking Meryl's hand was like holding a warm dishtowel. Demure and shy, she was not one for a solid handshake.

"This is my boss …well, and my friend, Oscar Logan," she said as the two men shook hands. "And these are Bev's—my daughter's bosses down at the Sportsman's Tavern, Chuck and Kate."

Hoffmann shook hands with everyone and took a seat on the sofa.

"Can I get you a cup of coffee from the kitchen?" Kate asked.

"No, but thanks," Hoffmann said, situating himself squarely on the sofa cushion. "I'm a little later than I thought, but I wanted to talk to a few other people before I came over."

Meryl's eyes welled up. Oscar nudged closer to Meryl on the sofa.

"This morning around six o'clock, we got a call from a resident of M-43 out here," he said gesturing back toward the road. "Several miles east of here, there was a single-car fatality."

Meryl moaned and buried her face in Oscar's shirt. Shawn, who sat on the other side of Meryl, began crying and burrowed into her mother's shoulder.

"The whole wreck must have happened at least an hour earlier, maybe even longer than that," Hoffmann said. "It looks like the driver swerved to miss a deer or something and wound up rolling the car and coming to a stop in the middle of a tree."

"Do you know who it was?" Kate asked from the opposite end of the room. "Do you know the sex of the victim?"

"Yeah. The victim got pretty burned up in the wreck, but the coroner was able to determine that it was a male, a tall male. But we still don't know who he was. Looks like he was driving some sort of Dodge, but even that isn't for certain yet, either," he said, looking directly at Kate. "The vehicle is really toasted."

"But he was the only person in the vehicle?" asked Oscar. Meryl had stopped crying and was hanging on the officer's every word.

"Yep, just him," Hoffmann said. "If this was the guy who gave Bev a ride home, she wasn't with him at the time of the accident."

"But Bev and John left around two a.m. anyway," Kate said. "It probably wasn't him."

"Maybe, maybe not," the sheriff said, pulling a small notebook and pen from his shirt pocket. "Now, you said the man that Bev left with was named—ah, let's see here—yeah, John Hanson?"

"That's right," Chuck chimed in. "A tall guy. Probably every bit of six foot or so."

"Yeah, and he was older," Kate said, glancing at Meryl. "He's probably in his thirties," she confessed.

Meryl's eyes widened. Oscar patted her hand.

"Has he ever been in your place up there before?" Hoffmann asked.

"Nope, and I know everybody who comes in there," Chuck said. "I overheard him tellin' Bev that he was working on a temporary basis somewhere up there in Lansing."

"Any idea what kind of business this guy was into?" Hoffmann asked.

"Nope, I didn't catch that," Chuck said, shaking his head. "We was really busy last night."

"Well, we can't even file a missing person report on Bev until she's been missing for twenty-four hours or so." Hoffmann flipped his notebook shut.

Tears slipped down Meryl's cheek.

"Now, I know it's hard, but try not to worry," Hoffmann added. "She's, what, 19 or 20?"

"She's eighteen today," Meryl said, suppressing a sob.

"Well, there you go. I bet she just got caught up in the celebration, and right now, she's probably trying to come up with a real good excuse." Hoffmann stood up.

"Do you have any phone numbers of her friends?" Kate asked Meryl. "Maybe we could give 'em a call."

Meryl turned to Shawn. "Do you know about that, Shawn? Does your sister have an address book with her friends' numbers in it?

"She does, but I think she keeps it in her purse," Shawn said. "I don't know though. It might be up in her room."

"We'll look around and start calling friends she knows around here," Kate said standing up from the sofa.

"That's a good idea," Hoffmann said. "I have two daughters myself, and I swear they're the reason I have all this gray hair. Here's my card. If she isn't home by this evening—say around seven or so—call this number and tell my deputy. I'll make sure he's brought up to speed on what's going on, and I'll tell him to contact me if you call him," he said. "I want to handle this whole thing myself if need be."

"Thank you, Sheriff," Oscar said, rising and holding out his hand.

"Yes, thank you, and I hope I won't be needing this number," Meryl said as her shaking hand took his card.

Hoffmann nodded and let himself out the front door.

Expressionless, Shawn went upstairs to her bedroom.

"We'll just hang tight with you this morning until Bev gets back," Kate said to Meryl and Oscar.

"Yeah. I want to hear the excuse that youngster comes up with," Chuck said, trying to lighten the mood.

10

It was nearly three in the afternoon, and moods were very somber around the old farm house. Rain continued to fall, Bev had been missing over twelve hours, and Meryl was ramping up into a mood reminiscent of the day her husband died.

"Her address book isn't up there," Shawn said, coming into the kitchen.

Kate busied herself in the kitchen, reorganizing cupboards and straightening up the junk drawer. Chuck sat at the table tapping his fingers.

Kate put down her dishrag. "Did you look everywhere you can think of, hon?"

"Yeah, me and Ma both. Bev must have put it in her purse 'cause there isn't anything up there."

"What did your mom find out from Sandy?" Sandy was a high school friend of Bev's.

"Nothin'," Shawn said, helping herself to a soda from the fridge. "Turns out Sandy is up north visiting her grandma. She called everybody we could think of that she might possibly meet up with, but nobody has seen her," she said looking at Bev's senior picture taped to the fridge.

"Don't worry, hon. We'll figure this out," Chuck said from the table.

Looking dejected, Shawn turned toward the living room. "I

better get back upstairs and try to help Ma think of more people to call."

"You bet, sweetie. We'll just be down here," Kate said.

"Do you think we should just shut the place down for the night?" Chuck asked Kate in a hushed tone.

Kate turned to look at him. "It's Saturday, and we'll be swamped tonight."

"'Specially if Bev don't show." Chuck wasn't known for his tactfulness.

"Jesus God, Chuck," was all Kate could respond.

"What?" Chuck said raising his eyebrows and shrugging his shoulders.

Oscar entered the kitchen with an empty coffee mug. "You two should go. You need to tend to your business. Really, just go. We'll be fine."

Oscar explained that he had the bases covered at the funeral home and would be staying with Meryl as long as necessary. "I'll just make a bed on the couch and stay here," he said.

"What if she don't show?" Chuck asked. Kate glared at him again.

"If she doesn't come home by seven, we'll do what Sheriff Hoffmann said: We'll call the number he gave us."

It was easy to see that Oscar, always calm and level-headed, had been in the funeral business a long time. Others couldn't help but relax when he was around.

Kate turned her back and continued wiping down the counter tops. "I just don't know what to think, you know?"

"Why, what?" Oscar walked over to the counter. "Is there something else we should know?"

"Well, I'm not sure," she said, voice cracking. "I can't decide what to think. It might be all my fault. I never should've let her leave with that guy."

"Hey!" Chuck said, as though a light bulb had just illuminated over his head. "Remember that fat loser we kicked outta there last night? You know—that Kelly feller who's always had a boner for Bev?"

"Yeah, 'course I do," she said, dabbing her eyes.

Kate stared at Chuck and dismissed his idea. "No, couldn't've been him."

"No, wait—what happened? Tell me," Oscar urged.

Chuck described last night's commotion to Oscar. "So you think this guy might've waited until that Hanson guy dropped Bev off in the driveway?" he asked.

"Maybe …who knows," Chuck said.

The more Kate thought about it, the more she began to embrace Chuck's theory. "Kelly Chapman knows where Bev lives," Kate said to both men. "He's always had a thing for her, and the more she turns him down …"

"The more pissed off he gets," Chuck said finishing her sentence.

"I think we should contact the sheriff with this information," Oscar said. "If there's a chance, we'd never forgive ourselves if it turns out that this Chapman fellow had anything to do with it."

11

It was nearly five that afternoon before the Eaton County sheriff's car pulled into the Deerfield driveway. Meryl and Oscar were surprised to see Sherriff Hoffmann and another officer climb out of squad car. They went to the door to greet the two men.

"Hello again. This weather is fit for ducks, isn't it?" Hoffmann wiped his big boots on a small doormat. "Still hasn't called or anything, huh?"

Oscar answered for Meryl. "No, I'm afraid not," he said. "We're getting pretty antsy about it all, as you can imagine."

"Yes, I can certainly understand that. This is Deputy Ralph Petty," he said, gesturing his tall, thin companion. "I brought him along just in case we have to go find somebody," he said, smiling.

Meryl invited them inside. "Both of you, c'mon in and have a seat." Both men moved toward the sofa, as the others found seats around the room.

"Officer Petty here says one of you called, and that Chuck and Kate had remembered something important."

"Well, maybe, maybe not," Chuck said settling into the recliner across the room. "Last night, this regular we got at the bar—Kelly somethin' or other … what the hell is his last name, Kate?" he asked, holding his hand up to his forehead.

"Chapman," she answered. "He used to work up there at Carl's

Drive In flippin' burgers 'til Carl caught him helpin' himself to one of the waitress's tits."

"That's right, it was Chapman," Chuck said. "I think he lives out toward Lake Odessa somewhere. He ain't from Sunfield or Mulliken."

Petty recorded the name in his notepad.

"And you say he comes in a lot?"

"Oh yeah. Probably at least three nights out of the week, wouldn't you say, Kate?"

"Yeah, maybe even more," Kate confirmed. "Chucky Junior might know more than we do, don'tcha think, Chuck?"

"Who's Chucky?" Hoffmann asked.

"He's my son that lives down by Mapes in Sunfield," Chuck said. "During the day, he's a furniture mover for Mapes, and he usually fills in as bouncer for us most weekends."

"Chucky ain't the most reliable kid," Kate said, glancing toward Chuck. "But you know what they say—blood is thicker than water."

"He's kicked Kelly's ass outta our place plenty o' times, and if anybody could give you the lowdown on that piece of shit, it's Chucky," Chuck said. "This other feller—the one that gave Bev a ride home last night—he's the one who jumped in and pulled Kelly offa Bev last night."

"Where can I get ahold of Chucky?" Hoffmann asked.

"He shacks up with some woman he met at AA," Kate said disapprovingly. "Since our bar is closed tonight, maybe you can reach him at their house."

Kate went into the kitchen for a pen and paper. "Here's his number," she said, handing Hoffmann a note.

"So what time did you throw this Chapman guy out?" Hoffmann asked.

"It had to be close to eleven, didn't it Kate? And it weren't us that throwed him out."

"No?" Hoffmann said, cocking his head and furrowing his brow. "Oh yeah—the other man, who was it?" Hoffmann flipped through his notes. "John …John Hanson, right?"

"Right," Kate and Chuck said simultaneously. "He coulda taken all three of those jokers," Chuck said confidently.

"OK .Well, let me see if I can track down this Kelly Chapman, and if I need anything more, I will call Chucky," Hoffmann said. "Do you know the other guys he was with?"

"Nah, I sure don't," Chuck said. "Do you happen to know, Kate?"

Kate shook her head. "Nope, I don't neither, but I bet Des might know."

"And Des is …?" Hoffmann said.

"The other waitress, Desiree Putnam. She lives with her boyfriend out there near Nashville," Chuck said.

"Well, let us get right on this Kelly Chapman thing and see if we can figure out what's going on. If we need to talk to Desiree, we'll either drive out there or give her a call."

"What should we do now?" Meryl said, fighting back tears.

"Just sit tight for another couple hours and I'll let you know what I find out. And try not to worry. She's probably just up in Lansing partying with her friends," he said, trying to ease the tension.

"I've called everyone I can possibly think of. Her address book isn't in her room, so I've been calling friends in the area mostly, but nobody has seen her," Meryl said.

"Did you reach anybody from school up in East Lansing?" Petty asked.

"No. I can't think of what her roommate's mom's name is,"

Meryl said. "She has a different last name than Stacey—Bev's new roommate. Bev talked to her a couple times on the phone, but other than that, they don't even know each other."

"Well, I know it's hard, but just try to relax. We'll get this sorted out and get your girl back," Hoffmann said sympathetically.

"He's right, hon," Kate said. Oscar draped his arm around Meryl's bony shoulders.

"Yeah, Mom, remember how she was really excited about her birthday?" Shawn said, squeezing in between Oscar and her mother. "She's probably on her way home with a huge excuse."

Hoffmann and Petty thanked everyone again, reassuring them they would be in contact as they headed out the door.

The officers climbed into an old black and white Ford Crown Vic and put the keys in the ignition. Thinking it would be a waste of time to drive all the way back to the office, Hoffmann picked up the police two-way radio and called in.

"Hoffmann to base. Do you copy?" He thumbed through his notes as he waited for a reply.

"This is base. Go ahead, Dan."

"Hey Dottie. I need you to run an address for me."

"Sure thing, Dan. What do you need?" Her voice echoed through the crude speaker.

"I need an address for a male suspect, approximately twenty-five years of age, a Kelly Chapman. That's Kelly, K-E-L-L-Y, Chapman, C like Charlie, H-A-P-M-A-N. I think he lives near Lake O. Do you copy?"

"Ten-four, Dan. Let me see what I can find."

Rain drummed on the roof of the squad car. "I doubt this guy has anything to do with it, but it's better to check," Hoffmann said, glancing over at Petty.

"Yeah. You just never know, though …I've had times where I

thought one way, and it turned out my gut instinct was wrong, so we just have to check it out," Petty said, taking off his wet hat. "Just goes with the territory, I guess."

The two-way radio crackled. "Base to Hoffmann."

"Go ahead base," Hoffmann responded.

"OK, Dan, I have one Kelly Chapman, age twenty-four, living at two zero four Lakeview, apartment two in Lake O. Do you copy that?"

"Ten-four. Thanks, Dot," Hoffmann said, scribbling down the particulars.

"Also, a Detective Alan Whitman called here just after you and Ralph left. He wanted me to tell you that the State Police verified the accident victim on M-43 this morning was a male, age thirty-two, by the name of John Charles Hanson. Over."

"Ten-four. There was just the one victim in the car, correct?"

"Ten-four, Dan. That's why Detective Whitman called. He knew you wanted to verify that."

"Copy. Thanks, Dot. We're on our way to Lake O."

"I think these folks could use a little good news," Hoffmann said to Petty. "You wait here. I'll just be a second."

Hoffmann climbed out of the squad car and walked back through the pounding rain to the Deerfield front door. Once again, he knocked.

"Did you find something out already?" Kate asked, bursting the screen door open. "Come in, come in!"

Meryl, Chuck, Oscar, and Shawn were standing in the living room.

"I just got off the two-way with my office," Hoffmann began. "I got Kelly's address and we're on our way over there. But before I go, I just wanted to give you some positive news."

"Please—please do," Meryl stammered.

"Dispatch said Al Whitman called just after we left to come here," he said. "Al is the detective with the Michigan State Police who handled that fatality out here on M-43 this morning."

"Well, what did he say?" Chuck said loudly. Kate sent a piercing glance toward Chuck.

"He said that the body was identified as a thirty-two-year-old male. Technically, I can't release his name until we notify his next of kin, but I think you know who I mean," Hoffmann said.

"But there wasn't anybody with him, right?" Meryl said, hands clasped at her neck.

"That's correct, ma'am," Hoffmann replied. "Probably swerved to miss a deer, just like we thought."

"Well, that's too bad about John," Chuck said.

"But it's good news that Bev wasn't any part of it," Kate said, turning to Meryl and smiling.

"Indeed," Oscar agreed.

Shawn hugged her mother. "See, I told you! She's probably in East Lansing getting to know Stacey."

"OK. Well, I'm going now to see if I can track down this Kelly Chapman. If Bev comes home, call my office number that I gave you, and Dot will reach me on the two-way."

"Will do," Chuck said, Chuck said, patting Hoffmann's damp shoulder.

12

The drive into Lake Odessa took only fifteen minutes. It was nearly six o'clock, so Hoffmann and Petty hoped to find Chapman at home eating dinner.

Despite the rain, Jordan Lake was a beautiful sight to behold. In contrast, the Lakeview apartments were a dive. Seeing overflowing trash cans and junk-laden balconies, Hoffmann and Petty knew what to expect.

The interior of the apartment complex stank of burnt grilled-cheese sandwiches and stale cigarette smoke. Chapman's apartment was on the lower level.

Hoffmann knocked on the door.

"Go the fuck away," a husky voice came from inside.

Hoffmann pounded louder. "Open up! It's the police, and we've got a couple questions for you."

Heavy footsteps approached from the other side of the door, causing Hoffmann to step aside and grasp his holstered Glock.

Abruptly the door opened, and Hoffmann stood eye to eye with a hung-over and disgusting Kelly Chapman.

"Yeah?" he said, scanning the two officers in front of him. Standing five foot ten and weighing at least two hundred seventy pounds, Kelly was unshaven, smelly, and dressed in a tight, grubby wife-beater t-shirt and grease-stained blue jeans.

"Are you Kelly Chapman?" Hoffmann asked.

"Yeah. Why?"

"We got a report that you were up at the Sportsman's Tavern last night. Is that true?"

"Yeah, me and a couple buddies of mine went. Why?" he asked defensively.

"Can we come in? We'd like to ask you a couple questions." Hoffmann said calmly.

"Yeah, I guess," Chapman said reluctantly. It's about that bitch, Bev Deerfield, ain't it?"

The officers stepped into an apartment that can only be described as a hoarder's paradise. Empty beer cans, potato chip bags, fast-food wrappers, and overflowing ashtrays littered the place. Dirty clothes were strewn down a short hallway, and moldy dishes filled the kitchen sink and counter space. The whole apartment smelled like garbage.

"Do you know Bev Deerfield?" Hoffmann asked, looking around. Petty moved further into the living room area.

"Yeah, I know who she is. She's a cock tease, that's who she is," he said.

Hoffmann noticed that Kelly's eyes were very bloodshot and his words seemed slightly slurred.

"Have you been drinking today?" Hoffmann asked.

"What's that got to do with anything? I didn't do nothin' wrong."

"I didn't say you did. Like I said, we're just here to ask a few questions."

Kelly wandered into the kitchen, and grabbed a beer from his harvest-yellow Frigidaire.

"So, tell me what happened last night at the bar," Hoffmann said, taking out his notepad. "Who did you go with? What are the names of your buddies?"

"I was with Doug Richards and Perry Hayes," Chapman said, arrogantly cracking his beer.

"Do they live around here?" Hoffmann asked.

"Doug does, just up the road here. Still lives with his old man. Hayes, no, he's not from around here, really. He lives up in Grand Ledge at that trailer park there, the Ravines."

Hoffmann wrote it all down.

"I heard you guys got thrown out of the Sportsman."

"Oh, so that asshole Chuck Preston called ya, did he?" Chapman took a big swig of beer.

"What happened last night? You were drunk and disorderly with a waitress, is that true?" Hoffmann asked.

"Oh c'mon, man! We was just having some fun."

"And that's when you got thrown out by a patron?" Hoffmann asked.

"Jesus Christ! I guess," Chapman said, clearly fed up with all the questions. "I don't remember who the fuck threw me out, but he punched me first—I do remember that." He pointed to his bloated face, where a small scratch and light purple bruising showed. "My buddies hauled me outta there, and we went into town to keep partying at the Barn."

"What time did you come out of there?" Hoffmann asked.

"How the fuck do I know? I didn't do anything wrong! I want you to leave. This is fuckin' stupid."

Hoffmann kept his cool. "So, what time did you leave the Barn?"

"Can't you hear nothing?" Chapman said, pointing to his head and moving closer to Hoffmann. "I said I want you to leave—and take Barney here with ya," he said, motioning to Petty.

Petty took a step forward and locked eyes with Chapman.

"I'm going to ask you one more time," Hoffmann said, a little more forcefully. "You can either answer it here, or you can come back to the station with us. What time did you leave the Barn?"

"Probably around two thirty, maybe a little earlier," he said, backing down. "What the fuck difference does it make?"

"Bev Deerfield never came home last night," Hoffmann said.

"And you were the one who had your hands all over her earlier," Petty chimed in.

"In fact, you and your pals are our main suspects, which is why I'm placing you, Kelly Chapman, under arrest. Please place your hands up against the wall."

"You're shittin' me, right?" Chapman said, as Petty slowly turned him toward the wall. "C'mon! This is bullshit, and you know it." Petty patted him down, cuffed him, and read him his rights. "I ain't saying nothin' else, goddamn it," Chapman spewed.

By now, a small crowd of neighbors had gathered in the hallway.

"What did he do this time?" one asked, as Hoffmann led him down the hallway to the awaiting patrol car.

13

By eight the next morning, Bev Deerfield was officially missing, and confined in two small holding cells at the Eaton County Sherriff's Department in Charlotte were Chapman, Richards, and Hayes.

Hoffmann and Petty had questioned the trio well into the night, but gave up shortly before eleven, electing to call in the Michigan State Police the next morning, and even the FBI if necessary.

"A lot going on here, eh?" Detective Al Whitman said, setting his wet briefcase down on Hoffmann's desk. He gestured to a plate of stale donuts in the main office. "Mind if I have one?"

"Nah—help yourself," Hoffmann said.

Returning with a cake donut, Whitman took a seat in Hoffmann's office.

"So, did you guys locate any family for John Hanson?" Hoffmann asked.

"No, but they traced him back to somewhere in the U.P. You'd think I'd remember the name of it," Whitman said.

"Oh, that's right, I forgot. You're from the U.P. aren't you?" Hoffmann said, sipping his coffee.

"Yep, and I worked at the Schoolcraft Sheriff's Department up there all the way through college, and after that for another ten years, before coming down here." While Whitman wasn't so keen on moving downstate, he was thrilled to be living the life he had always wanted—as a detective for the Michigan State Police.

"Turns out Hanson has a sister, but I'll be damned if we can find her," Whitman said. "No parents, no nothing, really. We ran a check on him, and he didn't have any outstanding warrants or anything. He was a 'Nam vet," he said, taking a bite of his donut. "He was honorably discharged in '68 after being wounded. It got him the Purple Heart, too. They'll probably turn his body over to the American Legion up there, and they'll figure out a place to plant him."

Whitman examined his donut. "My wife says I've got to give these things up. 'A moment on the lips, a lifetime on the hips,' she always says," he said stuffing the rest of it into his mouth.

As he wiped his fingers, Whitman turned back to Hoffmann. "So you've got these three yahoos in custody. What did you get out of them last night?" He began leafing through the case file folder from Hoffmann's desk.

"Basically nothing. We reefed on them one at a time until about eleven and finally gave up."

"Did you find any holes in their story?"

"No, not really," Hoffmann said with a sigh. "We interviewed them separately and questioned them pretty hard, but nobody told us anything. They all admit to the fight at the Sportsman's Tavern, but after that, all of them say they were at the Barn."

"Can anybody corroborate their story?"

"Wayne Bell. He's the owner over there, and he said that they came in around ten and left between two and two thirty," Hoffmann said. "That's consistent with what they told us."

"So the question is, what did they do after that?"

"Right."

Hoffmann sipped his coffee. "We've impounded Chapman's vehicle—they were driving that last night. I had Petty go over to the Deerfields' place yesterday evening and lift a set of Bev's prints out of her bedroom. If she was in their car, we'll be able to pin it on them."

"OK, well, I'll get an MSP forensics team out here to go over that car with a fine-tooth comb," Whitman said. "In the meantime, we have an APB out on Bev, and we're checking in and around East Lansing with the information we have. I talked to her mother— what's her name?"

"Meryl?" Hoffmann asked.

"Yeah, Meryl. Talked to her last night, and as of today, we're going over every detail and trying to find this kid. But I really think something is up with this one," Whitman said, shaking his head.

"Yeah?"

"Yeah. I've been in the police business for fifteen years, and you just sort of develop this sixth sense thing, you know?" he said, reaching for his briefcase. "I hope I'm wrong, but I really smell a rat."

Whitman snapped open his briefcase and produced a small cassette recorder, a legal pad and pen. "Set me up with those jokers. I want to talk to each of them separately."

14

"Well," Whitman said, returning to Hoffmann's office, "I got nothin'."

"Yeah, I was afraid of that," Hoffmann said. "We're going to have to release them, aren't we?"

"Yep, I think so," Whitman said. "The forensics team went over Chapman's car, and aside from finding a bunch of beer cans, a couple roach clips, and some girlie magazines on the floor, they didn't find anything indicating that the girl had been in the car," he said. "No hair, no fingerprints, no nothing. And everything I asked them about last night is backed up by your guy over there at the Barn. I think we need to start looking elsewhere."

"I'll have Dot begin the release paperwork," Hoffmann said, taking a seat at his desk.

Whitman settled into a chair facing Hoffmann's desk. "You know ... I was thinking about the timing of all of this. John Hanson was supposed to drop Bev off at her house on M-43 around two thirty or three, right? But he didn't crash his car until a couple hours later. What could he have been doing all that time?"

"His car was burnt to a crisp. There wasn't any way we could tell if a struggle occurred in the car. We know she was in there—she left with him," Hoffmann said, thinking aloud.

"What time does the Barn close?"

"Around two, two thirty, just like the Sportsman's Tavern."

"Maybe they went somewhere after they left the Sportsman's Tavern," Whitman said. "And with only one victim—John Hanson—left in the car, maybe there was a little foul play involved."

He got up and walked over to a huge map of the county adorning a wall of Hoffmann's office.

"Maybe we need to start looking for our girl somewhere close by," Whitman continued. "The Sportsman's Tavern is in a pretty rural area. There's probably a million places he could have taken her if that's what happened. Let's see here," he said, squinting at the map. "Ah ... yeah. The tavern is right here, eh?" he asked Hoffmann.

"Yep, right there. And just three miles up here to the east is the Deerfield place—right here." Hoffmann made an invisible circle on the map with his index finger.

"OK, so if we put a, say, ten-mile radius around the two known locations, there's a lot of areas he could have taken her," Whitman said.

"Oh yeah," Hoffmann said, nodding. "And just through town nearly to Portland is a huge wooded area called Shimnecon. Used to belong to the Indians."

Whitman turned to Hoffmann. "Oh, wow. So there's plenty of places back there, eh?"

"Sure, absolutely."

"That Shimnecon place—is that how you say it? If you draw a line due south to M-43, that's not all that far from where Hanson's car burned."

"It's a long shot, but we need to do something," Hoffmann said. "Time's ticking away."

"I'll get ahold of my boss and see if we can get an organized search going out here," Whitman said. "In the meantime, release those losers and tell them if we need them, we know where to find them."

15

"Torrential rain hasn't helped teams of officials from the Michigan State Police, Federal Bureau of Investigation, and many locals, as they comb the wooded areas in Danby Township in search of a girl who went missing over a week ago."

Shawn snapped off the TV and turned to look into the kitchen at her mother.

"Ma?" Shawn said gently. Meryl was seated at the kitchen table, sullen and absorbed. "Ma, can I fix you something to eat?"

Meryl snapped out of her trance and turned to Shawn. "What?"

"I said, can I get you something to eat?"

"No—no, I'm not hungry," she said abruptly.

"It's gonna be OK, Ma," Shawn said, trying to refresh any amount of Meryl's hope.

"They've been looking for her for days, Shawn." Her mother shifted away. "She's dead. I can feel it. She's dead."

Her emotionless eyes stared out the window into a gray and rainy sky.

Oscar entered through the front door of the old farm house with Detective Whitman.

"Hi sweethearts," he said as he entered the kitchen and took off his jacket. He leaned down and kissed Meryl's blank face. Shawn hugged Oscar before scurrying upstairs.

"You want a cup of coffee?" he asked Whitman.

"Sure," Whitman replied, as he entered the small country kitchen. "Hello Meryl. How you holding up?" He sat down across the table from her.

"I'm a wreck. My daughter is missing. Some monster took my daughter, and not you or any of your other damn professional police people can find her."

Oscar knew that Meryl, rarely one for swearing, was nearing the end of her rope. Placing his arms around her shoulders, he spoke to her calmly.

"Honey, you need some rest. Let's get you upstairs, and then I'll make you some soup."

"Get away from me," she said, pushing Oscar's hands away. "It's been almost two weeks and I haven't heard from my little girl!"

Meryl stood up. "I've been patient. I've talked to the newspapers. I've done interviews on TV. I've been sitting in this empty house waiting for somebody to tell me they found my daughter, and nobody—*nobody*—can tell me a single goddamn thing!" she said, slamming her hand on the table.

"Honey, you need to sit down and calm yourself," Oscar said, only to have his hands swatted away again.

Whitman nodded. "It's OK, Oscar, let her go. She needs to do this."

Her glare shifted to Whitman. "And now you're some damn psychologist?" she hissed. "You, who can't even do your own job right?" The vein in Meryl's forehead bulged with stress.

Oscar came around behind Meryl and wrapped his arms around her waist.

Again, Meryl pulled away. As she regained her composure, her anger dissipated into an eerie calm. "I have done my part," she said quietly. "I've given as much information as I know to the police,

I've listened and done as I've been advised. But I am *done* with it. I want to know exactly what's going on, and I want to know now."

"Fair enough," Whitman said. "Sit back down, and we'll talk."

"I'll get you a cup of tea," Oscar said to Meryl.

Meryl sat down and looked into the young detective's dark brown eyes. Whitman could see the exhaustion and worry etched into her face.

"Well, Meryl, this isn't going to be easy to hear," he said looking anxiously toward Oscar.

Oscar set a cup of tea in front of Meryl and took a seat at the table.

"It's been nearly two weeks, and to be honest with you, that's not good," Whitman began. "We've searched every wooded area, field, abandoned barn, swamp, you name it. We've searched an entire ten-mile radius around the bar and this farmhouse, and we've come up empty handed. The weather hasn't helped. Even if my theory is correct and Hanson had anything to do with it, if he left her somewhere out there, my dogs can't catch a scent—it's all been washed away."

Tears streamed down Meryl's tired face. "We've done all we can on this search," he said. "My boss has given me the orders to shut it down after five o'clock today."

Meryl slumped forward, her sobbing muffled by her work-worn hands. Oscar rubbed her back as Whitman sat helplessly witnessing Meryl's heart shatter.

"We'll keep the case open and hopefully find a clue that leads us to her. I'm just really sorry we couldn't turn anything up out there."

Whitman went into the living room to get his jacket, and Oscar followed.

"Thanks for everything you've done, Al," Oscar said, shaking his hand. "We'll get through this. I'll be here for them," he said.

"You've got my card, right?" Whitman asked.

"Yeah, right here."

"It's never easy when a case comes to this point." Whitman shook his head.

"Things like this are never easy," Oscar said. "But we do thank you for all you've done. You've really gone above and beyond."

Whitman nodded. "We'll be in touch," he said, and he pushed the old screen door open into the rain.

16

Julie sat curled up in the passenger seat reading a book as her mother drove their beat-up '88 Ford Festiva westbound on M-43.

Slapping her book closed, Julie looked down the highway. It was a beautiful August day.

"I can certainly understand why you'd want to move closer to Lansing," Julie said. "There's so much wide open space and so many freaking wild animals."

"Oh c'mon, Jules, it ain't that bad," Shawn said, pawing through her purse while she continued driving. "I can remember being five or so, riding with my dad on his tractor and scaring all the deer out of the corn."

Pulling out a cigarette, she placed it between her lips and pushed the cigarette lighter.

"Oh, come on, Mom! I just took a shower," Julie protested. "Grandma's going to smell smoke on you and start ragging on you again," she said in an almost parental tone.

Shawn pulled the lighter out of the dashboard and held it to her cigarette. "What do I care? She's never been happy about anything I do, so a little smoke won't hurt."

After the search was called off for Bev in September of '72, Meryl's overwhelming grief left Shawn pretty much to her own devices. Teen drinking, smoking, hanging out with the wrong crowd, and an unwanted pregnancy in her late twenties left Shawn and her mother on the outs most of the time. Julie's dad was in the picture long enough to cradle his new infant daughter in his arms one time at the hospital. Since then, nobody had seen or heard from him.

"God, I'm so dreading this," Shawn said, thinking aloud.

"Dreading what?" Julie asked.

"You know—this whole game we play at Meryl's house."

"Mom, you should really call her Mom. You know she hates it when you call her by her first name."

"Yeah, whatever." Shawn exhaled. "Friggin' Oscar is gonna be there, and to make matters worse, today is the thirty-fifth anniversary of when my sister went missing."

"Oh, no," Julie moaned. "Really?"

"Yeah. Would have been her fifty-third birthday tomorrow, too."

"Aw, poor Grandma. That must be so hard for her."

"Jesus, you really do sound like my sister," Shawn said as she flicked an ash into her overflowing ashtray. "Bev used to really dote on my mom, that's for sure."

Before turning into the Deerfields' long gravel driveway, Shawn pitched her fuming cigarette butt out the window.

"Just don't mention what day it is to Meryl," Shawn said. "Maybe they've forgotten about it."

17

The old farmhouse looked pretty much the same as it did over three decades earlier. Oscar Logan had become Meryl's husband more than fifteen years prior, following the death of his wife, Elizabeth.

Elizabeth battled early onset dementia for many years, and eventually Oscar was forced to move her to a nursing home. His daily visits to his ailing wife were part of what Meryl loved so much about Oscar. After Elizabeth died, Oscar sold his home and business, married Meryl, and moved in with her.

Shawn drove up the long driveway. "Looks like they're both working in the garden."

Shawn and Julie got out of the car and walked toward the back of the house. Oscar and Meryl clapped the dust from their garden gloves and walked to meet them.

"Hey, look who's here!" Oscar chirped.

"Hey, Oscar, hey Ma," Shawn said, leaning forward to hug her mother. Meryl's gray hair was pinned neatly in a bun and topped with a straw gardening hat.

"Oh my, I'm afraid I'm a little sweaty from working in the garden. There's my girl!" Meryl pulled Julie into a bear hug.

"Hi Grandma. You look summery today," Julie said. "And Oscar—you look great, too."

"Thanks, doll," Oscar said, planting a delicate kiss on Julie's cheek.

Meryl put her arm around Julie's shoulder. "Come inside and tell us all about your new roommate at college. Have you met her yet?"

Oscar held open the rickety back screen door as they filed in one by one.

"Yeah, I met her at orientation and we've been swapping email over the summer. She seems like a nice girl, and she's pre-med, just like me."

"Would you two ladies like a cold glass of iced tea?" Oscar asked, as he followed them into the kitchen. The layout of the kitchen had never changed. The old table where Meryl sat sobbing 35 earlier still stood in the corner.

"You got a beer?" Shawn replied with a wink to her mother. "Just kidding!"

"Tea would be great, Oscar," Meryl replied. "Now, you were saying, Bev?"

At that moment, it was as if the world stopped turning.

"Oh goodness," Meryl said, holding her hands to her sun-smacked cheeks. "I can't believe I said that." Shawn's face flushed in anger, but she held her tongue.

"It's OK, Grandma. You always say I remind you of Aunt Bev—I consider it a compliment."

Shawn glared at her daughter.

"Aren't you sweet," Meryl said, caressing her granddaughter's face. "You do so remind me of her," she said, beginning to mist up.

"Aw, Grandma, don't be sad." Julie put her arm around her grandmother's shoulders.

"It's just that I've been thinking about her so much this week." Meryl sat down at the table. "You know, today is the…"

"I know, Grandma. It's OK," Julie said, taking a seat by her grandmother.

"Here's the iced tea." Oscar set the tall glasses down one by one on the table.

"I can't believe it's been so long," Meryl said, before taking a sip of her tea. "Seems like it was just yesterday."

"That it does," Oscar said. "But let's talk about something happy, shall we? Now Julie, tell me: Does that scholarship you got pay for everything through 2011 when you graduate?"

Julie was a member of the National Honor Society, a straight-A student, a member of the school band, Spanish club, and student council. With an outstanding score on her ACT, Michigan State University was happy to recruit her.

"Yeah, pretty much," Julie replied. "As long as I keep my grades up, they'll cover all my expenses."

"Oh honey, I know you'll keep your grades up. You've always been such a good student," Meryl said. "Just like your Aunt Bev always was."

"Yeah, well I've been pulling double shifts at the nursing home to put more money away in our rainy-day fund," Shawn said, trying to gain a little attention from her mother.

"If you ever need any 'mad' money, sweetheart, you know I always have a special little stash for you," Meryl said to Julie, ignoring Shawn's declaration.

"Hey Einstein—why don't you come out to the garden with me and let me show you my award-winning crop of corn." Oscar stood up from the table.

"That'd be great, Oscar," Julie said. "That'll also give Mom and Grandma a little time to chat," she said, staring directly at her mother.

The back door slammed as Oscar and Julie went outside. Meryl and Shawn, seated opposite one another at the table, sat in silence for several minutes.

Shawn finally spoke up first. "So, how's it been going, Ma?"

"OK, I guess. This last week has been a rough one for me," she said, before taking a sip of tea.

"Why? This thing with Bev's anniversary and all?" Shawn asked abruptly.

"Yes," Meryl said quietly. "It was a hard time, and the anniversary of it always brings back a lot of memories for me."

"Well, that's understandable, Ma." Shawn gulped the last of her tea. "But we all know she's safe in heaven, don't we?"

"I suppose," Meryl said, eyes welling with tears. "But it doesn't get any easier …nobody should ever have to lose a child."

Shawn rolled her eyes, stood up, and went to the sink.

"What's that look all about?" Meryl asked sternly.

"It's just that we always have to go through this," Shawn said as she rinsed her glass. "It doesn't matter if it's the fifth anniversary or the thirty-fifth—same old same old."

"My, my, my." Meryl shook her head. "I just can't understand why you think so little of your big sister. You meant the world to her, don't you remember that?"

"Of course I do," Shawn snapped. "You tell me that every single time I'm here. I'm just sick and tired of you constantly reminding me how great she was and what a fuckin' loser I am."

"You'll not use that disrespectful language in my house," Meryl retorted, voice cracking.

"That's right, I won't. Because we're leavin'."

"What about Julie? You just got here," Meryl pleaded. "Oscar and I have been waiting all week for her to come."

Julie walked into the kitchen with Oscar. "That really is some of the best corn I've ever seen, Oscar!"

"We've got to get going, Jules," Shawn said. "I have to work tonight."

"But I'm making Julie's favorite garden-fresh dinner," Meryl said, gesturing to the stove. "All fresh veggies her granddad and I have grown ourselves."

Shawn ignored her mother's pleas.

"I thought you were going to look for another job," Oscar said sitting down at the kitchen table.

"Yeah, I was, but I've worked my way up through the ranks," Shawn said. "I'm a senior member of the staff now, and I've been doing more management stuff for the last six months or so. I don't have to wipe quite as many butts as I used to."

"Oh, Shawn," Meryl said disapprovingly. "I don't know where you came across this sarcastic way of talking."

Shawn acted as though she hadn't heard her mother's criticism and made her way toward the door. "Thanks for the tea. Jules, say your good-byes. We gotta hit it."

Julie looked confused by her mother's request for a quick exit. "Mom, Grandma's right. We just got here."

"I just remembered a bunch of things I need to do before work tonight," Shawn lied. "Really. Tell your grandparents you'll catch 'em next time for dinner."

"Well, it's been great seeing you and grandma," Julie said, hugging an elderly Oscar.

"It's been so great to see you today, too, dear," Oscar said. "It really makes your grandma's day. You're a ray of sunshine in her life." As he released her, he added, "You're so grown up these days. Just look at you—you're a young woman, now."

Oscar saw the image of Julie's late Aunt Bev, though a bit taller and thinner. With the dark complexion of her father, dark hair and crystal-blue eyes, Julie was stunning

"Don't be a stranger once you get up there to that mean old town!" Meryl hugged her granddaughter. "Call me collect if you have to, you hear?" she said as the duo opened the old screen door.

"Grandma! Nobody calls collect anymore, but I'll call you on my cell phone. And if I don't see you beforehand, I'll look forward to seeing you at Thanksgiving."

"You bet," Meryl said. "I'll make us the best homemade Thanksgiving dinner in the county. And I'll make you a cherry pie, too— I know that's your favorite."

"Aw, Grandma, you're the best," Julie said, looking behind. "You two take care! I love you both."

Meryl felt a lump swell in her throat. "Love you, too, babe," she croaked.

Oscar put his arm around Meryl as they both waved and watched the old car drive off.

"Let me guess—you and Shawn got into it again." Oscar continued to wave.

Sadness overwhelmed Meryl as she nodded at Oscar's hunch.

"Julie is really growing up into a nice young woman," Oscar said, trying to brighten the mood.

"She really is," Meryl said quietly. "She's just like Bev was at that age: sweet, kind, and considerate. Sometimes it's hard to believe that Shawn is her mother."

"Now, Grandma," Oscar said. "Be nice."

18

A week later, it was time for Julie to move into her new dorm at MSU.

"I hope you know where you're going," Shawn said from the passenger seat.

"I do, I do. Try to relax." Julie flipped on her blinker.

"You still make me really nervous when you're driving," Shawn said as she dug through her purse for a cigarette.

"I just thought it would be easier for me to drive, since I do know where I'm going and you don't. It's just up here on the right: Wonders Hall."

"Oh, right here?" Shawn pushed in the lighter.

"Yep. I'll just pull up, and we can unload."

Julie's belongings consisted of a hard plastic suitcase containing all of her clothing, a laundry basket filled with sheets, towels, and mementoes from her bedroom at home, the laptop computer Meryl and Oscar had bought her for graduation, and several shirts and sweaters hanging on hangers.

"I've already got the key, so we should be able to get this stuff up there in one trip," Julie said.

"OK, sure. And I'll come back and move the car after we drop this stuff off," Shawn replied.

Wonders Hall and the sidewalk outside were like Grand Central Station on a busy day. Students buzzed about moving suitcases, random pieces of loft bedframes, microwaves, and other personal items to their dorm rooms.

Shawn and Julie rode the elevator up to the third floor. "This is it," Julie said fidgeting with her dorm key. "It's just down this way."

The door to her dorm room was ajar. "Hello?" Julie pushed it open.

Nobody answered.

"Somebody's been here, obviously," Julie said, opening the closet and hanging her clothes on the empty side.

"I'm here," said a young woman as she emerged from the bathroom, drying her hands on the thighs of her jeans. Pattie's face appeared ordinary. Dishwater blonde hair and a ruddy complexion made most guys miss the rest.

"Sorry, I didn't hear you! I'm Pattie, Pattie Robbison, Julie's roommate." Pattie reached out to shake Shawn's hand.

"Nice to meet ya. I've heard a lot of good things about you."

"Really? Well, that's nice to hear! How have you been doing, Julie?" Pattie leaned forward to give Julie a brief hug.

"I've been well, thanks," Julie said. "Is it OK if I set up shop over here?" She gestured to the empty desk nearest the window.

"Absolutely," Pattie said. "It's all yours. I hope you don't mind that I took the top bunk."

"Oh no, that's not a problem. The bottom bunk is good enough for me."

"Jules, I'm gonna go move the car, then come back and help you unpack," Shawn said.

"Mom, that's really nice, but I think I can manage. Why don't you head home? I know you have to work tonight."

"Are you sure?" Shawn said, already halfway out the door.

"Yeah, really, it's fine." Julie looked over at her new roommate.

"Pattie and I can yack while I unpack, and we can get to know each other better."

"Well, if you're sure. Give me a hug."

Julie embraced her mother. "You know how to get home from here, don't you?" Julie asked in a protective tone.

"Oh yeah, not a problem" Shawn said. "I'll give you a call on your cell phone Monday night to see how your first day went."

"OK, sounds good."

"Nice to meet you, Pattie, and good luck to both of you on Monday," Shawn said. "It's gonna be a big day for you guys."

"Thanks," the girls said in unison.

Shawn turned and let herself out of the dorm room, reveling in her distinct sense of freedom.

19

It didn't take Julie long to unpack her suitcase and stow her perfectly folded underwear, jeans, and t-shirts in the dorm-supplied dresser. After stashing the suitcase in the closet, she moved on to making up her bunk.

"Wow, you sure are efficient," Pattie said from her perch on her desk as she drank a soda.

"I guess I do keep a pretty tidy room," Julie said, putting an ironed pillowcase on her pillow. "That's one thing I won't miss about living with my mom. Our apartment is always a little on the messy side for me. I guess that's why I spend so much time in my room. What about you? Are you going to miss home?"

"Yeah, I do already," Pattie admitted. "My little brother and I are really close. He's fifteen now, so I'll miss him. My parents are divorced and I lived with my mom. My dad is shacked up with some ho."

"Aw, that sucks." Julie gathered her folded towels and toiletries and took them into the bathroom. "Where did you go to school, again?"

"Right here in town: East Lansing. I could have lived at home, but figured I'd make my dad pay for everything he's done to the family by living on campus and making him fund it all."

"He doesn't mind?" Julie turned her attention to her laptop and reference books.

"I'm sure he's not happy with footing the bill, but what can he say? He'll do anything to win me back," she said smiling. "So I just take advantage of it. What about your dad?"

"Never knew him."

"What? Are you serious?"

"Yeah," Julie said nonchalantly. "My mom had a brief affair with him, became pregnant with me, and when my Grandma wouldn't allow her to give me up for adoption, my sperm donor, I mean dad, dumped us and never looked back."

"Wow. That's sad."

"I'm used to it. Never knew anything different." Julie placed a picture of Meryl and Oscar on her dresser.

"Who are they?"

"My grandparents," Julie answered. "I took it last summer at Grandpa's eightieth birthday party."

"So, what are you going to do tonight?" Pattie asked, changing the subject.

Julie hoisted her college dictionary to the shelf above her desk. "Probably just hanging around and reading."

"Oh, c'mon!" Pattie hopped off the desk and pushed the power button on her CD player. "It's our first night in the dorm. We should go do something fun."

"Like what? Going to the library?"

Pattie laughed. "Oh my God, are you shitting me? No! I'm talking about going to the bar."

"But we're not old enough to drink."

"Oh, that's not a problem—I know the bouncer. He was friends with my older brother and graduated four years ago. Besides, everybody knows Slippery's is a dive, and they cater to underage partiers, if you know what I mean."

"Nah ...I don't know," Julie stammered. "I'm not much of a party girl."

"Awww, c'mon. Have some fun. Finish up here, and we'll go grab a bite to eat before going out."

"Man, I don't know. I don't really have much to wear," Julie responded, with another excuse.

"It's OK. It's a dive, really. Just wear tight jeans and a low-neck t-shirt. Guys love that shit," Pattie said, laughing. "Once you have a couple drinks, you won't care."

"Oh, all right ...but let me get all this stuff organized before we go."

"Julie, you won't regret this. We'll have a blast!"

20

The first six weeks of her first semester went by in a blur for Julie. Between staying current on her homework and trying to stay in touch with her mom, she found herself a bit envious of her roommate. For Pattie, college seemed a whole lot easier.

Maybe it was Pattie's tumultuous upbringing that had taught her how to go with the flow, but Julie couldn't believe how easygoing Pattie was. Julie occasionally witnessed her studying, but on the weekends, Pattie rarely cracked a book.

"Don't you have a test to study for?" Julie asked as Pattie headed for the door one Friday evening in mid-October.

"Yeah, but in case you haven't noticed, it's Friday." Pattie beamed a beautiful smile in Julie's direction. "Why don't you come with us? You haven't let up from your books since you got here."

Julie put down her pen and rubbed her eyes. "I would, but I've got a huge test on Monday, and I'm struggling with it as it is." Julie yawned.

"You owe yourself a little downtime," Pattie said. "Might make ya sleep better, too."

Over the last six weeks, sleep had been a rollercoaster for Julie. Plagued by insomnia for days at a time, she'd eventually crash heavily, dreaming so vividly that Pattie would have to awaken her.

"Who knows? Maybe a little playtime would make you do better in school?" Pattie suggested.

Julie jolted upright. "What makes you think I'm messing up with school? I've got a straight four point going on here." Julie glared at Pattie.

"Jesus, Jules, lighten up, will ya?" Pattie turned toward the door. "I'm just trying to help! Go ahead, stay here and study. I could give a shit less," she said, slamming the door behind her.

With the sound of the slamming door resonating in her head, Julie slumped backward in her chair.

"Why do I do that?" she thought. "She was just trying to be nice, and I had to turn it into a fight."

Disgusted with herself, Julie shook her head, got up, shuffled over to the fridge, and helped herself to a Coke. "Looks like it can be an all-nighter for me," she said aloud. "I'm sure Pattie won't come back tonight. She never does."

21

"Tell me you haven't been sitting there the whole time I've been gone," Pattie said as she danced into the dorm room on Sunday morning.

"Tell me you haven't been partying all this time," Julie shot back sarcastically. "Hey, listen, about Friday night ..."

"Forget it, it's fine. I know you take your studies really seriously." Pattie took off her jacket and walked over to the fridge. "I need to take a page out of your book."

"And I could probably take a page or two out of yours," Julie said, closing her book. "I'm too uptight about things. I had no right to snap at you."

Pattie flopped down at her desk and propped her feet up. "Tell ya what," she said, taking a drink of her soda. "Let's make a pact. I'll study all week—I'll morph into a freakin' bookworm—if you promise in return to come with us next Friday to the Halloween costume party at Slippery's."

"Oh, man, I don't know. I don't have a costume or anything." Julie stood up and helped herself to a bag of pretzels from the shelf.

"They have a ton of costumes at the sorority house," Pattie said enthusiastically. "We can dig up something for you to wear, not a big deal."

A smug smile appeared on Julie's face. "You're really going to study this week?"

"Absolutely," Pattie said with a stern look.

"I mean really study, starting right now," Julie said, popping a pretzel into her mouth.

"Yep, right after a shower." Pattie got up from her desk chair.

"OK, then it's a deal. But if you screw up, I reserve the right to say no to the costume party."

"Deal," Pattie replied, holding her hand out.

The roommates shook hands. "Again, sorry to have been such a bitch on Friday," Julie said.

"Don't worry about it." Pattie headed for the bathroom. "You can make it up to me by being the life of the party on Friday."

22

Julie stepped out from the bathroom of their dorm room. "I feel like a moron wearing this."

"Are you kidding? You look hot. The guys are gonna be all over you at the bar," Pattie said, taking a sip of beer. "How do I look?" she asked, sporting a sleazy Playboy bunny costume.

"You look ...very perky," Julie said, looking at her roommate's chest.

Pattie smiled and looked into the mirror. "Yeah, it's a size too small, but what the hell do I care, right?"

"I still wish they would have had less-promiscuous-looking costumes at the house." Julie picked up her feather duster and a small black purse. "I mean, not only do I feel stupid dressed this way, I don't even know any French." She glanced at herself in the mirror. "Shouldn't a French maid at least know the language?"

"Dressed like that, all you gotta know is the language of love," Pattie said, laughing. "Like, 'Voulez-vous couchez avec moi se soir,'" she sang in her best Pattie La Belle voice.

"What's that mean?"

Pattie was smiling broadly. "Just memorize it. You're gonna need it," she said slamming the rest of a beer. "It means, 'Will you sleep with me tonight.'"

Julie laughed. "Oh man! Who needs Berlitz when there's you?"

***

By eight that night, Slippery's was rocking with students. A line of patrons, most of them in costume, was already beginning to form outside of the popular campus nightspot.

Pattie parked the car and stuffed her purse under the driver's seat. "I'm just going to take some cash, my cell, and my ID in with me. Take your driver's license: Pete will look at it and act like we're legal."

Following Pattie's lead, Julie also took out her cash and ID. "I've got my cell phone, too," she said, patting the front pocket of her apron.

"Wow, this place sure is busy," Julie said as they got in line.

"It's their annual Halloween bash. What did you expect?"

"What about a cover charge?" asked Julie.

Pattie summoned her best *Goodfellas* accent: "Fogettaboutit!" Julie beamed.

Julie soon found herself standing in front of a mountain of a man—Pete, Pattie's friend and resident bouncer at Slippery's.

Dressed like Frankenstein, Pete leaned down and growled into Pattie's face. "Hey, little P." He broke into a grin and wrapped huge arms around Pattie. "How you doin'?"

"How does it look like I'm doing?" Pattie thrust her chest forward and looked straight up at his handsome face. "Can you get me and my new roommate, Jules, in tonight?" she asked.

For a moment Pete acted as if he wasn't going to allow it, but then his smile returned. "Mais oui," he said in a French accent. "Of course. Just don't drink too much and get me into trouble," he added in a hushed tone.

After a perfunctory look at their IDs, Pete waved them through.

The inside of the bar was packed with partying college students. A band was setting up, as the jukebox blared.

"What do you want to drink?" Pattie shouted.

"I don't know," Julie shouted back. "What are you having?"

Pattie hesitated a moment, looked at one of the twenty-dollar bills she'd brought inside, and smiled. "Probably whatever is on special tonight."

Julie smiled back. "Me too," she shouted.

The roommates snaked their way through the crowd up to the bar. "What's on special tonight?" Pattie yelled to a Dracula-clad bartender.

The bartender pointed to a whiteboard behind the bar. Kamikazes were the drink of the night.

"What's a Kamikaze?" Julie yelled to Pattie.

Pattie leaned close to Julie's ear. "It's vodka, triple sec, and lime juice. They're pretty good."

"OK, I'll have one."

Holding up two fingers, Pattie ordered two Kamikazes.

"Three bucks," the bartender shouted as he placed two small cocktails on the bar.

Pattie again leaned over to Julie. "They look small, but they pack a wallop. Cheers!" The roommates clinked glasses.

Julie watched as her roommate slammed the drink, then gulped hers down in two chugs.

"How was it?" Pattie yelled. All Julie could manage was the thumbs-up sign.

"Good! Let's order two more," Pattie suggested.

"Here's my money." Julie said before Pattie could order. "I'm going to go find us a table."

Locating a table near the rear of the bar, Julie sat down and started looking around. College students of all ages and sizes were in the bar, some wearing costumes, and most in a party mood.

It took her ten minutes, but eventually Pattie returned to the table. "Here we go," Pattie said loudly as she approached the table with a large pitcher of margaritas and two glasses.

"What happened to the drink specials?"

"I thought to hell with it and splurged on a pitcher of margaritas for us." She sat down and poured out two glassfuls. "My mom loves these things."

"What is it? It looks really fruity."

"Yeah, it's strawberry margarita mix, ice, and tequila, mainly," she said as she took a sip of hers. "Try it." Julie took a taste. "Do you like it?"

"Mmm," Julie said. "It's good, yeah."

"Oh my God!" shouted Pattie as she lurched out of her seat and began running toward two guys who lumbered toward their table. "I can't believe you're here!"

Pattie collided with the skinnier of the two and proceeded to hug and kiss him. "Oh my God," she repeated. "What are you doing back?"

The two men followed her back to the table and sat down. "Jules, this is Bart and his friend …?"

"Greg," the handsome companion said.

Julie nodded to the young men, who were dressed like Fred Flintstone and Barney Rubble.

"Bart graduated two years before me and went into the service right after high school."

"Oh, wow," Julie said. "It's nice to meet you. I love your costumes."

Bart smiled. "Thanks. Yeah, it was Greg's idea, since we're such good friends. I made it back from two years overseas," he said. Judging by the haircut, Julie figured he hadn't been back too long.

"Are you OK?" Pattie asked. "You look great," she said, stroking the arm of the handsome young GI.

"Yeah, I'm OK." He took a drink of his beer. "I was in Iraq for the last six months. That kinda fucked me up, but I'm doing OK now. It's hard to get used to being back."

"Are you going to school here?"

"No, me and Greg have an apartment off campus, and I'm working as a security guard at a credit union. I am taking classes at Lansing Community College, though, and I'm hoping to get accepted into the Michigan State Police program."

"That's great," Pattie said. "You certainly are built for it!" she said flirtatiously. "What about you, Greg?"

Greg sipped at his beer and answered, "I go to LCC, too. And I work for the same security company as Fred here—I mean Bart," he chuckled.

"Oh, so that's how you met?" Pattie asked Bart as she snuggled closer to him.

Bart nodded. "You're smokin' in that bunny costume, Pattie. You wanna dance?"

"Sure," she said, giggling as Bart pulled her out onto the dance floor.

Julie remained behind, quietly sipping her margarita. "So, uh, what do you do?" Greg asked her.

"I just started here at State this fall."

Greg nodded. "MSU is a great place, that's for sure."

"Yeah. I usually spend most of my time studying. But Pattie— she's my roommate—she wanted to go do something wild tonight, so she talked me into coming here."

Greg smiled and took another slug of his beer.

They both directed their attention to the dance floor, where Bart and Pattie were dancing and laughing.

"Looks like they're ready to rekindle whatever happened in high school," Greg said.

Julie shifted on her chair. "Yeah ...well, I think I'm gonna get going."

"What? You're leaving already?" He gestured to the half-full pitcher of margaritas. "From the looks of it, you just got here."

"To be honest, this isn't really my bag," she murmured, gazing at her margarita.

"No, no, no, you can't leave yet." He flagged down a waitress. "This margarita ain't workin' for her," he said as he tilted his head toward Julie. "Can you bring her a Long Island Iced Tea? And grab me another one of these while you're at it."

"Iced tea," Julie thought. "That's better. I can handle a glass of tea ...finally a guy who gets it!"

"You'll like that a lot better."

"Thanks, I appreciate that."

"So, what are you studyin' at MSU?"

Julie sat up straighter and stated, "I'm in pre-med."

"Wow! Hot *and* a brainiac, huh?"

Julie blushed at Greg's compliment. "I want to be a pediatrician, I think, but we'll see."

Greg's eyes widened. "That's a fancy word for foot doctor, right?" Greg said, trying to charm Julie.

"No, no, it's just a fancy word for a kid doctor."

Every bit of six feet tall, sandy blond hair, good teeth, and a muscular build, Julie noticed. Although judging by his grammar, Julie was certain there wasn't a lot going on upstairs.

"What about you? Do you want to be a policeman like Bart?"

"Nah, I don't think so. Not nearly enough money for me."

"So what do you want to do?"

"Not really sure. I love to skateboard, so I was thinking about opening up my own skateboard shop and park or something like that."

Julie felt like rolling her eyes. "Ahhh," she responded, trying to look connected. "Cool."

He reached for his wallet as the waitress appeared. "It's gonna take me some time to be able to afford it, but yeah, we'll see."

"Here you go." The waitress set the drinks on the table. "That's $8.50."

Julie reached for her purse. "No, I'll get it." Greg handed the waitress a ten. "Keep it," he said, winking at the waitress.

Julie looked at her drink and thought it must be some different type of iced tea. Taking a big gulp, she nearly blew it out her nose when she tasted the strong liquor.

"What's the matter?" Greg chortled. "Are you OK?"

"I'm fine," Julie said, embarrassed. "It just went down the wrong way."

In an attempt to help her stop coughing, Greg patted Julie on the back. His hand lingered longer than necessary, and Julie finally realized she was being hit on.

"Here, take another sip," he said as he lifted the glass to her lips.

Julie didn't know what to do. She'd never been on a real date, let alone in a bar where guys would hit on her.

Feeling pressured, Julie took a big gulp.

"Good? Huh?"

Julie nodded.

"Well, well, well," Bart said as he and Pattie returned to the table. "We leave for a couple dances, and look what happens?" Pattie giggled.

When Pattie draped her arm around Bart's shoulder, Julie knew she wouldn't be getting a ride back to the dorm from her that night.

The drinking continued, and not wanting to appear prudish, Julie attempted to keep up.

After a second and third round of drinks, Bart and Pattie got up to dance again.

"You wanna dance?" Greg asked Julie.

"No—no, I don't think so," she said shyly. Julie's face was flushed from the alcohol.

"Me neither." Greg took another swallow of his drink. "I'm not much of a dancer. You wanna get out of here?"

For Julie, the room was spinning. All she could do was nod.

"OK, wait here. I'll go tell Bart and Pattie that we're leaving. Pattie drove, right?" he asked a drunken Julie.

"Yeah," she said, trying to appear sober. "Yeah, Pattie drove us here."

Greg smiled, knowing full well that his impromptu date was tanked. "OK, Bart can grab a ride with her, then." He headed out to the dance floor.

Julie watched Greg as he walked away from the table. She gulped the last bit of her third Long Island iced tea and looked around the room. The hazy smoke made Julie feel as if she were swimming in a giant fish bowl.

"God, I must be really drunk," she thought. She found that she sort of liked this detached and loose feeling.

When Greg returned to the table, he asked, "You ready?"

"Where are we going? What time is it?" Julie said.

"It's about ten thirty or so. You wanna go back to my place and watch TV?"

"No, you should probably take me back to the dorm."

"Oh, c'mon," Greg said, placing his arm around her waist. "It's still early. Let's go have some fun."

Julie rested against Greg as he helped her navigate through the wall of people standing at the rear of the bar.

The cool autumn air felt good after being in the hot, smoky bar all evening. "C'mon, Julie, I'm just parked over here."

23

"This is a cool Jeep," Julie said loudly as the vinyl top of his old Jeep Wrangler flapped against the roll bar. Greg headed down Michigan Avenue to East Grand River.

"Yeah, I bought it from my brother a year ago," Greg said, snapping on the stereo. "It's great when it's warm enough to have the top down."

Belted into the passenger seat, Julie slumped forward.

"Hey girl!" Greg averted his eyes from the road momentarily and nudged Julie's arm. "Wake up!"

Julie popped her head up and shot him a crooked grin.

"You're feeling pretty good, hey?" he said with a laugh. Julie just closed her eyes and drifted back out of consciousness.

Turning left into the Village Apartments, Greg roared his Jeep into a carport.

"Where are we? Are we at my dorm?"

"No, baby." Greg came around the back of the Jeep. "We're at my place, remember?"

"Oh yeah," Julie slurred. "I 'member now." Greg opened her door, unbuckled her seat belt, and scooped her up into his big arms. "What are you doin'?" Julie squealed.

Greg laughed again, and carried her into his apartment and flopped her down on the couch.

The apartment opened into a moderate-size living room with a sliding glass door leading to a patio. The living room was cluttered, and the carpet rarely got vacuumed. Adjoining the living room was the kitchen and dining area, and straight down a long hallway from the front door led to two bedrooms and a bathroom.

"I gotta pee," Greg said as he moved down the hallway. "Don't go anywhere. I'll be right back."

Julie had already leaned her head back on the couch and passed out.

Within a couple of minutes, Greg returned wearing jeans and a t-shirt and walked into the kitchen to grab a longneck.

"You want one?" he said as he came into the living room. Julie didn't respond.

Greg placed his cold beer down on the table and went over to sit on the couch by Julie. "Hey…" Greg patted her cheek softly. "I've heard about being a cheap drunk, but this is ridiculous."

Julie's eyes fluttered open and before she could say anything, Greg's tongue was already in her mouth.

Julie kissed back for a moment before pushing him away.

"What's wrong?" Greg said softly, caressing her hair and staring into her drunken eyes.

"Nothin'," Julie slurred. "I jus' wanna get to know you first, that's all."

Trying to regain her composure, Julie sat up on the couch and adjusted her short skirt.

"Do you wanna beer?" Greg said, getting up to grab his drink.

"Nah—I think I've had enough."

"How about one of these?" Greg pulled a joint out of the small pocket on his t-shirt and set his beer down on the coffee table.

"What is it?"

"Are you kiddin' me?" Greg grabbed a lighter off the end table. "What are you? Freakin' Mother Theresa, or what?"

She giggled. "I just … you know, never do this kinda stuff …"

Greg sat down next to her and placed the joint between his lips. "Well, Julie, this is a joint. You know—a doob, a marijuana cigarette."

Greg clicked the lighter and lit the joint. "And after a couple hits on this, you'll be feeling really good." He then took a long drag. Holding the smoke in his lungs, Greg held out the joint and nodded for Julie to take it.

"What do I do?" she asked as she took the joint delicately between her thumb and index finger.

Greg finally exhaled and gave instruction.

"Just do what I did. Hold it carefully so you don't burn your finger, and take a big drag off it," he said. "Then hold it in as long as you can." Julie leaned forward and took an awkward hit off the joint. Within seconds she convulsed in a fit of coughing and hacking.

Greg couldn't help but laugh. "That's OK. It happens to everyone on their first try." He took another hit himself and held the smoke in his lungs for a bit, while Julie finally stopped coughing. Then he handed her back the joint.

"Now try it again." Julie grasped the small joint and took another hit. This time she held it at least ten seconds before exhaling and coughing again.

"Good, that's better. See? Doesn't it feel good?"

Julie was surprised by her immediate sense of lightheaded euphoria. "Wow. That *is* cool!"

Greg took another hit, leaving just a little bit more marijuana for Julie.

Taking the joint from him, Julie took a drag and held it even longer.

Greg smiled broadly and then exhaled as he moved closer. "I

told you we'd have fun over here." Easing his hand onto Julie's thigh, he took the remaining roach from Julie and stubbed it out in the ashtray on the coffee table.

Julie staggered to her feet. "Now I gotta pee."

"Down the hall. Last door on the right," Greg said, leaning forward and grabbing his beer.

He followed her down the hall and walked into his bedroom. Greg's unmade queen-size waterbed dominated the room. After snapping on the television, he closed the double doors to hide his messy closet. Taking off his shoes, he fluffed his pillow and settled in to watch TV.

Julie popped her head around the corner. "What are you doin'?"

"This is where I watch TV," Greg said, setting his beer bottle on the nightstand. "C'mon in. I won't bite," he said patting the warm mattress.

Julie stumbled as she took off her high heel shoes.

"You're really wasted, aren't ya?" Greg watched the beautiful young woman weaving as she tried to stay vertical.

"If that's what you call it, then yeah, I guess I am," she said, smiling and looking over at him.

"Oh wow!" Julie sounded as though she had discovered gold. "Is this a waterbed?" Carefully, she sat down on the bed.

"Come on over to me." Greg bounced on the mattress, making a huge wave. Julie laughed as she lost her balance and rolled over toward Greg.

"Wow…it's so warm, too," She reveled in the moment. Julie lay flat on her back and felt the waves slowly dissipate. Random thoughts tumbled in her mind like warm clothes in a dryer, as she listened to the ever-fading drone of the TV.

Greg rolled over onto his stomach and leaned closer into Julie's face. "Just close your eyes… just ride the waves and let them wash you away," he whispered.

The last thing Julie remembered was feeling Greg's warm kisses on her neck and his fingers trying to remove her fishnets. She was too far gone to resist anything.

24

Julie's eyes snapped open as she found herself lying alone in the waterbed. Struggling to remember what had happened, Julie discovered that beneath the sheets she was naked.

Her French maid costume, fishnets, and underwear lying next to the bed began to tell the story. She felt a burning sensation in her groin. Slowly emerging from the warm confines of the waterbed, she saw blood stains on the sheets as she attempted to get up. A blood-stained hand towel was wadded and thrown near the foot of the bed.

Julie felt like crying as she began to think about what must have happened. "He raped me," Julie thought. "I passed out and he raped me." Glancing around the room, she noticed an empty carton of condoms and several torn plastic wrappers on the nightstand. "At least the son of a bitch had the decency to use condoms."

With nothing else to wear, Julie put on her soiled underwear and the wrinkled maid's costume and stuffed the fishnets into her purse. She helped herself to one of Greg's large sweatshirts, throwing it on over her costume.

In the dining room, Julie discovered a note on the table. Expressionless, she read it.

"Didn't want 2 wake U up. Had 2 go 2 work. Lock up when U leave. C U later. G."

Julie didn't bother to lock the door behind her. Walking through the rain into the parking lot, she doubled over and clung to the bumper of a car, emptying her stomach.

Using the sleeve of Greg's sweatshirt to mop up the remnants of vomit around her mouth, Julie composed herself and walked into the convenience store across the road. Gazing through the fogged glass of the refrigerator section, she decided on a fruit punch.

"Will that be it?"

Julie scanned the cigarettes behind the counter. "Nah, give me a pack of those Marlboro Lights," she said, adding a disposable lighter to her order. "Is there a bus stop around here?" she asked.

"Yeah, it's up the road maybe a mile or so. That's gonna be six dollars and eighty-six cents."

Julie handed the cashier a wrinkled ten-dollar bill.

"Rough night, huh?" he said, winking at Julie.

Julie didn't smile or acknowledge his comment, grabbed the change and her items, and walked out to the parking lot.

Sitting down on the curb, Julie opened her pack of cigarettes, placed one between her lips, and lit it. After last night's joint, the cigarette felt like breathing fresh air. "What would Grandma say if she could see me sitting here like this?" she thought. "Why the hell am I even smoking?"

Standing up, she put the lighter and cigarettes into her purse, and grabbed her fruit punch. Heading westward up East Grand River, she knew it was a long walk back to the dorm.

Misty rain continued to fall as she walked and tried to recall what had happened after she left the bar.

Julie took a long drag on her cigarette. "I remember being in his car," she thought. "It was a Jeep, I think." Julie took another hit off her cigarette. Traffic sounds and any immediate awareness of what was happening around her disappeared as her thoughts raced.

"We smoked a joint... on the couch." Julie took a swig of her punch. "He tried to kiss me. His hands were all over me. I didn't know what to do!" Julie struggled to remember what happened next. "Did I go to the bathroom? Was that what I did? How did I get into the bedroom?"

Julie's thought process was broken by the ringing of her cell phone. It was Pattie calling.

"Hello?"

"Hey girlfriend! You must've had some night, right?" said Pattie cheerfully. "Where the hell are ya? You still with Greg?"

"I'm—I'm not really sure." Julie began to cry.

"Ooooh, you don't sound good. Are you OK? What's wrong? What happened?"

"No, I'm really not OK," Julie said sobbing.

"Where are you? I'll come get you."

"Somewhere on Grand River," Julie said weakly. "I... I really don't know. My head is pounding so hard... I'm somewhere near where Greg and Bart live. All I know is, I'm walking west of that convenience store across from their apartment."

"OK, hold tight. I know exactly where you are, and I'm coming for you right now."

25

Within fifteen minutes, Pattie had spotted Julie. Pulling over, Pattie opened the passenger door for Julie.

"C'mon, get in. What the fuck happened to you?" Pattie looked plenty concerned as Julie slid into the passenger seat and slammed the door. She slumped forward, head in hands, sobbing.

Pattie maneuvered the car into a neighboring lot and parked. Unbuckling her seat belt, she turned toward Julie and tried to embrace her. Julie's mournful sobs came from the very depth of her soul.

"Tell me, Jules... what happened?" Pattie pulled Julie's hair away from her face.

"It's all my fault," Julie said, trying to stop crying.

"What's your fault? What's your fault?"

"What happened last night! I got so drunk—didn't know what I was doing, and went home with Greg." Julie continued to cry.

"OK, so you went home with Greg," Pattie said. "That's not a crime, Julie—it's OK."

"No! You're not listening to me!" Julie couldn't quite catch her breath as she sobbed. "I never should have agreed to go to the fucking bar with you. I would be fine right now if I hadn't gone to the bar."

"What happened at Greg's?" Pattie probed. "Julie—look at

me." She gripped Julie by the shoulders. "Look at me! Now, what happened?"

Julie looked like a little girl who had been busted for doing something bad. She took a few breaths to compose herself. Looking up, Julie wiped her nose with the back of her hand.

"He raped me."

Saying nothing, Pattie stared compassionately into Julie's eyes before leaning forward and holding Julie while she continued to sob. "It's going to be OK." After a few moments, Pattie's compassion transformed to anger. "You've got to go see a doctor. That fucker is going to pay."

"No!" Julie wailed. "No—if my Grandma finds out, if my mom finds out—they'll never let me stay here at school," she said, crying. "Promise me you won't say a word to anyone. Promise me. We've got shit insurance … my mom would definitely find out."

"Julie, I just think you should get checked out. What if you're pregnant? What then?"

"I'm not—he used condoms. They were all over the fucking nightstand." Julie slowed to a sniffle, and reached for her pack of cigarettes.

"Oh, Julie—I'm so sorry," Pattie said. "This is my fault. I never should have left you alone with a guy neither of us knew," she said. "I didn't know you smoke." Pattie watched as Julie fumbled with her lighter.

"I do now," Julie sneered as she cracked the window and exhaled smoke. "Can you take me back to the dorm now?"

"Yes, of course." Pattie reached for her seat belt. "But I still think we need to go to Sparrow Hospital," she said, starting the car.

"This is my goddamned decision! Now promise me you won't say anything to anybody," Julie demanded.

"OK, I won't, I won't. You're right. It's your body, it's your decision. I won't tell anyone."

"Not even Bart," Julie said, taking another drag on the cigarette.

"I doubt I'll even see Bart again. He's too arrogant for me. And anybody who hangs around with scumbags like Greg isn't up there on my list, you know?"

26

Julie headed directly for the shower after she and Pattie arrived at their dorm room.

Closing the bathroom door behind her, Julie stripped down and cranked on the hot water in the shower, climbed in and pulled the curtain behind her.

A hot steamy waterfall cascaded from the top of her head to her toes as she replayed the evening's events over in her head once again. Feeling violated and dirty, Julie reached for the soap and began scrubbing every inch of her body. The rusty-colored suds generated by washing her tender and bruised privates caused Julie to begin crying again.

Julie's body slid downward along the wall, leaving her sitting knees to chin on the shower floor. She sobbed quietly for nearly a half hour, until she heard a loud knocking on the bathroom door.

"Jules, are you OK?" Pattie called.

"Yes," Julie yelled back. "I'm fine. I'll be out in a minute."

"You sure?"

Julie heard her trying to open the locked bathroom door. "I'm *fine*, Pattie. Really. I'll be out soon," she said, getting to her feet.

Pattie didn't respond, but stood vigilantly outside the door straining to hear what was going on.

Julie shut off the water, opened the curtain, and grabbed one of her freshly folded towels. Carefully, she dried her body and then used it to wipe steam off the bathroom mirror.

Her exhausted face reflected from the mirror. Leaning forward, she stared into her weary eyes. "The windows to one's soul," she found herself thinking, as she noticed something different about herself.

"You don't look the same," she thought. "Yesterday you were normal: responsible, bright, and friendly." She furrowed her brow and looked closer. "Today, you're a monster." It was as if another personality spoke from within.

Pattie banged on the door again, startling Julie out of her deep and troubled thoughts.

"Jesus Christ, Pattie," Julie screamed. "I told you—I'll be out in a fucking minute!" She listened as the echo from her outburst rang into complete silence. Pattie said nothing.

Wrapping the towel around her slim body, Julie gathered her clothing and opened the door. Pattie was sitting on her bunk, looking worried and on the verge of tears.

"I'm sorry. I just—I just need some time to figure this all out," Julie said, opening her closet door and placing her soiled clothing into her laundry basket. "I really appreciate that you're concerned about me, but this is something that I have to work through on my own. I'm exhausted. I'm hungry. And I have a full load of classes to get through tomorrow. It's overwhelming."

Pattie nodded and sniffed.

"It's not exactly how I wanted our fun night out to go, you know?" There was a chill in her voice. She opened the top drawer of her dresser and took out underwear and a nightshirt. "I'm going to change into this, get a cup of soup, and get into bed and read," Julie said quietly.

"Is there anything I can do?" Pattie asked, sitting up and swinging her legs off the top bunk of the bed.

"You can help me by acting like this whole thing never happened," Julie said, before retreating back into the bathroom.

27

"It's open," Julie heard as she jingled her key in the lock of her dorm room door that afternoon. Pulling her key out, she twisted the knob to find Pattie leaning back on the chair of her desk, talking to a girl from across the hall.

"Hey Julie. How did it go at the library today?"

"Uh, pretty good," she said, tossing her backpack onto her desk.

"Jules, this is Sarah from across the hall. She's a junior psych major. I don't know if you've ever met."

"Hey," Julie said to Sarah.

"How you doing?" Sarah replied. "I heard you guys had a pretty wild night out on Saturday."

Julie glared at Pattie. Pattie's eyes were wide as she shook her head, indicating that she had not mentioned anything of the incident to Sarah.

Julie's phone rang. "Hang on." Julie dug through her backpack and then glanced up at Sarah. "Nice meeting you," she said as she flipped open her phone and looked at the number.

"Yeah, you too," Sarah said.

"It's my mom. I'm just going to go in the bathroom and take this." She closed the bathroom door, sat on the toilet, and answered her phone.

"Hello?"

"Jules—hey, how are you doing? Didn't hear from you this last weekend."

"Oh, hi Mom. Yeah, I went to a Halloween gig with my roommate. Had a late night and studied most all day yesterday," she lied.

"Good, I'm glad you're out having a little fun," Shawn replied. "So, everything is going well with your new roommate and the dorm?"

"Oh, yeah. We're all settled in and doing fine." Julie tried to sound confident and upbeat. "Pattie is a nice girl."

"And classes are still going pretty good for you?"

"Yep, fine. Doing well in all my classes."

"That's awesome. I told Meryl and Oscar that you were probably just too busy working and having fun to call."

"I'll try to call them this week," Julie said. "And I'll see them over Thanksgiving. I was thinking that I might stay overnight with them for a night or two."

"They'd love that. I'll probably have to work most of the time anyway, so it would give you more company if you stayed out there with them. I'm sure they wouldn't mind."

"I'll give Grandma a call this week or on the weekend," she said. "Will you be picking me up on that Wednesday before Thanksgiving?"

"Yeah, of course. What time is your last class?"

"I'll be done around noon that day. If you came around one, I'd be ready to go."

"OK, but we can figure all that out as we get closer to the day," Shawn said. "I better let you get back to your studies."

"OK. Well, thanks for calling," Julie said. "I'm just probably going to stay here this next weekend if you don't mind."

"Oh no, that's cool. But if you change your mind, let me know and I can come up there and get you."

"No, I'll be swamped with homework anyway. I'll just plan on hanging here."

"OK… well, if you're sure… good. I'll give you another call toward the end of the week," Shawn said, making an effort to be motherly.

"All right then – I'll talk to you in a few days."

"Sure thing—I'll talk to you later. Bye."

"Bye." Julie flipped her phone shut.

If anyone would understand her plight, it would probably be her own mother. Still, Julie had no intention of sharing Saturday night's events with anybody.

She emerged from the bathroom to find Pattie reading her biology book at her desk.

"What's with you telling this Sarah chick my business?"

Pattie looked up from her text. "I didn't. She just heard about it from some of the other girls who went to the bar. Her boyfriend is in a fraternity and knows a bunch of the girls I hang with."

"Oh. OK. I just thought maybe you were dragging her over here because she's a psych major and I'm all fucked up, that's all."

"I promised you I wouldn't tell anyone, and I won't. Are you feeling better today?"

"I'm all right." Julie produced her pack of cigarettes and lighter from her backpack. "You don't mind if I crack the window and smoke, do you?"

"Nah—no problem. I just thought you hated smoking."

"I *did*." Julie glowered at Pattie. "But that was before your boyfriend's loser of a friend fucked me without my permission."

Julie's statement shocked Pattie, but she elected to not respond. "That's fine, Jules, smoke a cigarette if it makes you feel better." Pattie buried her head in her book.

Julie jerked a cigarette out of her pack and lit up. "I'm tired. I didn't sleep worth a shit last night," she said, taking a long drag to calm herself.

Pattie put down her book again. "I know. You must have had bad dreams all night long, huh?"

"Why? How would you know that?"

"I do sleep in the bunk above you, Jules. I heard you mumbling and crying several times during the night."

Julie simply looked out the window and exhaled smoke.

"I thought you were working out what happened on Saturday night," Pattie said. "You know what I mean?"

"Yeah, I guess. I don't remember any dreams, but I do know that I didn't sleep well."

"Have you considered going to the free counseling center?" Pattie asked.

Julie paused for a moment. "I—I just don't think I'm ready for that. I really don't feel like talking to anybody about it."

Pattie searched the top drawer of her desk. "Well, in the meantime, maybe you should try one of these. I swiped it from my mom's stash. It's a sleeping pill."

"Does it work?" Julie asked.

"Does it work? Are you kidding me? Absolutely. You'll sleep like a baby! You'll feel much better tomorrow and be able to put this whole mess behind you."

Julie took the pill and threw her cigarette butt out the window to the grass below. "Thanks, Pattie," she said as she squeezed Pattie's shoulder. "Sorry I've been such a bitch today. I'm just tired, I think."

"It's OK." Pattie directed her attention back to the book. "You wanna go to dinner around five?"

"Yeah, I guess."

28

"Do you have any homework tonight?" Pattie asked Julie as they were walking down the hallway to their dorm room after dinner.

"Nah, I don't think so,"

"Wow, that's a first." Pattie unlocked their door.

"Yeah, I'm pretty well caught up," Julie said, walking in after Pattie. "I'm beat, and I was actually thinking about going back to Slippery's for a drink."

Pattie stopped hanging up her coat. "You're kidding me, right? After what happened, you want to go back there?"

"I didn't get raped at the bar. Remember? Your buddy kidnapped me and fucked me at his apartment."

"I don't want to start anything with you," Pattie said carefully. "I know you've been through a lot, but I don't think it's real fair to keep blaming this whole thing on me. I think you need some counseling."

Julie went to her desk and pulled out her pack of cigarettes. "Oh, really? Wasn't it you who flagged those losers over to us in the first place?"

Pattie slammed her book down on the desk. "Yeah, I suppose it was. But I didn't pour those drinks down your throat, and I didn't advise you to go back to the scumbag's apartment, did I?"

Julie's eyes narrowed in anger. "I told you on Saturday afternoon that I felt like an idiot in that fucking costume and didn't want to go to the goddamned bar, but no, you wouldn't have it," she said exhaling smoke. "You just nagged and nagged and nagged until I agreed to go with you."

"You're a big girl, Jules," Pattie said condescendingly. "I figured anyone who has the brains to get a fucking full ride at MSU certainly has the brains to figure out if she wants to go to the bar, you know?"

Julie stormed into the bathroom, dropped her half-smoked cigarette into the toilet, and flushed. "Don't wait up," Julie said, coming back into the room and grabbing her purse, keys, and cigarettes off her desk.

Julie's unbridled rage told Pattie that she had overstepped her boundaries. "Jules—don't go. Come on—I shouldn't have said that."

Julie leaned down and looked directly at Pattie. "You're goddamned right you shouldn't have."

Pattie thrust herself back in her chair. "You're freakin' me out, Jules." Pattie began tearing up. "Back off! I mean it!"

"I should have known all along," Julie taunted. "You're nothing more than Daddy's little girl. You can't stand up for yourself or think for yourself." Pattie froze, certain Julie would strike her.

Tears rolled down Pattie's cheeks as she sat paralyzed at her desk. "Look at you—you can't even speak. You're pathetic," Julie said, easing away. "Like I said—don't wait up."

Pattie cowered in her chair as she watched Julie slam the door on her way out.

29

Slippery's wasn't nearly as busy as it had been on Saturday, but it was still pretty packed for a Monday.

"You got any ID?" came the voice of another bouncer at the door, as big as Pete and then some. Julie wondered if he played football for the Spartans.

Julie tried to act cool. "I, I'm a friend of Pete's."

"Oh yeah? A friend of Pete's, eh?" The bouncer shouted toward the bar. "Hey, Pete! You know her?"

Julie saw Pete pop his head up from behind. "Yeah—sure. Absolutely, it's cool."

Without looking at her ID, the bouncer waved Julie in.

Julie made her way up to the bar and took a seat. "Thanks, Pete," Julie said, locating a twenty in her purse.

"Almost didn't recognize you without the maid outfit," Pete said jokingly. "What's it gonna be tonight?"

"What's the special?" Julie asked as if she were a regular.

"Monday nights, it's Slippery's famous Boilermaker. A shot of whiskey in a pint of beer—like he's doin' right now," Pete gestured to another patron. "For a buck and a half, you can't beat it."

Julie watched as another person at the bar dropped the shot glass into the beer and chugged it down. His bar buddies cheered after he swallowed the last bit.

"Yeah—why not?" Julie said. "I'll try it."

Within a minute, Pete produced a mug of beer and a single shot glass containing an ounce of the hard stuff.

Julie smacked her twenty-dollar bill on the bar and turned her attention to the waiting drinks.

Daintily, she plopped the shot glass into the beer, and hoisted the mug in the air.

"Careful not to chip a tooth," an onlooker said, smiling.

One big breath and several gulps later, Julie had finished her first boilermaker like a pro.

Others at the bar nodded in approval and went on about their small talk. Holding up her empty glasses, Julie signaled Pete for another round.

"That was pretty good," Julie said. She liked the smoky sweet taste of the whiskey as it blended with the cold beer. "What is that you put in there?"

"Whiskey—a shot of whiskey." Pete collected her glasses and scurried to the other end of the bar.

Julie lit a cigarette and did a little people-watching while she waited for the second round.

"So where's Pattie?" Pete asked as he placed round two in front of Julie and took the money off the bar.

"She had homework to do," Julie said exhaling smoke and rolling her eyes.

"I hear ya," Pete said. "I should be doing my case studies, but I'm trying to make a little extra dough this week. I'm saving up for a new laptop."

Julie nodded and finished up her cigarette, and started working on her second drink.

30

"Jules," Pete called from the other side of the bar. "It's really late. You're not driving are ya?" He sounded like a protective older brother.

"No," Julie said belligerently. "I gotta take the bus—or a taxi—whatever—back to Wonders." She attempted to stand up and poke in her pocket for a cigarette.

"How about if I give you a lift back to the dorm?" he said in a concerned tone. "I don't usually make it a habit of driving total strangers home." Pete winked at her. "But you look like you could use some help tonight."

"No, no—no," Julie slurred. "I'm not makin' that misssstake again."

"What mistake?" Pete asked as he continued cleaning up.

"Nothin'," Julie said angrily. "I'm just not takin' a ride with somebody I don't know."

Pete held up his hands and backed away. "Suit yourself. But I could get you back to your dorm around two thirty or so. Good luck finding a bus or a taxi that's going out that way this time of night."

Julie sat watching Pete busy himself behind the bar and, in her inebriation, realized he was right.

"OK… I'll take a ride from you." She staggered off her barstool. "But if you lay one hand on me, you're dead."

Pete laughed. "OK, deal." He held out his hand to her. "I promise I'll be a total gentleman."

Julie ignored his hand and pawed through her purse for her lighter. Lighting her last cigarette, she sat back down and waited as Pete finished work.

Snapping off the light behind the bar, Pete was finally ready to go. "You ready?" Julie drunkenly dropped the remains of her cigarette on the floor and scrubbed it out.

"C'mon," Pete said, holding the door open for Julie. Julie teetered on the curb as she waited for him to lock up.

"I'm right over here." Pete gestured to a parked car in the rear of the neighboring parking lot. "It ain't much, but it's paid for," Pete said, laughing about his ride. "My grandma used to own it. Then it belonged to my dad, who kept it covered with a tarp in our garage for twenty years and never drove it! I inherited it after my dad passed away two years ago. I needed a car, so I began driving it. Runs like a top."

Pete unlocked the passenger side door and stood by as Julie climbed in. Too drunk for small talk, Julie listened as Pete jabbered on.

"Dodge built these for several years. My dad used to work for the company, and he helped my grandma get a deal on this one. Grandma didn't put many miles on it, and when she retired and moved in with my folks, she just gave it to them."

Pete started the car and put it into drive. Julie gazed around the pristine relic. "Itsss pretty clean," she managed. "It reminds me of something …" She struggled to remember. "I think … I think Ossscar had one of these."

"Who's Oscar?"

"Oscar is my granpa … Well, he's not my granpa, but he's my granma's husband. Yeah, he had one of these. I think."

RAGING SOUL

"You don't see too many of them anymore. They made these, and then in the seventies, changed the name to the Dodge Swinger. I've always thought they were kinda cool."

When they arrived at Wonder's Hall, Julie had passed out. "Jules. Wake up, Jules." Pete tugged on her arm from the passenger side of the vehicle. "C'mon, we're back at your dorm."

Julie emerged from the car, stumbling drunk and disoriented. "Do you have your keys?" After rummaging through her purse, Julie found her dorm room key. "Right here," Julie giggled, waving it. In the brief ten minutes it took to get back to the dorm, Julie's mood had gone from irritable to giddy.

Pete supported Julie to the front door, pressed the security buzzer, and helped open the door when the guard appeared. "Do you know where you're going?" Pete asked protectively.

"Yeah. Uh, thanks fer tha ride home. You really are a nice guy," she gushed.

"I'll see to it that she gets to her room," said the guard, shaking his head. "Doesn't seem like a good way to start off a week of school, but it takes all kinds." He tried to help by taking Julie's limp upper arm.

"Let go! Let go of me." Julie pulled away from the security guard and turned toward her new friend. "I see you, Pete."

Pete smiled. "OK, Jules. Get some rest. I'll see you later."

The security guard watched Julie stagger to the elevator and pressed the up button. "I'm in 306. I know where I'm goin'."

Pattie looked at her illuminated clock radio. It was 2:39 when she was awakened by the loud clanking of keys in the lock of her dorm room door.

In stumbled Julie, hammered and reeking of alcohol and cigarette smoke. Tossing her keys and purse onto her desk, Julie kicked off her shoes and flopped down onto the bottom bunk without undressing or turning down the bed.

Pattie lay silent in her bed above, listening as Julie gurgled off into a deep and drunken slumber.

31

Sunlight streamed in through the dorm window, and Julie heard the laughter of students coming from the hallway. Struggling to sit up on the edge of the bed, she squinted at her alarm clock.

"Oh shit," she said aloud, realizing that she had missed her morning classes. It was one o'clock in the afternoon.

Julie rubbed her forehead, stood up, and shuffled into the bathroom. Her mind-bending hangover prevented her from getting any thoughts straight. Hovering over the bathroom sink, she splashed cold water on her face before going for the Advil in the medicine cabinet. She tossed three tablets into her mouth and washed them down with water she cupped in her hands.

Closing the cabinet, Julie looked into her face. "You sure have screwed things up," she said quietly to herself in the mirror. Gazing at her bloodshot eyes, she remembered the argument with Pattie and boilermakers at Slippery's. Everything else was pretty much a blur.

"You need to pull your act together, or —you're going to screw this up and be no better than Shawn."

With that thought resonating in her pounding head, Julie undressed, turned on the shower, and climbed into the stall for a long soak before hitting her last two classes of the day.

32

Pattie was sitting at her desk studying when Julie entered the dorm. Abruptly, she slammed her book shut and grabbed her backpack.

"Where are you going?" Julie asked as she heaved her backpack onto her desk.

"None of your business. To the library, I guess. Anywhere away from you."

"Pattie, listen. I've been a complete idiot." Julie sat down at her desk. "I—I think I owe you a huge apology. I'm very sorry for the things I said yesterday afternoon, and for all the shit I've put you through in the last few days."

Pattie stopped what she was doing and looked at Julie. "You've been a complete bitch," Pattie said frankly. "Your whole attitude, your personality—it's all changed in a matter of days."

Julie rubbed the back of her right hand while she thought about what to say next. "I had a chat with myself this morning, and I promise you, I'm done with all the crap. I'm going to get my shit together," she said, glancing over at Pattie. "You know?"

Pattie nodded.

"I'm just really sorry and I'm hoping we can maybe, I don't know …start over?" Julie said, still rubbing the back of her hand.

"What's wrong with your hand?" Pattie asked.

"Not sure. Probably did something to it in my moment of stupidity last night."

Julie shook her head. "Really. I'm done with all that shit, Pattie. I have too much riding on this—my whole college career and my life after that. You have every right to be completely pissed off with me."

"It's partly my fault, too," Pattie said. "This whole thing for you started because of our night out on Saturday."

"Yeah, but you were right yesterday. You didn't force me to go to the bar—or force me to go home with Greg, you know?"

Pattie held out her hand. "Let's just start over then. Let's shake on it."

"Yes! But careful of my hand," Julie said, grinning and holding out her sore right hand.

"OK, so it's full steam ahead." Julie picked up her book bag. "I have everything I need in here, so I'm probably going to go down to the lobby and read."

"Why don't you stay here? I'm just studying, too." Pattie unzipped her backpack and found her book.

"Yeah, OK, I'll hang here a while. But I have a feeling that I'm going to be up reading all night, trying to catch up with what I missed today. I kept you awake enough last night. Really, it's cool. I'll just go down to the lobby when you're ready to knock off for tonight."

33

By the following week, Julie was feeling more like her old self. Having refocused on her studies, she had completely caught up on the homework she had missed, and then some.

"So, what are you up to this weekend, Pattie?"

"Some girls I know are going to a party at the Chi Sig house," she replied. "They want me to go with 'em. What about you?"

"Uh, probably nothing," Julie said. "I'll probably just hang around and study to get prepped for a trig test I have next Wednesday."

"Yeah, I need to study for my math, too. I suck at trig."

Julie went through her backpack and spotted a half-smoked pack of cigarettes and her lighter.

Watching Julie consider a smoke, Pattie remarked, "I thought you gave all that up."

"Yeah, I did. But just one cig won't hurt, right? I'll crack a window."

Julie perched on the window ledge, slid open the window, and lit up.

"So what do you think?" Pattie asked. "You wanna join me and the girls for a little party with the Chi Sigs on Friday night?"

"I probably shouldn't. Like I said, I should study for trig."

"Aw, c'mon. You can study all day Saturday and Sunday. And

you don't have to drink: you can just hang with us and have fun, get outta here for a night, you know?" Pattie teased.

"I'll think about it." Taking another puff, Julie thought back to that Sunday night at Slippery's, remembering how good the whiskey had tasted.

"Yeah, I might join you girls. I'm a grown woman. I'm a freshman at MSU! I can handle myself at a party."

"Yeah? I don't want to force you into anything you don't want to do."

"Sure! I won't make the same mistakes I made a week ago—that I promise you," she said.

"If you're cool, I'm cool." Pattie closed the cover of her book. "It's a plan, then. Sarah—you know, the psych major across the hall—well, her boyfriend is a Chi Sig and that's how I got, we got invited."

Julie flicked her butt out the window, closed the window, and went into the bathroom to wash the smoky smell off her hands. "God, my hand is still killing me," Julie said from the bathroom sink.

"Maybe you pulled a tendon or something," Pattie said as she scrounged through her dresser drawer looking for a nightshirt.

"Yeah, maybe. Here, does it look swollen to you?" She showed the back of her right hand to Pattie. "It's really achy."

"Holy shit, Jules," Pattie said, staring at Julie's puffy hand. "Maybe you have carpal tunnel. My mom had that from all her years as a secretary on the computer. You should go to the health clinic and get an x-ray," she suggested. "I have some zipper baggies on the shelf, and there's that tray of ice cubes in the freezer part of the fridge. Make yourself a bag of ice and put it on your hand tonight."

"That's probably a good idea, *Doctor* Robbison. Why didn't Doctor Deerfield think of that?"

Pattie laughed. "One day when we're colleagues at our medical clinic, I'll remind you of the day I prescribed ice for your hand." Pattie changed into her nightshirt.

Julie continued carefully rubbing her hand. "It is sore as heck," I just cannot figure out what I must've done to it."

Pattie climbed into the top bunk and turned on her lamp. "I'm going to read for a while. I'm not tired yet. I'll probably read for a couple hours, if that's OK with you."

"Absolutely," Julie said, taking a baggie to their mini fridge. "After all the studying I've done for the last week, I'm ready for a good sleep. You won't bother me in the least."

Julie made an ice bag, changed into her nightshirt, and slipped into bed.

34

Pattie had been reading for nearly an hour before she noticed Julie's unsettled breathing pattern from below. Hanging her head over the top bunk, she looked down at her roommate.

Julie lay flat on her back, eyes at half-staff, breathing erratically—apparently asleep. Pattie studied her roommate's face, thinking how creepy Julie looked. Chalking it up to exhaustion, Pattie started reading again.

Moments later, Pattie's concentration was interrupted by Julie's clear voice.

"Bitch," she said plainly. "You bitch."

Pattie hung her head over the bed again. Julie's eyes were still half open, but her breathing had settled down.

"Jules?" Pattie said quietly. "Jules?" No response. Puzzled by what was going on, Pattie shrugged and went back to reading.

A few minutes later, the bunk bed shook violently as Julie tossed over to her side. As suddenly as it began, it stopped.

"Get up. Bitch—get up!"

Pattie listened intently for more words. Julie's breathing again became labored. She tossed again to the other side, then sputtered and woke up. Breathing hard, Julie got out of bed and made her way to the bathroom.

"Are you OK?" Pattie asked her. "You must've been having some intense dream."

"I was," Julie said from the bathroom. "I was in a house or something."

"You didn't have the best language, in your dream." Pattie sat up on one elbow. "You kept saying 'bitch.' At first I thought you were talking to me."

Julie laughed. "No, really?" Hmm …yeah …I was definitely dreaming that I was in a house… no place that I recognize, though. And I don't recall calling anyone a bitch."

"You looked really creepy, too. No offense."

"What do you mean?" Julie said, flushing the toilet.

"You were sleeping flat on your back with your eyes half open. You looked possessed."

Julie washed her hands, came out of the bathroom, and opened the top drawer of her desk. "I'm going to try this sleeping pill you gave me. You're serious, these really work?"

Pattie leaned forward off her bed. "Yeah, absolutely. If you can't sleep after taking that thing, you've definitely got a problem."

"I've never had problems sleeping before." Julie popped the pill and drank it down with a slurp from the bathroom faucet.

Climbing back into bed, she rolled onto her side and placed the half-melted ice bag on the back of her hand. "How long will the pill take to kick in?"

"Maybe a half hour, forty-five minutes tops," Pattie said from above. "But you're tired already. It probably won't take that long for you."

"Night," Julie said, closing her eyes.

"Good night, Jules. I hope you can get some good rest." Pattie turned the page in her book an went back to reading.

Less than an hour later, Pattie heard a stirring from the bottom bunk. Although Julie was turned over on her side, her breathing had taken on the same ragged edge, sounding as though she were frightened.

Julie mumbled something into her pillow, and Pattie strained to understand what she was saying. Looking at the clock radio across the room, Pattie saw that it was nearing midnight. The pill had apparently rendered Julie's body motionless, but the dreaming continued for the next hour or so.

Mumbling aside, Pattie noticed that Julie would occasionally cough without waking. Raspy and wheezy, the cough sounded like it was deeply seated in her lungs. Eventually, Julie's coughing calmed down, and her mumbling subsided enough for Pattie to close her book and go to sleep. It was nearly two by then.

35

Julie was up and around by six thirty, and at seven fifteen was dressed and loading last-minute essentials into her backpack.

"What time is your class this morning?" a groggy Pattie asked from her upper bunk.

"My first one is at eight-ten. Next term, I'm either taking Fridays off altogether, or scheduling my classes a little later in the day!"

"How'd you sleep?" Pattie asked.

Julie rubbed the back of her right hand again. "Uh, OK, I guess. But I kept dreaming about that damn house, all night long."

"The same house that you dreamt about earlier?"

"Yeah, I think so. An old farm house of sorts."

"Hey, are you feeling OK?" Pattie asked. "Do you have a cold or something?"

"No, I don't think so. My hand hurts like hell, but I'm pretty sure I'm not coming down with a cold. Why?"

"Besides talking in your sleep—mumbling, really—you started coughing a bunch of times."

Julie froze for a moment, and then said, "You just jogged my memory. The house I was in: It was on fire. There was heavy black smoke, and I was covering my nose with my shirt." Julie's eyes were immobile and glazed.

"Really? Are you messing with me?"

"No, no—I'm serious, Pattie," Julie continued to stare at her.

"The house in my dream was on fire." She took a sharp breath. "Oh, and I was trying to get out!"

"That's some serious shit you're dreaming." Pattie flopped back onto her pillow. "Maybe you shouldn't take any more of my mom's sleeping pills."

"Yeah, maybe not," Julie said, still shaken by the sudden vivid memory.

Julie produced a cigarette from her backpack. "I've still got time before class. You mind if I light up and think about this?" She opened the window.

"Have at it. I'm going to get up and take a shower."

36

"Yo," said Pattie, bursting through the dorm room door late that afternoon.

Julie sat on the window ledge smoking a cigarette. Her right hand was wrapped in an Ace bandage.

"Did you get your hand looked at today?" Pattie tossed her keys and backpack onto her desk.

"Nah, I just bought an Ace bandage at Rite Aid."

"Does it help?"

"Not yet. I guess the bandage makes me remember not to bump it."

"You really should get an x-ray."

"Yeah. If it isn't better by Monday, I will. I really think I just strained something. So what's the plan for tonight?"

"Well, Sarah said the party over there starts around seven thirty or eight. And I happened to run into my old buddy Pete today, and talked him into buying us this." Pattie produced a paper bag from her backpack.

"What is it?" Julie asked, tossing her fuming butt to the grass below.

Pattie pulled a fifth of Jack Daniels from the bag. "Our old buddy JD. You know: Jack Daniels."

Julie's face still looked blank.

"Whiskey. Hello? Anybody home?"

"Oh, whiskey. It's a good thing it's this week and not last," Julie said, laughing. "I couldn't look a bottle of that stuff in the eye."

"Really? You were drinking whiskey on Monday?"

"Well, sort of, yeah. The special was Boilermakers."

"Isn't that with beer or something?" Pattie said as she twisted off the top of the bottle.

"Yeah, you take the shot of it and dump it—glass and all—into the middle of the beer and toss it down the hatch," she said smiling.

Pattie raised her eyebrows. "And you liked 'em?"

"Well, yeah, I guess," Julie said. "Believe it or not, I sort of like the taste."

Pattie grabbed two shot glasses off her bookshelf and, using her shirttail, wiped the dust from them. Carefully, she poured two shots.

"Here. Let's have a drink," she said, handing a shot to Julie.

"To a better weekend." Julie hoisted the small glass into the air and clinking it against Pattie's.

"Amen sistafriend," Pattie replied, before tossing the drink back. She grimaced at the taste.

"Ah," Julie said, downing hers. "What's up?" she said. "You don't like whiskey?"

"Oh, yeah, I like it," Pattie grabbed the bottle. "I just like it better after a couple."

Julie laughed and went for her cigarettes. "I bought a new pack today. I know I said I don't smoke, but I think I kinda like it. My mom won't care—she'll be glad that I finally joined the dark side."

Pattie and Julie were laughing when they heard their door open.

"Knock, knock?" Sarah poked her head around the door. "What are you girls doin'?" she asked playfully.

"What's it look like, Sarah?" Pattie reached for a third shot glass on the bookshelf. "We're getting' ready for your boyfriend's big party."

"So I see." Sarah took a seat on Julie's desk.

"You remember my roommate, Julie, right?" Pattie handed Sarah a shot.

"Oh sure," Sarah said, smiling at Julie. "What is this?"

"JD," Pattie said. "Turns out JD is one of Julie's favorites, too. Who knew!"

Sarah was a girl everyone liked. Despite her petite four-foot-eleven frame, her curvaceous figure and bubbly personality filled a room. With fine facial features, a flawless complexion, and curly brown hair, it was easy to understand why Sarah was never lacking in the boyfriend department.

Even Sarah's brightly polished fingernails reflected her vibrant personality, as she grasped the small shot glass with her perfect manicure.

"Down the hatch," Sarah said, tossing the drink back. "I told Mike we'd be there around seven thirty," Sarah said putting her shot glass down on the desk.

"Mike is the president of the Chi Sigs," Pattie explained to Julie. Julie nodded and exhaled smoke out the window.

"Everybody loves Mike," Sarah said. She reached for the bottle of booze and poured another round for everyone.

"How long have you guys been going out?" Julie asked, tossing her smoldering butt out the window.

"Two years, six months, and five days," Sarah answered as she picked up her shot glass. "But who's counting?" Pattie and Julie laughed.

"So, you're thinking he might be Mr. Right?" Pattie asked.

"Well … who knows, really," Sarah said thoughtfully. "We've

still got a lot of school ahead of us, but after that, I hope we're still together."

"That's so cool," Pattie said dreamily. "I hope I meet a good guy while I'm here."

"Not me," Julie said, closing the window.

Sarah directed her attention toward Julie. "No? Why not?"

"I don't know. My mom never had much luck with men, and quite frankly, never had too many good things to say about 'em. My grandma's boyfriend, Oscar, is a good guy, but even he was foolin' around on his dying wife for a long time."

"What? What are you talking about?" Pattie asked.

Julie pointed to the portrait on her dresser. "Oscar—over there. His wife had dementia for years, and he put her in a home because he couldn't work and take care of her at the same time. He'd go visit her every day, but if she only knew what he was doing behind her back, you know? That's what my mom said, anyway."

"What do you mean?" Sarah asked, placing her shot glass on the desk.

"After the accident—it was in 1966—my mom was only six." Julie reached for her cigarettes. "My grandma was a total wreck, I guess. Oscar was the undertaker who handled my Grandpa's burial, and he went a little further than just comforting my grandma, if you know what I mean."

Julie lit her cigarette, cracked the window again, and sat back on the window ledge.

"What accident?" Sarah asked, becoming more interested.

"Yeah, back up the bus," Pattie said. "You never told me any of this."

"A farming accident—a pretty gruesome one, too, from how my mom described it. My Grandpa was out harvesting the corn in the fall. He stopped when a cob became stuck in the picker. He'd been a farmer for his whole life, so you'd think he'd have known better, but I guess he figured he'd been doing it so long, he could just reach in there and pull out whatever it was without stopping the blades."

"Oh, God," Pattie said, covering her mouth.

"His shirtsleeve got caught in there, and it just pulled him in, right up to his shoulder," Julie said, staring out the window and taking a drag off her cigarette.

"Aw, God, I'm so sorry," Sarah said.

"Well, by the time Grandma and Aunt Bev noticed that his tractor was stalled in the field, it was too late. He bled to death before anyone could help him." Julie stared out the window. "Grandma never forgave herself for that."

An awkward pause ensued as the girls visualized the horrific events of that day. "Then six years later, my mom's sister—Aunt Bev—never came home from her job." Julie took another puff of her cigarette. "If it weren't for Oscar there, my mom's pretty sure Grandma would have lost her mind."

"What happened to your aunt?" Pattie asked as she freshened the drinks.

Julie took a long drag on her cigarette and exhaled. "They're not really sure. They searched for her body for something like two weeks and never found any sign of her." She leaned forward to pick up her glass.

"Could she just have run away?" Pattie asked.

"No. It's a really long story, but no. Some guy gave her a ride home from where she worked. They think he dropped her off in the driveway, but don't really know what happened after that."

"What about the guy?" Sarah asked. "Did they track him down and ask him questions?"

"Well, it turned out that he was in a really bad car accident soon after he dropped her off," Julie said, and took a swig from her glass. "A deer ran out in front of him, his car flipped, and he burned up in the crash. Aunt Bev wasn't in the car, so they couldn't prove he had anything to do with her disappearance." Julie put her shot glass back down on the desk. "It remains a mystery to this day."

"God, what a story. Your family sure has been through a lot," Sarah said, looking truly sorry.

"Yeah," Julie said, staring thoughtfully out the window for several minutes. As suddenly as she had begun sharing the story, Julie ended it. "We should probably get ready to go."

"Thanks for the drink and a half," a slightly tipsy Sarah said. "Come over to my room when you're ready. The cab will be out front around seven fifteen."

37

Every light in the huge Chi Sig house was on as the taxi pulled up front. After paying the driver, the trio of tipsy college co-eds made their way to the front door.

"Should we have arranged a time for him to pick us up?" Julie asked her companions.

"Nah," Sarah said as they made their way toward the porch. "We can either sack out here, or Mike's friend Dave can give us a lift later. He doesn't drink, and if he's around, he's always a good guy to hit up for a ride."

Without knocking, Sarah walked into the elaborate foyer. The house heaved with college students, mingling throughout the house, beers in hand.

"Hey, hey," came a booming voice from the living room. Mike was remarkably handsome. Curly brown hair, a six-foot-four frame and good looks, it was no wonder Sarah was smitten.

"Hi sweetie," he said kindly as he bent down to hug Sarah. "How'd you guys get here?"

"We split a cab," Sarah said. "We had a couple shots back at the dorm, you know? Mike, this is Pattie and Julie. They're roommates and live across the hall from me."

"Welcome to Chi Sig," Mike said, proudly swooping his muscular arm outward. "Make yourselves at home. The keg's in the kitchen, the hard stuff is on the bar downstairs. C'mon with me, Sarah. There's somebody I want you to meet."

Sarah nestled into Mike's embrace. "I'll catch you guys in a bit," she said cheerfully. "Have fun, make yourselves comfortable."

"You wanna get a beer in the kitchen?" Pattie asked.

"I think I'm going to go down to the bar and see if I can scare up a shot of whiskey. I'll meet you back up here."

Julie went down to the walkout basement and found herself alone in a beautifully furnished rec room, complete with a fully loaded bar, music, and a pool table. A comfy leather couch and love seat were situated around a fireplace at the end of the room. The bar was strategically positioned between the two areas.

Julie bee-lined it to the bar and found a full bottle of Jack Daniels ready and waiting. Instead of opting for a shot glass, Julie found a cocktail glass, loaded it with ice, and poured JD over the rocks.

By eleven o'clock, Pattie finally went looking for Julie. The Chi Sig house was bursting with students, and with Julie nowhere to be found in the basement or on the main level, Pattie began to wonder if she'd maybe taken off early.

"There you are," Pattie said, stepping into the backyard from the basement walkout. Julie was clustered with several other students as two young men attempted to start a campfire.

Pattie came up behind Julie. "What's up? I thought you were going to come find me." The smell of marijuana hung in the air.

"I must've forgot," a drunken Julie said. "You been having a good time?"

Pattie shivered and rubbed her arms. "Yeah. But I'm kinda tired. You ready to go?"

"What time is it?" Julie slurred.

"It's about eleven," Pattie replied.

"Wow—eleven already." Julie rubbed the back of her left hand. "Why don't we grab just one more drink, then we can go."

"OK, but I'm going to see if I can borrow a jacket if we're out here. And I'll call for a cab to come get us in about a half hour, OK?"

Julie nodded and headed back inside. "Do you want a shot?" she asked Pattie as she slid the door open.

"Mmm… OK, yeah, why not?" Pattie flipped open her cell phone and hit redial for the taxi company while Julie went behind the bar and fetched two clean shot glasses.

"Yeah, the Chi Sig house, that's right," Pattie said into her phone. "About a half hour? OK. Good. Thanks."

Pattie shut her phone and turned to the bar. "They'll be here in about a half hour."

Julie had poured the drinks. "Wow, you sure seem to know what you're doing now," Pattie said, laughing.

"Cheers!" Julie said as she raised her glass into the air. "Cheers!" Pattie clinked her glass and took a dainty sip.

Julie downed her shot and quickly poured another. Pattie's initial impulse was to comment on how fast Julie could toss back a drink, but based on her previous experience with Julie's ever-changing disposition, she decided to skip it.

She was flat-out wasted again, and Pattie knew it.

Pattie took another sip of her drink. "Do you want to go back outside to the campfire?"

"Nah. The booze is in here, right?"

Julie reached in a pocket and pulled out her cigarettes.

"I don't think they allow smoking in here," Pattie said, apologetically.

"Screw 'em," Julie said as she searched for her lighter.

"Really—Jules—you'll get yelled at and they'll kick us out of here. It's a rule they have, something to do with home insurance and their fire policy."

Julie rolled her eyes and lit up. "Honest to God, Pattie. You really don't have any balls, do ya?"

Pattie stepped back. "I'm sorry?"

"What I mean is," Julie said, exhaling smoke and taking a drink of JD, "you're so afraid of insulting anybody, you can never think for yourself."

Pattie calmly placed her drink on the bar. "I think you've had enough to drink, Julie."

"Oh really?" Julie said, flicking her ash onto the carpeted floor. "Here we go again with the Mother Patricia thing."

"What's going on you guys?" asked Sarah as she descended the stairs. "Sorry, Jules, but if you're going to smoke, you're going to have to go outside."

Julie glared at the girls, and went outside.

Sarah looked at Pattie. "Jesus, what happened to her?"

"She's hammered again. I found her outside smoking a joint with some of the others, and when I suggested that we should maybe get going, she said we could go after another drink." Pattie pointed to her glass. "She's had way too much tonight."

"Wow. Did you know she had a drinking problem?"

"That's the thing. When she arrived at MSU in September, she'd never even been to a bar before. She had never even tried a drink!"

"No shit," Sarah exclaimed.

"And the more she drinks, the nastier she gets." Pattie glanced toward the patio. "When she lit up in here, I told her that there was a no-smoking policy, but she went all mental on me about it."

"Yeah, she's definitely had too much to drink," Sarah said.

"Mike's friend Dave hasn't had a drink all night. Do you want him to drive you guys home?"

"I've just called a cab. They're coming at eleven thirty. I just hope we can get Julie to come with me."

"If she gets nasty about it, I'll handle it and have Dave give her a lift," Sarah offered. "Really. If you want to go back to the dorm, just go. I can handle Julie."

"I'll just wait five minutes or so and then approach her," Pattie said. "If she gives me any shit about it, I'll let you know." Pattie shook her head. "I'm never going to bring her to another party again. This is bullshit, you know?"

"Yeah. But from the sounds of it, she's had a pretty rough life, too," Sarah said.

"I know, but this is ridiculous. We're supposed to be having fun, and she just ruins it by getting so shit-faced."

Pattie finished most of her drink, and then with Sarah, opened the sliding glass door onto the patio.

Julie stood alone, staring into the fire. The rest of the students had walked further out into the yard to play a nocturnal version of hide-and-seek. So deep in thought, Julie didn't notice that Pattie and Sarah flanked her by the fireside.

The flickering light of the fire danced on Julie's face, exposing a sad and forlorn expression.

"You OK?" Sarah said, touching Julie's elbow.

"Huh?" she said, looking side to side. "Oh, yeah—I'm fine. I was just thinking."

"About what?" Sarah asked.

"I don't really know," Julie said, still staring into the flames. "Just a bunch of stuff, really."

"It's been a rough week for everybody," Pattie said, patting Julie's shoulder.

"Oh—it's been pretty rough on *you*, has it?" Julie said, now looking away from the fire and directly at Pattie. Pattie and Sarah could feel Julie's seething anger.

"C'mon Julie, let's not argue," Sarah said diplomatically. "I think we all should go back to the dorm. It's really late."

Julie looked away from Pattie and back into the fire.

"The cab will be here in a few minutes. Let's call it a night," Pattie said.

"I need to go to the bathroom." Julie turned to walk back into the house.

"OK, go to the bathroom and meet us at the front door, OK?" Sarah said cheerfully.

Julie nodded and said nothing.

Sarah and Pattie watched as Julie stumbled up the stairs.

"She is so fucked up," Sarah said. "Something is deeply wrong with her, I just know it."

"She freaks me out. She gets so pissed off at me, and I don't even know her that well."

"Yeah. And what was all that about, at the fire?" Sarah asked.

"It's way too long to go into right now, but let's just say she's had a tough few weeks on campus," Pattie said quietly.

"I think the best thing to do is to get her back to the dorm and get her to bed," Sarah said. "She is so fucked up right now that if she gets any drunker, we could really have a problem on our hands."

38

In the ten-minute ride back from the party to the dorm, Julie had passed out in the backseat of the cab. Together, Pattie and Sarah roused Julie enough to get her to stagger back to their dorm room virtually unassisted.

"I can't believe you made me leave the party," Julie slurred as she lurched into their room.

"Let me help you get ready for bed," Sarah said, trying to help.

"Get your hands off me, bitch," Julie yelled.

Sarah threw her hands up. "That's it. I'm outta here!"

"Fine—leave, tha's what I want you to do—get outta my room." Julie flopped onto her bed. "Both of ya—get the fuck outta here."

Sarah and Pattie went into the hallway. "Do you want to stay in my room tonight?" Sarah whispered. "She's definitely whacked. I think you should see about changing roommates."

"Honestly, Sarah, she's not like this when she's sober. She's actually a pretty nice person. It's like she turns into someone else when she's tanked. Besides, she'll pass out, and that will be that. She probably won't remember a thing about it in the morning."

"If you change your mind, just knock," Sarah said.

"Thanks! But aren't you going back to the party to spend time with Mike?"

"Nah, I told him I was going to stay here. It's late, anyway. I've got some reading I should do, and I'm still wide awake."

"Yeah, me too," Pattie said.

"If you need anything—if she pukes all over or… I don't know, whatever—come get me."

"Thanks, Sarah." Pattie gave her a hug. "I owe you big time."

"What are friends for? I'll see you tomorrow."

Pattie crept back inside the dorm room and quietly locked the door. The low buzz of Julie's breathing told Pattie that her roommate was officially knocked out. Grabbing a nightshirt out of her dresser, she quickly changed clothes, flipped off the lamp, and climbed up the frame of the bunk into her awaiting bed.

The clock radio on her desk shelf read 12:13 a.m. Clicking on her small reading light, she settled in and began reading her textbook. To the hum of Julie's rhythmic breathing, she quietly read a chapter of her psychology book, highlighting important facts with her purple highlighter as she went.

By twelve fifty-five, she had read half of her assignment. She wasn't really tired, and although she hadn't planned to study, was glad it had worked out that way. Reading her psych assignment into the wee hours of Saturday morning would allow her to focus on trig the rest of the weekend. Turning back to her text, she began to read again.

Within ten minutes, Pattie heard a difference in Julie's breathing from below. Much like the other night when Julie had taken a sleeping pill and fallen asleep, her breathing took on a raspy and hurried sound.

Pattie stopped reading and began listening. Gradually, Julie's respiration increased, sounding much like a person who was running scared.

Julie moaned in her sleep and turned violently onto her back.

Pattie popped her head over the bunk and stared down into Julie's face. Eyes wide open, Julie's chest heaved as she exhaled booze breath into the air.

In an instant, Julie sat bolt upright in bed, her eyes still wide open and mouth gaping. So startled was Pattie that she nearly fell out of the upper bunk. She scurried to the end of her bunk bed and climbed down quietly.

Julie pushed herself into the corner of her bottom bunk, gathered the bedspread to her chest, and emitted a low, whining sound, much like a wounded animal would do.

Pattie waved her hand in front of Julie's open eyes. No response. Quietly, Pattie let herself out of the dorm room and knocked on Sarah's door.

"What is it?" Sarah said, cracking the door open.

"It's Julie," Pattie said urgently.

"What's wrong?" Sarah said as she opened the door. Sarah's hair was mussed and it looked like she had been sleeping soundly.

"It's Julie. She's asleep but is having some weird dream again, this time with her eyes open, and she's sitting up."

Sarah made sure her door was unlocked and followed Pattie back to her room.

Julie remained balled up in the corner of her bunk, eyes wide open and seemingly terrified.

"She's having a night terror," Sarah said quietly. "They're worse than nightmares, and in the morning, she probably won't remember a thing about any of it. Usually little kids have them, but occasionally adults will."

Julie's mouth was closed, but her breathing was heavy and labored. Tears streamed from her eyes, yet she didn't cry.

"Julie. Can you hear me?" Sarah said calmly. Julie didn't respond.

"Jesus—what happened to her hand?" Sarah asked Pattie. "It's all swollen."

"I know," Pattie said. "She doesn't know what she did to it, but it's really been bothering her."

"Julie, can you hear me?" Sarah asked.

Julie's eyes darted back and forth, apparently trying to figure out who was talking.

A husky voice came from Julie's throat. "Fuckin' bitch. This will teach ya." Julie pushed herself further into the corner and wadded the blanket in her hands.

Sarah sat back and didn't know what to say. "Did she just say what I think she said?"

Clearly overwhelmed by the situation, Pattie cowered behind Sarah as she continued to push Julie to respond. "Maybe we should call an ambulance," Pattie suggested.

"No, it's OK," Sarah said. "My niece had one of these when I was babysitting and I got her through it."

Julie's hair was becoming stringy, as sweat began to run down her forehead and cheeks.

"I'm scared," Pattie confessed. "This is all too weird for me."

Sarah turned to Pattie. "It's OK, really. She's just having a dream. We can get her through this."

"Julie? Can you hear me?" Sarah asked again.

The sound of Sarah's voice agitated Julie, causing her to thrash about and mumble. "Fire—it's hot—fire," was all Sarah and Pattie could understand.

"She had a dream about a fire just the other night," Pattie whispered to Sarah. "Her eyes were open like this, but she also started coughing."

"Get out," Julie said clearly, but in a deep, raspy voice, different from her own. "Hot—smoke." She coughed and gagged as she continued wringing the bedspread with her hands. "Blood! So much blood!" Julie became more frantic.

Looking troubled, Sarah struggled to remain calm.

"Let's call 911," Pattie repeated.

"Julie, wake up. Julie! It's only a dream!" Sarah said, clapping her hands. "Wake up."

Julie's eye movement ricocheted like the steel ball in a pinball machine. Suddenly, her eyes rolled backward into her head. A guttural voice came from deep within Julie's throat. "Viiiii-let," she hissed.

"Oh my God. What did she say?" Pattie said urgently. "Why is her voice like that?"

Sarah looked rattled and shook her head in confusion. "It sounded like the word 'violet,'" she said.

"Viiiii-let," Julie repeated in the same deep voice.

"Do you think she's possessed?" Pattie whispered to Sarah.

"Jesus, no! I think she's having a bad dream." Pattie's constant questioning was beginning to annoy Sarah. "Julie—can you hear me? You need to wake up," Sarah said again.

Julie's eyes returned from the back of her head and began darting back and forth again. Carefully, Sarah touched Julie's shoulder and tried to awaken her. Julie grabbed Sarah's wrist with her right hand and clenched it tightly.

"Viiiii-let," she hissed, twisting Sarah's wrist further with her sweaty hand. Sarah struggled to pull away, but Julie's grip was too strong.

"Pattie, help me," Sarah said, trying not to panic. "Help me loosen her grip."

Pattie grabbed Julie's right hand and pried her fingers off one by one. Julie thrashed and once again pushed herself into the corner of the wall.

"Are you OK?" Pattie asked as she watched Sarah examine her wrist. Pattie could see a bruise already forming on Sarah's fair skin.

"I'm fine," Sarah said, focusing back on Julie.

"Julie! Wake up!" Sarah said in a louder voice. "You're dreaming, Julie. Wake up."

"Fuck you Viiiiiii-let," Julie continued in a guttural voice. "Die Viiiii-let."

Julie's eyes fluttered and shut.

"This is so creepin' me out," Pattie said, retreating to her desk.

"I think she's over it." Sarah watched as Julie's breathing leveled out. Julie slid down the wall and back onto her pillow. Her grasp of the bedspread released.

"That's the weirdest thing I've ever seen," Pattie said, looking at Sarah.

"Yeah," Sarah said quietly, looking at a now peaceful Julie. "This girl has some issues. Did you catch that last thing she said?"

"Die Violet?" Pattie asked. "Yeah. What do you think that's all about?"

"Hopefully, just a bad dream, but it kinda makes you wonder about all the crap she's been through over the years, doesn't it?" Sarah headed for the door. "I think you should come sleep in my room. She's probably done for the night, but I'd feel safer knowing you're over there with me."

Pattie nodded. "Yeah, OK, you're right. I'll grab my pillow and comforter." Pattie climbed up into her bunk, grabbed her bedding, and snapped off her reading light.

"I'll be back in the morning before she comes to, I'm sure."

39

The makeshift bed in Sarah's room hadn't allowed Pattie to sleep well. As a result, she elected to get up early and head for the library with Sarah and Mike. Julie was still sleeping when Pattie went back to their room, and would undoubtedly not feel too well when she did awaken. After showering and grabbing a quick Pop Tart, Pattie collected her backpack, grabbed her keys, and locked the door behind her.

Sarah was waiting in the hallway. "Was Julie still out?" she asked as they walked toward the elevator.

"Oh yeah," Pattie said. "Out like a light. She's probably gonna feel like 100 percent shit today."

"No doubt. Mike's picking us up. He's got a lot of studying to do for his criminal law class."

Pattie nodded as the two rode the elevator down. "I'm really concerned about Julie, but at the same time, I don't know if I really feel like putting up with all this shit. I mean, I've known the chick for what? Six or eight weeks? Seems like a lot to deal with when it's coming from a person I hardly know."

"Yeah, I understand what you're saying," Sarah said. "Maybe you should check into getting a new roomie, you know?"

"Mm-hmm," Pattie said. "I've been thinking about that a lot lately—especially over the last couple weeks or so. She'd had a few bad dreams prior to Halloween, and she's talked about how her sleeping habits have changed since she got here, but she hadn't had any of the drinking binges and that sort of thing prior to Halloween."

Sarah gestured to Mike's car parked in front of the building. "There's my man now." The two made their way to Mike's awaiting car.

"Morning, sweetie," Sarah said, climbing in and kissing Mike's handsome face. "You don't mind if we give Pattie a ride to the library, do you?"

"No, not at all! That's exactly where we're headed. And by the looks of this case study I'm doing, I'm going to be there most of the day."

"What is it this time?" Sarah asked.

"Just this old case study on a murder that was never solved. It's part of my criminal law class."

"Ooh, that sounds cool," Pattie chimed in from the backseat. "Sounds a hell of a lot better than trying to figure out trigonometry."

"Yeah, I guess it would be," Mike said.

"What are you studying, Mike?"

"Criminal justice. But ultimately, I'd like to become a detective for a state agency or maybe even the FBI. It's always been my dream."

"Yep, he's gonna look pretty good in a police uniform, don't you think?" Sarah said, rubbing his big shoulder.

Mike blushed. "C'mon, Sarah."

"Well, it's true! So what's the case about this time?"

"Well, my instructor is a retired Michigan State Police detective. He used to live in the U.P. before moving down state forty years ago."

"Man, he must be old, huh?" Pattie said from the backseat.

"He's probably in his mid-60s, but he really knows his shit. And he's so interesting—I really shouldn't be complaining about this case because it's fascinating and I always learn so much from him."

"That's cool," Pattie said.

"So…" Sarah said, rolling her wrist to get Mike to continue.

"So, he likes to write up his own case studies from old cases that were never solved up there in his day. This one he has us working on looks like it's gonna be a doozy." Mike pulled into the library parking lot and parked his car. "It happened in some weird little town—can't remember the name of it, but from the sounds of it, it's in the middle of nowhere."

"Every place up there is in the middle of nowhere," Sarah said.

"Well, this is an unsolved arson and murder case. I just skimmed over the information yesterday afternoon, but today I really have to dig into it," he said as they entered the library.

"My instructor says we probably won't be able to solve the cases that he provides for us, but that it's a good way for us to learn how to think like detectives."

"That's so cool, Mike," Pattie said. "Well friends, I'm going to go upstairs and let you guys study alone."

"Come with us, Pattie. We're just gonna camp out at one of the tables here and study ourselves. It's no fun to study alone, right Mike? Come on!"

"I just don't want to be a fifth wheel."

"It's not like this is a date," Mike said, smiling. "We're here to do exactly what you're doing, and if we get bored or hungry, we can hop in my car and go to McDonald's or something."

Reluctantly, Pattie agreed.

"But if you have any questions about trig, don't ask either one of us. We suck at math, don't we, Mike?" Sarah quipped.

"Yeah, pretty much. That's why I wanna be a cop and you wanna be a shrink."

40

The trio of scholars quickly found a quiet reading area and sacked out in the leather-upholstered chairs surrounding a coffee table. Mike began reading through his case study packet.

"What are you studying, Sarah?" Pattie asked as she paged through her trig book.

Sarah produced her highlighter from her backpack. "I'm doing a paper on schizophrenia, so I'm just trying to read up on it and get my thoughts in order. It isn't due for another three weeks, but I like to get a good start on stuff."

"Seney," Mike said aloud, head in his case study packet.

Sarah looked up. "What, honey?"

"Seney—that's where this whole thing happened. In 1964."

"I've heard of Seney before," Pattie said.

"Really?" Mike looked over at her.

"Yeah, my stepdad is a total backasswards type of guy. He bear hunts or something like that up there. I know I've heard him talking about Seney before."

"Weird. Who bear hunts, anyway?" Sarah rolled her eyes. "What kind of person gets into all that?"

"Really." Pattie agreed. "That's what I've always said to my mom—who the hell bear hunts?"

"So, what's it about, Mike?" Sarah asked.

"Well, I'm not very far into it, but it's about this old woman who rented out one of the upstairs rooms of her farmhouse. I guess the police never really knew who the renter was."

"Why wouldn't they know that?" Pattie asked.

"He hadn't been renting all that long, and the old lady never did a lease or anything. He was just a drifter of sorts who paid to use the room and the bathroom in her second story."

Both girls looked confused.

"Remember, you guys, this was back in 1964. Things were a lot different back then, and people actually trusted strangers," he said, looking back at the information in his packet.

"That's true enough, I guess," Sarah said. "Especially up in the U.P., where there weren't so many people."

Pattie was gaining interest in Mike's story. "You're so lucky— your work is actually interesting. Maybe I should change my major from pre-med to criminal justice. So what happened next?"

"Well, just hold on, Dr. Pattie. I'm just getting to the medical part of it all."

"What do you mean?" Pattie put down her calculator.

Sarah stopped her work, too, listening intently to the details of Mike's case study.

"Well, this drifter guy—the police think he went to a local bar, got totally shit-faced, then came back to the house. It happened on a Friday night in the late summer."

Mike scanned the text. "When he got back to her house, the police think the landlady probably gave him some shit about being so loud and coming in late. They don't know if he had forgotten his key, or if he was just loud, but the people who knew the old lady said that she'd had trouble with him coming in drunk and rowdy on a few other occasions. And Violet didn't like it."

"Who's Violet?" Sarah said, looking at Pattie, whose mouth had dropped open.

"The old lady," Mike said, continuing to read.

Neither Pattie nor Sarah said anything.

Mike noticed the silence and looked at the two girls. "What? You guys look like you've seen a ghost."

Sarah recovered. "No—it's OK Mike, go on," she said, shaking her head. "It's just a weird thing that her name would be Violet."

"Why?" Mike asked. "Why is that weird?"

"Oh, it's nothing, really," Pattie said. "My weird roommate—you know, Julie?"

"Yeah. The one who got so wasted at the party last night?" Mike asked.

"Yeah. She had this totally whacked dream last night, and she kept saying the word "violet.""

"'Die, Violet,'" Sarah added. "'Fuck you, Violet.'"

"What?" Mike scrunched his nose as he stared at Sarah. "Are you kidding?"

"No, it's true," Pattie said. "Her voice got all weird, too."

"You're kidding." Mike was now thoroughly enthralled in the girls' story.

"She was wasted, Mike, that's all," Sarah said, trying to reason with her boyfriend. "It's just odd that she'd use that name. It's not all that common of a name, you know?"

Sarah went back to reading.

"So what happened?" Pattie probed.

"Well, I guess this fella was pretty pie-eyed, and the police think that when she went all ape shit on him, he grabbed a huge carving knife off the kitchen counter and buried it in her chest."

"Oh, my God," Pattie gasped and faced Sarah. "Sarah, did you hear that? Mike said the guy buried a knife in the old lady's chest."

"Yeah, so?"

"So, remember in Julie's dream? Remember when she talked

about blood? Remember her saying something about teaching somebody a lesson?"

"When? Now you're just making shit up, Pattie." Sarah sounded a little rattled.

"C'mon Sarah—you remember. She said something like, 'blood—so much blood.'"

Sarah hesitated and thought back.

"Did she really?" Mike leaned forward in his chair.

"I'm thinking," Sarah said.

"It was right before her eyes rolled back into her head and her voice got all freaky," Pattie said, reliving those moments.

"Yeah, you might be right. I do remember her saying something about blood, but I was more focused on her body, her thrashing and all that. She was all over the place, and I didn't want her to hurt herself."

"Wow—this is really weird," Mike said.

"Go on, Mike. What happened next?" Pattie urged.

"OK. So the police say the large knife completely split this woman's sternum," he went on, pointing to his breast bone. "They said he must have used tremendous force, like he hit the knife on the very end with the palm of his hand and just jammed the knife into her chest."

"Oh, how gross," Pattie said. Sarah didn't say anything.

"They think he must have realized what he had done, because they say he then dragged her body from the kitchen into the first-floor bedroom and put her on her double bed."

Pattie shook her head. "Oh, man. How could anyone do that?"

"You'd be surprised what some people can do," Sarah reasoned.

"After that, they think he went out to the barn and got a big can of gasoline," Mike continued. "He dumped it all over her and around the bed and lit it up with a match."

"Oh," Pattie said, covering her mouth. "I can't fuckin' believe this. Can you, Sarah?"

Sarah remained silent, staring at Pattie.

"What?" Mike leaned forward and touched Sarah's knee. "What, babe? Can't believe what?"

"Julie—last night," Pattie said, looking frightened at this point.

"What now?"

"She said something about hot fire and smoke in last night's dream. A couple nights ago, she remembered another dream where she was in a house that she didn't recognize... and it was on fire," Pattie explained.

Mike sat back in his chair. "Wow, this is all pretty strange."

"Yeah, she did," Sarah agreed. "She did say something about smoke and being trapped."

"It's weird indeed," Mike said. "They never found the guy or located anybody who could give them a decent description of the guy."

"What do you think, Sarah?" Pattie said, looking at her decidedly shaken friend.

"I just think it's weird. And I think we all have incredibly overworked imaginations!"

41

It was nearly four that afternoon when Mike dropped Pattie and Sarah back at the dorm.

"I'll come back after I get done helping Dave." Mike tenderly kissed Sarah's lips. "We'll go grab some dinner, OK?"

"Sure—that would be great."

"Thanks for the rides today, Mike," Pattie said from the back-seat. "I'll keep you posted on my strange but interesting roommate."

"Thanks, Pattie. Can't wait to hear it."

Pattie walked back inside the dormitory with Sarah. "So, do you really think there's any connection between Mike's story and Julie's dreams?"

"No, way," Sarah said. "I mean, as a psych major it would be great if there was actually something to it, but frankly it's just a huge coincidence"

"I wonder if she's totally hung like a big dog today," Pattie said getting onto the elevator.

"She's gotta be. She had a zillion drinks last night, so she's got to be feeling like hammered shit."

The elevator doors opened on their floor. "Just keep me in the loop. I'm thinking Mike and I will go out to eat around seven, but we shouldn't be out late." Sarah unzipped her purse. "If anything happens, you have my cell number, or if I'm back—and I probably will be—just knock on my door."

"Will do." Pattie opened the door to find Julie sitting at her desk typing up a report on her laptop.

"Hey, hey," Julie said cheerfully. "Where you been all day?"

"At the library." Pattie was astonished that Julie was even conscious.

"What's up?" Julie asked. "You look surprised to see me or something."

"I thought you'd be so hung over after last night that you'd still be in bed," Pattie said, flopping her backpack on her desk.

"Nah, I wasn't that drunk. I was just feeling good."

"Are you shittin' me?" Pattie took off her jacket. "You were so shit-faced, you passed out in the car."

"I was just resting my eyes," Julie said turning back to her laptop.

"C'mon Jules. Honest to God, you were absolutely hammered!"

"OK, OK, I admit it. But I handled it, didn't I?" Julie stood up and reached for her pack of cigarettes on the bookshelf.

"God, your hand still looks awful," Pattie said, changing the subject.

"Yeah, and it's still pretty sore." Julie removed a cigarette from the package. "I think I'm going to have to get it x-rayed."

"So what's the last thing you remember about last night?" Pattie grabbed a soda out of the small mini fridge.

Julie cracked the window and thought for a second. "Hmmm—I remember being outside by the fire," she said, lighting her cigarette. "I remember the fire… that's about it."

"You don't remember anything after the fire? Are you serious?"

"'Fraid so," Julie said before taking a long drag off her cigarette.

"And yet you feel OK today?" Pattie was in total disbelief.

"Yeah, I feel fit as a fiddle." Julie exhaled and relaxed into a smile. "I had a smidge of a headache when I first woke up, but for the most part, I'm good."

Pattie took a sip of her soda. "That's unfuckinbelievable."

Julie flicked an ash out the window. "Was I really that bad?" she asked, looking a bit worried.

"You didn't barf or anything, but you got kinda agitated at Sarah and me," Pattie said, taking care to not rile Julie.

"Oh. I'm sorry," Julie said. "I need to stay away from the JD, I guess."

Pattie took a seat at her desk. "You had another one of those really weird dreams, too."

"I did?" Julie asked, as she exhaled. "I don't remember a thing. I just feel like I got some good rest."

"Wow. Yeah, you were having a—oh, what did Sarah call it?" Pattie said.

"Sarah was here?" Julie said in an annoyed tone.

"Well, yeah," Pattie said nervously. "A night terror! Yeah, that's what you had, a night terror."

"What the fuck is a night terror?" Julie said tossing her fuming butt out the window. "And what genius made that diagnosis?"

"There isn't any reason to get mad, Julie," Pattie said defensively. "We were worried about you. You were all curled up in the corner of your bunk bed crying—eyes wide open and talking in your sleep again."

"Oh, my God," Julie said, sitting down at her desk. "I must really be losing it or something."

"It *was* pretty creepy," Pattie admitted. "But it's probably just the stress from your first term here."

"My eyes were open and I was crying?" Julie asked.

"I swear to God." Pattie set her soda down on the desk. "Sarah said it was a textbook night terror. Go talk to her about it."

"No, absolutely not! I don't want to," Julie said. "It's embarrassing enough."

"C'mon, Jules," Pattie said, playing the diplomat. "We're all friends here. I still think you might just be having adjustment problems."

"Yeah, maybe." Julie stood up and walked into the bathroom. "What did I say?" Julie stared at herself in the mirror.

Pattie hesitated. "Huh?"

"I said, what did I say, last night when I was asleep?" she repeated, while still staring into her own dark eyes.

"Oh, just stuff about smoke again," Pattie stammered. "Sorta like the other night when you had that dream about the farmhouse that was on fire."

Julie didn't say anything, but continued to stare into the mirror at a face she didn't really recognize. Although she looked the same, she sensed that something deep inside had shifted. Her eyes, normally warm and friendly now reflected the opposite – cold, ominous, menacing.

"I honestly don't remember," Julie said. "I don't know why I keep dreaming about fire. I don't know what's happening to me."

Julie walked out of the bathroom and sat down on the edge of her bunk. "It's like last night, too. The fire—I couldn't stop staring at it," she said. "I sort of remember feeling scared, but can't remember specifics as to why I felt that way."

Pattie turned and looked at her roommate, and for a moment she considered telling Julie everything.

"Look, Jules," Pattie began, before reconsidering and backing off. "You're ...you're probably just overly tired."

"Yeah, you're probably right." Julie sprawled out on her bed. "Can I have another one of your mom's sleeping pills tonight?"

"It's OK with me, but are you sure you want another one? I mean last time, you had your first nightmare."

"Yeah ...I really don't think that was because of the pill," Julie said, staring at the ceiling. "I don't know what to think, really." Julie paused. "I think I just need a shot of JD."

"What? Are you shittin' me?" Pattie asked. "After last night?"

Julie sprang from bed to her feet. "Yeah! What do they call it? A little hair of the cat or something?"

"It's hair of the dog," Pattie said. "The rest of the bottle is on my bookshelf. I'm going to take a shower."

"You don't want any?" Julie said, reaching for a shot glass.

"No, thanks, not right now. But you're welcome to it." Pattie grabbed a fresh towel from her closet and headed into the bathroom.

Julie heard the shower come on as she poured herself a shot of JD and reached for her cigarettes again. Perching on the window ledge, she cracked the window and lit up. After savoring a long sip of the JD, she leaned her head against the cinderblock wall and stared into the court yard.

Julie's thoughts swirled around in her head like autumn leaves on a windy day. In the last two weeks, her lifestyle had done a complete about-face. Non-smoking, non-drinking Julie in Potterville would never have dreamt she'd be sitting on a window ledge, smoking, drinking, and pondering an ever-changing personality. Was this part of being a college student? Did everybody's personality change the minute they hit campus?

Julie took a hefty drag off her cigarette and thought some more, exhaling smoke from her nostrils as she sat in silence.

"Knock, knock," Sarah said as she popped her head around the door.

"Do you always have to do that?" Julie asked from her perch. "Can't you just knock like normal people do, waiting for someone like me to say, 'Come in?'"

"Sorry," Sarah said. "Do you want me to come back later?"

Sarah noticed the bottle of JD and pack of cigarettes laying on Julie's desk.

"No, no," Julie said. "I'm sorry. I'm just being a bitch. Come in, of course."

"I didn't expect to find you vertical, much less smoking and drinking again." Sarah said.

"Yeah, well, it's been one of those kinda days, I guess." Julie tossed back the last bit of JD.

"What's wrong?" Sarah asked. "You're probably pretty hung over today, eh?"

"Actually, no." Julie hesitated, flicking an ash out the window. "I had a late lunch around three, did a lot of studying and typed up a report …it's been pretty productive."

"Wow," Sarah said. "That's amazing! I mean—you know."

"Yeah, I heard I was sorta out of control again last night," Julie said apologetically. "I'm kind of embarrassed about the whole thing, you know?"

"Aww, don't worry about it," Sarah said. "I've seen people have wild dreams like that before, during my internship last summer."

"Oh, you mean in the fuckin' looney bin where you worked?" Julie asked sarcastically. "Is that what you think about me? That I'm some sort of nutcase?"

Julie threw her cigarette out the window and slammed the window shut.

"No, not at all," Sarah said calmly. "Never mind, Julie. I was just trying to make conversation. I actually came over to talk to Pattie."

"She's in the shower." Julie poured herself one more shot and placed the bottle back on Pattie's shelf. "Look, in the future, I'd appreciate it if you don't come over here and use me as a fuckin' lab rat the next time I have a bad dream, OK?"

"Pattie came and got me," Sarah said angrily. "You were thrashing all over the place and she was scared. She had never seen something like that."

"Well, if it happens again, just wake my ass up," Julie said, picking up her drink. "Why is that so fuckin' hard for people to do?"

"Maybe you should get your own room," Sarah suggested.

"Yeah, and maybe I should buy a fuckin' yacht and sail around the Mediterranean, too," Julie snapped. "I don't have a rich daddy to pay for everything, and unfortunately, my scholarship doesn't pay for me to live solo."

Sarah watched Julie slam the shot, and fumble for another cigarette. "I know you don't want to hear this—you're angry and all—but your roommate really does care about what's going on with you."

Julie lit her cigarette, cracked the window again, and refused to make eye contact with Sarah.

"And you're right, there are a lot of things I don't know about, but I can see when somebody is struggling, and I see that in you," she said. "Right now it's pretty hard to like you, but Pattie seems to think you're a nice person. I'm always around if you want to talk." Sarah turned and let herself out of the room.

42

"I can't believe you have to work tomorrow. It's Thanksgiving!" Julie said as she rode along with her mom westward toward Mulliken.

"That's the way it goes when you're in the old fart business," Shawn replied. "Somebody has to be around to wipe the asses after eating turkey all day."

"Mom!" Julie tried to suppress a laugh. "That's not even funny. You know Grandma and Oscar are getting up there!"

"I know, I know. Hand me a cig, will ya?" she said, cracking the window and pushing in the lighter. "We rotate holidays, which means I'll be able to hang out with you on Christmas. Besides, tomorrow I'll earn double time. Can't beat that, can ya?"

Julie handed her mom a cigarette.

"What? You're not going to complain about my smoking?"

Julie remained expressionless. "Nah, why bother?"

"You're kidding, right?" Shawn lit her cigarette. "After all the years of shit you've given me for smoking, suddenly you're OK with it?"

Julie shrugged her shoulders. "It's your life."

"Wow. College must be changing you after all," she said, exhaling smoke into the small car.

"So, you're having dinner with us and then you're going back home, right?" Julie asked.

"Yeah, that's right," Shawn said. "It's nearly three o'clock now and knowing ma, we'll probably eat around five thirty or six so I can be outta there by seven. I know they're both looking forward to having you stay over tonight, and are really happy to have you all to themselves tomorrow."

"Yeah ...it'll be good for me, too," Julie mumbled.

"What's wrong? You seem sad today or something," Shawn said, glancing over at her daughter.

"No, no...I'm not sad. School's just taking it out of me, I guess. What I mean is, it'll be nice to have a break and be back in familiar surroundings, you know?"

"Yeah, definitely." Shawn took one last toke on her cigarette. "I better get rid of this and air out before we get to their house," she said, sounding much like a deceitful teenager.

"When do you think you're going to grow up enough to just tell Meryl and Oscar to stick it?" Julie asked abruptly.

Shawn threw her cigarette out the window and stared at her daughter blankly. "What is with you? What have they been putting in the water at MSU?"

"What do you mean?" Julie asked. "What?"

"I mean—first of all, you never stick up for me when it comes to smoking, and secondly, you never refer to your grandparents by their first names. I do, remember?"

Julie managed to smile. "I don't know." Julie wistfully gazed out the window. "I think I'm just growing up or something. I'm just changing, I guess."

"Well, we knew it was bound to happen," Shawn said, turning into her parents' driveway. "Here we are, so put on a happy face, will ya?"

"You'll need it more than me," Julie responded. "You're the one who hates your mother."

Shawn brought the car to a halt. "What are you talking about?" Julie's flippant responses were beginning to anger Shawn.

"What?" Julie said. "You do, don't you?"

"Of course not," Shawn said. "I just don't always see eye-to-eye with the woman. Doesn't mean I hate her."

"Whatever," Julie said, unlatching the door.

Meryl and Oscar stood huddled on the back porch, shivering in the cold November air.

Slamming the driver's door, Shawn looked at Julie across the roof of the car. "We'll talk about this later," she said sternly. "I really don't like your attitude."

Julie rolled her eyes and waited for her mother to unlock the hatchback. "I need my stuff," she said impatiently.

"Seriously, Jules, you better get your shit together. If you treat your grandparents this way, I'm the one who's gonna hear about it." Shawn popped the hatch.

"Oh yeah, I forgot—it's all about you. It always is."

Shawn's angry expression softened to one of concern as she pondered her daughter's sudden mood swing.

"Hi Grandma," Julie said walking toward the house with her suitcase and backpack. It was as though Julie could switch anger on and off.

"Oscar, go help our girl with her bags," Meryl said, nudging him toward the wooden steps off the porch.

"I can get it, Grandpa," Julie said politely.

"No, no! Now let me do something here. Your Grandma gave me strict instructions. Don't get me in trouble, now."

Julie handed Oscar her small suitcase and put her arm around his shoulder. "It's good to see you, Grandpa. You're looking great."

"Thanks, Toots," he said as he made his way up the stairs. "Isn't our girl growing up?" Oscar said as he walked past Meryl.

Meryl smiled and held out her arms.

"Hi Grandma," Julie said, hugging the frail old lady. "We better get inside! It's freezing out here."

"Hi Ma," Shawn said as she brought up the rear.

"Oh hi, dear. You two made good time getting out here," Meryl said. "I'll just put the kettle on the stove."

"Yeah, Jules was all packed up and ready to go when I got there." Shawn took off her jacket and slung it across the back of a kitchen chair.

"Honey, why don't you put Julie's things up in Bev's old room," Meryl instructed her husband. "You don't mind staying in your aunt's old room now, do you?"

"No, of course not. I'm sure Aunt Bev would love for me to stay there," Julie said looking over at Shawn.

"She can stay in my old room," Shawn said defiantly.

"No, dear, I use your old room for storage now. She'll be more comfortable in Bev's room."

Meryl's cavalier announcement that her room had been relegated to a storage room bothered Shawn. "I store my sewing stuff and other boxes of old pictures and things in your old room," Meryl said, not realizing that her words and actions devastated Shawn.

Even in death, Bev would always win out over Shawn when it came to their mother's affection. Shawn was beginning to realize that she was also taking a distant third to her own daughter.

"You got any beer?" Shawn said, heading for the fridge.

Meryl's expression quickly changed to one of disapproval. "You have to drive home tonight," she reminded her daughter. "And work."

"Yeah, I know I do, Ma," Shawn growled. "Never mind."

"OK, kiddo," Oscar said, entering the kitchen. "Your things are up in Bev's room."

"Thanks, Grandpa." Feeling the tension, Julie tried to redirect the conversation. "So, what's for supper tonight, Grandma? It smells great in here."

"Well, I figured you would be pretty tired of eating that dorm food, so I'm making you one of my famous meatloaves with all the fixings," Meryl said. "It was one of your Aunt Bev's favorites, wasn't it Shawn?"

"Yeah, I guess so." Shawn plopped down at the kitchen table. "I don't really remember. I've moved on with my life."

Meryl chose to ignore her daughter's comment, while Oscar scurried to the stove as the kettle began to whistle. "So, tell us all about your classes, Julie."

"Oh, they're all going pretty well." Julie looked out the back door toward the field. "I'm pretty busy all the time, but my studies are going great. I'm keeping a straight 4 point," she said, turning back to Oscar.

"You hear that, Grandma? A straight four point!" Oscar reached for the mugs in the cupboard. "That's our Julie," he said. "Do you want some tea, hon?"

"No, thanks," Julie responded.

"I'll take some, Oscar," Shawn said from the table.

"So, school's going fine. What about your roommate?" Meryl said, wiping her hands on a dish towel.

"Pattie? Oh, she's good," Julie replied. "She's pretty cool. She's pre-med, too, but doesn't study as much as me."

"Here you go," Oscar said, setting two mugs of tea on the table. "Oh, she's a party doll, eh?"

"No, I wouldn't say that." Julie pulled up a chair. "She goes to a few things on the weekends and stuff, but she just doesn't seem to study as much as I do."

"Few people probably do," Shawn added.

"Well, I have a pretty heavy load," Julie said, an edge in her voice. "Of course, you wouldn't understand, not having gone to college and all."

Shawn said nothing, but stared directly into her daughter's eyes. "I guess you're right," Shawn said. "But thanks to your Grandma here, I didn't go." Shawn stood up from the table. "She said an abortion was out of the question."

"Shawn!" Meryl looked toward her expressionless granddaughter. "She didn't mean it, honey."

"So, how about them Lions?" Oscar said, trying desperately to change the subject.

"I gotta go," Shawn announced.

"I thought you were staying for dinner," Meryl said.

"No, sorry, I have to work at six."

Julie knew her mother didn't work until eleven, but said nothing.

"Oh, I could have sworn you said you were staying," Meryl said, looking a little confused.

"Nope. Well, have a happy Thanksgiving." Shawn gave her mother an obligatory hug. "I'll come by on Friday morning and pick you up."

Shawn slid into her jacket and headed for the door. "See ya Friday, Oscar. Have a great turkey day."

With a slam of the door, Shawn was gone.

"She didn't mean what she said," Meryl said, patting Julie's hand.

Julie snatched back her hand and rubbed it.

"Oh, my," Oscar said looking at Julie's hand. "What the devil did you do to your hand there?"

"I don't know," Julie said, sounding a bit annoyed. "It must be from all the typing I'm doing at school."

Meryl cocked her head and stroked Julie's long hair. "Why don't you go upstairs and have a good long soak in the tub? You're just exhausted from school. By the time you've had a nice warm bath, dinner will be ready."

"Grandma's right," Oscar said. "There's plenty of fresh towels up there. Just have a good soak—it's just what the doctor ordered."

Julie stood up from the table. "Thanks, you guys," she said, bending over to kiss Meryl gently on the cheek. "You're right. It's been a heck of an adjustment at MSU. It probably *is* just what the doctor would order." Julie patted Oscar on the shoulder before heading for the stairs.

43

Meryl's small upstairs bathroom was tiled green and yellow, and had been as long as Julie could remember. A large towel cupboard in front of the toilet held perfectly folded towels and an assortment of toiletries from the last thirty years.

Julie walked over to the mint-green tub, put the stopper in, and turned the porcelain hot and cold water handles simultaneously. Grabbing an old bottle of bath beads and a fresh towel from the cupboard, Julie tossed three beads into the tub, and remembered she'd forgotten to retrieve something from her suitcase.

The old farmhouse's hardwood floor creaked as she entered her Aunt Bev's old bedroom. It was like stepping back in time. The twin bed Bev once occupied had the same frilly purple bedspread on it, accenting the now yellowing and faded purple flowered wall paper.

Curled black and white pictures of her aunt with high school friends were still stuck into the frame of her old dressing table mirror, exactly as she had left them in 1972. Bev's golden hair still entwined the bristles of her old brush that laid exactly where she'd left it on the nightstand.

"Jesus Christ," Julie mumbled as she made her way to the bed. "It's like a freakin' shrine in here."

Julie retrieved her roommate's half-drunk bottle of JD from her suitcase. "Thanks, roomie," she said quietly as she closed her case.

The steam of the water warmed the small bathroom. Julie shut the door, peeled off her clothes, and eased into the awaiting tub.

After several minutes, Julie twisted the porcelain handles in opposite directions, turning off the water. Resting back into the tub, she took a long sip of JD from the bottle. While the heat of the water warmed and relaxed the exterior of her body, soothing sips of JD warmed her throat and chest. As her body and mind relaxed, Julie began to enjoy the numbness JD always offered.

Julie twisted the cap back onto the bottle of JD and sat it on the corner of the tub. Closing her eyes, she eventually drifted into the foggy area between consciousness and sleep.

An hour later, Julie was awakened by the sound of her grandmother's voice and several loud knocks on the bathroom door.

"Are you OK in there, honey? It's nearly five o'clock—you've been in there for over an hour."

Water splashed everywhere, as Julie jolted awake, her arm sending the capped bottle of JD thumping down onto the bathmat in front of the tub. Julie's heart pounded and her head spun from the disorientation of her bathtime buzz.

"Yeah," Julie sputtered. "Yeah, Grandma, I'm fine. I must have fallen asleep in the tub."

"What's all that noise in there? Are you alright?" Meryl shouted through the door from the hallway.

"I'm fine, Grandma," Julie said. "I fell asleep in the tub, and when you banged on the door, it startled me." Julie pulled the plug on her now lukewarm bath water.

"It's been so long that your Grandpa and I were getting worried," Meryl repeated.

"I know, I know. I'm getting out right now."

"What was all that noise?" Meryl asked again. "It sounded like a bottle or something."

"No—no," Julie said as she stepped out of the tub. Bending down, she picked up the bottle. "I knocked my shampoo off the tub," she lied. "It's a big bottle of shampoo."

"It's not in a glass bottle, is it?" Meryl said doubtfully. "Because it sounded like glass."

Taking a deep breath, it took everything for Julie to answer without yelling. "Nope. It was my huge bottle of shampoo, Grandma—it's huge."

Well, as long as you're OK, dear. I—we were just worried when you didn't come out."

"Sorry, Grandma. I just fell asleep," she repeated again. "Give me ten minutes and I'll be down."

"'Take your time, sweetheart." Meryl reluctantly backed away from the door.

Julie listened intently as she heard her grandmother descend the wooden staircase. After drying off, Julie got dressed and concealed the bottle of JD in her damp towel before entering the hallway.

From the hallway, Julie could hear her grandmother repeating the story to Oscar in the kitchen below. Shutting the bedroom door behind her, Julie unwrapped the bottle and took another big swig before stowing it in her suitcase.

44

"Well, there she is," Oscar announced from his regular position at the table. Pouring milk into the awaiting tumblers, Meryl hovered around the table, much like a hummingbird darting from bloom to bloom.

"Sit down, sweetie." Meryl placed the milk carton on the kitchen counter. "Do you feel more rested now?" she asked as she took her seat at the table.

"Yeah—I told you two I was tired." Julie rubbed her eyes. "It's been so long since I've had a good hot bath, it just knocked me out."

Oscar winked at Meryl. "I told you, Grandma, nothing to worry about. Shall I say the blessing?"

The three grasped hands. "Dear Lord," Oscar began. "Thank you for this wonderful fall day and for bringing our granddaughter home to us safely."

Julie opened her eyes and watched as her grandparents prayed. "Thank you for this meal and bless this food for our use, that it might rejuvenate our tired souls, Lord. In Jesus' name, we pray, Amen."

"And aMEN," Julie blurted as she let go of her grandparents' hands.

Oscar and Meryl stared at their normally reserved granddaughter.

"What?" Julie said, picking up her fork. "Good prayer, Oscar!"

Oscar beamed. "That's what I like to hear," he said, trying to dispel Meryl's growing concern over Julie's unusual behavior. "A little enthusiasm over an old man's prayer—that always makes my day!"

"And Lord knows we could use a few rejuvenated souls around here, eh?" Julie placed her napkin in her lap. "You really shouldn't have fussed," she said as she helped herself to a piece of meatloaf. "I mean, tomorrow, we're gonna pig out anyway, right?"

"Nonsense," Meryl said, passing Oscar the peas. "I don't usually get to cook for anyone besides your grandfather and me. It's nice to have company, and besides, you probably haven't had a good home cooked meal in a long time."

"You're absolutely right." Oscar piled peas onto his plate. "Nobody makes a better meatloaf than your Grandma, either."

Julie took a bite of the homemade entree. "Mmm," she said, closing her eyes. "I don't care what mom says about you, Grandma. You are a good cook, and always have been."

Meryl put down her utensils and stared at Julie. "No, I guess I don't know what your mom always says about me," she replied in an annoyed tone. "Would you care to tell me?"

"What? Are you kidding me? Help me out here, Oscar."

Oscar shrugged his shoulders, unsure of how to respond.

"What I meant was—Jesus," Julie said becoming a little flapped. "You know what I meant. You and mom are always sparring about something." Julie picked up her glass of milk and took a huge gulp before continuing.

"Right, Oscar? I mean, you two never agree on anything." Julie studied Meryl's sad and wrinkled face. "Look, Grandma, I didn't mean anything by it. I was just trying to make conversation."

"What's gotten into you today?" Meryl picked up her plate and retreated to the kitchen sink.

"Now, now, Mother," Oscar said, standing up. "Bring that plate back over here and sit down. You need to eat more than that. Let's not ruin our nice evening together with our granddaughter."

Like a pouting teenager, Meryl reluctantly brought her plate back to the table and sat down.

"I really didn't mean to upset you," Julie said, grasping Meryl's aged hand. "I love you, you know that."

"Yes …I know you do, dear," Meryl sighed. "It's just been a rough road with your mother, and when I hear somebody say it out loud, it just upsets me, that's all."

"Sorry, Grandma," Julie said. "It's my fault."

"It's nobody's fault," Oscar chimed. "Now let's eat our dinner and talk about other things."

45

"Where did you guys learn how to play such cutthroat Scrabble?" Julie joked as she put away the game. After tidying the kitchen, she and her grandparents had played three straight matches.

"Oh, I guess it must be all the crossword puzzles your Grandma and I do." Oscar rinsed his glass in the sink.

"There isn't a lot for a couple of old codgers like us to do in the fall," Meryl said as she stretched her arms high above her head. "In the summer, your grandfather and I'd still be out in the garden weeding, wouldn't we, hon?"

Oscar glanced at the clock above the kitchen sink. "I reckon we would. Stays light in the summer almost until ten o'clock or so. I think I'm going to turn in, if it's OK with you kids."

"Sure, hon," Meryl said. "It's getting late, and we've got a big day ahead of us tomorrow. I thought we'd go to the church service tomorrow morning, if that's alright with you," she said, looking at Julie. "Gladys Smith can't wait to see you. It's been so long since your mom and you have gone to church with us."

"Church on Thursday?" Julie questioned. "I mean, that's totally cool with me. Just seems odd to have church on a weekday."

"Well, our congregation believes we Americans have a lot to be thankful for, so Pastor Ed always does a Thanksgiving Day service."

"Yeah," Oscar said. "It's real nice—nice for us folks who stick around here, anyway."

"So, what time does it start?" Julie asked.

"Ten," Meryl responded. "But I'll be up long before then getting supper started."

"Oh, you can expect to hear a pan or two clankin' away in here, to be sure," Oscar said with a wink. "Hope you don't mind, Tootsie Belle."

"Nah, I'll come down to help you," Julie promised.

"No, sweetheart." Meryl's face softened into a smile. "You need your rest. That's why you're here with us. You just stay up there in bed as long as you want. I'll get you up in time for church."

Julie reached out to hug Meryl. Memories from the past surged through Julie's mind as the two embraced. As a child, she could recall no safer place to be than in the arms of her grandmother.

"I love you, Grams," Julie said as she rested her head on her grandma's bony shoulder.

"Oh, I love you, too, sweetheart," Meryl said locking eyes with Oscar. "You go on up now and get some rest."

"I will, Grandma." Julie turned to hug Oscar. "Goodnight Grandpa. Tomorrow you're going to feel my wrath in our next Scrabble match."

"What is it you kids say?" Oscar said, trying to think of the expression. "Oh, yeah—bring it!"

Julie exploded into laughter. "You got it," she said. "And I will."

"Goodnight, sweet pea," he said, turning to head up the stairs.

"You know where the remote is. We have cable out here now, so you can probably find something on television," Meryl said.

"Nah," Julie said. "I'm with you two. I'm going to head up to bed and maybe read for a while."

"Whatever you want to do, sweetie." Meryl began climbing the stairs. "Sleep tight, and I'll see you in the morning."

Julie flipped off the lamp on the end table in the living room, and followed her grandmother upstairs to her awaiting bedroom.

Julie turned on a reading lamp by the bed and closed the door. Unzipping her suitcase, she broke out the bottle of JD, flopped back on the bed, and propped herself against the wall. With a quick twist, the cap was off, and Julie took a long sip of the booze.

"Mmm," she said quietly to herself. "Much better."

Bottle in hand, Julie got off the bed and began snooping around the room.

Dusty stuffed animals and old 4H trophies lined a shelf above the bureau. Faded ribbons of assorted colors hung from thumb tacks stuck into the wood. A four-by-six-inch framed black and white photograph sat next to a blue ribbon.

Julie took a swig of JD before taking the framed photograph off the shelf. Setting the bottle on the bureau, she wiped dust from the glass to take a closer look. It was a picture of Aunt Bev and the grandfather she'd never known. Bev looked to be about 10 years old. She clung proudly to the first-prize 4H ribbon as her father looked on.

The 4H fair was something that Julie had never really heard her mother or grandmother discuss. By the time Shawn would have been old enough to enter the fair, her father was long gone. Meryl never had the strength or ambition to help her with it. It was just another milestone of childhood her mother had missed.

Julie stared into the faded black and white face of Jasper Deerfield. Having seen very few pictures of him over the years, it was at that moment that she realized how much her own mother resembled him.

Carefully, Julie placed the photograph back on the shelf.

Julie sat back down on the bed and watched the clock radio as it flipped over to 10:47. Not tired in the least and feeling a little buzzed, Julie contemplated her options. She remembered that the old Sportsman's Tavern where her Aunt Bev had worked was no more than a mile's hike west on M-43. Shawn had mentioned many times before that sometimes Bev would actually walk home from work at two in the morning.

Careful to be quiet, Julie unlocked the window and slid it upward. It would be a short step to the porch roof, and then a quick climb down the trellis to the front yard. She unzipped her backpack and took out her pack of cigarettes, a lighter, and about thirty dollars in crumpled bills.

Suddenly, Julie remembered that she'd left her jacket downstairs in the living room. She quietly opened her aunt's old closet. Stuffed with old coats and clothes from the 60s, it looked like a rack from the Salvation Army.

"Damn!" Julie exclaimed after pulling a pair of wildly patterned bell-bottoms out of the closet. "Too bad I didn't come out here before Halloween," she thought. Just then, Julie felt a floorboard shift under her foot.

"What the hell?" Julie whispered, kicking back the old throw rug in Bev's closet. Using her toe, she jiggled the loose board and removed it, revealing Bev's old childhood diary.

Julie took the diary out of the closet and into the light to examine it. Blowing dust off the cover, she flipped to the bookmarked page. It was Bev's October 4, 1966, entry.

Julie's fingertips lightly traced the handwritten and blood-smudged heart on the page as she sat on the edge of the bed and read her aunt's entry. "Just before he died, my dad told me I have a brother in the Upper Peninsula. I still don't understand what he meant. How could this be?" Julie read.

"Holy shit," Julie said aloud after reading her aunt's written words. "Grandpa had a son?" Julie sat in disbelief and re-read the entry several times, pausing after the last. Over the years, Jasper Deerfield's status had risen to that of a saint as far as Meryl was concerned, and Julie knew instinctively that the news of a child from a previous relationship, should her Grandma learn of it, would devastate her. Julie slid the old diary into her backpack, replaced the floorboard and slid the throw rug over it. "It's our secret, Aunt Bev," she said quietly and resumed her search for a coat to wear.

A faded jean jacket looking to be about Julie's size hung near a section of several miniskirts and other bell-bottomed pants.

"As long as I'm keeping your secret, I'm sure you wouldn't mind if I borrowed this," Julie said, sliding into the jacket. For the most part, it fit perfectly, but Julie's longer arms left the sleeves a little short. "It'll work," she said stuffing her cigarettes, lighter, and money into one of the pockets.

Julie turned off the light, grabbed the bottle of JD, and stealthily climbed through the open window to the awaiting roof. After sliding the window nearly shut, she scrambled down the trellis to the awaiting sidewalk.

With no cloud coverage, the crystal-clear November evening was a bit chilly. Julie buttoned up her borrowed jacket, jogged down the long driveway to the highway, and began walking west.

46

The gravel parking lot of the Sportsman's Tavern was half full as Julie strolled in off the shoulder of M-43. The tavern itself hadn't changed much over the years. An elongated log cabin structure, it had served as Mulliken's watering hole for close to 70 years.

Taking a last gulp of JD, Julie hurled the bottle over the hood of a truck into the awaiting bushes before heading for the front entrance.

Julie pushed the door open and felt immediate relief as the smoky warmth of the interior soothed her chilly hands and face. Seeing no bouncer at the door, Julie made her way to an empty stool at the end of the bar.

The main room held a smattering of drunken locals celebrating tomorrow's day off from work. Two waitresses and one middle-aged bartender worked hard to keep everyone happy.

"What can I get for ya?" the bartender said as he quickly placed a cocktail napkin in front of Julie.

"Boilermaker," Julie said without hesitation, and forgetting she wasn't legal. Julie took her cigarettes and lighter out of her pocket, lit up, and eased onto her barstool.

"You wanna run a tab, hon?" The bartender placed a mug of cold beer and a shot of whiskey in front of her.

"Yeah, please," Julie said.

"Hey, Junior," a neighboring patron said to the bartender, "Can I have another one of these?" he asked holding up an empty mug.

"You got it, KC," Junior responded.

"You ain't from around here, are ya?" the barfly asked Julie with a creepy wink.

"Nope," Julie said, slamming the shot. "I'm not." Julie picked up the mug of beer and took a few long gulps. The patron's greasy hair, unshaven face, and stained t-shirt told the story. "Fuckin' redneck," Julie found herself thinking.

"Well, well, well," he said, moving down a couple stools toward Julie. "It sure looks like you know what you're doing. But you ain't old enough, are ya?" Julie glared at the middle-aged jerk.

"Don't worry don't get all mad at me," he said. KC reached for his cigarettes in his t-shirt pocket. "I ain't the law or nothin' I just know an underage drinker when I see one."

Julie's defensive glare changed to one of disdain. With solid lumps of black grease underneath his fingernails, KC played with his lighter.

"KC here," he said, holding out his pudgy hand. "C'mon now, I won't bite."

Reluctantly, Julie shook KC's filthy hand. "Julie," she said without further explanation.

"So, Julie," KC said, lighting a cigarette. "What brings you here tonight?"

"Look—KC, is it?" KC's flurry of nods was similar to that of an eager puppy waiting to be fed. "I'm not trying to be rude or anything, but I'm not interested."

"Here you go," Junior said placing another beer in front of KC.

"Get her another one, will ya? On me," he said, gesturing to Julie's half empty beer.

"No, that won't be necessary."

"Now why don't you just let me be neighborly?" KC asked. "I'm just trying to make conversation here, that's all. Shit, I'm old enough to be your daddy."

Julie stubbed her cigarette out in the ashtray. "Look. Like I said, I'm not interested, and I don't need a 'daddy,'" she said making the finger quote sign and getting up from her barstool. "I gotta pee."

"Well, ain't you sassy," KC said in an annoyed tone. "I was just trying to be nice." Julie walked past him toward the end of the bar. "Little bitch," he muttered.

Julie ignored his comment and went around the bar, past the pay phone, and down the long hallway toward the bathrooms. A framed black and white photograph hung at the end of the hall between the men's and women's restrooms.

"Holy shit," Julie said, looking at the picture. An older woman wearing an apron had her arm draped around her Aunt Bev's shoulder. The picture had been taken in front of the bar. "In memory of our beloved employee Beverly Deerfield," read the small tarnished plaque beneath the picture. "Aug. 25, 1954 – Aug. 25, 1972."

Until that moment, the story of her aunt's disappearance from the bar had seemed like a legend of sorts. Having heard the story so many times before, Julie had detached herself from the reality of it. Seeing her aunt in the picture and standing in the actual bar where she once worked shook the very depth of her soul.

"I knew the little bitch in the picture," a smoky voice came from behind her. It was an intoxicated KC, invading Julie's personal space. Before Julie could turn around, she felt the pressure of KC's weight pin her to the paneled wall. His scratchy beard grated on her cheek as he whispered in her ear. "She was hot, too." His hot booze breath blew in her face. "You kinda remind me of her. She had nice tits like yours," he said, grappling for her breast.

"Get the fuck off me!" Julie delivered an elbow to his midsection and turned to face him. Before he could react, she sent a well-aimed kick to his groin. KC screamed in agony and fell to his knees, clutching his crotch.

"What's going on out here?" a husky voice came from down the hallway. It was Junior, who had stepped out of the kitchen.

"I was looking at this picture and this bastard came up behind me and pinned me to the wall," Julie said angrily. Julie directed another swift kick into his fat ass.

"Ouch, you little bitch," KC yelled, lunging toward Julie.

"That'll be enough, KC," Junior shouted. Junior stepped between the two and gave KC a shove. "I told you. You start this shit again, and I'm callin' the cops. Either you get up and get your sorry ass outta here, or that's exactly what I'm doin',"

Butt crack showing, KC struggled to his feet, still laboring to catch his breath after Julie's ball-breaking blow. "Kick her outta here, too!" he bellowed. "She's a complete cock tease—you seen her at the bar."

A crowd of rowdy do-gooders was forming at the top of the hallway. "I'm not gonna tell you again, KC," Junior warned. "There are plenty of guys in here tonight who can help me kick your miserable ass outta here."

"I'm takin' off," KC said, sending a mist of spit into Junior's face. A greasy strand of hair flopped over his eyes as he attempted to pull up his sagging Levis. KC bumbled down the hallway, pushed his way through a group of men, and exited out the rear door into the parking lot.

"Thanks, guys," Junior said, waving to the men. "The next round is on me." Turning to Julie, Junior's voice softened. "Are you OK, hon? Did he hurt you?"

"No," Julie said, adjusting the shirt underneath her jacket. "He just tried to grab my…"

"It's OK," Junior said, interrupting her and touching her hand. "KC has been a problem as long as I can remember. He was drunk off his ass. I shoulda cut him off."

"I told him I wasn't interested at the bar. He followed me back here and started pushing me around."

"Yeah, he gets a few drinks in him and gets all horny," Junior said, staring at the old black and white picture hanging on the wall. "He don't know when to take no for an answer. Why, even Bev here had a run-in with the fucker the night she went missin'. My dad told me all about it."

"Really?" Julie said, looking back at the photograph.

"Yeah. I'd tell ya 'bout it, but I gotta get back behind the bar."

"It's OK," Julie said. "I'm fine, really."

"You sure?" Junior glanced back toward the kitchen.

"Yeah, really."

"Well, the rest of the night, the drinks are on me. Deal?"

"Deal," Julie said.

Junior returned to the kitchen as Julie stood in the hallway staring at the picture of her aunt. News of KC's involvement with her Aunt Bev didn't come as a surprise, for some reason. "You're just drunk," Julie said aloud to herself before heading into the bathroom.

47

It was eleven thirty, and many of the patrons had considered the long day ahead and called it a night. A cold beer and a shot of whiskey were already waiting for Julie as she returned to her place at the end of the bar. Holding up the shot of JD, Julie caught Junior's eye and nodded in appreciation before downing it.

"Things are winding down here, Sugar," Julie overheard Junior telling his veteran waitress. "Do you think you could run things for a few minutes while I talk to the young lady at the end of the bar?"

Julie watched as the waitress looked in her direction and nodded. Junior removed his apron and filled a large tumbler with Coke for himself, before coming down to her end of the bar and taking a seat next to her.

"Whew, what a night, eh?" Junior took a long sip of his cola.

Julie nodded and grabbed a cigarette out of her pack on the bar. Reaching into her jean jacket pocket for a lighter, she instead produced an old tube of lip gloss. Bev's closet was becoming a bit of a time capsule, containing clothes she once wore as well as everyday items she must have used. Julie examined the label. "Maybelline Kissing Slicks," it read. The flavor was "Sinnamon Sin," and some of the reddish-brown lip gloss was still in the tube.

"Well I'll be darned," Junior said, looking at the antiquated tube. "I haven't seen a tube of that in—gosh, I don't know how long. Can I see it for a second?"

Looking confused, Julie handed Junior the lip gloss.

"Yep," he said, trying to untwist the top of it. "I'm pretty sure it's the same stuff." After decades of congealing, the cap was difficult to remove. Finally Junior opened it, revealing a coppery-colored lip gloss with the scent of cinnamon.

"It still even smells the same," he said sadly. "Where did you get this?"

Julie shrugged her shoulders. "It was just in this jacket," she said, picking up her beer. "I—I kinda borrowed it."

Junior looked puzzled. "Borrowed it?"

"It's a long story, but this jacket belongs to my aunt," she said. "She must have left it in the pocket."

"Ah," Junior said. "But this stuff is really old. I know, because I used to know a girl who used this exact brand," he said.

"You're—you're kidding!" Julie said, beginning to see the connection.

"Nope. In fact, you know that girl in the black and white photo back by the bathrooms?" Julie felt her stomach flutter. Her eyes widened as she nodded.

"That was her... Bev... I had the biggest crush on her, but she never knew it," he said putting the cap back on the lip gloss.

"I used to bounce here for my dad, back in the seventies," he said. "I'd sit up here at the bar on my break and just watch her smear this stuff on her lips. She was such a beautiful girl."

"Well, I've got a little confession to make," Julie said, pounding back the rest of her beer and trying to gather up her courage to tell. "The reason I was looking at the picture is because she's my aunt. This was her jacket. I'm staying with my grandparents for the holiday, and they've got me staying in her room. I knew my grandma would have a shit fit if she knew I went to the bar, so I snuck out after we all went to bed."

"Well, I'll be damned," Junior said waving at the waitress. "Sugar, can you get me a beer, and her another round, please?" Junior stared at Julie intently. "I just can't believe it. So must be Shawn's your mama?"

"That's right," Julie said. "But you can't tell her I was here, either."

Junior shook his head. "No, 'course not. What happens at the Sportsman stays at the Sportsman."

The waitress brought the drinks to Junior and Julie. "Now that you mention it, you do sorta look like her. Your hair and skin coloring are different, but your features are similar." Junior tasted his beer without taking his eyes off of Julie.

"That's what my grandma says." Julie reached into her blue-jeans pocket for her lighter.

"I've never forgiven myself for that night," Junior said, setting his drink on the bar.

"What do you mean?" Julie lit her cigarette.

"Well, I didn't show up to bounce that night. Me and Big Lou— that was the other bouncer— we'd switched schedules, and I forgot all about it and didn't show up for work that night," he said. "My dad and Kate, they blamed it on Big Lou, because they thought he was supposed to be working, but it was me who shoulda been here the night she went missing. Do you mind?" Junior asked reached for Julie's cigarettes.

Julie slid the pack and her lighter over to him. "What's to forgive?"

"C'mon! You must've heard this story." Junior's hand shook as he lit his cigarette.

Julie drank half of her shot of JD. "Don't get all upset," she said, placing her drink on the napkin. "We're talking about something that happened over three decades ago."

"Well ...there was this fella in here—his name was something like Joe—was it Joe?" Junior said, scrunching his forehead and exhaling smoke.

"John," Julie said.

"Yeah, that's it—John. So you have heard the story."

"I haven't actually heard the story—I've just heard the name," Julie said, feeling a little antsy. "Hanson. John Hanson."

"That's right. John Hanson," Junior repeated. "Well, he was in here that night, and he actually saved your aunt from being molested by that same guy that was all over you tonight." Junior stopped and shook his head. "Ain't that weird? KC does the same damn thing to you that he did to your aunt?"

"What do you mean?" Julie said. "That guy's gotta be in his late fifties. There's no way that could be the same guy."

"No, actually he's in his sixties now," he said. "He's about my age. Kelly Chapman—goes by KC. He was five or six years older than your aunt."

Things were finally starting to make sense. Julie took a long drag of her cigarette. "Tell me more."

"KC always had a thing for your aunt," Junior said. "Well, there weren't many of us who didn't. Not only was she gorgeous, but she was nice, funny, and smart." Junior took a sip of beer. "You know—the whole package."

Julie nodded and flicked her cigarette in the ashtray.

"Obviously, I wasn't working when it happened, so this John fella stepped in and kicked the livin' shit out of KC," he said. "My dad told me later that this John guy was a mountain of a man—in his late twenties or early thirties, and he just cleaned KC's clock. Your aunt, I guess, sorta took a shine to him after that." Junior took another drink of his beer. "God, I wish I'd been here."

"That son of a bitch has been at it way too long," Julie said angrily. "Somebody should kill the motherfucker."

"Settle down, hon. He's gone, and he won't be back," he said. "And you really kicked his ass tonight anyway."

Julie's anger dissipated. "I guess I kinda did, didn't I?" she smirked. "It's just weird that he'd still be around—and that he happened to pull that shit on me, too." Julie shook her head while considering the irony of it all.

"Yeah, it is pretty coincidental, I'll give you that," Junior said. "Well, you know the rest, I bet," Junior extinguished the butt of his cigarette. "That John guy took your aunt home. Or, so they thought."

"Yeah, my mom said they thought he might have had something to do with it, but that he was actually killed in a car accident later that night —well, early the next morning," she said, taking a drink of her beer.

"Yeah, that's right," Junior said. "East of here a few miles west of Grand Ledge. They think a deer must've run out in front of him, and he rolled his car into a tree. He and his car burned to a crisp, but it was only him in the car, so they really don't think he had anything to do with your aunt's disappearance."

Julie seemed to be in a trance of some sort as Junior talked.

"Are you OK, hon?" Junior asked.

"Hmm? Oh, yeah, I'm fine," Julie said recovering. "I guess I was just lost in the thought of it all."

"Shit, there's been all kinds of theories and rumors about what must have happened that night, but I still think about it," he said. "Usually if I was working, I'd give her a lift home instead of Kate and my dad droppin' her off. She liked me alright, but I guess I wasn't her type back then," he said shaking his head. "I gave up and started dating an older lady. Didn't take."

"So what were some of the theories?" Julie scrubbed her cigarette out in the ashtray.

"Well, one was that he dropped her off and KC and his buddies were waiting in the weeds for her," he said. "But the police pretty much ruled that out."

"Uh-huh. I've heard that one before." Julie took the last gulp of her JD. "The cops checked 'em all out. They had gone to some other bar or something?"

"Yeah, The Barn, in downtown Mulliken," Junior said. "Then there was the one that said she'd just had it with everyone and ran off—just left life here and started a life in another state, but I don't think that's true. I think she was too dedicated to her family," he said. "And she seemed to be genuinely happy with the way her life was turning out. She loved kids and couldn't wait to start college and become a teacher somewhere," he added. "Shit, her life was just starting! She wouldn't run off from all that."

"Yeah, from what my mom's said, they really don't think that's what happened," Julie said.

"No way. It just wasn't her style."

"Then …there was the theory that I mighta had something to do with it," Junior said, raising his eyebrows.

"What? You're kidding." Julie picked up her beer.

"No, I'm serious. Your mom never told you this part?"

"No! No way," Julie said.

"It's a small community, and it was pretty obvious that I liked your aunt," he said. "When they couldn't find her, folks started saying that I had planned the whole thing by switching shifts with Big Lou so that he wouldn't be around. Some folks thought I was actually waiting for her when she got home."

"C'mon. You?" Julie said, shaking her head.

"Yep, me. I was at friend's house that night—over at Bob Carr's place," Junior said. "The cops checked it all out, and Bob vouched for me. I'd never have done anything to hurt your aunt," he said.

"But boy, were my dad and Kate pissed that Meryl even let 'em check into my whereabouts."

"She probably had no choice, right?" Julie asked.

"Yeah. The fella that ran the investigation—not the guy from the Sherriff's Department…" Junior paused, trying to think of a name. "He was actually a detective with the Michigan State Police. He's the guy who came and talked to me. Al somebody is all I can remember."

"Must've been pretty upsetting for you," Julie said. "Especially being innocent and all."

"Yeah, it was. Because I really loved your aunt." Junior paused and took a drink of his beer. "I mean, I was upset enough about her missing—and then when the focus shifted to me, it was just really a helpless feeling."

"I can imagine," Julie said. "But what about the obvious theory? You know—what really happened that night, but the cops were too stupid to figure out?" Julie lit another cigarette.

"What do you mean, exactly?" Junior asked. "You mean the theory about this Hanson guy having something to do with it? The cops conducted a huge search for weeks, but never found anything. And nothing linking her to John Hanson," he added. "What makes you so sure he did it?"

"I don't know," Julie said, exhaling and flicking her ash into the tray. "Just a little voice or something, telling me he did."

Junior stared curiously at Julie for a few moments.

Julie broke the pause. "I mean, c'mon. It rained and rained and rained after Aunt Bev went missing. Any trace of anything would have been washed away. It's hard to pin a crime on somebody when you can't find a body," Julie said matter-of-factly. "I think this Hanson guy knew exactly what he was doing, and I bet he dumped her body somewhere right around here, but where nobody would ever find it."

A chill ran down Junior's spine as he listened to Julie's thoughts on what happened to Bev.

"You've probably heard your grandma and grandpa talking about this, huh?" Junior probed.

"Nah, hardly ever." Julie took another drag off her cigarette. "I can't explain it. It's just something that I know in my gut."

"Well, either which way, it's a shame," Junior said. "And I still should've been here that night."

"Woulda happened if you were here anyway," Julie said coldly.

Junior raised his eyebrows. "Really? You think?"

"Sure." Julie continued smoking. "She had the hots for this John guy, and she let him take her home. She was askin' for it from him. She wouldn't have had you take her home—she wasn't interested in you."

Junior looked hurt. "Asking for it?" Junior exclaimed. "You gotta be kidding me! Your aunt wasn't that kind of girl."

Junior was truly puzzled by Julie's theory on what had happened, but chalked it up to youth, inexperience, and too much liquor.

"Yeah, whatever. Maybe. It's getting late. I think I should be headed back to the farmhouse." Julie looked at the clock behind the bar. "Shit, it's nearly one o'clock."

"Do you have a car?" Junior asked.

Julie smiled. "No, I'm a Deerfield, remember? I walked."

"Are you kidding?" Junior asked.

"I snuck out," she said. "I already told you that."

"Let me give you a ride," Junior said, finishing his beer. "These guys can lock up. I have to go to church in the morning, anyway."

"Me too," Julie said rolling her eyes.

"Meryl?" he asked.

Julie nodded and snuffed her cigarette out in the ashtray.

"She and Oscar are good Christians," Junior said.

"If I see you there, you gotta act like you don't know me," Julie said seriously.

"I know, I know," Junior said. "I promise. I remember what it was like with parents and grandparents when I was your age. Just let me just check on a couple things, and then we'll go."

"I'm gonna hit the bathroom before we leave." Julie gathered her things and stepped down off the stool. Feeling a little tipsy, she headed down the hallway.

The second waitress was busy mopping the floor of the small women's room.

"Just use the men's room," the waitress instructed Julie as she waited in the doorway. "It's all clean—nobody's in there, and there's a toilet."

Pushing the door to the men's room open, the stale stench of urine and cigarette smoke overwhelmed her senses, giving her an instant urge to vomit. She'd definitely had too much to drink.

Julie burst into the small stall and hunkered over the bowl. Her stomach heaved, yet nothing came up. After several waves of nausea with nothing to show for it, Julie stood up and leaned against the wall of the stall. Dizzy, she closed her eyes and wiped spittle from the corners of her mouth with the sleeve of her jacket.

Julie shuffled over to the small sink and turned on the water. Gathering her dark hair into a pony tail with one hand, she bent forward and cupped her other hand, splashing cool water onto her face. She turned off the water and looked into the small, smoky mirror.

For a second, the tanned face of a dark-haired man stared back at her in the mirror, and then the image was gone.

"Jesus Christ," Julie said, scrambling backward into the trough urinal. In a flurry, Julie wheeled around to view the man who she thought stood behind her, but nobody was there.

"You OK, hon?" came the waitress's voice from the other side of the door.

"I'll be right out," Julie said loudly. Her hands shook as she ran them through her hair, trying to make sense of what she had seen. "You are so fuckin' drunk," she said quietly to herself. "You've had way too much to drink tonight. You're losing it, that's all."

Julie collected herself and stepped out of the men's room into the long hallway. Junior was waiting near the kitchen door.

"You ready, hon?" he asked kindly. "You OK?"

"I'm fine," Julie said. "Just had too much to drink, I think. This place isn't haunted, is it?"

"What?" Junior said, furrowing his brow. "We'll getcha home in a jiff," he said, jingling his keys. "You need to go to sleep."

48

"You can just drop me off here at the bottom of the driveway. Now remember, tomorrow in church—don't let on like you know me," Julie reminded Junior.

"I know, I know, hon," he said. "Knowing Meryl like I do, I'd get in just as much trouble as you. How are you gonna get in? Do you have a key or something?"

"No, no," Julie whispered, as if she were going to wake up her sleeping grandparents. "I'm gonna climb up the trellis real quietly, slide the window open, and climb in."

Junior smiled. "Save your whispers for when you get inside. Good luck getting in without waking them up."

"Thanks, Junior," Julie said "I'll see you tomorrow."

"Yep, see you at church."

Junior lingered for a few seconds as he watched her run up the driveway. For so many nights during his youth, Junior had watched as young Bev Deerfield ran up the same driveway.

"Doesn't seem possible," Junior mumbled to himself before slowly pulling away from the house.

With little effort, Julie scrambled up the trellis and quietly slid the cracked bedroom window open. Once inside, she shut the window and pulled the shade. Snapping on the small table lamp, Julie emptied the contents of her jacket pockets into her backpack and hung the jacket back in Bev's closet.

After shucking off her smoky clothing and stuffing them into her suitcase, Julie put on a nightshirt, turned off the light, and climbed into bed. Within seconds, the bed began to spin, sending her into the upright position.

Julie got up and made her way to the bathroom. As she weaved her way down the hallway, she noticed that the door to her mother's old bedroom was ajar. Quietly, Julie pushed the door open and went inside.

The full moon shone brightly into the room, allowing Julie to see that her mother's old bed was piled with old clothes on hangers, bolts of fabric, stacks of old books, and a big box that had once held bananas. To enhance the limited lighting, she turned on the small lamp near her Grandmother's sewing machine. She then lifted the carton and brought it closer to the light. Sifting through the box was like looking at a cross-section of her aunt's life. Meticulously organized, the box contained files that were labeled "Baby Pictures," "Baptism," "Baby Book," "Grade School Pictures," "Report Cards," "Class Pictures," "Letters," "Middle School Pictures," "Church Events," "High School," and "Graduation."

Julie pulled out Bev's 1954 baby book. Meryl had diligently filled out all of Bev's firsts: first foods, first sounds, first words, even a snippet of Bev's golden locks from her first haircut. Through the age of five, Meryl had documented everything, including shots, illnesses, and doctor visits.

"Jesus," Julie said quietly. "I bet she didn't do one of these for Mom." Placing the book back into its folder, Julie then pulled out several grade school pictures and report cards. With the letter "E" for "Excellent" scribbled next to every single topic, it was like looking at one of her own.

Flipping open the high school folder, Julie mainly found pictures of Bev with her friends, and even a smaller version of the exact black and white picture that hung on the wall at the Sportsman's Tavern. Julie turned the picture over and examined the writing on the back: "Bev and Kate, June, 1972". "It must've been taken just a couple months before she died," Julie thought, placing the photograph on the sewing table.

Julie noticed another picture, presumably also taken at the tavern. In the picture, Bev was standing between two boys of similar age. Beverly's smile radiated in the picture, and Julie could understand Junior's comments about her aunt. She was stunning. On the back of the photo was written, "Big Lou, me and Chucky, summer '71." Julie surmised that "Chucky" was in fact Junior. She kept that photo as well.

As Julie placed the remaining pictures back into the proper folders, she saw an unsealed manila envelope peeking out of the back of the box. She slid the packet out, raised its flap, and peered inside to find several neatly folded yellowing newspaper clippings.

Carefully, she unfolded the first article. Published by the *Lansing State Journal,* it was dated August 28, 1972. "State and Local Law Enforcement Band Together in Search for Missing Youth." Bev's graduation picture was shown, and the two-column article explained the initial details of the alleged abduction.

Realizing that she was too drunk to comprehend all that the article offered, Julie began to refold the article. A picture of a handsome man on the opposite side of the clipping caught her attention. Julie's hands began to shake uncontrollably as she picked up the fragile news copy and began reading the other side. "What the fuck is this?" she whispered aloud as she stared at the picture of John Hanson.

A separate article had appeared in the same issue of the paper, identifying the victim and detailing the events of John Hanson's fiery crash along M-43. The military photo accompanying the article showed a younger John Hanson, but Julie immediately recognized him as the man she had seen in the mirror at the Sportsman's Tavern.

"I must be losing my mind." Julie frantically skimmed the article. "How can this be?" Julie put the article down and took a few deep breaths to get her bearings. "OK. You're trashed, you're looking through all kinds of creepy stuff, and it's just your imagination," she told herself. "You're too fucking drunk to comprehend this stuff. It's very late. Go to bed."

Still, the photograph of John Hanson awakened a feeling in the pit of her stomach. Julie placed the article back into the envelope with the other articles and photos she'd collected and took it to her room to read later.

49

"Happy Thanksgiving, honey," Meryl said from the stove. "I'm just getting your plate ready. Did you sleep well?"

"Like a rock," Julie said, joining Oscar at the table and staring at a tall glass of milk. "Do you think I could trade this in for a coffee?"

"Sure thing." Oscar pushed back in his chair and prepared to get up.

"No, don't you get up," Julie said. "I can get it."

"I guess I didn't know you were a coffee drinker." Meryl carried a steaming plate of biscuits and gravy over to Julie's place at the table.

"Well, with all the late-night studying I've been doing, I sort of developed a taste for it, I guess," Julie lied. The fact was, after a long night at the bar, Julie thought a little caffeine might help her get through the morning. Grabbing a mug from the cupboard, she poured herself a hot cup of black coffee, no cream.

"Shall we say the blessing?" Oscar said, holding out his hands. "Dear Lord, we thank you for this day as we celebrate Thanksgiving together with our granddaughter. Thank you for the many blessings you bestow upon us, and for the plentiful food we will eat today. In Jesus' name, amen."

"Amen," Julie repeated. "So, what time do we have to leave for church?"

"Oh, probably around nine thirty or so," Meryl said. "I always like to get our usual seats, and lately Ruby Beldoff has been encroaching on our pew."

"Oh, now, Mother," Oscar said gently. "You can get the same message from any pew in there. Your grandmother is a creature of habit."

"Well, that's just how I am, Oscar." Meryl savored her first bite of breakfast. "C'mon, honey, eat up. It's your favorite."

Julie used her fork to cut a piece of biscuit soaked in gravy. Reluctantly, she crammed it into her mouth and swallowed. "Mmm," she said, smiling, raising her eyebrows and washing it down with coffee.

"What's the matter, sweetheart?" Meryl put down her fork. "Don't you feel well? Are you sure you slept alright? Because you honestly look bone-tired."

"No, I'm fine." Julie cut another piece of gravy-soaked biscuit. "I'm just not caught up on my sleep, I guess."

"Well, you must have slept for nearly eleven hours last night, hon," Meryl said sympathetically. "Maybe we need to get you over to Doctor Robert's before you go back to school? Maybe you're anemic, or maybe you have mono or something."

"No, there's no need for that," Julie sputtered. "Truly, I'm fine." Julie shoved another forkful of breakfast into her mouth.

"Doc wouldn't mind," Meryl said. "He might actually be at church today. He and Lucy usually stay around over the holidays."

"I said no," Julie said, slamming her fork down onto her plate. She could feel herself on the verge of completely losing her temper, but struggled to stay calm.

Meryl and Oscar recoiled from the sudden outburst and stared at their granddaughter.

"Look, I don't mean to be rude, but I don't need to go to the doctor," she said quietly. "I'm really fine. Just still a little tired from my new routine at MSU, that's all."

"She's right, Mother," Oscar said, resuming his role as the peacekeeper. "She's still got today and tonight to rest up. She's not even been here for a whole day."

Julie smiled gratefully at Oscar and picked up her fork again. "Yeah, that's right," she said, lopping off another piece of biscuit. "I have all of today to rest up."

Meryl quietly shook her head and took a sip of coffee. "Sometimes, I..." Meryl began. "Never mind."

"What? Sometimes you what?" Julie said with her mouth half full.

"Sometimes I wonder where our Julie went," she said mournfully.

"Oh, my God." Abruptly, Julie got up from the table and took her half-eaten plate of food to the sink. "Why doesn't anybody seem to understand that I'm not the same person?" Julie slammed her plate on the counter. "I'm growing up! And I get sick of all this shit about living in the past." Julie stormed out of the kitchen into the living room.

Meryl's eyes were glassy with tears as she listened to her granddaughter thump up the stairs.

"Now, Mother," Oscar said, getting up from his seat at the table. "You just pushed her too much is all. The girl obviously has a lot on her mind about school."

"I know, I know." Meryl dabbed her eyes with a napkin. "She's just like Shawn was, I suppose. It's just so disappointing."

"Shhhhh," Oscar said. "We'll have none of that talk. Let's give her a few minutes to settle down, and then I'll go talk to her. She's just tired, and I don't think either one of us realized how stressed she is right now."

Meryl shook her head. "Maybe you're right."

"Of course I am," he said. "When I think back to my first year in college, I remember how overwhelming it was. That's what our girl is going through right now, so we need to just let her have some space. She knows we're here when she needs us."

"I know. You're right." Meryl got up from the table. "It's just that her behavior has been so very different this visit. She seems like a different person."

"She's young, Meryl," Oscar said. "She's trying to figure it all out. Remember what that was like?"

Meryl began scraping breakfast scraps from the plates into the trash. "Yes, I guess I do, but it's just so out of Julie's character. Having her around is usually very comforting to me because ... I don't know, I guess I sort of feel that for those hours when Julie is here, I have my Bev back in some way," she said, voice cracking.

"I know, sweetie." Oscar walked over to his wife and wrapped his arms around her shoulders. "It's still hard, isn't it?"

Julie appeared in the kitchen doorway as Oscar held Meryl.

"I'm really sorry, Grandma," Julie said, inching into the kitchen. Tears streamed down her young face as she moved toward her grandparents.

"Oh, Tootsie Belle," Oscar said, opening his arms and inviting Julie into their hug. "You don't need to cry about all this. What am I going to do with you girls?"

Meryl turned to Julie and tenderly wiped away her tears. "It's going to be OK." Meryl looked deeply into Julie's bloodshot eyes. "Whatever is going on with you right now—it's going to be OK."

Julie broke down and sobbed in her grandmother's arms. "I don't know what's going on with me—that's the whole problem."

"Oh, honey," Meryl said, stroking her granddaughter's dark

hair. "It's just a bad patch, that's all. Nobody likes change, but things will get better."

Julie stopped crying. "I just don't know why I treat people—why I treated you like I did just then. It's like I just can't stop it, and I hate myself for it."

"Honey, I think you're just overly tired," Oscar said. "We sometimes don't realize how tired and fatigued we can be. You've got a heavy load at school, and you're stressed out."

"Maybe you're right," Julie said, sitting down at the table and wiping her eyes with a napkin. "I do have a lot going on at school. And there's the pressure to keep my grades so high, so I won't lose my scholarship, that's always on my mind, too."

Meryl sat next to Julie at the table. "You have a lot on your plate," she said. "What does your mom say about all of this?"

"Nothing," Julie said flatly. "We don't talk about it. She doesn't know I'm upset about anything."

"Well, maybe you need to talk to her," Meryl said.

"Mother, now that's really for Julie to decide," Oscar said cautiously.

Julie nodded. "I don't really want to talk to her about any of it. She'll just think … well, I really don't care what she'll think."

"Maybe you need to talk to somebody at school—a counselor or somebody," Meryl suggested.

"No, I don't need that, either." There was an edge of anger in her voice.

Meryl looked up at Oscar with true concern in her eyes.

"Sweetie, your grandma and I aren't trying to tell you what to do. Please know that," he said. "We just want you to be happy."

"I know you do," Julie said apologetically. "I'm just so screwed up right now."

"Listen—let's skip church today," Oscar said. "I think it would be better if you just rest up."

"No, no, absolutely not," Julie said emphatically. "I want to go to church with you guys. It will probably do us all some good." Julie stood up from the table.

"Are you sure, sweetheart?" Meryl asked. "It really won't bother me one bit if we miss it."

"No, let's go," Julie said. "You've been looking forward to it, and it will give me something else to think about."

50

It was nine fifty when Oscar turned into the driveway of the Mulliken First United Methodist Church. Flanked by cornfields, the single-story white plank board structure looked a little like a one-room schoolhouse from the road.

"Looks like Ruby's here," Oscar said as he negotiated his black Crown Vic into a parking space next to a shiny red Buick.

"Yep, that's Ruby's ruby-red car, all right." Meryl gathered her purse. "I bet she's already sitting in our spot, too."

Julie's mind was flooded with distant memories of the past as she stepped into the old church. She had attended Sunday school there for much of her childhood, always a visitor with her grandparents while her mother worked weekend shifts.

A center aisle divided two rows of wooden pews. Four simple stained glass windows on each side of the sanctuary led up to a slightly raised platform consisting of an altar, two short rows of seats for the choir, and a podium.

"Happy Thanksgiving," Junior said, holding out his hand to Oscar.

"Same to you," Oscar said cheerfully. "Junior, I don't know if you remember her or not, but this is Shawn's daughter, Julie. She goes to MSU and is visiting us for the holiday."

"Well, ain't that nice." Junior smiled broadly. "Julie, it's nice to meet you," he said, delivering an Emmy Award–winning performance and holding out his hand.

"Nice to meet you, too," Julie said, returning the handshake.

"Junior here is the son of Chuck Preston—owned the bar where your Aunt Bev worked," Meryl said coldly. "Are your folks here?"

"Yeah, they're right over there." Junior pointed in their direction, a few rows down. Meryl had never quite trusted Junior's role in the disappearance of her daughter, and it still showed thirty-five years later.

"C'mon," Meryl said to Oscar and Julie. "We should find our seats."

Julie could feel Meryl's annoyance as she saw Ruby Beldoff sitting smack-dab in the middle of Meryl's favorite seat. Before Meryl or Oscar could do anything, Julie bee-lined into the pew and bent down to speak privately with Ruby.

"Ruby, you're gonna have to move," she said without emotion. "See, for some reason you like to sit where my grandparents do, and it's making everyone mad."

Ruby's eyes widened and she looked toward Oscar and Meryl, who anxiously looked on.

"Now, if you could just slide your ass down to the end of the row, we can all sit here, OK?"

"Why …" Ruby muttered, glaring at Julie.

Julie stared intently back, causing Ruby to reconsider a rebuttal. "That's it … thank you," she said as Ruby began scooching all the way to the end of the row. "Here we go," Julie said, taking Ruby's seat and gesturing for her grandparents to sit on either side of her.

"What did you say to her?" Meryl whispered in Julie's ear.

"I just told her that it was our family seat and that it upsets you when you can't sit here," she explained. Oscar seemed troubled by his granddaughter's take-charge attitude, but based on the morning's earlier interaction, he chose to shut up and take a seat. Meryl's nervous wave in Ruby's direction went unacknowledged.

Julie looked around the congregation, recognizing people she hadn't seen in years. "Isn't she dead yet?" Julie whispered after seeing Gladys Smith wobble down the aisle on her walker. Oscar suppressed a smile while Meryl looked disapprovingly at Julie for her comment. Julie smiled and touched her grandma's arm. "C'mon Grandma—lighten up already. I'm just kidding."

As they continued to wait, Julie continued with the commentary. "Jeez, it's like God's waiting room in here—everybody's so freakin' old."

Oscar furrowed his brow. "I Ion, please," he whispered in Julie's ear. "We're so happy to have you with us, but please try to not upset your grandma."

51

Oscar stepped into the kitchen from the back porch. "Oh, it smells so good in here!"

"It sure does," Julie agreed. "When's dinner, Grandma?"

"Oh, I thought we'd eat around two or two thirty," she said, glancing up at the clock. "It's going to be another three hours or so, so if you two are hungry, you better grab a snack."

"Nah, I'm good." Julie took her jacket off. "Is there anything I can help you with?"

"No, sweetie, I don't think so." Meryl tied an apron around her waist. "The bird and the stuffing are in the oven—your favorite pie needs to go in around one—Oscar is handling the mashed potatoes and gravy—and the rolls go last."

"That all sounds so good," Julie said.

"Why don't you just relax and take it easy?" Oscar said, grabbing a bag of potatoes out of the pantry. "Your grandma and I have things under control. Go grab a nap or something, or watch the parade on TV—just rest, Tootsie Belle."

"If you're sure, then I'll just go upstairs and read for a while."

"Sounds like a good idea, hon," Oscar agreed.

Meryl and Oscar listened until they could hear Julie close the door to her bedroom. "I'm really concerned about her," Meryl whispered.

Oscar dug a half dozen potatoes out of the bag and placed them in the sink. "I know you are, hon, but there really isn't anything for us to do. She's just going through a phase."

"Well, I don't like it," Meryl replied frankly. "Did you see how Ruby left the church as we were singing the last hymn? That's not like her—not like her at all." Meryl reached for the flour canister on the countertop. "She loves to have coffee after the service and visit, 'specially on Thanksgiving and all."

Oscar used a brush to scrub the potatoes in the sink. "Yeah, I know it isn't," he said, turning on the water. "I noticed that, too, but I didn't want to risk causing a scene at church. We'll have a word with Ruby on Sunday after Julie goes home."

"I just can't help but wonder what's really going on," Meryl said. "Shawn was moody, but she wasn't as feisty as Julie's been, and Julie has never been this way."

"Kids are different these days," Oscar said. "They're raised differently than we were, and they're allowed to get away with it. I'm sure she'll outgrow it."

"I hope it's that simple," was all Meryl could say.

52

Julie cracked the window in her bedroom and flopped down on the unmade bed. With her hands behind her head and lying flat on her back, she closed her eyes and thought about all that had happened in the last two days. The trip back to familiar surroundings, which was designed to even things out for her, was having the opposite effect.

Julie started thinking about the stash of old articles and photographs that she had discovered in her grandmother's sewing room. Who was John Hanson, and why did she recognize his face in the photograph as being the same "ghost" she had seen at the Sportsman's Tavern?

"Was I that drunk?" Julie wondered. Maybe it had been a combination of things: the old photograph of her aunt in the bar hallway, talking to somebody who'd actually known Aunt Bev *and* felt responsible for her death, and inadvertently running into the same drunken asshole who tried to molest her aunt. It was a lot to fathom.

Julie slid off the bed and quickly straightened the bedspread and pillow. In last night's drunkenness, she had stuffed the envelope of old photographs and articles haphazardly into her backpack.

Julie removed the large envelope from her backpack and spread its contents across the bed. Carefully, she unfolded each article and arranged them by date.

After turning on the small reading lamp, she read the first of four articles. It was published in the *Lansing State Journal* on Monday, August 28, 1972.

State and Local Law Enforcement Band
Together in Search for Missing Youth

MULLIKEN, Mich. — *State and local law enforcement officials continue the search for 18-year-old Beverly Ann Deerfield. Deerfield was reported missing on Saturday by her mother, who said she never returned home after working the late shift Friday evening at the Sportsman's Tavern in Mulliken.*

Preliminary reports say Deerfield left the M-43 establishment around 2 a.m. Saturday morning after accepting a ride from a patron.

"We know for a fact that Beverly Ann Deerfield left the Sportsman's Tavern with a patron around 2 a.m.," Eaton County Sherriff Dan Hoffmann said. Hoffmann identified the patron as John Charles Hanson, 32, of Germfask, Michigan.

Hoffmann said the timeframe of the case is troubling. "We know John Hanson was going to drop Beverly Deerfield off at her home around 2 a.m.," he said. "The trouble is, there is no indication that she ever showed up, and approximately three hours later we got the report that a single car had been in an accident on M-43." Hoffmann said it was later determined that Hanson's car was involved in the accident, and that Hanson was killed in the wreck.

Extensive background checks on Hanson indicated

that he was a war veteran with no known living relatives, Hoffman said. He was honorably discharged in April of 1968 after being wounded in action in Vietnam and earning the Purple Heart.

"He was the only person in the car, but the question then becomes what happened to Bev Deerfield, and more specifically, what happened between the hours of 2 and 5 a.m.?" Hoffmann said. **(Continued on page 2A)**

Julie flipped the article over to continue reading. John Hanson's intense stare into the camera was the same one Julie had seen in the mirror at the bar.

(Continued from 1A)

After ruling out criminal involvement of several other suspects, Michigan State Police Det. Alan Whitman said the focus of the case was turning back to John Hanson.

"Here's a guy who it would appear had a stellar record," Whitman said. "We're trying to dig a little deeper into his past, but without relatives or any known friends, it's a difficult task, as you can imagine."

Whitman said the State Police and other local law enforcement personnel and volunteers would be targeting an area having a ten-mile radius in the vicinity of The Sportsman's Tavern, the Deerfield residence, and the site where Hanson's car was found.

Whitman said the only suspect continues to be Hanson. "He came from the rural area of the Upper Peninsula and served in Vietnam. Obviously, he knows something about negotiating wooded areas," he said.

"The Shimnecon region near Mulliken is about as remote as you can get, so we're pinning our hopes on this theory, and hope that we can give the Deerfields some answers."

Anyone with information concerning the whereabouts of Beverly Deerfield or any information that might assist officials in the case are urged to call the Eaton County Sherriff's office or the Michigan State Police.

Julie rubbed her eyes and wondered why her mother and grandparents never made a particularly big deal out of John Hanson's possible role in her aunt's disappearance. More than that, she wondered if the previous evening's image of John Hanson was an invention of her drunken imagination, or perhaps his ghost trying to sort out unfinished business. Julie felt a shiver go up her neck as she considered the possibilities.

The second *Lansing State Journal* article was dated a week later, on September 4, 1972.

Bad Weather Slows Search for Missing Teen

MULLIKEN, Mich. — *Torrential rains and high winds have slowed teams of law enforcement officials and volunteers as they comb miles of wooded area in Eaton and Ionia Counties' Shimnecon region looking for signs of what may have happened to Beverly Ann Deerfield, 18, of Mulliken. Deerfield was reported missing on Aug. 25 by her mother, who said she never returned home after working the late shift Friday evening at the Sportsman's Tavern on M-43.*

"The rain has really slowed our progress, not just on the ground, but also from the air," Det. Alan Whitman of the Michigan State Police said. "We've got an eye in the sky, but it's so foggy and rainy, it's almost impossible to see anything." Whitman said the helicopter was grounded all weekend due to high winds and driving rain.

"Our K9 units aren't picking up anything either, and we haven't found any trace of anything, I'm sorry to say. The bad weather couldn't have come at a worse time."

Owners of the Sportsman's Tavern, Kate Danaker and Chuck Preston, are among the hundreds of volunteers searching the area, and have a very special reason for helping out.

"She is our employee," Danaker said, choking back tears. "I was the last one to see her. It's the least I can do to be out here trying to find a clue or something that can help figure out what happened."

Eaton County Sherriff Dan Hoffmann says the search has been well organized, but both bad weather and the extreme conditions of Shimnecon have made their efforts very difficult. "You've got just about every type of pitfall Mother Nature can throw at you back there. From the woods to the thorn thickets to the vast and mucky swamp area, it's darn near impossible to walk through there. I can't imagine anybody negotiating that kind of a landscape on the best of days, to say nothing of in the middle of the night."

Whitman said the search will continue for the rest of the week before Michigan State Police officials make a *determination of whether to continue on with the search or not.*

"We'll be out there for several more days anyway," Hoffmann said. "If the weather breaks, hopefully we'll find the answers we're all looking for."

Anyone with information concerning the where-abouts of Beverly Deerfield or any information that might assist officials in the case are urged to call the Eaton County Sherriff's office or the Michigan State Police.

"Kate Danaker—she was at church today," Julie thought. It was suddenly all making sense. "Chuck and Kate owned the Sportsman's Tavern, and Junior is Chuck's son, the guy who bounced in 1972," Julie realized.

Julie turned her attention to the third article. Published on Saturday, September 9, 1972 the headline completed the series of articles.

Search Ends for Local Teen: Beverly Deerfield Feared Dead

MULLIKEN, Mich. — *Michigan State Police Det. Alan Whitman told reporters that the statewide police agency was officially calling off the search for Beverly Ann Deerfield, 18, on Friday.*

Deerfield was reported missing on Aug. 25 after not returning home following completion of the late shift at the Sportsman's Tavern.

Teams of local and state police officials and hun-dreds of area volunteers have spent the last two weeks combing the 10-mile area surrounding the Shimnecon region of Ionia and Eaton Counties. Bad weather, high winds and extreme conditions in the region hampered the search.

"It was a difficult call to make," Whitman told members of the press at a conference held at the Eaton County Sherriff's office. "We've spent thousands and thousands of dollars in man hours and equipment, and unfortunately we've come up empty-handed. I certainly don't like to see cases go unsolved, but we'll stay on it and see if we can find another lead somewhere else."

While he was cautious to state his beliefs in the case, Whitman said he feared foul play. "I've been a cop for a long time, and from the very beginning, I suspected malfeasance. I'm still not convinced John Hanson didn't have something to do with Miss Deerfield's disappearance, but unfortunately, we can't prove it at this point."

Hanson, 32, allegedly dropped Deerfield off at her residence sometime around 2 a.m. on Aug. 25, but hours later was killed in a single-car crash along M-43 in Eaton County.

Whitman thanked all police agencies and volunteers for their hard work, hope and prayers over the last two weeks. "It truly has been a joint effort on everyone's part to bring some closure to the Deerfield family, and I hope in some way we have helped," he said.

Meryl Deerfield, mother of the victim, was not available for comment.

The last article was Bev's obituary, dated one year later, August 25, 1973. Julie remembered her mother telling her about her grandmother's reluctance to declare Bev deceased. The year after Bev's abduction, Shawn said, had been some of her mother's darkest days.

Julie gathered the articles and pictures and placed them back into the envelope and slid them back into her backpack. All the reading and thinking had left Julie sleepy. Crawling back up onto the bed, she drifted off to sleep within minutes.

Julie's sputtering and coughing awakened her from a dead sleep. With black smoke billowing into the small room from underneath the bedroom door, Julie jumped to her feet. Turning the cool brass doorknob, Julie moved into the hallway and was overcome by fumes. Julie covered her mouth and nose with her shirt as she stumbled down the staircase and into the living room.

The thick smoky air made it difficult to see, yet her eyes didn't sting. Desperately, she made her way to the kitchen, but found neither people nor a fire—just smoke. "Grandma! Grandpa!" she tried yelling, but her voice made no sound.

Confusion and panic filled Julie's consciousness as she tried to determine the origin of the smoke. Julie turned and raced back through the living room to the staircase. Taking two steps at a time, she made it to the upstairs hallway. Struggling to call for her grandparents, Julie still couldn't utter a sound.

Standing in front of her grandparents' closed bedroom door, Julie looked down and saw what appeared to be water flowing from the room into the hallway. As she opened the door, the overpowering fumes told her it wasn't water but gasoline. Horrified, Julie looked up and saw the mutilated bodies of her grandmother and Oscar lying on a bed dripping with fuel.

Julie approached the double bed and looked at her grandparents' broken bodies. Meryl's half-opened eyes gazed upward toward the ceiling as her blood-soaked and motionless body lay twisted and fractured on the bed. Julie poked at her frail frame in an attempt to awaken her, but it was too late. She was dead.

Oscar lay bruised and broken beside her. A bloodied baseball bat lay by the side of the bed. Eyes closed, Julie was unable to determine if he, too, was dead. Bending down for a closer look, she shrieked in agony when he grabbed her hand.

Julie's eyes snapped open as she awakened screaming from a dream.

"Hon, hon, it's me, Grandpa! You're having a bad dream, that's all." Oscar perched next to her on the bed. "She's OK, Mother. She's fine." Meryl was pacing in the hallway, not wanting to enter Bev's old room.

"What's going on?" Julie cried. Her heart pounded double time in her chest.

"Sweetie, calm down. You were just having a bad dream, that's all," Oscar said. "Your grandmother and I could hear you all the way downstairs, and we thought something was wrong."

Julie sat up, hair mussed and face streamed by tears, and took a deep breath.

"Mother, can you get our girl a nice cold glass of water, please?" Oscar said gently, slipping into his undertaker mode. "You've just had a nasty dream, hon," he repeated calmly. "Grandma will get you something to drink."

Julie's throat felt raw. "Here you go," Meryl said, trying not to spill the full glass of water. "Are you OK, hon?"

Julie nodded.

"What were you dreaming about?" Meryl asked, troubled once again by her granddaughter's freakish behavior. "Do you remember?"

Julie could remember, but shook her head and acted as though she didn't.

Oscar took the drink from Meryl and handed it to Julie. "Here you go, hon—take a drink."

Julie took a few gulps of water and her expression softened. "I'm really sorry," she said hoarsely.

"What?" Oscar said. "Nonsense. You had a bad dream—that's not your fault. Are you OK now?" Oscar sensed that Julie wanted to recover alone.

"Just take your time. Finish your water and clean up," he said, softly stoking her hair. "Your Grandma and I will be downstairs if you need us." Oscar joined Meryl in the hallway and shut the door.

The whole dream had seemed so real, and Julie's lungs and throat felt as if they had actually been seared by the hot smoke. Julie's right hand, the one Oscar had grabbed in the dream, was swollen again and very sore.

Julie remembered her grandparents' bodies lying on the double bed—the absence of life in her grandmother's eyes, and the battered, bleeding, and broken body of Oscar. Physically, she felt like she'd been there.

"What's happening to me?" she said quietly. Holding her head in her hands, Julie silently wondered what would make her mind come up with a scenario like that. Further, why in the dream had she been more curious than upset?

Julie sat up on the bed and grabbed her backpack. Removing her cell phone, Julie dialed her mother.

"Shit! Voicemail," Julie said aloud. Julie left a message.

"Yeah, mom, it's me. You're probably working—it's close to 2 o'clock. We haven't eaten yet, but I'm wondering if you could come get me tonight instead of tomorrow. I'm—I'm just getting kind of tired of doing the grandparent thing," she said. "I don't think Grandma and Oscar will mind if I go tonight. Call me back, or just come. But don't let on that I called you, OK? Thanks."

Julie flipped her cell phone shut and headed to the bathroom to clean up.

53

"Well, it's all paid for—I'm stuffed," Oscar said, slapping the side of his retiree paunch and leaning back in his chair at the table. "And can I say that you simply outdid yourself, Mother?"

Meryl smiled and looked at her granddaughter across the table. "Julie, did you get enough to eat?"

"Oh absolutely, Grandma, thank you. It was really great. Best meal I've had in, well, I guess as long as I can remember."

"And you're sure you're OK now?" Meryl asked, looking intently worried.

"I told you guys, I'm fine. It was just a bad dream. But I feel better now that I've eaten." Julie got up and began clearing the table.

"Oh sweetie, you and your grandfather go in there and watch football while I do up these dishes," she said. "You know how he loves the Lions, and I don't know one side of the field from the other." Meryl gestured toward the living room. "Shoo, both of you. Go enjoy the game."

Oscar grinned and looked at the clock. "Your grandmother is right. It's just after three, so they're probably in the last quarter of the game. Let's see who's ahead," he said. "It's not that often I get to watch football with anybody—your grandma hates it." Julie put the dishes in the sink and dutifully followed Oscar into the living room.

Oscar turned on the old 24-inch Zenith TV in time to watch as the Lions were losing to the Green Bay Packers. "Just as I suspected,"

Oscar said, settling into his recliner. "We're losing by more than two touchdowns. We need a new quarterback."

Julie stretched out on the couch and began watching the game. "The Lions need a helluva lot more than a new quarterback, Grandpa," Julie said confidently. "The Packers, now there's a team! Brett Favre is probably the NFL's best quarterback ever."

"I guess I didn't know that you followed football all that closely," Oscar said, taking notice of Julie's sudden interest.

"I don't really. I just know a little about how crappy the Lions are and how they can never beat the Packers," she said. "They're a downright embarrassment to us Michiganders."

Oscar was somewhat surprised by his granddaughter's opinions on NFL teams, but given the day they'd had already, decided to keep his mouth shut.

Julie and Oscar watched as, with less than five minutes to play, the Lions' Calvin Johnson used his height to catch two perfectly aimed passes, narrowing the Packers' lead to nine points.

"See! Now that John Kitna isn't all that bad," Oscar said excitedly as he watched the Lion's kicker boot the extra point. "We're only trailing by eight, and if we can get the ball back, who knows?"

"Oh my God, Oscar," Julie said arrogantly. "Don't tell me you've drunk the Lions Kool-Aid, too!"

Oscar didn't smile. "What do you mean?"

Julie sat up on the couch. "I mean, how many years have you been a Lions fan, would you say?"

"As long as I can remember, I guess," he said, gently rocking in his chair.

"And of all those years, have they ever had a winning record or gone to a Super Bowl? No."

"They sure had a heck of a team back in '57," Oscar said

reminiscently. "Joe Schmidt, Yale Lary, Dick 'Night Train' Lane," his voice rising. "Those were the days!"

"Thank you," Julie said slapping her hand on her knee. "You just made my point. They've been rebuilding for the last frickin' fifty years. Helllllooooo? I'd bet you a tenner that the Lions will wind up losing this one. Historically, they always do."

Oscar didn't respond to his granddaughter's chiding.

With two minutes to go, the Packers would march the ball back down the field to pop another goal through the uprights, putting another loss on the Lions' record and giving Lions fans throughout the state of Michigan cause for indigestion. "I told ya," Julie said, clapping her hands together. "The Lions totally suck."

Oscar got up out of his recliner and headed to the kitchen. "Need a beer after that one, eh?" Julie joked as he shuffled by.

"Is the game over already?" Meryl asked cheerfully as she wiped the last of the dishes.

"Yeah, we lost," Oscar said, pouring himself a cup of coffee.

"What's the matter, hon?" Meryl noticed a distinct difference in Oscar's normally chipper demeanor.

"Shhh," he said waving toward the living room.

"What?" Meryl repeated.

Oscar gestured to his wife to come nearer. "Julie's at it again," he said quietly. "She's acting aggressive and arrogant, this time about football. I shouldn't let it bother me, but it's been a long couple of days. I guess I'm too old for this stuff."

Before Meryl could say anything, she saw Shawn's car pull into the driveway.

"I didn't think she was coming until tomorrow morning," Meryl said, untying her apron. "I wonder why she's here."

Oscar set down his coffee and called to Julie. "Julie! Did you know your mother was coming this afternoon?"

Julie walked into the kitchen and played dumb. "No, I didn't," she lied. "She must be missing me or something."

54

"Thank God you checked your phone messages," Julie said, buckling her seat belt.

"I was kinda surprised you called." Shawn put the key in the ignition and started the car. "Wave to your grandparents and look happy. So what gives?"

"I don't know," Julie said, looking out the window. "They were just driving me nuts."

Shawn's face relaxed into a smile. "Yeah, they seemed a little weird tonight. Maybe it was because I came unannounced. They certainly didn't seem too disappointed that you were leaving. Are you sure everything went all right?"

"Yeah, of course it did," Julie said, trying to blow off her mom's question.

"What did you guys do last night?"

"We had three bitchin' games of Scrabble," Julie said sarcastically.

"Julie Ann Deerfield," Shawn said in her best motherly tone. "What has gotten into you?"

"No, we did," Julie eased the seat back in a semi-reclining position. "God, I'm stuffed," she said unsnapping her pants. "Meryl fixed the biggest damn turkey I've ever seen."

"What is with you, Jules?" Shawn put a cigarette between her lips. "You just seem so—so not you, you know what I mean?"

Julie just rolled her eyes and shook her head. "I'm fine. Just too much quality time with the old farts, I guess. So, what do you know about that guy named John Hanson?"

Shawn's eyes diverted from the road as she looked at her daughter. "What are you talking about?" she said defensively. "I haven't heard that name in years."

Julie sat up in her bucket seat. "Well, I found all the old articles about it in a box at Grandma's and read 'em."

Shawn cracked the window and lit up her cigarette. "Did your grandma know you were doing that?"

"Hell, no!" Julie exclaimed. "I was bored. There wasn't anything else to do," she said, trying to convince her mom it was nothing more than curiosity that caused her to read the articles. "I mean, it just seems like Grandma or you would have said a little more about this guy, John Hanson, you know? He's probably the guy who did it."

"Oscar and Meryl went 'round and 'round about that," Shawn said reminiscently. "Oscar really thought that Hanson guy did it, but Ma just focused on Chucky Junior."

"The bouncer?" Julie asked.

"Yeah—how would you know that?" Shawn said, taking a puff of her cigarette.

"I …I met him at church today," Julie stammered. "He goes by Junior now."

"Chucky? At church?" Shawn said, smiling. "Seriously?"

"Yeah. He was the handshaker or whatever you call it," Julie said. "The greeter—his folks were there, too, but Grandma wouldn't talk to 'em."

"Yeah, see?" Shawn said, flicking her ash. "Ma was convinced that Chucky was hiding in the weeds when that John Hanson guy supposedly dropped her off," she said. "But in reality, Chucky had arranged to switch with Big Lou, the other bouncer."

Julie tried to act like she hadn't heard the story before. "So you think that was the truth?"

"Of course it was the truth," Shawn said, tossing her cigarette butt out the window. "Chucky is a lot of things, but a murderer he ain't. He had a crush on Bev, but he'd never have hurt her, I'm sure of that."

"Yeah, he didn't seem like the type to me, either," she said without thinking.

"How could you tell that? You met the guy at church?" Shawn said, laughing.

"Oh, yeah, uh, right, I know, but I was just thinking to myself, he didn't look the type at all," Julie said. "So Oscar thinks it was the John Hanson guy who actually did it?"

"Jules, why the sudden interest in dredging up all this old shit?"

"Just after reading those articles, you know, and being submerged in all of Aunt Bev's things—it's just been on my mind all weekend." Julie stole a glance at her mother to see if she'd been convinced.

"Ah! Yeah, now I get it. She made you sleep in the shrine."

"Yeah. And it was crazy!" Julie smiled. "But at least now I can say I slept in a time capsule."

"So is that what the trouble was at their house?" Shawn asked curiously.

"Yeah, probably," Julie said. "That, and I'm just stressed from school, I think. It just didn't feel right there."

"Well, you've got Friday and Saturday back at our apartment. Maybe that will feel more like home."

"Yeah, maybe," Julie said. "I have homework to do, anyway."

55

Opening the door to her old bedroom, Julie felt an immediate sense of relief in the familiarity.

"Feels good to be home, huh?" Shawn stood in the doorway of her daughter's room.

"It really does. I've had a lot on my mind with school, and it just feels good to be back in my own space. I should come home more often."

Shawn smiled. "You know you're always welcome here, kiddo. What's on the docket for tonight?"

"Well, I think I'm going to do some homework here." Julie snapped on the small lamp at her computer desk. "I'm gonna fire up the old PC and have at it, I guess."

"Why don't you just relax?" Shawn asked. "It's not even Friday yet. Just take a break from all the homework for the evening."

"I will. I'm not going to work too hard tonight," she said, pushing the power button on the tower.

"Well, I'm just chillin' here tonight, too," Shawn said. "If you're hungry later on, maybe we could run out and grab a bite."

"Nah," Julie said. "Nothing's gonna be open. Besides, I'm stuffed from today. It'll be nice to just hang here."

"Good point," Shawn said, turning to go toward the kitchen. "Whatever you want to do. There's pop in the fridge, and I got you your favorite ice cream, too."

"Thanks," Julie said as she went to close her bedroom door. "I'll talk to you in a bit."

Julie removed the manila folder from her backpack and settled at her desk. With no intention of doing homework, Julie hoped to learn more about John Hanson. She flipped to the August 28 article that provided the most details about him. "OK, let's see here." Julie scanned down through the article. "Germfask. Where the hell is Germfask?"

Taking a road atlas down from her shelf of reference books, Julie thumbed her way to the Michigan map, where she directed her attention to the Upper Peninsula. "Germfask … Germfask … there it is." Situated near the center of the Upper Peninsula, it was halfway between the towns of Seney and Blaney Park.

"Jesus, talk about backwoods," she said as she Googled for a newspaper in the area. "Nothing," she said, after looking up Seney and Blaney Park.

With limited knowledge of the Upper Peninsula, Julie examined the map again. A larger town called Newberry was slightly north and east of Germfask. She typed "Newberry, Michigan newspaper" into the Google search engine.

"Voila!" she said as the link for the *Newberry News* website popped up on her screen. "Since 1886. This might just work." Julie clicked in the search box and typed "john hanson." She then clicked "Advanced Search" and entered January 1, 1968 as the first parameter of the search, followed by September 1, 1972.

Not expecting to come up with anything, Julie was surprised when two articles popped up on her screen.

"Germfask Welcomes War Hero Home," dated Wednesday, May 8, 1968. Julie clicked the link.

NEWBERRY — The Newberry High School Marching Indians led the way as residents of Newberry and the surrounding area welcomed back one of their own, war hero John Hanson of Germfask.

Private Hanson served in Company B, First Battalion of the U.S. Marine Corps in Vietnam and was honorably discharged late last month and awarded the Purple Heart after being wounded while fighting North Vietnamese forces in the Quang Nam Province of Vietnam.

Hanson voluntarily joined the Marines in 1964.

Humbled by the outpouring of gratitude, Hanson was reluctant to speak. "I realize how lucky I am to have the support of the community," Hanson said. "Lots of my brothers don't get the same treatment, and it's a shame. They gave their all, just like I did."

In spite of having no immediate relatives left in the area, Hanson said he would make his home in the Newberry area. "I'm not sure what I'll do with the rest of my life, but I'm coming back to where I know, somewhere close by up here. I'm hoping to put some distance between me and 'Nam now that I'm back."

Julie wrote down the name of John's battalion and where he served in Vietnam, before clicking to the second article, dated Wednesday, August 30, 1972.

Local War Hero Dies in Crash

EATON COUNTY — John Charles Hanson, 32, of Germfask died Saturday, Aug. 26 from injuries sustained in a car accident in the Lower Peninsula's Eaton County.

According to a Michigan State Police report, it is believed Hanson was driving eastward on M-43 near Mulliken in the early hours of Saturday morning when he lost control of his vehicle. Hanson's car rolled over several times before crashing into a tree and becoming engulfed in flames.

Hanson was a decorated war veteran, having served three years with Company B, First Battalion of the U.S. Marine Corps in Vietnam. As a survivor of an attack on his battalion in the Quang Nam Province of southern Vietnam, Hanson was awarded the Purple Heart in 1968.

Jake Redmond worked with Hanson last summer at the Seney Wildlife Refuge, both serving as seasonal park rangers. "We became pretty good friends that summer," Redmond said. "He was a big outdoorsman, so working at the refuge was right up his alley." Redmond said Hanson had lived in the greater Newberry area most of his life, and had spent much of his youth in the woods. "He loved to hunt," Redmond said. "He wasn't much of a talker, but he'd hunt anything. I could always get him to start talking when we were in the woods. I'm going to miss him."

Funeral services for John Hanson will be held at 11 a.m. on Monday Sept. 4 at the Beaulieu Funeral Home in Newberry. A military graveside service will follow at Forest Home Cemetery in Newberry. Memorial contributions can be made to the Germfask Doran-Keating VFW Post 6030.

Julie wrote down all the particulars, including Jake Redmond's name. Closing the website, Julie returned to Google, where she looked up "Company B, First Battalion, U.S. Marines, Quang Nam, Province."

"Declassified papers show atrocities went far beyond My Lai." Julie clicked on a summary of a 2006 article that ran in the *New York Times.*

> *"The men of B Company were in a dangerous state of mind. They had lost five men in a firefight the day before. The morning of Feb. 8, 1968, brought unwelcome orders to resume their sweep of the countryside, a green patchwork of rice paddies along Vietnam's central coast. They met no resistance as they entered a nondescript settlement in Quang Nam Province. So Jason Stoddard, a 23-year-old private, set his rifle down in a hut, unfastened his bandoliers and lit a cigarette."*

Julie felt her guts churn as she read on.

> *"Just then, the voice of a lieutenant crackled across the radio. He reported that he had rounded up 19 civilians, and wanted to know what to do with them. Stoddard later recalled the company commander's response: Kill anything that moves.*
>
> *Stoddard stepped outside the hut and saw a small crowd of women and children. Then the shooting began.*
>
> *Moments later, the 19 villagers lay dead or dying."*

"Kill anything that moves," Julie said quietly to herself. "Why do I know this already?" she thought. "Did I study this in school? Did one of my friends tell me this once?"

Troubled by the fact that the story was so familiar, Julie read on.

"Back home in Ohio, Stoddard published an ac-
count of the slaughter and held a news conference to air
his allegations. Yet he and other Vietnam veterans who
spoke out about war crimes were branded traitors and
fabricators. No one was ever prosecuted for the massacre.

Now, nearly 40 years later, declassified Army files show
that Stoddard was telling the truth about the Feb. 8 killings,
and a series of other atrocities by the men of B Company.

The files are part of a once-secret archive, assembled
by a Pentagon task force in the early 1970s, that shows
that confirmed atrocities by U.S. forces in Vietnam were
more extensive than was previously known."

Julie pushed away from her computer and rubbed her eyes.
"Slow down, Julie," she said aloud. "Let's think this through."

Julie got up from her desk, opened her bedroom door and
walked into the kitchen. With her mother asleep on the couch and
the TV blaring, Julie helped herself to one of her mother's long-
necks. Quietly closing the fridge door, Julie returned to her room
and closed the door.

Twisting the cap off her beer, she sat back down, put her feet up
on the desk, and leaned back in her chair to think.

"OK, so we've got John Hanson who was clearly a member of
Company B," she thought to herself. Taking a cold chug of beer, she
continued thinking. "If he was a member of this company of men,
why then wouldn't the state police have known that he may have
had a track record of murdering innocent people?"

Suddenly it all made sense. "They didn't know about this back
in '72, you idiot," she said aloud to herself. The declassified files had
been under lock and key until 2006. Julie put her beer down and sat
back up in her chair to continue reading.

The documents detail 320 alleged incidents that were substantiated by Army investigators, not including the most notorious U.S. atrocity, the 1968 My Lai massacre.

Though not a complete accounting of Vietnam War crimes, the archive is the largest such collection to surface to date. About 9,000 pages, it includes investigative files, sworn statements by witnesses and status reports for top military brass.

The records describe recurrent attacks on ordinary Vietnamese—families in their homes, farmers in rice paddies, teenagers out fishing. Hundreds of soldiers, in interviews with investigators and letters to commanders, described a violent minority who murdered, raped and tortured with impunity.

Abuses were not confined to a few rogue units, a Times review of the files found. They were uncovered in every Army division that operated in Vietnam."

"Jesus God. No wonder the dude was fucked up."

Attempting to wrap her mind around the whole issue, Julie printed a copy of the article for safekeeping and folded the two-page article in half and placed it in the manila folder with the other information she had taken from her grandparents' home.

Julie turned off her computer, put the manila folder back into her backpack, grabbed her cell phone, and flaked out on her comfortable double bed. For some unexplained reason, delving into John Hanson's past had precipitated a feeling of peace that she hadn't experienced in months. It was a good feeling.

Flipping open her phone, Julie scrolled down to Pattie's number and hit send. The phone rang a couple of times before Julie heard the familiar lilt of her roommate's voice.

"Hey," Pattie answered cheerfully.

"Hey yourself," Julie replied. "Happy Thanksgiving."

"You, too," Pattie said. "Are you still at your grandparents' place?"

"No. I had my mom come pick me up tonight. I only stayed one night."

"How'd it go?" she asked. "Are you feeling better?"

"Yes and no," Julie said honestly. "It's a long story about all that happened at Grandma's place, but I'll fill you in next week."

"Uh, actually, I won't be there until Tuesday," Pattie said. "My grandpa in Arizona died last night. My mom's a wreck, so we're flying out there first thing in the morning."

"Oh, Pattie, I'm sorry to hear that. Is there anything I can do on this end?"

"Nah, it's OK," Pattie said. "He had heart problems for a long time. We knew it was coming, you know?"

"Yeah," Julie said. "But it's still a hard thing to lose somebody."

"True enough," Pattie said. "I can't blame my mom for being upset. As much as I complain about my dad, I still love him, you know?"

"Sure, absolutely," Julie said. "So you're leaving tomorrow?"

"Yep. The funeral is Monday, so we're going to take the red-eye back, and I'll be home in time to catch my ten o'clock on Tuesday morning."

"OK. Tell your mom I'm sorry, OK?" Julie said sweetly.

"I will. Oh, and I left something on your desk yesterday before I came home," Pattie said. "Pete came by with a bottle of JD for you. I think he has a crush on you."

"Are you kidding?" Julie asked, feeling herself begin to blush.

"Honestly," Pattie said. "I'm not making this up. He's a nice guy."

"Well, I'll have to thank him," she said. "It would be nice to have a boyfriend, especially an enabling boyfriend, but…"

Both girls laughed.

"You sound a lot better today," Pattie said. "Back to your old self, sort of."

"Yeah, whoever that is," Julie said sarcastically.

"What do you mean?" Pattie asked.

"Nothing—I've just been doing a little … reading and stuff, and …oh, I don't know what I'm saying. It's just been an interesting forty-eight hours, let's put it that way."

"Well, whatever's going on, it's good to hear you sound so upbeat," Pattie said. "I have to get going; gotta pack my funeral outfit and stuff."

"OK. Have a safe trip, and again, pass along my condolences to your family," Julie said.

"I will, thanks, Jules. See you on Tuesday."

"Talk to you later, Julie said flipping her phone shut.

"Jules?" Shawn said, nudging the door slightly open. "I'm tired. I got up at four this morning. Do you mind if I go to bed? I know it's early, but …"

"No, no, go ahead, mom," Julie said kindly. "I'm just going to grab a shower and do the same thing. Two days with the grandparents really takes it out of a girl."

"OK, well, good night," she said, beginning to close the door. "Oh, and Jules?" Shawn said.

"Yeah?"

"It's good to have you home."

56

The rest of the weekend at home and the ride with her mother back to MSU had gone without incident, and Julie was still feeling like she had somehow managed to free something from within. It was something that had been gnawing at her for months, yet she still had no idea what that was. Even so, it felt a little like the old Julie had returned.

Just as Pattie had said, a big bottle of JD was waiting on the desk with a note attached.

"Thinking of you on Thanksgiving. See you next week. Pete."

"Wow," Julie said aloud. "Who knew?" She put down her backpack and tossed her suitcase onto her bottom bunk.

Noticing that the room was a bit dark, Julie threw back the curtains and let the brilliant sunshine of a Sunday afternoon flood the room. It felt good to be back, almost like a fresh start. Although the weekend hadn't gone as Julie had planned, it still had served the purpose: clarity, direction, and peace.

Julie was unzipping her suitcase when she heard a light knock on the door.

"Knock, knock," came the familiar voice of Sarah from across the hall. "Hey Julie. How was your Thanksgiving?"

"Pretty good, Sarah. How was yours?" Sarah's involuntary flinch indicated she was noticing a new attitude in the room.

"Mine was fabulous. So, what's up with you?" she said, flashing her contagious smile. "You seem different."

"Really?" Julie said looking up from her suitcase. "I feel different."

"What happened at home? Did you see your grandparents?" Sarah sat down in Pattie's desk chair.

"Yeah, I did, but I didn't stay as long as I thought I would have. It was weird. It's actually a long story, what happened. It was all pretty strange, but whatever it was seemed to have worked itself out."

"Well, what happened?"

"Honestly, Sarah, it's a really long story," Julie said, closing her empty suitcase.

"Well, I have all afternoon," Sarah offered. "You just seem more at peace with things."

"I think I am back to normal. But …" Julie said.

"But what?"

"But I don't know why." Julie slid her case underneath the bunk. "I have no idea of what happened to make me feel this way. It was strange."

"Hey, come over to my room. Mike bought me a pack of wine coolers. We can chat and figure this out." Sarah stood up.

"I don't know. You're going to think I'm nuts."

"Oh, please," Sarah said. "Help me help you," she said imitating her favorite line from the movie *Jerry Maguire*.

Julie laughed. "I loved that movie, too! Oh, all right. But don't think I'm a psycho bitch from Hell when I tell you, OK?"

"Deal," Sarah said. "What time will your roomie be home?" she asked, moving closer to the door.

"She won't be here 'til Tuesday," Julie said. "Her grandfather in Arizona died, and they flew out on Friday. The funeral is Monday, but Pattie will be back in time for her ten o'clock on Tuesday."

"Oh, I'm so sorry to hear that," Sarah said. "Is she really upset?"

"Her mom is, but I guess the guy had some serious heart stuff going on, so Pattie wasn't all that surprised. I got this for all of us to sign," Julie said, holding up a sympathy card.

"Aw, that's great, Julie," Sarah said. "Something is definitely different with you. Give me a half hour, then come on over. I have to give Mike a call about tomorrow."

"OK," Julie said. "I'll pop over in a bit."

57

It was nearly nine o'clock by the time Julie finished telling Sarah the entire story, even going back into the history of her aunt's death.

Julie poured herself a shot of JD as Sarah folded the last of the articles contained in Julie's manila folder. "What a trip," Sarah said. "You sort of look like your aunt."

"Yeah, I get that a lot from family members."

"So, let me get this straight—you went to the same tavern your aunt worked at and were served by the same guy who was supposed to bounce that night in 1972?"

"Yep."

"And the drunken asshole at the bar follows you to the restroom and tries to molest you in the hallway, and it turns out it was the same guy that did the same thing to your aunt the same night she went missing?"

"Yes. As hard as it is to believe, yes," Julie said from her perch on Sarah's desk. "I know it's a lot to digest."

"You got that right." Sarah went to the fridge for her third wine cooler.

"So talk more about what happened in the bathroom before Chuck Jr.—was that his name?" Julie nodded. "— before Chuck Jr. took you back to your grandparent's place."

"OK. I was drunk, *really* drunk, mind you, but it's still incredibly vivid to me. I tried to go to the women's restroom, but one of the waitresses was mopping and told me to use the men's room. She said she'd already cleaned it and that nobody was in there."

"OK," Sarah said, twisting off the top on her cooler. "Then what?"

"When I got in there, I just remember smelling the fumes of piss and cigarettes, to be honest," Julie said almost apologetically. "It made me gag, so I ran into the stall and puked."

"Ew," Sarah said, making a face. "OK, go on."

"Yeah, I know. It wasn't one of my finer moments," Julie said. "So I went to the sink and needed to rinse out my mouth and splash my face, you know? Because the room was just spinning. And after I turned off the water and stood up, I looked in the mirror and saw a man staring at me. Just staring at me."

"Was he behind you, or ..." Sarah asked, trying to get more details.

"I—I don't think so, and I do remember looking behind me. But when I think about it now ...it was more like I was looking into my own face ...except it wasn't me. Does that make sense?"

Sarah shifted her eyebrows and smiled. "No, not really, but it's good. It's all good," she said confidently. "So what you're saying is that, for a brief instant, you were looking into your own face, but it wasn't you."

"Exactly," Julie said, taking another sip of her booze and snorted. "I told you that you'd think I was a psycho bitch."

"Stop! I don't think that." Sarah took a sip of her cooler. "So how did you feel? Did it scare you? Were you mad? What?"

"It scared the shit out of me," Julie said with a smile.

For the first time in weeks, Sarah looked at Julie with compassion. Before when she'd heard details of what had been happening, she'd just chalked the behavior up to typical freshman drama.

"I bet it does," Sarah said, making eye contact with Julie. "So it scared you because you didn't recognize the man, right?"

"No, I didn't know him, and I looked behind me and

everything—nobody was there. The only thing I could think of was that it was a ghost or something, you know?"

"Sure," Sarah said. "That's probably what most people would think."

"Ya think?"

"What? That it was John Hanson's ghost?"

Julie nodded.

"I'm still not sure what I think. Are you sure it was John Hanson?"

"Yeah, absolutely. Without a doubt, it was him."

"OK. So, you just thought it was John Hanson's ghost after that? That he'd come back to the bar where he had last been?"

"Well, I didn't really know what to think," Julie said. "I still don't really—but it certainly is the easiest solution, you know?"

"Yeah, it is," Sarah said. "It's really hard to buy into the whole ghost thing, though."

"I know!" Julie said, looking confused.

"But let's not lose our focus." Sarah adjusted her position on her twin bed. "You said that it wasn't an apparition—that it was like looking into your own face, except it was John Hanson's face."

"True," Julie said. "What could that mean?"

"I'm not really sure ....um, this is going to sound freaky," she warned.

"What is?" Julie asked.

"What I'm about to suggest. Now it's me asking you not to think I'm some psycho," Sarah joked. "I'm just throwing stuff out there, OK?"

"Absolutely. Go for it," Julie said.

"Do you believe in reincarnation?"

"Reincarnation? You mean the idea that we've all lived past lives, and that kind of thing?"

"Yeah, that's exactly what I mean," Sarah said.

"I guess I've never really given it much thought. Why?"

"I don't know if I told you this or not, but my aunt moved back from California to Grand Ledge. You know where that is, don't you?"

"Yeah, of course I do. It's right up the road from Mulliken."

"Well, she moved back here to be closer to family; she's in her 70s now. But she's a well-known psychic, and she does past life regressions on the side," Sarah said. "She's even written a few books on the subject, too."

"So?"

"So, I can hook you up, and we can get to the bottom of it. If you've had a past life that's interfering with this one, she might be able to help you."

"What are you talking about?" Julie asked. "What can all of this possibly have to do with reincarnation?"

"What I mean is, what if what you saw *wasn't* a ghost, but rather a part of you?"

"Oh jeez," Julie said standing up from the bed. "I'm not so sure about that. I mean, it sounds really crazy—plus I don't have the funds to pay for something like that."

"I'm my aunt's favorite," Sarah said. "She'll do anything for me. She doesn't have any kids, and she really digs the fact that I chose psychology based on my interest in her studies. She always says I'm the closest thing she has to a daughter. For me, I think she'd do it for free. Besides, I need a topic for my term paper, and past life regression would be an awesome subject."

"Oh, sorta like 'help me help you,'" Julie said jokingly. "Thanks, but no, I don't think so. It's really nice and all, but..."

"But what? After everything you've told me, I really think

there's something to all this," she said. "It could be that your higher self is trying to come to terms with something. You trust me, right?"

Julie nodded. "Of course I do."

"Then trust me on this one. Meet with my aunt—just one meeting. If anybody can help you figure this out, it's her. And what can it hurt, right? Do you have a better plan?"

"No..."

"And you want to feel better, right?"

"Yes, absolutely."

"Then take me up on my offer," Sarah pleaded.

"Oh, all right. You're right, I have nothing to lose. And thanks for all your help today. I honestly do feel better."

"You look better," Sarah said. "Even just since you got here this afternoon. You look more relaxed. I'll call Aunt Shirley tomorrow. Mike can take us."

"Us?"

"Yeah! You don't think I'd miss out on this one, do you? You might be the topic of my master's thesis—who knows!"

58

"Sorry to knock so early," Sarah said, as Julie answered her door the next morning. "How did you sleep last night?"

Julie looked inquisitively at Sarah. "Fine, I guess. Uneventful for a change."

Sarah broke into a smile. "Just as I suspected."

"Huh? Did I miss something?"

"Never mind." Sarah pushed the door open and entered Julie's room. "I called my aunt last night, and she's really into meeting with you."

Julie smiled and shook her head. "You know, I've been thinking more about this. I really don't know if I..."

"Shhh," Sarah said, taking a seat at Pattie's desk. "Before you say no, please let me finish. My aunt doesn't often get the opportunity to do this type of work anymore. People in Michigan aren't as open minded as they are in California, you know? My aunt is as crunchy as they come—a hippy in every sense of the word."

"I don't know..."

"She is an expert in reincarnation and past life regression," Sarah said. "I mean, I don't know if you really understand just how qualified she is. Here, you can check out her web site at this address." Sarah handed Julie a piece of paper. "You'll probably understand it a lot better after you read up on it. Anyway, she and I talked until midnight last night. I told her everything we discussed, and she truly thinks we may be onto something."

"Great," Julie said sarcastically.

"So, how about tomorrow?" Sarah asked. "I'll blow off my classes if you'll blow off yours."

"Oh, man! You know how I hate to miss school. My life depends on good grades."

"C'mon, just this once," Sarah begged. "Mike doesn't have class on Tuesdays because he works late on Mondays, so he can drive us. Besides, he'll just be happy to wait and have some quiet time to read his criminal justice case studies."

"What time?" Julie asked as she brushed her hair.

"Well, Aunt Shirley said any time after nine a.m. is good," Sarah said.

"How long will it take, did she say?"

"It depends on what happens," Sarah said. "I'm excited, because I've never seen a real past life regression before. It's going to be really cool!"

"Oh, God," Julie said with a sigh. "What have I gotten myself into?"

"C'mon Jules, you should be happy."

"And what happens when we find out that I'm not a reincarnation of John Hanson? Huh? Then what?"

"I really don't know, Julie. But all we can do is try."

"Nine o'clock?" Julie asked, almost surrendering.

"Yeah, Mike can come by here and pick us both up. I know exactly where we're going in Grand Ledge."

Julie sighed. "Oh all right."

"That's the spirit!" Sarah said. "I know you're reluctant, but I think you'll be amazed. My aunt rocks. You won't regret it."

59

"Here it is—turn here," Sarah said, directing Mike onto one of the charming tree-lined streets of Grand Ledge. "I love Grand Ledge. The downtown is really cool, and the ledges—man, you should see 'em."

"You should!" Mike agreed. "Sarah and I took a walk on the ledges last fall, and it was amazing."

"What are they?" Julie asked.

"They are sandstone rock formations that rise up along the Grand River," Sarah said. "Sort of like the Wisconsin Dells, but not as commercialized."

"My mom used to date a guy from here," Julie said. "We never visited the ledges, but we used to go to that place down on the river for ice cream … what was the name of it?"

"Lickity Split," Sarah answered nonchalantly.

Mike glanced over at Sarah and smiled. "That's right! You made me drive you way the hell out here for one of their famous banana splits when you were on your period once," he said laughing. "I remember now!"

"Shut up, Mike." Sarah playfully slugged him in his muscular shoulder. The three of them laughed.

"OK, it's just up here on the right," Sarah said. "The house covered in ivy here."

The huge old fieldstone home was surrounded by mature oak

trees. Ivy climbed the pillars of a sprawling front porch, giving it a secretive feeling. Several lawn chairs surrounded a small clay chimenea. Wind chimes and incense burners backed up Sarah's "crunchy" description of her aunt.

Mike parked the car and the three of them got out.

"Well, look who's here," Shirley said, opening the massive oak front door. "Don't mind my mess out there—come in, come in."

Shirley was a young 70-something and most assuredly colored her hair bright red. Wearing silky paisley pants, wool socks, and Birkenstocks, she topped off her ensemble with an oriental-style Nehru jacket.

"Welcome, welcome," she said, closing the door. "You kids must be freezing— It's so cold and windy out there today."

"Oh, it's so good to see you, Aunt Shirley," Sarah said, giving her a long hug. Shirley then reached for Mike.

"Come here and give your aunt a hug, Mike." Shirley reached up around Mike's neck. "Mmm, don't you smell good?"

"And you must be Julie," she said, holding out her hand. Julie nodded and shook Shirley's hand. "Thanks for seeing me today," she said shyly.

"Oh gosh, that's my line of work," Shirley said. "I hope I can help you get to the bottom of all this."

Julie looked around. "Your house is beautiful." An oak-banistered staircase led directly from the front door to the upstairs, while a parlor opened to the right, and straight down the hallway was the kitchen.

"Come in, come in," Shirley repeated, gesturing to the parlor. "Can I get you kids some tea? I have all kinds of blends for whatever ails you."

"No, thanks, I'm good," Julie said nervously.

"We're fine, too, Aunt Shirley," Sarah said, speaking for Mike as she took a seat on a small floral sofa. Mike sat down next to her and leaned his backpack up against the furniture.

Julie sank into a recliner near the sofa, while Shirley took her designated seat across the room. Candles blazed at several locations in the small antique-clad parlor.

Julie was distracted when a loud meowing cat began rubbing against her leg.

"I hope you're not allergic to cats. I've got five of 'em. That's Hercules there," she said, gesturing toward the calico cat wrapped around Julie. "Male calicos are very rare, you know, and he's been with me for six lifetimes now. He just keeps popping up. He has a wonderful soul."

Julie glanced nervously over in Sarah's direction, but Sarah refused to engage her.

"Really? I guess I didn't know animals can be reincarnated," Julie said.

"Oh yes, dear. All living things can be reincarnated. Hercules and I first met in ancient Rome. I was touring the bowels of the Coliseum," she said, as if it were no big deal. "He was scavenging for food, and it was love at first sight for us. It's as simple as that."

Julie tried not to smile, and avoided looking in Mike's direction for fear they would both laugh out loud. "I took him directly to my home and he's been with me on and off ever since." Shirley bent down and snapped her finger. "Come here, Hercules—come."

A pregnant pause ensued. The three college students were at a loss for words, watching Hercules pad over to Shirley. "He still likes raw meat, too. He thinks he's a lion, it would seem," she said, smiling. "I love him enough to buy him meat at the store," she said as she scrubbed him under his chin. "And I'm a vegetarian."

Shirley sat up in her chair. "Sarah told you I am a regressionist,

I understand—but first and foremost, I'm a psychic. When I lived in California, it's how I made my living."

"What do you mean? You did psychic readings for clients?" Mike asked.

"No, I worked as a psychic detective with law enforcement agencies all across California. I did it for nearly thirty years. And I helped them find the bodies of twenty-seven victims."

"Wow," Mike said. "Sarah, you never told me that."

Sarah blushed. "I was afraid you'd think it was weird."

"That's the problem with a profession like mine. Lots of people simply refuse to believe it."

"I can imagine," Julie said. "It must be hard."

"I've worked with a lot of detectives, and some of them aren't comfortable talking about it. Some of them don't even want their department to know about it. But after six to eight weeks of looking for a body and coming up with nothing, the department has pretty much done all it can. Often, that's the point where I come into it."

"I think it's intriguing," Mike said. "Especially when you've found the bodies to back it up."

"Mike, believe me about this. I can sit there and tell them every nuance about the victim—pages and pages of stuff—and they'll still come back and say, 'yup, that's right, but where's the body?'"

"But you usually found the bodies, didn't you, Aunt Shirley?" Sarah asked.

"Usually, yes. There were only a few that I couldn't find." She shifted in her chair. "But we're not here for all of that. We're here to do a little regression today, is that right?"

"Uh-huh," replied Julie.

"So, tell me, Julie. Why are you here?" Shirley sat back in her chair and studied Julie.

"I'm here, really, because Sarah thought you could help me."

"I see. And how can I help you, do *you* think?"

"I guess ...I'm not really sure."

Sarah interrupted. "Aunt Shirley, she really doesn't know much about reincarnation. We're really here because I suggested it."

"I understand that, dear," Shirley said. "I just want to hear what your friend has to say about it. It's important that I listen to Julie herself." Sarah nodded, and sat back.

Julie took a breath and began. "I know you and Sarah talked at length, so I think you've got most of the details, right?"

"Yes, that's correct."

"OK. So, I'm here because if it's true that this John Hanson and I are somehow connected, I want to understand it. I need to, so I can move on with my life. You know? Resolve whatever it is that needs resolving."

"Excellent," Shirley said. "Then you and I are, as they say, on the same page. Let me give you the general rundown on how we do this, OK?"

"I'm going to sort of give you the Reincarnation 101 speech. I want you to understand what past lives are, and why they have an impact on our current life."

"This is great," Sarah chimed from the sofa. "Mike, can I borrow one of your notebooks? I should have brought one."

Mike handed his girlfriend a notebook and pen.

"Well, simply put: A past life is a life you lived before your current life. It's basically that simple. You had a different body, you may have been a different gender, you may have had different skin color, different family members and friends, you may have been a different religion, had different goals and a different belief system—different skills, different tastes, different fears—all that."

Julie had that deer-in-the-headlights look as she tried to comprehend what Shirley was saying.

"I know it's a lot to take in, but bear with me," Shirley said. "If you meet your former self, you might not recognize him or her, but parts of that self remain in your subconscious and continue to influence your current life, for good or for bad, just as your current life will influence your future lives."

"I love this stuff," Sarah said, scribbling down her aunt's thoughts. "It's intriguing."

"It really is," Shirley said. "Having written a few books on the topic, I obviously find it intriguing as well."

"How do people tap into their past lives?" Julie asked.

"That's a good question. It really depends on the person. Some people can do it on their own without any help. They might experience it through meditation, dreams, or maybe they've traveled somewhere that has triggered a past-life memory. The hints are all there. An unexplained love for a certain kind of music is a strong indicator that you lived in a different culture; different types of clothing can give us clues, too."

"What do you mean?" asked Julie.

"Well, let's say you like silky clothing. That might suggest that you led a life of wealth in India or China. A preference for dark, plain clothing might suggest a past life as a nun, or a monk, or a serf—hints like that. The possibilities are endless, but you get the general idea, right?

"Yeah …but it sounds pretty crazy."

"I know it probably does, and that's OK," Shirley said. "But there are other things that give us clues—unexplained fears in our current lives. Fear of drowning, burning, starving, or being buried alive are all fairly common. Wounds can be indicators, too."

"Like what?" Julie asked.

"Well, if you died of a specific wound—like if you were a Jewish Holocaust victim who died in a gas chamber—you might, for instance, have residual respiratory ailments in this lifetime. Any place on your body that might be marked by illness or an increased sensitivity at the sight of that earlier death wound."

Sarah piped up. "Hey! Sorta like your hand, huh Julie?"

Julie glanced at her slightly swollen right hand and then at Shirley. "Well, I have had this thing with my hand lately. I really think I just bumped it or something, but periodically, it becomes bruised and swollen for no apparent reason."

"Interesting," Shirley said. "When does it happen usually?"

"The last time I saw it happen was when you were having that night terror, Julie," Sarah said. Julie looked uncomfortable, glancing at Mike as they discussed her hand. "Do you want me to go in the kitchen?" Mike gallantly volunteered.

"No, it's OK, Mike. It doesn't matter anymore."

"Jules, what's wrong?" Sarah leaned forward on the sofa. "There's nothing to be embarrassed about or ashamed of."

"That's right," Shirley added. "We're all here to help you through this, OK?"

Julie nodded, sighed, and rubbed her right hand.

"Now about this hand. It got swollen during a what? A night terror?"

"It's gotten swollen a lot lately, and yeah, it usually does occur after a bad dream or something like that," Julie responded. "It's still slightly swollen right now, from when I had a bad dream while I was staying at my grandparent's last week. I woke up screaming my head off—nearly gave my grandparents coronaries."

Shirley got up from her chair and examined Julie's right hand. "Mmm-hmm, I see. And can you remember what that dream was?"

"Yes ..." Julie kept her gaze on her hand.

Taking her fresh young face in her hands, Shirley looked directly at her. "Stop feeling ashamed of all this, Julie. You have absolutely no reason to apologize or feel badly. Let's work through this; I believe it might help."

A tear slipped from one of Julie's eyes. "Here's a clean tissue," Aunt Shirley said, reaching into her jacket pocket. "Now, tell me about the dream," she said, returning to her seat across the room.

"I was in my grandparents' house, and in my dream, I had awakened from a dream, if that makes sense."

Shirley nodded and recorded a few notes on her clipboard.

"I was in the exact same room where I was staying, and in fact, I didn't know it was a dream—I thought I was actually there," Julie said.

Mike glanced over at Sarah, who was completely engrossed in the story.

"Smoke was coming in from underneath the door, so I thought the whole house was on fire, you know?"

"Yes," Shirley said. "Go on."

"I went downstairs to find my grandparents, but when I got to the kitchen, they weren't there. And there wasn't actually a fire, it was just smoke. But it didn't sting my eyes. And when I tried to call their names, nothing came out."

"I've had dreams like that before," Mike said. "I'll be running or something and getting nowhere."

"Yeah, just like that, Mike—very frustrating," Julie said. "So I turned and went back upstairs, and then I found myself standing in front of their bedroom door."

"What did you do?" Shirley asked.

"I looked down and saw what I thought was water coming out from underneath their door. But when I opened the door, I saw that it wasn't water—it was gasoline."

"How did you know it was gasoline?" Sarah asked.

"I could smell it, the fumes."

"And yet you couldn't feel the sting of the smoke, nor could you make an audible sound when you tried to speak." Sarah said, jotting down a couple of notes just as she did in her psychology training.

"Is that how the dream ended?" Shirley asked.

"No …" Julie whispered. "My grandparents were lying on the bed …they'd been beaten and battered …soaked in blood."

Sarah's gasp from the sofa brought dirty looks from both Shirley and Mike.

"The worst part of it was…" Julie began crying. "I wasn't really upset! I …I was more curious than anything else."

"Is that when you woke up?" Shirley asked.

"No. I saw that my grandmother was dead, so I moved to the opposite side of the bed to look at Oscar, my grandfather—and he grabbed my hand, and I screamed out," Julie said. "But in reality, my grandfather was actually grabbing my hand; he was trying to wake me up."

Sarah looked up from her notepad. "Wow. You didn't tell me about that on Sunday."

"I was so embarrassed," Julie said. "Why would I dream of such a despicable thing and then be more curious about it than upset?"

"Based on what I've heard here, we have some work to do," Shirley said. "I do think it is all in some way connected to a past life. I'm very curious to see what we find out. The part with your hand is particularly interesting, because it does fit in with our past-life theory. Let me ask you a question: Did you see yourself in the dream?"

"What do you mean?" Julie asked.

"I mean, did you look in a mirror, or perhaps look at your hands or any part of your body, and recognize it as your own?"

Julie thought for a moment. "No, I guess not. I don't recall thinking anything about it, to be honest. Why?"

"Well, I'm just thinking out loud, but Sarah told me about your experience at the bar near your grandparents' home. She said you looked into a mirror there and saw the image of a man—the same man you saw in the newspaper clipping. I was just thinking that if you'd seen him in the dream, too, we'd have another connection."

"Aha," Sarah said. "I was wondering where you were going with all that."

"Time will tell," Shirley said. "Not to worry."

"So you think this might help?" Julie asked, wiping her nose with the tissue.

"I think it may give you some insight, but it's ultimately going to be up to you as to what you do with the information. The universe can only do so much. You have to be willing to do some of the work, too. If you're willing to work with the information, it could bring whatever resolution your soul seems to be seeking."

"How do we do it?" Julie asked.

"You mean, how does the whole past-life regression thing go?" Shirley asked.

"Yeah. How do we do it, and how long will it take?" Julie asked.

"Well, it really varies from person to person. It really depends on how receptive you are to it all. Regressing is one way of accessing information that comes from earlier lifetimes."

"I think I understand that part. But exactly how do I get there?" Julie asked.

"I'm going to help get you into a light trance state," Shirley replied. "Once you're in it, you'll go back or regress to discover the roots of skills, relationships, problems, or other blocks that have formed in previous incarnations."

"I see," Julie said nervously. Looking apologetically at Sarah, she added, "But I really don't know if I'm going to be able to do this."

"Don't worry about it, Julie. Just give it a try. There isn't any pressure here," Sarah said.

"Sarah is right," Shirley added. "Just give it a try. There are no 'rights' or 'wrongs.'"

"I just think I'm too uptight to actually go into a trance, you know?" Julie said, pulling her sweater zipper up and down.

"If I had a dime for every client who's told me that over the years, I'd be a very rich woman," Shirley said. "And usually—not all the time, but usually—the client is surprised at how successful they are."

"If I can manage to slip into the trance, how do I get the information?"

"Again, it's going to depend. Some clients have vivid images, can hear sounds or tastes. Some experience it through different emotions. We just won't know until we get you there. Everybody is different."

"Seriously, I just don't know if I'm capable of this, you guys," Julie said, pushing out of her chair.

"Come now, Julie, please sit down and relax," Shirley said. "You're getting yourself too worked up over this. We're only here to help you."

"Um, what do you do in all of this?" Julie asked.

"Like I said, I'm going to help you get into a light trance, and then I'll assist you in moving forward and backward in the 'story' you begin to tell me. I'll ask you questions as though I'm interviewing you. Whatever past-life information and emotions that do come through, it all comes from you, not me."

"I'm …I'm just scared about what we'll find out, you know?"

Sarah stepped in. "Yeah, it might be scary, that's true. But Julie, you can't go on like you've been doing for the last two or three months."

"Yeah, I know. You're right, but this is so …"

"Crazy?" Mike piped up from the couch.

"Mike!" Sarah hissed. Mike's comment succeeded in lightening the mood, and allowed Julie to break into a smile.

"It's not crazy, Shirley!" Julie said. "Please don't think I'm judging what you do."

"Nonsense," Shirley said. "I wouldn't think that for a moment. You're here, aren't you? That speaks volumes. And now, let's get to work."

60

"I converted one of the old bedrooms into my office up here," Shirley said, climbing the old oak staircase. Julie and Sarah followed close behind, while Mike stayed in the parlor and worked on his homework.

"Are you sure it's OK that I observe, Aunt Shirley?" Sarah asked, rounding the top of the staircase.

"As long as you sit there and stay very quiet—don't interrupt or ask any questions—we should be fine. But if for some reason your energy begins to interfere with Julie's regression, I may have to ask you to leave, understood?"

"Yep," Sarah said. "You won't even know I'm here. Julie, are you sure you're OK with my staying?"

"Yeah, I want you to stay," Julie said. "I'd just feel more comfortable with it."

A neatly made twin bed, a small desk, and a recliner filled the medium-sized bedroom, while a variety of East Asian pictures and decorations adorned the walls.

Shirley closed the blind and turned on a small reading lamp on the desk. "I'm going to sit here at the desk; Sarah, you can have the recliner; and Julie, I want you to lie down on the twin bed and get comfortable."

Julie removed her shoes and sat awkwardly on the edge of the bed.

"Don't be shy," Shirley said. "It's up to you: You can lie on top of the bed and use the afghan to cover up, or you can get right into the bed. The sheets are all clean. Just get comfortable."

Julie swung her legs onto the bed and laid back. "I think I'm good just on top of the bed, if that's OK."

"Well, at least use the afghan to cover up. Often the body cools down when we do regressions. That's why I have all the bedding available for you to use," she said.

Julie settled in with the afghan and stared at the ceiling. "Just relax," she told herself. "They don't think you look stupid doing this, so just go with it."

"When you're ready to get going, just close your eyes for me, and concentrate on your breathing. Is this light bothering you?"

"No," Julie said quietly, closing her eyes.

"Good. The first thing I want you to do is to pick your favorite place. It might be a beautifully sun-kissed beach in Mexico where the water is a brilliant turquoise blue. Crystal-clear waves crash onto the beach as a light breeze blows through your hair …."

As Shirley spoke, Julie let all thoughts drift out of her mind, instead paying attention to images produced by her brain.

"… Or maybe your favorite place is a lush green meadow. You're sitting down on the grassy banks of a small stream, the sky is clear, and you feel complete solace …. or maybe you have a place of your own. Which place do you want to choose, Julie?"

"I think I'm going to my own favorite place," Julie said quietly, yet confidently.

"Good. And where is that? Can you describe it?"

Julie remembered a trip she had taken to the Grand Canyon with Meryl and Oscar when she was ten. "I'm standing on the banks of the Colorado River. The Grand Canyon is all around me. I'm completely surrounded by the orange-colored walls of stone."

"And what are you doing there?" Shirley asked.

"I'm just standing in the shade of the wall behind me, looking at the beautiful emerald-colored water," she said.

"What time of day is it?"

"It's in the morning. It's still cool down by the river, but if you walk into a spot of sunshine, it warms you up." Julie could actually envision the image in her head.

"Excellent. Why don't you walk along the bank and enjoy your surroundings."

Even though Julie could see the scene plainly in her mind's eye, she was still very conscious of Shirley and Sarah's presence in the room.

"Are you walking along the shore now?" Shirley asked.

"Yes," Julie replied.

"Now what are you seeing?"

"Water …beautiful, cold, green water rushing around the rocks in the water. It's not exactly a rapids area, but there are a few boulders sticking out of the water here and there."

"And how do you feel?"

Julie hesitated. "I feel good, I guess ….I'm pretty relaxed."

"Just take a few minutes to enjoy the scenery."

Within a minute, Julie's breathing had evened out, and Shirley saw that she was beginning to go under. "OK Julie …I want you to continue walking up the river until you see a magnificent orb waiting for you. It looks like a big bubble, beautiful and iridescent, but big enough for you to climb into. Do you see it there, up ahead?"

"Mm-hmm …I'm walking and see it up there a ways. I'm having trouble keeping my eyes closed. Is that normal? Am I doing all right?"

Shirley smiled. "You're going under further than you think you are. I know it seems odd, but your eyes are in REM, which is a clear indication that you're going under."

"I don't feel under. I hear everything you're saying, and yet I can see where I am, too."

"That's right—that's how it should be," Shirley said reassuringly.

"Hmm ...weird."

"OK, have you reached the orb?"

"Yes. It's right here."

"On the other side, you'll find a little door. Go to the door of the orb and open it... Get in; can you do that? It's comfortable inside with a seat to sit on... nothing to fear."

"Mmmm-hmmm." Julie spoke more and more slowly. "Yes, I'm in now... and I've closed the door."

"Good. The orb is a time machine of sorts. It's going to lift off the ground and go way into the sky   is it lifting off the ground right now?"

"Yes. But I'm really having trouble keeping my eyes shut."

"Put your hand over your eyes—it's OK to do that," Shirley said.

It was all Julie could do to lift her right arm. "Wow... my arm is almost completely numb... but I can do it. This is so weird."

Shirley smiled and winked at Sarah, who was enthralled with the whole process. "OK, Julie, is that better? Your eyes?"

"Yes... much."

"Your orb is high above the Colorado River, and you can see the Grand Canyon sprawling out below. You're going higher and higher, away from the Earth, but you're not afraid. You're enjoying the trip and marveling in the beauty of the Earth."

"Mmmm-hmmm ....it's beautiful. The Earth is beautiful."

"OK, now you're traveling high above the Earth in your orb. I want you to just go with the flow, and tell me where you're going to land. It can be anywhere in the world, any year. There are no guidelines."

"Hmmm," Julie said. "This is weird."

"That's fine. Just let it go, and tell me what you're seeing." Sarah was amazed by her aunt's ability to consistently deliver calm and relaxed requests and instructions.

"For some reason, I'm thinking Wisconsin," Julie murmured.

"OK, that's fine. Your orb is now descending toward Earth …. When it lands, you're going to open the door and get out. Is your orb landing back on Earth?"

"Yes. I'm opening the door and getting out."

"And where are you?"

"I'm in a field of soybeans."

"Soybeans... are you sure?"

"Yes, they're just like they are at my Grandma's house. They're soybeans, all right."

"Good. Do you know how old you are, or what year it is?"

"I believe I'm younger than I am in this life—like maybe ten?"

"OK, so you're a child?" Shirley asked.

"Yes," Julie replied.

"Can you tell if you're a boy or a girl?"

"I really have no idea," Julie said. "I sense I'm a child."

"Can you look at your clothing? Are you wearing boy's clothes or girl's clothes?"

Julie hesitated. "I'm wearing overalls, and worn-out leather boots, very dirty. I don't have a shirt on under my overalls, so I assume I'm a boy."

"Very good. So you're standing in a field of soybeans. Is there anything around?"

"There's a barn, probably 200 yards away, and I can see a cow fenced in outside. There's a house in the distance; it probably goes with the barn."

"Good. I want you to walk toward the barn, OK? Just keep walking until you get to the barn."

Julie was silent for nearly two minutes. "OK, I'm at the barn now. It's not a huge barn. There's hay in the loft, and an old tractor parked inside, very old tractor. Outside there's one lone cow. She's thin, doesn't look real healthy."

"How do you feel? Are you OK?" Shirley asked her.

"I feel OK, but just sad, really, and I don't know why. It just feels like we have no money, like something important is missing."

"Let's move toward the house. Can you do that?"

It was nearly five minutes before Julie answered. "I can't seem to get there. I'm just catching glimpses of it, really."

"That's fine. Why don't we do it this way: I'll count backwards from five, and when I get to one, you'll be standing inside the house. Shall we try that?"

"Mmmm-hmmm."

"Five... four... three... two... one. Are you in the house?"

"Yes, but it's troubling!"

"Why is it troubling?" Shirley asked, jotting down notes.

"It's just a one-room cabin, really. It's very dirty and very sad. There's a woman with a baby... she's crying."

"Who's crying? The woman or the baby?"

"Actually, both. There is a man here, and it looks like he's mad at the woman."

"What do you mean?"

"He looks angry, and he's moving around like he wants to hit her. He's drunk."

"Do you know him? Is he your father?" Shirley asked.

"No! No, he is *not* my father. There's no way this man is my father. I... I'm filled with hate for him right now."

"OK, just go with it. What else can you tell me?"

"I think it's my mother and baby sister...." Julie hesitated for a minute. "I just feel so sad right now." Julie's voice began to crack. "The baby just isn't right."

"What do you mean?"

"The baby is… mentally challenged. The mother seems to be at the end of her rope, and the man isn't helping the situation at all. She's looking at me like I should do something to help."

"Are you the man of the house?"

"I wish I was! But no, this man won't have it," Julie replied, tears streaming down her cheeks. "I just—I just feel so much pressure. I hate him!"

"That's a lot for a young boy to handle, isn't it?"

"Yes… and… I also feel so frustrated and angry with my mother for allowing this to go on!"

"Let's move ahead in your life. I'm going to count backwards from five again, and when I get to one, you're going to be a young man. Five… four… three… two… one. Now what do you see?"

"I'm standing in the kitchen of an old farmhouse. I'm older— maybe early twenties or …" Julie took a long pause. "Sorry, I'm not really sure."

"That's fine. Where is the farmhouse? Do you know?"

"I think I'm in Michigan. That's the feeling I have. I can't explain it—it's just what comes to mind."

"And what are you doing at the house?"

Julie hesitated.

"Are you OK?" Shirley asked.

"Something is wrong. Something is *really* wrong. The kitchen is smoky, and it's like I'm trying to get out of the house," Julie said, rustling under the afghan and becoming alarmed.

"Do you feel like you're in danger? Like the house is burning down around you?"

Julie had begun breathing rapidly. "I was in the kitchen, but now I'm just seeing snippets of it. Feeling snippets of it, really."

"All right," Shirley said. "The universe is slowing things down for you... just go with it... take your time."

Julie didn't speak for nearly three minutes.

"Are you still with me, here?"

"Mmmm-hmmm," Julie responded.

"What's going on now? Are you still at the house? Is it on fire? What are you seeing or feeling?"

"I'm... I'm just seeing bits and pieces of stuff. Something bad happened here. All I can see is the purple haze of smoke in the kitchen... it's just purple, purplish gray."

"What else are you seeing?" Shirley asked. "Just take your time."

"I'm angry! So pissed right now."

"Why are you mad? What's gotten you so upset?"

"I don't know. It's something about this old lady—this old lady who is missing her right hand. She just came at me through the smoke."

"And she's missing her right hand? Can you say more about that?"

Julie hesitated again. "Oh, my God! She's coming at me—swinging this hook thing at me," Julie shouted urgently. "Ow!" Julie cried. "My chest—it's really hurting."

Shirley took a quick breath. "Let's move out of this. Let's move ahead. I'm going to count backwards from five, and when I reach one, you'll be an older man and in a different part of your life. Five... four... three... two... one. Are you still with me here?" Shirley asked.

"Mmmm-hmmm. But I'm not sure where I am. It looks like I'm with some sort of military group... I'm in a tropical village of some kind, very primitive."

"Are you afraid for your safety?" Shirley asked.

"No… well, not much. But I have a feeling of dread. Like we're about to do something I know in my gut is wrong."

"What do you mean? Who are you with?" Shirley asked.

Sarah sat in the corner, furiously scribbling notes in her notebook.

"I'm with a group of men. There's a bunch of us. We're all following the one guy, who's going toward some hut or something… oh, I really don't like this," Julie said, tearing up and beginning to tremble.

"Try to relax—just let it come to you."

"Oh God… God, no," Julie moaned.

"What's wrong, Julie? Should we move ahead?"

"No, no… I just saw the front of my uniform! My last name is Hanson."

Shirley looked over at Sarah. Remaining completely calm, she delivered her next instructions.

"That's all right; that's fine. Let's move forward."

"He's lining up innocent kids… oh, God… just making them get on their knees and pointing a machine gun at them! It's horrific—really, really wrong."

"I'm going to count backwards from five now. When I hit one, you'll be at another point in your life. Are you with me?"

"Mm-hmm," Julie said.

"Five… four… three… two… one. Are you with me now?"

"Yes," Julie whispered. "I'm still in a jungle or something, but my back hurts so much. I'm lying in shallow water… there are bodies floating everywhere." Julie began weeping. "I'm bleeding… hurt, but not dead. The water is… bright red."

"Do you feel like you're going to die?" Shirley asked. "Is this the end of this lifetime?"

Julie hesitated. "Um… no, but I'm badly injured."

"OK, let's leave this. I'm counting backwards again: five… four… three… two… one. We're out of the jungle now, and you're in another phase of your life. Where are you now?"

Julie was silent for a couple minutes as her breathing evened out.

"Can you tell me where you are?"

"I'm in the woods again, but it's not a jungle. It's Michigan again."

"Good, so you're home?" Shirley asked.

Julie's voice cracked. "I don't think so."

"What's wrong? Can you tell me?"

"I'm not sure where I am …somewhere different than where I'm used to, but yet familiar."

"Familiar how?"

"Familiar because it's the woods."

"OK, good. Why are you in the woods? What's happening?"

"I'm coming out from underneath some trees, and I see a car parked near a field. It's dark, and I'm wet," she said, shivering.

"Is it your car?"

"Yes, definitely. But I'm cold, so cold and dirty."

"Go on up to the car. Can you tell me anything about the car?"

"Yes: It's old, like from the 50s or 60s. I don't know. I'm not into cars, really."

"That's fine. Don't worry about it. What else can you tell me about it?"

"It's white—it's a white car—very shiny. Uh, this may sound strange, but I don't have a shirt on."

"Oh. Are you injured? Can you tell if you're hurt? Why don't you have a shirt on?"

"I really don't know, but it feels like …" Julie hesitated for several seconds. "It feels like I've done something wrong again. I feel really pissed off again. Pissed, but sad—regretful. Things are sketchy again …I'm just seeing snippets again."

"That's fine. Just take your time."

"I'm seeing flashes of a swamp or something—very thick and wooded," she said. "My skin is scratched and bleeding, and my hand is throbbing."

Shirley looked at Julie's right hand, which was covering her eyes. It had become slightly more swollen than earlier.

"Hang tight. Just take your time, and keep going if you can."

Minutes passed before Julie spoke again.

"Oh, God! My legs are burning up!"

"OK, Julie, that's it. I'm going to bring you back to the current moment," she said calmly. "I'm going to count backwards from five again, this time a little more slowly, and with each number, you'll find yourself waking up, feeling a bit better, and coming back to the present day."

"OK," Julie gasped, tears streaming down her face.

"Five… you're pulling out of that timeframe. Nothing is hurting you now, Julie… Four… with each number, you're becoming a little more aware of what's going on around you…. Three … feeling stronger and more awake… Two… you're almost awake, and soon you'll feel like you've awakened from a long nap, but you'll remember everything we discussed… One."

Julie rubbed her eyes. "Oh, my God," she said groggily. "I'm so …I feel so odd."

"That's normal, Julie. Just lie there for a few moments and get your bearings," Shirley said, glancing at her niece. "You've had quite a session."

Although Julie chose not to say anything, tears continued to fall to the pillow case.

"When you feel like you're able, just sit up on the edge of the bed, hon," Shirley said kindly. "I know we have a lot to talk about, but you take your time and wake up fully. I'm going to go brew us a pot of tea. You girls come downstairs when you're ready."

Looking sad and distraught, Julie gradually pulled herself upright on the edge of the bed.

"Are you OK?" Sarah said, plopping down next to her.

Julie shook her head. "Why did I let you talk me into this?"

Sarah put her arm around Julie's shoulder. "None of this is your fault; you know that, right? Remember what Aunt Shirley said: It's not about the information you gain, it's what you decide to do with the information to resolve whatever the block is."

"Yeah, that's true, I guess," Julie said, rubbing her right hand. "Wow, my hand really hurts."

"Can you stand up?"

Julie's legs felt as wobbly as a newborn foal's as she attempted to stand. "Man, this is so weird. I feel like …I don't know how to explain it. Just drained, I guess."

"You ready to go downstairs?" Sarah grabbed her notebook.

Julie nodded. "Thanks, Sarah," she said meekly. "I really don't know what I'd do without a friend like you right now," she said, wiping tears away.

"It's all good, Jules," Sarah said, trying to lighten her friend's mood. "Let's see what Aunt Shirley thinks. If anyone can help us figure out your next move, it's her!"

61

"How'd it go?" Mike asked, giving his upper body a big stretch from the sofa. "You guys had a long session—nearly two hours."

"God, really?" Julie asked. "Seemed like we talked for a half hour! I can't believe it took two hours."

"Yep. It's nearly noon now," Mike said. "I was able to really dig into these cases for my Criminal Justice class, so it was great for me."

"Here we go, a nice pot of tea," Shirley said, interrupting their discussion. "I've also put some muffins, boiled eggs, and fruit on the tray for everyone. But Julie, I insist: I really want you to eat and drink something. Going under as far as you went really takes a toll on your body."

"Thanks, Aunt Shirley," Sarah said, pouring herself a cup of tea. "This is so nice of you to help us with this. It's been, well, pretty disconcerting these past couple months."

"It's what I do," Shirley said cheerfully. "And we have a lot to talk about, don't we?"

"So it went pretty well?" Mike asked again.

"Yes, I'd say we came away with some fairly significant information. Wouldn't you say so, Jules?" Sarah said, picking up a banana off the tray.

Julie nibbled on a blueberry muffin and nodded.

Shirley handed her a cup of tea. "Julie dear, please drink something, too."

"Thanks." Julie accepted the cup and took a few sips before continuing. "Yeah, it was really something else, that's for sure."

"How are you feeling now?" Shirley asked Julie.

"I'm just sort of dazed or something... can't explain it."

"I understand. The first time is always quite the experience."

"I mean—it was just weird. I knew you were there and were asking me questions. I knew I was Julie. But at the exact same time, I was having glimpses of things and feeling emotions... just having more of a sixth sense, really, about whatever I was seeing, you know?"

"I know just what you mean," Aunt Shirley said. "That's what I was trying to explain to you earlier, but you really can't fully understand it until you experience it."

Julie shook her head. "I don't even know where to start with it all or what to do next."

"Well, I took really good notes while you were under," responded Shirley. "Why don't we review them together, and then if you happened to see something else that you can remember, Julie—something that you didn't share during the session—either you can share it with us now, or just file it for future reference, OK?"

Julie nodded.

"OK. You went under fairly quickly. It was funny, because I could see your eyes moving and I knew you were headed into the trance—you just didn't happen to know," Shirley said laughing.

"Yeah, I couldn't figure out why my eyes wouldn't stay shut. It's a very odd sensation."

"That it is," Shirley said, picking up her notepad. "Let's start with your first vision. You described yourself as a ten-year-old boy, in some sort of a farming community."

"Yeah, in Wisconsin," Sarah offered, taking a bite of her banana and looking back over her notes.

"I just saw the shape of the state in my head, and the word 'Wisconsin' popped into my head," Julie said.

"That's how it often happens." Shirley buttered a muffin and read from her notes. "We didn't really know what year it was, but I'm guessing you may have sensed something. You said you recognized the woman and baby as family, but that the abusive man in the room was not your father."

"Yeah," Julie said sadly. "That was the feeling I got. Seemed like it was before my time, but not like the 1800s or anything that far back. Seemed like it was the 1950s or so. I don't know why, though."

Shirley nodded. "That's fine, dear—many times it's more of a gut feeling than anything else."

"I wonder if any of that matches up with John Hanson's story," Julie said, thinking aloud.

"Let's not get ahead of ourselves here," Shirley said. "We have plenty of time for research. Eventually, you may want to check on all that, but let's move on through this for now." Shirley shifted in her chair and scanned her notes.

"So you lived on some farm in Wisconsin with your mother and mentally challenged sister, all under the rule of an abusive alcoholic; that's what I have in my notes, anyway. And after you saw the woman and the baby, you became pretty emotional. At that point, I counted you through to the next part of your life, which was equally interesting,"

"Yes. I felt conflicted, really—sad, but also pissed."

"Right," Sarah said, putting her banana peel on the tray and wiping her hands. "And after you got through that count, I have it that you said you sensed you were in Michigan, maybe in your twenties, but you couldn't really tell."

"That's correct," said Shirley, verifying in her notes.

"Yeah. That was pretty weird," Julie said, hesitating. "I knew it was Michigan, probably because I've lived here my whole life …something about it …I just knew I was back here."

"In Lansing or Grand Ledge?" Sarah asked.

Julie took another sip of tea. "No, just Michigan in general. No idea where, though."

"That's OK," Shirley said. "The universe would have told you specifically if it had wanted to," she said.

"Why do you think it held back?" Sarah asked.

"It's not necessarily that it withheld information from Julie," Shirley said. "It could be that Julie already knows—or that the universe was showing her something symbolically."

"Hmmm," Julie said.

"What? Did you remember something?" Sarah asked.

"No. I was just thinking about that hook thing the old lady was swinging at me."

"It was some sort of hook? That's new," Sarah said. "Was it some kind of a prosthetic device, do you think?"

"Yeah, I think so. I was just catching glimpses of it, but it was like this old-style wooden thing with a hook, and some sort of cables attached to it."

"Eew," Sarah said, making a face.

"This old lady, she had the straps slung over her shoulder …some sort of harness thing that was over her old dress. That much I did see. Oh, and that she was absolutely pissed off about something—coming at me with the freakin' hook."

"At one point, you said your chest hurt," Sarah reminded her.

"Yeah, like I'd been hit in the chest. Maybe I was sensing that she actually connected with the hook? I don't know," Julie sighed.

"That's very possible," Shirley said. "In regression, sometimes we tend to sense things more than we actually see them."

"And all that smoke …it was very strange," Julie said.

"Was the house on fire or something?" Mike asked.

"I'm not really sure, Mike. I think so, but I'm not a hundred percent," Julie said.

Mike shifted in his seat. "This is going to sound weird, but it sort of reminds me of that one case study we were talking about that one day at the library," he said to Sarah.

"You mean the one that happened in the U.P.?" Sarah asked him.

"Yeah." Mike dug for his Criminal Justice folder. "Several of 'em happened in the U.P., but this one was …"

"What are you talking about?" Julie interrupted.

"Remember that night you had the night terror in your room after the Chi Sig party, and Pattie came over and got me?" Sarah asked.

Julie blushed. "Yeah, I guess."

"Well, the next day, Pattie and I went to the library with Mike, and he was telling us about this unsolved case where this lady was murdered and then how whoever did it torched the body," Sarah said. "The lady's name was Violet, and because it matched the name you had been saying in your dream, we just thought that was weird."

"And you know what else? It seems like there was something about her arm." Mike shuffled through his papers, and then looked up from the folder. "Holy shit. Now I remember. The case study doesn't specifically talk about a hook, but in the forensic report, the coroner stated that this burned-up white female—Violet—was missing her right arm from her elbow down."

"Her hand!" Sarah and Shirley said simultaneously.

"Oh, my God." Sarah stared at Julie, and then turned to her aunt. "Could this be connected, do you think?"

"I suppose it could be. The universe definitely works in mysterious ways." Suddenly, Shirley's face fell.

"I just thought of something. What did you say the victim's name was, Mike? Violet?" Shirley asked.

Mike nodded. "Yeah, Violet Swansen."

"And what color was the smoke in the kitchen, Julie—do you remember what you told us?" she continued.

"Yeah, of course. It was purple. Purplish-gray, really." In that instant, Julie understood where Shirley's line of questioning was headed. "It was violet-colored smoke."

"Exactly," Shirley said. "Remember what I said about symbolism?"

Julie's face slumped in astonishment. "But how could this be? You have to admit this is pretty far-fetched, isn't it?"

"Dear, one thing you have to remember about the universe: Everything happens for a reason. The universe made sure your path would cross with Sarah and Mike. This could be the reason."

"My head is spinning," Julie said, standing up and pacing into the hallway.

"Sweetheart, try to settle down. Sit down and finish your tea," Shirley said. "We'll figure this out."

Mike turned back to Shirley. "Wow. So let me understand this. If Julie was somehow also John Hanson, and she can provide more details about this particular lady, then she might be able to solve the case, right?"

"So this is an actual case study, Mike?" Shirley asked.

"Yep. The murder occurred in the winter of 1963."

"OK, so let me just think about this for a second," Shirley said, turning to a blank page in her notepad. "If John was ten in 1950, let's say, that means he was born in 1940. Does anyone know the actual year he was born?"

Julie, stunned, was unable to speak.

"It was around then," Sarah said. "I forget exactly, but yeah, it's close."

"OK. Then by 1963 John would have been twenty-three years old, right?"

"That's probably right," Sarah agreed.

"So, we're still in the ballpark. I wouldn't expect us to figure this out exactly at this point, but our theory is still plausible," Shirley said.

"So, if after we research this further and everything checks out, then what?" Mike asked.

Julie walked back into the parlor and flopped down into the recliner. "Guys—this is really freaking me out. This can't be real."

"Hold on here." Shirley tried to regain control of the discussion. "Honey—Julie—this is all speculative at this point. We are just trying to figure out where all this is going. Please remember, we're all trying to help you."

"I know," Julie said sadly. "I'm probably getting ahead of myself, but if I was really John Hanson at one time..." she said, getting teary eyed, "Well, it's just upsetting!"

Sarah moved closer and touched her hand.

"If I was really John Hanson ..." Julie took a deep breath and looked at Sarah. "It means I killed my aunt! My mom's sister!"

"Wait, Julie—we don't know that," Sarah replied. "We don't even know that John Hanson did anything wrong at this point."

"Sweethearts, all of you, listen to me," Shirley urged them. "Even if it turns out that we can link all this up, *Julie* didn't commit a crime—John did."

Julie grabbed a tissue. "But can you imagine what my family is going to do when I drop this bombshell on 'em?" Julie paused and blew her nose. "Can you even imagine? 'Oh, by the way, Grandma, it turns out that I'm a reincarnation of the bastard who killed your favorite daughter.' Yeah, that will go over real well. They'll hate me forever." She began sobbing.

"Let's slow down here," Shirley said. "We're all pretty emotional about this right now."

"Has this ever happened to any of your other clients before?" Julie asked. "Has anybody else ever realized they were a monster in a former life?"

"First of all, I don't believe John was a monster, as you call him," Shirley said. "All along, he said he knew whatever he was doing was wrong. But for whatever reason, he continued to make the wrong decision—or perhaps he was forced into something he didn't want to do. I've had clients who have found that they were celebrities or historical characters before, but no, never this. There's a first time for everything, and we're going to help you through this, if it turns out to be true," she said. "We still don't know anything for sure at this point."

Mike stepped in. "OK, let's think this through. Is there something I can do to help? It's my case study—what can we learn from it?"

"In all honesty, I don't really know, Mike," Shirley said. "Why don't you tell us a few other things about the case?"

"Fair enough." Mike sifted through the case study. "Like I said, it happened in 1963 near the small town of Germfask in the Upper Peninsula."

"Jesus Christ," Julie burst out. "That's where John was from! Remember in the articles, Sarah?"

"What?" Sarah said. "What am I missing?"

"What are you missing? Germfask! That's where John was from. I can't believe you didn't remember that."

"Actually, it was Pattie who had heard of Germfask," Mike interrupted. "Her stepdad hunts up that way, remember, Sarah?"

"That's right, now I do remember that," Sarah replied. "But I've never heard of the place before. Really, Julie, it didn't stick with me."

Julie sat back down in her seat with a grunt of annoyance.

Shirley followed Mike and Sarah's lead. "So it sounds like we have yet another connection with it."

"Damn right we do," Julie said, getting more worked up by the second.

"Right," Mike said. "We talked about the arm. The victim was 69 years old. She was a widow for many years and continued to run a farm up there, and she often took in workers to help her keep things going. My instructor was a detective in the case. He worked for the Schoolcraft County Sheriff's Department at the time as a cop, and he said that they thought the perpetrator was one of those guys she took in at the time. But he said he had interviewed many people from Germfask who knew of her, and she had a reputation for being kind of a bitch."

"If she took him in and let him live in her house, why didn't the police have a name?" Sarah asked.

"I asked the same question," Mike said. "Professor Whitman said it was the early 60s in the U.P., and everybody trusted everybody. They just had a verbal agreement, and this old lady would pay him a little bit of money and let him stay at her house in return for his work. That was a pretty common way to do business back then, at least on farms."

"Wait a minute," Julie said, straightening up in her chair. "Who did you say? Professor Whitman?"

"Yeah, my instructor at MSU. His name is Al Whitman, and he was a cop in Schoolcraft County for the Sheriff's Department before he became a detective with the Michigan State Police down here."

"Oh, my God," Julie said, holding her head in her hands again. "You guys are never going to believe this."

"Now what, Jules?" Sarah asked. "What's wrong?"

"Doesn't that name ring a bell with you, Sarah?" Julie said, sitting up. "Did you even read those articles I gave you on Sunday?" she asked angrily.

Sarah hesitated and thought. "I read them, but no …I'm sorry, but it really doesn't ring any bells."

"Alan Whitman was the detective in my Aunt Bev's case. I don't know if it's the same guy, but… after everything that's happened today, I wouldn't be surprised if it was." Julie was crying again.

"But that's your aunt's case," Mike said. "The two can't be connected."

"Let me ask you three something," Aunt Shirley interrupted. "What's the common denominator here?"

"John Hanson," they all said in unison.

62

It had been a long ride back to MSU, with Julie not saying much from the backseat of Mike's car. Mike had dropped the girls off and headed back to his place.

Julie unlocked the door to her room, and Sarah followed her inside without being asked.

"Well, look who's here," Pattie said from her desk. "I've been wondering where everybody went."

"Don't ask," Julie said throwing her coat onto her bunk and moving toward the fridge for a Coke. "How are you doing, Pattie? Did the funeral go OK?"

"Yeah, it was very nice, thanks. My mom is doing better, and I think she was just glad to get back to Michigan after all of that."

"I can imagine," Sarah said.

"So, what's up with you guys? Where have you been?"

Sarah looked at Julie questioningly. Julie gave the nod and opened her soda.

"We've been over in Grand Ledge, meeting with my aunt," Sarah said. "She did a past-life regression on Julie."

"She did a what?" Pattie gasped. "A past-life what?"

"Regression," Julie said calmly from her bunk.

"What does that do?"

"My aunt has written two or three books on the matter," Sarah began. "She used to live in California, but moved back here a few years back to be closer to family."

"Uh-huh," Pattie said closing her text book. "So?"

"So she's an expert in all this stuff, and after what happened to Jules over the Thanksgiving weekend at her Grandma's, I suggested that we maybe see if my aunt could regress her."

"Jeez, Julie, what happened at your Grandma's?" Pattie asked. "You didn't tell me anything!"

"It's such a long story, Pattie," Julie said, flaking out on her bed. "Can I explain it all to you later? I'm just pooped right now."

"You should rest, Julie. Just remember what Aunt Shirley said," Sarah said, sounding a little like a mother hen. "You'll sleep really soundly tonight, but tomorrow you might have some really vivid dreams, and you'll need to get up and write them down so that we can figure more stuff out."

"Aw, come on! Figure what stuff out?" Pattie said.

"Have you had dinner yet?" Sarah asked Pattie.

"No, and I'm starving."

"Then Jules, do you mind if I fill Pattie in on everything at dinner, while you rest? Since she's your roommate and all—and this is potentially some pretty serious shit you're going through—she really should be in the know."

Julie yawned "That's fine. I'm cool with it. I'm too tired to think about it, quite honestly."

"OK, then, you get some rest. Pattie, let's go."

"Sarah? Thanks for helping me with all of this," Julie said sleepily from her bottom bunk, turning over toward the wall.

"It's OK, Jules." Sarah grabbed a light blanket off the back of Julie's desk chair and threw it over Julie. "Just rest up. Everything is going to be fine."

63

It was nearly eight o'clock before Pattie returned to the dorm, finding Julie buried in her books studying.

Pattie and Sarah had opted out of the regular dorm-food fare and enjoyed a Mexican dinner and drinks at El Azteco in downtown East Lansing, a favorite hangout for many college students.

"You're awake," Pattie said as she entered the room. "I thought you were down for the count."

"Yeah, I got up around seven. I feel much better now. I just passed out, dead to the world."

"That's good. From everything Sarah told me, you had quite a day."

"Did Sarah tell you everything?" Julie asked, pushing away from her text books.

"Yeah. I can't believe how much has happened in a week. And this whole thing about Violet! Jesus Christ, it's unbelievable. I was here and saw you go through that whole thing. I know how scary it was."

"Yeah, it's a bit freaky, isn't it? It sort of explains a lot, though."

"Are you going to do more research on all of this?" Pattie asked.

"Yeah, that's the plan. But Mike is going to talk to this Whitman guy first and see if there really is a connection; that'll be our next step. Part of me hopes it isn't the same guy. Because if it is..."

"Oh, Jules, don't go there right now," Pattie said. "Just take one step at a time. But if this Whitman guy is the same guy who handled both crimes—that would just be way too weird."

"I know," Julie said, engrossed in thought. "It's almost too much for me to think about right now." Julie returned her attention to her books. "And thank goodness I've got about an hour more of reading to do."

64

"Be sure to study those three cases," Professor Whitman told his class as they reached the end of the hour. "If you focus on all aspects of those cases—and I mean everything—you'll do OK on the exam," he said with a gentle smile. "I have office hours every day this week from two until four. Have a great day."

Mike gathered his belongings and made his way to the front of the auditorium.

"Professor Whitman? Do you have a minute?"

"Sure Mike. What's up?" he asked as he put his materials back into his brief case.

"Well... I'm not sure where to begin," Mike said. "It's a really long story."

"Uh-oh. Did you get into trouble over the weekend or something?"

"No, no, nothing like that. Actually, it has something to do with one of the old cases we studied."

"Really?" Whitman turned his complete attention to Mike. "Which one?"

Mike hesitated. "It's, uh ...you wanna grab a cup of coffee in the cafe, and I can walk you through it?"

Whitman glanced at his watch. "Sure. I don't have another class for a couple hours."

"Great. It's a long story, and you'll probably have a lot of questions," he said as they turned to walk out of the auditorium.

"So which case is it?" Whitman asked.

"It's the one that happened in Germfask with that old lady, Violet Swansen."

"Wow! That *is* an old one. What can you possibly know about that, Mike? That happened way before you were born."

The small café at the end of the corridor was virtually empty. "Have a seat," Mike said, gesturing to one of the small tables. "What kind of coffee do you want?"

"Just grab me a regular black coffee."

As Mike went to the coffee counter to get their drinks, Whitman rummaged through his briefcase, looking for the Swansen case study.

Mike returned with two black coffees and a couple of Danishes.

"Oh, God," Whitman said, eyeing the pastries. "You're going to make a great cop one day."

"I love these things," Mike confessed. "I didn't have any breakfast this morning."

"OK, so what's on your mind about this case study?"

"Well, let me ask you this first," Mike said, removing the lid from his coffee. "Did you ever work on a case in a town called Mulliken where a young woman never returned home from working in a bar?"

Whitman cocked his head and looked inquisitively at Mike. "Yes, I did," he said, taking a sip of coffee. "That was one of the first cases I worked on as a lead detective with the Michigan State Police. But what does that have to do with the Germfask case?"

Mike hadn't really expected Whitman to confirm his suspicion; he looked rattled at Whitman's remark.

"What's wrong, Mike? You look like you've seen a ghost."

"Sorry. This is just really weird. I guess I didn't know what I expected to hear."

"Why? What's going on with all this?"

"OK ...let me back up here," Mike said, before taking a bite of his Danish. "Do you believe in reincarnation?"

"Jeez, Mike, you're all over the place with this."

"I know, I know. Just bear with me for a minute." Mike hesitated for a couple seconds. "So, do you? Believe, I mean."

"Well, I don't really know a lot about it, but I've read a few Shirley MacLaine books, yeah. My wife really believed in it." He laughed. "She thought our dog was a reincarnation of the poodle she had when she was a little girl—Mr. Twinkles."

"OK, good," Mike said with a nervous laugh. "Well, I'm just gonna lay all this out here."

"Good. That's what I like people to do."

"All right. My girlfriend, she's a student here at MSU, too, and she has a friend who's been having some severe problems with bad dreams ...and personality changes." Mike said. "In fact, this friend is the niece of Beverly Deerfield, the victim in the Mulliken case you worked on."

"Is that right? That must mean that—oh, what was Bev's little sister's name? Sharon? Was is Sharon?" Whitman said to himself. "No, it was Shawn... yeah, Shawn Deerfield! Is that your friend's mother?"

"Yes, I'm pretty sure that's her name."

"OK," Whitman said, intently listening.

"Well, Shawn's daughter—Julie is her name—started having all these visions and stuff. It really began to disrupt her life, and so yesterday, my girlfriend Sarah, hooked her up with a person who does past life regressions," Mike said.

"Whoa! Hold on, Mike. In the detective world, we rely upon facts, and facts only, you know?"

"Yeah, I get you. But if you'll just hear me out, I think you'll be amazed by the connections of it all."

"OK, well go on, then. I'm all ears."

"Well, the whole Violet Swansen connection came after the actual regression," Mike said. "I happened to be listening into what they were talking about, and I questioned it."

Mike took a bite of his Danish and referred to his case study.

"As a result of the regression, they believe that Julie is actually a reincarnation of a man named John Hanson," Mike said.

Whitman sat up in his seat.

"John Hanson was the man who was ..." Mike began.

"...with Bev Deerfield the night she went missing, yes!" Whitman said, finishing his sentence.

"That's right," Mike said. "But did you know that he was also from the Germfask area?"

"I do recall that they shipped his body up there to Newberry," Whitman said. "But we did extensive background checks on him, and he came back cleaner than a whistle. He even won the Purple Heart for bravery or some damn thing."

"That may be true," Mike said, "But Julie's done some research on his old Marine battalion, and it turns out they did some pretty awful things to innocent Vietnamese people on his watch. The report on all this stuff didn't even get released to the public until last year. That's why you never had reason to suspect that Hanson might have been a little screwed up."

"Hmmm." Whitman took out a notepad and pen. "It's an interesting theory, that's for sure. What was the name of the battalion and all that?"

"I don't have it all with me, but I'm sure Julie would talk to you."

"OK, so I understand the connection here with the Deerfield case, but what does this have to do with the Swansen case?" Whitman asked.

"Well, when they were going through this regression yesterday, Julie saw the name 'Hanson' on his uniform. He was in some tropical village sort of place," Mike said.

"Wait— didn't Julie already know about Hanson? If she already knew the name, don't you think she could have just said that? That she could have just made that up?"

"Why would she do that? Believe me, if anybody was hoping that wasn't true, it was Julie. Can you imagine what her mother and grandmother would do if they heard that news?"

"I see—I understand. Meryl Deerfield was a mess back then. I can only imagine what dredging up this crap would do to her. So, why Violet?"

"Well, in another part of the regression, Julie said she thought she was young man, maybe in the earlier part of his 20s," Mike said, referring to Sarah's hand-written notes. "She said she sensed that he lived in Michigan, but couldn't give an exact location."

"OK," Whitman said, picking up his half-drunk coffee.

"She said she ... *he* was in a kitchen of a farmhouse of some sort, and that some lady came at him swinging this hook thing," Mike said. "We suspect that she may have actually connected on him, because her chest was aching during this part of the regression, and the regressionist told us later that often that's what happens."

"I do recall that the victim did wear a prosthetic device, and I believe—I'm not a hundred percent sure, but I believe it was in fact a hook," Whitman said, making a note.

"But the other thing she said was that the house was filled with smoke."

"Which it was, because the perp stabbed her in the chest with an enormous kitchen knife, dragged her body into the bedroom off the kitchen, drenched her body with gasoline on the bed, and touched it all off with a match," Whitman said. "How's that for a memory?"

"Right, but what Julie said that was particularly interesting was that the smoke was purple," Mike said.

"The smoke was probably more black than anything."

"I'm sure it was," Mike said. "But the regressionist seemed to think Julie was using symbolism here—for Violet's name."

"Well, that's certainly an interesting theory," Whitman said, leaning back in his chair. "But unfortunately, it takes a hell of a lot more than that to convince a jury."

"I know, I know. I just want to give you all the details."

"All right. But did she say anything about her aunt's case?"

"She never saw her aunt in any part of the regression, but the last thing she said was that she, or he, felt cold and dirty, and was walking out from underneath a canopy of trees," Mike said, reading from Sarah's notes. "He was walking toward a car that she described as an older model car, say from the fifties or sixties, and that it was white."

Whitman raised his eyebrows and scribbled notes down on his notepad. "What else? Is that it?"

"Not quite." Mike struggled to read Sarah's writing. "At the end of the session, she said his legs were on fire, and the regressionist intervened and brought Julie back out of it."

"Well …I mean, Julie probably knew the guy had been burned to death, right?"

"Yeah, probably," Mike said. "But if you just met with Julie— you'd see. She's not making this stuff up. I can usually tell when somebody is selling me a load of crap, and she's not. I wouldn't be talking to you if I doubted her for one minute."

"Fair enough. Well, Mike, I'll tell you what," Whitman said, flipping his notepad shut. "I'm going to be honest with you. I wouldn't normally do this, but not being able to solve the Deerfield case has always bothered me. I felt so bad that we never figured out what happened."

"I can imagine. It must've sucked."

"It did. But it sucked, as you say, far worse for Meryl Deerfield and her daughter. They had already been through so much, with the farming accident and all that."

"Yeah, Sarah told me about that, too," Mike said.

"I always suspected that it was Hanson, yet I couldn't prove it," Whitman said. "I kept just about everything on the case, and I still have it in a big file cabinet at home. I do want to talk to Julie, and then I'll go back through my notes again. I have everything: notes, the autopsy on Hanson, interviews with witnesses—and I know for a fact that I have Hanson's old military file."

"Oh, man. Wouldn't it be sweet if you can actually figure this out, after all this time?"

Whitman handed Mike a business card. "Have her call me. But I wouldn't get your hopes up, Mike. This is all pretty …"

"Speculative?"

"Yeah, and weird, too," Whitman said, standing up. "I'll see you next week. And don't forget what I said about the exam—learn those cases inside and out."

"Will do. Thanks for talking to me and for hopefully helping Jules out. I'll be interested to see if anything comes of it."

"Me too," Whitman said. "I guess that's why I'm willing to look into it. Even if there's a remote chance that we can bring closure to this, nearly 40 years later …Bev and her mama deserve that."

As he watched Whitman walk away, Mike called Sarah with the good news.

65

Julie and Whitman met for the first time nearly a week later. Having spoken on the phone, she knew him to be a kind, older gentleman, very much tuned in to what her family had gone through thirty-five years earlier.

"You must be Julie," Whitman said, joining Julie at the same table and same café where he'd met Mike. "I'd recognize you as a Deerfield anywhere," he said, smiling and holding out his hand.

Aside from his graying hair and more pronounced laugh lines, at sixty-eight Whitman looked good for his age.

"It's great to meet you," Julie said, shaking his hand. "I still can't believe all of this. The dreams, regression and all that, and then this—having a connection back to you through Mike."

"Yeah, it's strange how things work sometimes," Whitman said, putting Julie at ease. "It's like I told Mike—it's a long shot. Actually, it's longer than a long shot. But if there is a remote chance that we can give your grandmother some closure on all of this, then it's worth it."

"Well, thanks. Like I told you on the phone, it's been a rough go for my grandma all these years," she said. "She did marry Oscar, though."

"She did? Oh, that's great. He always seemed like a nice guy."

"He is. He really is."

"So, what does your grandmother think of all this reincarnation business?"

"Are you kidding?" Julie stammered. "I haven't told them any of it. The only people who know are you, Sarah, Mike, the regressionist, and my roommate Pattie."

"So what happens if we actually get onto something here? What are you going to do? I can't imagine that your grandmother is going to be real happy with you," Whitman warned.

"You know, I haven't even gotten that far yet. I have to take it all one step at a time, or I begin to lose my mind, like I did earlier this fall."

"Fair enough," Whitman said. "Let me bring you up to speed on where I am in all of this, and then you can tell me any additional stuff you may know—or think you know."

Whitman reached into his briefcase and pulled out the notepad that contained notes from his conversation with Mike, notes he had taken during his initial phone conversation with Julie, and the thick folder from his original case file.

"What did you find out?" Julie asked.

"Well, I was able to bring up those articles on the Internet from the *Newberry News* that you were talking about."

"Oh, good," Julie said. "Did any of that help you?"

"Well, it may have, actually." Whitman put on his reading glasses. "Back in my file here, I have the original interview I did with Jake Redmond," he said. "He's the guy who worked with Hanson at the wildlife refuge. He was a couple years older than John, and would be seventy-six by now. I thought it would be good to talk to him again—see if he could remember John ever saying anything about Violet Swansen."

"Oh, I see. Because back in 1972 when you interviewed him, you had no cause to link him up with her death."

"Exactly. I still might not have any reason to link the two, but I thought I'd ask."

"So what did he say?" Julie asked excitedly.

"Well, nothing. Turns out he died three months ago."

"Oh shit. What timing, eh?"

"Actually, our timing was still pretty good. You're never going to believe this, but I spoke with his wife. She's a little younger and sounded pretty spry on the phone. Anyway, it turns out that she was cleaning out her attic just this last week. She said it had taken her that amount of time to come to grips with going through her husband's old stuff. While she was up there, she came across this old footlocker from the Marines—and you'll never guess whose name was on it."

"No way ..."

"I couldn't believe it either. J. Hanson—U.S. Marines."

"No fuckin' way," Julie said. "Oh—please excuse my language."

"Honey, I've heard far worse than that in my day. And I know this is a real shocker. Back in his original interview, I specifically asked him if he had any belongings of John Hanson, and he said no," Whitman said pointing to his notes. "So I got to thinking... why would he lie to me?"

"Maybe he forgot?"

"Maybe—maybe not," Whitman said, as only a detective could. "I've seen it all in my day. If somebody doesn't tell you something, there's usually a reason."

"Yeah, I guess."

"Well, the wife there was pretty friendly with me," he said. "She said she would be happy to put the footlocker aside for me."

"You're kidding."

"Nope—she said she was just going put it out for the garbage collector anyway. She doesn't even know what's in there. It's probably just blankets and military belongings, but the fact that Jake left it out of his original interview is enough for me to want to take a look. I called my niece—she goes to school up at Michigan Tech in Houghton Hancock."

"Oh, really?"

"Yeah, and it turns out she's headed home for Christmas break this weekend, so I sweet-talked her into stopping by the Redmonds' home on her way through. She'll bring me the footlocker on Saturday."

"Wow, that's awesome," Julie said taking a sip of coffee.

"Like I said, chances are it's nothing, but we'll check it out to be sure."

"So then what?"

"Well, if by chance there turns out to be something in there connecting him to Violet—and let's face it, the chances of that are probably one in a billion—then we'll have something to go on."

"In other words, you'll be more apt to believe my whole regression thing if you can connect him to Violet Swansen."

"Well, yeah, I guess," Whitman said. "Because—and please don't take this the wrong way, but over the years you've heard the story of your aunt's case over and over. You probably don't even realize how much you've heard …"

"It's not that way. My mother and grandmother really didn't go into the details with me. It was always way too painful for my grandma."

"Be that as it may, I still want to see where this gets us. I don't have any idea of what we're looking for, but if it's like all the other cases I've worked on, I'll know it when I see it."

"Do you still want to hear my version of the regression about Violet?"

"Of course I do. Look, Julie, there's no reason to get gloomy about all of this. Finding Hanson's footlocker is huge. Even if we can't connect him to the Swansen case, it might give you and your family more information. You just never know."

"I know, I know. And I appreciate you taking the time to do all of this for us. I know how crazy it all sounds."

Whitman patted Julie's hand. "Just tell me what happened in the regression. I'm all ears."

"All right. Well, it all started when I was about 10 years old. I was a little boy standing in a field," she said. "And from what I felt, I got the impression that I was in Wisconsin."

Whitman got a serious look on his face. "Mike didn't tell me any of this. You mean that you think you regressed back to Hanson's early beginnings?"

"Well, we think so. Shirley—I mean the regressionist— walked me through different ages during that particular lifetime. The first one happened at age ten or thereabouts."

Whitman shook his head and shuffled through his briefcase for a file folder. "This is John Hanson's military record. It tells everything we know about him: where he was born, when his birthday is, all that stuff. I didn't really look at that and it's been so long … Ah, yes, here we go."

"Hanson, John Charles," he read from the report. "Born April 30, 1940 in Kingsford, Michigan."

"Ugh! Already that doesn't match up with what I saw in my regression."

"Not so fast, honey. Obviously you don't know your Upper Peninsula very well. First of all, Kingsford is just across the river from Aurora, Wisconsin. Secondly, there isn't a hospital in Aurora. So, many folks from that area are actually born in Michigan, but wind up living in Wisconsin."

Julie dipped her head in acknowledgment. "But we still don't know that to be the case."

Whitman returned to the report. "According to Hanson's school information, he graduated from Beecher Dunbar Pembine High School—and see here—that's in Pembine, Wisconsin."

Julie's eyes widened. "I couldn't have possibly known *that*, Professor Whitman."

Whitman nodded. "What else did you see in that portion of the regression? Did you gain any other details about his life?"

"I—he—was in a field of soybeans. Overalls with no shirt, leather boots. There was a barn with a very old tractor, and a cow that was fenced in."

"What about a house? Did you see a house?"

"Yes, the regressionist asked me to go to the house, which actually looked more like an old cabin. I couldn't quite get there in the vision, so Shirley counted me inside."

"What does that mean?" Whitman asked, looking up from the report.

"She told me she was counting backwards from five, and when she got to one, I was inside the cabin," she explained.

"So you were inside, and then what?"

"Well, there was a younger lady there. She had her hair drawn into a tight bun, and she was dressed in black. She was crying and holding a baby, and I'm guessing, but the baby was probably a little over a year old."

"Was that all you saw? Anything else you can tell me?"

"The baby was crying, too, and there was a man in the room— he didn't seem like the father, because he was an abusive man." Julie fought against tears. "I'm sorry. Even thinking about it gets me upset."

Whitman cocked his head and stared at Julie. "Why so emotional?" he asked, like a true cop.

"I have no idea. It was the same way during the regression. I felt so sad when I saw the woman and the baby—my mother and sister—and intensely angry with the man."

"John Hanson never knew his father," Whitman said, clarifying her thought. He scanned through the military record and stopped to read part of it. "Jesus," he said quietly, looking back up at Julie. "The report says Hanson had an alcoholic stepfather who died of alcoholism in 1957."

"Hmmm," Julie said, beginning to tear up again. "I knew he wasn't the father."

"Either you're really a reincarnation of Hanson, or you're one amazing con artist," Whitman said, half smiling.

"He also had a sister, nine years his junior," Whitman said. "Let's see here …her dad, James Gregory Addison, died in '57. Must have been the stepdad in question," Whitman mumbled. "In 1958 his mother, Ernestine Bradley Hanson-Addison died of cancer at the age of 35."

"By then, John would have been what? Eighteen?" Julie asked.

"Yep. And little sis, name of Barbara Sue Addison, would have been nine. His record says he took over as his sister's guardian …awful young to be looking after a little sister, but he was her only kin. Hmmm," he said, reading on.

"What?"

"I don't remember this from before. Says here little sis was deaf, and that John knew American Sign Language—bet that came in handy in the Marines. Anyway, when she turned sixteen, they parted ways," he said. "She went to live with a family from church."

"How do you know all this?"

"It's right here in his military record. They ask these guys everything about family and prior work experience when they enlist," Whitman explained. "Looks like from '58 until the time he enlisted, in January of '64, he lived near Newberry."

"So far, my regression seems to be pretty consistent with the actual John Hanson, don't you think?" Julie asked.

Whitman hesitated. "Let's move ahead," he said, refocusing on the report. "When did you see the name 'Hanson' in your regression?"

"That actually came after the part about Violet," Julie answered confidently. "I felt like the whole kitchen scene with the handicapped lady happened as a relatively younger man, like early to mid-20s maybe—not sure, just something I sensed at the time."

"Hanson was nearly twenty-four when he enlisted," Whitman said. "Of course, with his sister and all, he would have been unable to go into the service until '58 at the earliest. His records say he did 'odd jobs,' during that time," Whitman said, making air quotes and smirking. "That could be anything."

"That's consistent with Violet Swansen's case," Julie said. "I mean, you even said she took in guys to help out in exchange for a little money and a place to stay. Theoretically, it could have been Hanson."

"So what else can you tell me about the kitchen or about the lady, Violet, if it was her?"

"Well, she had this prosthetic device or hook type of thing on her right arm. In my vision, she was swinging the thing at me like crazy—just flailing it at me."

"I'm sure Mike told you this, but Violet was actually missing her right arm from her elbow down. However, they never found a prosthetic device in the charred remains of everything."

"Really? He told me about the missing arm, but he didn't tell me the device was missing after the murder. That's strange, isn't it?"

"Yeah… It was a very troubling aspect of the case, as I recall. We had spoken with several local folks, but they didn't really know her well enough to comment on her personal habits with the device. I do know that she lost her arm in a car accident in 1952. Her husband died in the crash, and if she'd been a recluse before that, she was even worse after. The preacher at her church told me that."

"How sad, to live until you're nearly seventy and not have a soul in the world give a damn about what happens to you in the end."

"Yeah, it was a sad case in that way."

"What kind of a hook was it?" Julie asked.

"Well, why don't you tell me?" Whitman said with a laugh. "You're the only one here who's ever seen it, right?"

"From what I could see, it had a double hook type of head on it, curved and sharp. It was sort of, I don't know, strapped on around her shoulders and over her dress. Does that sound weird?"

"No, that's how some of 'em worked back then. Mike said you thought she hit you?"

"I didn't actually see anything hit me, but at the time that the scene was playing out in my head, I felt a dull pain right here," Julie said, pointing to the area just below her left collarbone with her right hand."

"Let's see." Whitman flipped though Hanson's military file to the medical portion. "If Hanson was sliced open with a hook, he'd have a scar, right?"

"I don't know if he got cut," Julie reiterated. "I just had a pain there."

"Well, I'll be damned," Whitman said, shaking his head as he looked up from the report. "Check this out." He turned the report around for Julie to see.

The doctor who had performed Hanson's pre-enlistment physical on January 15, 1964 marked a prominent scar on the frontal body diagram, just below the collarbone and on his left side.

"Oh, my God," Julie gasped, as she read the scrawled handwriting. The physician had written that Hanson had sewn up the four-inch-long gash himself with nine crude stitches, but that it had healed well with no signs of infection. A small notation at the bottom of the page indicated that Hanson had told the physician that he had been injured in a farming mishap over the holidays.

"Holy shit," Whitman said. "Now I can't wait to see what's in that footlocker. This could get pretty darn interesting, eh? All right, back to my original question: when did you see Hanson's name?"

"After Shirley counted me out of the farmhouse, I found myself dressed in military gear, with a group of men in a tropical place—warm, palm trees, and all that."

"OK, and we know Hanson served in Vietnam, so again, that is consistent with the theory. What were you doing?"

"I was following the group of men. There was a person in charge telling us what to do," Julie said, becoming misty eyed. "I felt like—like we were doing something we knew was wrong. I watched as women and children got on their knees when they were told. We were in a village of some sort. And then ..." Julie choked back a sob.

"Hang on, hon, it's OK. If this is too hard, we don't have to go through it."

"No, it's OK," she said, regaining her composure.

"What did you see?" Whitman asked kindly.

"Men killing women and children," she said flatly. "Gunning down innocent people for no fucking reason," she said, beginning to become angered by the questions.

"And you saw the name 'Hanson' on your uniform in the original vision, right?"

"That's correct," she said.

"So then what happened?"

"Shirley counted me out of that situation. I guess I was getting pretty upset, like I did just now," she said, blushing slightly and wiping a rogue tear.

"It's OK," Whitman said reassuringly. "I'm just trying to figure out what this could all mean."

"Right, I know. So, the next vision. I was lying in some shallow water, bodies floating all over the place, red water, and I had a huge ache in my lower back and left hip," she said, pointing to her buttocks.

"And John Hanson was wounded in the lower back and buttocks," Whitman said.

"Really? I mean, I know he was the sole survivor of an attack, but I didn't know where he had been wounded."

"Yep, that general region," Whitman said, matter of fact. "So then what?"

"Shirley counted me out again, and I was back in Michigan—or at least that's what I thought."

"Why did you think that? Did you see a map in your head, or..."

"No, it was just something I sensed. You know, I've lived in Michigan my whole life—it just felt like home."

"Where were you?"

"I'm not sure where in Michigan, but coming out of some woods."

"Do you know what year it was?"

"No, not exactly. But by the looks of the car in my vision, it could have been in the 60s or so. I'm not really up on my cars, so I'm not sure."

"Do you think if you looked at some cars from that time period, you could recognize it?"

"Probably. Probably I could give you a ballpark idea, yeah. I know it was either white or a light color of some sort."

Whitman nodded. "Do you know what time of day you were coming out of the woods?"

"It was dark," Julie said, thinking back to her vivid regression. "I was cold and very dirty. And I know this is going to sound weird, but I don't believe I had a shirt on."

Whitman took a long pause. "I think we have enough to go on right now."

"What's wrong?" Julie asked. "Did I say something wrong?"

"No, of course not. I just think we've discussed enough today. It's all pretty remarkable, that's for sure. Let's see what happens with the footlocker and go from there."

"Sure," Julie said, gathering her materials. "Like I said, I'm going to meet with Shirley again on Friday, and may even do another regression with her if you think it will help."

"Hang on there," Whitman said. "Let's hold off on another regression until we can regroup. I want to take a look at a few more records I have at home and wait until my niece Joanne drops off the footlocker on Saturday."

"OK. Thanks again for taking the time to meet with me," Julie said, holding out her hand.

"Whoa. What the hell did you do to your hand?"

"I don't really know. It's something that's just came about this fall. The swelling comes and goes. The strange thing is, I have no idea what I must have done to it."

"Huh. Well, give me a call if you think of anything else. And I'll give you a buzz on Saturday night, after I have a chance to look over Hanson's footlocker."

66

S hirley opened the heavy oak front door. "Come in, come in. Did Mike and Sarah bring you?"

"They did," Julie said, stepping into the foyer and taking off her coat. "But they're going to do a little Christmas shopping at Ledge Craft Lane downtown, and then go out for dinner at the Chinese place they love so much."

"I see. So, we have a couple hours, yes?" she said as she took Julie's jacket and guided her to the parlor. "Can I get you a cup of tea?"

"No thanks. Wow! What a great Christmas tree!"

"Thank you. I collect ornaments from all over the world. They now serve to remind me of some pretty incredible journeys."

"I bet," Julie said, continuing to gaze.

"Speaking of incredible journeys, how's yours going?" Shirley took her regular seat in the parlor.

"Oh, you know," Julie said, shrugging her shoulders as she sank down into the recliner. "Same old, same old, I guess."

"Sarah called me and told me everything that happened with you and Mike's instructor! Isn't the universe grand?"

"I guess it all depends on how you look at it …I mean …I guess I just wish all this would go away. I have no idea what's going to happen, and even less idea of how my mom or grandparents will handle it."

"One thing you need to keep in mind is that you must take just one step at a time. You'll tell them when the time is right."

"Yeah, I hope you're right …Shirley, I know you said I would have a vivid dream after the regression, and I did dream, but I just can't remember much of it," Julie said.

"Let's start with what you can remember." Shirley leaned forward in her seat. "Did you write it down?"

"Yeah, it's here," Julie said, taking a piece of notebook paper out of her back pocket and unfolding it.

"Did you just have the one dream?"

Julie nodded. "The only one I remember, anyway. Pattie said I've been talking a lot in my sleep again—shouting, sometimes whimpering, I guess—I don't really know. It's all so embarrassing."

"You must stop being embarrassed about this," Shirley said sternly. "There is nothing you can do to control it. It's trying to come out. Let's begin with the dream you have there, and then we'll talk about what it might mean and what our game plan is going to be."

"OK. But it just doesn't make any sense."

"Oh dear," Shirley said, getting up from her chair. "Your hand is quite bad today. Your body is trying to give you a big clue here, Julie—that's why it swells up and hurts. Would you like some ice for it?"

"Nah. I guess I'm getting used to the pain. I hardly even notice it anymore. It hurts, but it's just becoming part of me."

Shirley sighed heavily and returned to her chair. "We're going to have to see about that. But let's move on with this for now."

"I just wrote down snippets that I remembered," Julie began. "I'm telling you, though, none of this is going to make any sense."

"Just read it, Julie, really. It's fine. I've heard it all, believe me."

"In my dream, I was driving down the highway by my grandmother's home in Mulliken," Julie said.

"Was it your mom's car, or a different car?"

"Actually, it was Ruby Beldoff's car."

Shirley looked confused. "Who?"

"Ruby Beldoff, this old bat who goes to my grandparents' church. She drives a red Buick, and I saw it when I went to church with my grandparents on Thanksgiving. See? I told you this was stupid."

"Nonsense," Shirley said, taking notes. "Do you know Ruby Beldoff?"

"No. Well, not really, I guess," Julie said, beginning to blush. "It's a long story, but I kicked her out of my grandparent's pew at church that day. She always encroaches on their space."

"OK, go on."

"So, I'm headed toward their house on M-43 with my old dog Mac when I see a storm developing, and just as I look across a field, I can see a huge tornado coming right at me. Mac died when I was nine. He always stayed at my grandparent's farm."

"Interesting. So, what did you do?"

"Well, there weren't any homes around—it was all farmland—so I pulled off under an overpass. And in reality, there are no overpasses on M-43."

"Then what?" Shirley asked.

"I was terrified of the tornado, but I got out of the car, and went outside of the overpass and laid on my stomach in the ditch. I was really worried about Mac, but left him in the car, thinking he'd be safer there, I guess. I don't know why I didn't stay in the car, too, if I thought it was safe enough for Mac."

"All right. So were there other cars there?"

"No, just mine. Debris was flying through the air—tree limbs, straw, dust and dirt, all sorts of stuff. I just hunkered down and laid on my stomach there in the mud. The rain and wind were so strong that it lifted my car and swept it away with Mac." Tears were running down Julie's cheeks unnoticed. "I felt hopeless in the dream when Mac was gone. I didn't give a shit about the car, just Mac."

"Of course."

"When the tornado was gone, I stood up, and oddly it felt like it was early morning. The sky had that pinkish glow, and it was peaceful, even though the tornado had torn everything up," she said. "Then I woke up."

"Hmmm." Shirley got up to pour more tea. "Tornado dreams are indeed interesting. Have you ever experienced a tornado before?"

"A couple times, but we always rode it out in my grandma's cellar," Julie said. "Grandma and Oscar had a tree fall on their car in the driveway once, but we never lost the barn or anything like that."

Shirley placed her teacup on the table and sat down again. "Even though you think this dream makes no sense, I think it makes perfect sense."

"Really?" Julie said. "How so?"

"You were driving down the same highway where John Hanson lost his life. And you weren't in your own car. You were in somebody else's car. Somebody you knew, but didn't particularly like."

Julie nodded.

"Let's see if I can explain this. I would interpret the part about you driving another person's car as John Hanson's way of saying that he may be in familiar territory—on M-43, a road both of you know—but he's in a different 'vehicle,'" she said in air quotes. "He was in you."

"The fact that your old dog Mac is in the car with you tells me that you're longing for the past or some sort of security. Presumably as a little girl, Mac made you feel secure. Am I right?"

Julie reached for a tissue as she noticed the tears trickling down her cheek. "I loved that dog. He was my best friend. Followed me everywhere, and kept me safe."

Shirley nodded compassionately. "So you pulled up under a shelter, left your dog in the car, and then went outside of the shelter and laid down in a ditch as a violent tornado approached. This is really just telling us what we already know to be true."

"How?" Julie said, wiping her nose.

"It's all about your ongoing inner struggle. You parked under a structure that you felt was safe—safe enough to leave your most prized possession there. Then you proceeded to leave Mac alone in the car, and take your chances in an open ditch, with flying debris, wind, rain, and God knows what else. Your security was swept away, and you felt vulnerable and alone, yet still on a familiar road."

"I guess I didn't think about it that way."

"But the end of your dream tells it all." Shirley walked over to where Julie sat and took her hand. "You said that after the storm, it felt like it was morning, right?"

Tears streamed down Julie's cheeks as she nodded. "You know deep down in your soul that there may be some stormy weather ahead, but in the end, it will be a new day. You'll have hope again."

Julie began to sob and buried her face in Shirley's shoulder.

"You've been without hope long enough," Shirley said. "The part of you who was John Hanson and who caused so much of the hopelessness is trying to make things right. Listen to him. Let him show you the way."

67

Joanne Whitman's 1984 VW Golf roared into her uncle's drive-way just before three o'clock Saturday afternoon. Alan Whitman walked out to her car as she popped the hatchback open.

"Look who's here! When did you get this little buggy?" he said, gesturing to her small blue car.

"I bought it from a guy up in Houghton. It runs pretty good, but either I'm tired from the nine-hour trip or there's a problem with the exhaust system. I've been fighting to stay awake the whole time."

"So either way you're exhausted, huh?" Whitman said with a wink. "And you got the trunk, I see."

"Yeah. Those people up there were a little on the strange side."

"Really?" Whitman said, grabbing a handle of the footlocker and sliding it outward.

"Here, let me help." Joanne grabbed the other end. "Yeah, a little backwoodsy out that way for me," she said, laughing. "What's in here, anyway? It's kind of heavy."

"I don't really know," Whitman said as they walked up the sidewalk toward the house. "But we're going to find out. Can you stay for a cup of coffee?"

"No. I'd love to, but I have to get going. It's another hour or so to Jackson, so I better hit it. My parents can't wait to see me. I stayed at school through Thanksgiving, so it's been a while."

"Oh well. Thanks so much for picking this up for me. Tell your dad I'll be giving him a call in the next week or so, will ya?"

"Will do," Joanne said, giving him one last hug. "Have a great Christmas if I don't see you."

"Merry Christmas to all of you, too. Drive safe."

Whitman watched the blue fog emerge from the tailpipe of his niece's car as she sped off. It seemed like yesterday when he would give his little niece rides in his State Police-issued squad car.

Closing the front door, Whitman turned his attention to the footlocker. Dragging it out of the living room, he hoisted it up onto the kitchen table for a better look.

Whitman examined the exterior of the footlocker and took notes.

"J. Hanson – U.S. Marines" was written across the top of it, followed by his seven-digit service number. With Hanson being a relatively common last name, Whitman then compared the service numbers on the footlocker and in the military records to verify that it was the same man. They matched.

A large gold-colored clasp, centered at the front of the foot-locker and secured by a tarnished padlock, was flanked by two un-locked hinges. After examining the old padlock, Whitman fetched a pair of bolt cutters. Positioning the jaws of the bolt cutter on one side of the lock, he clenched down hard on the handles. The sharp blades of the hand tool sent the heavy lock tumbling onto the table. Setting the bolt cutters aside, Whitman unclasped the hinges and opened the box.

The musty smell of over thirty years filled the kitchen nook as Whitman put on a pair of latex gloves and began to rummage through the contents of the upper compartment tray.

Contained in the left portion of the tray were what seemed to be all of John Hanson's military mementoes: his dog tags, a pistol holster, a crude wooden box containing several military medals and bars, a tarnished Marines lighter, and a yellowing envelope containing black and white pictures of a few war buddies.

On the right side of the tray were his military personal effects: an old tin of shoe polish and a rag, a bristle brush, some old shoe-strings, a U.S. Marine-issued belt buckle, a small canteen, and a stash of Vietnamese coins.

Whitman reached for his digital camera and photographed its contents. Next, he recorded everything in his notepad. Then, grabbing the center compartment divider, he carefully lifted out the tray and set it aside.

Military t-shirts, pants, and jungle shirts were neatly folded and stacked in the bottom of the trunk. Whitman snapped a picture before removing the apparel piece by piece from the footlocker. He lost his breath as he discovered what remaining items lay in the bottom of John Hanson's foot locker. While there were several items in the box, what grabbed his attention was an old arm prosthesis and bloodied strap.

"I'll be damned," he said, carefully removing the device with his gloved hand. Dried blood could be seen on the curved two-prong hook. As he examined the dirty shoulder strap and the flesh-colored sleeve in which the stub of an arm would go, he saw that the entire device was spattered with blood.

"Good God. Julie is telling me the truth," he muttered. "There's no way in hell she could have known this."

Whitman went to the fridge and retrieved a beer, cracked it open, and let his mind work through the details.

After a long gulp, he set the can down on the table and continued looking in the footlocker. Carefully, he extracted what looked to be a small Oriental jewelry box. Ornately detailed, the delicate box was made of wood and covered with leather. It had copper handles, a hand-painted dragon on the front, and two drawers.

Whitman opened the top drawer and found a small piece of paper folded in half, along with a small topaz ring. On the paper was written a single word: "danhtu." Whitman snapped a picture of the drawer and its contents.

The bottom drawer contained a single pair of Lennon-style sunglasses. Whitman examined the glasses a bit closer, noticing well-buffed scratches on the pale green lenses before snapping a picture. Whitman pushed the bottom drawer back into the box and set it aside.

A canvas zippered bag remained at the bottom of the trunk. Whitman photographed it before picking it up. He unzipped the bag with care.

"Hmmm," Whitman said aloud as he took out a case containing a cassette tape, and a women's gold Omega watch, perhaps dating to 1960. Whitman set the watch aside and turned his attention to the tape. Aside from looking dated, the tape appeared to be in excellent condition.

"JCH talks – August 18, 1972" was scrawled in messy handwriting across side A of the tape.

68

"Thank God you were a pack rat, my love," Whitman said, pulling open the lower drawer of the nightstand on what was once his wife's side of the bed. It had been several years since Grace Whitman died of breast cancer. Whitman had never quite been able to go through her things.

The vintage '70s Panasonic tape recorder worked as well as it did the day Grace bought it. Whitman brought it into the kitchen and plugged it in near the kitchen table.

Settling in at the end of the table with his notepad, pen, and half-drunk beer, Whitman wrote "JCH Talks – 8/18/72" at the top of the page, placed the tape into the old tape recorder, and pressed play.

Whitman strained as he listened to what initially sounded like the tape recorder being set down and slid across a table or floor. Footsteps going away from the recorder could be heard, followed by the squeak of a door opening.

"C'mon in," a man's voice could be heard in the background. "Can I get you a beer or somethin'?"

A second man's voice said, "Sure. But I've been nippin' on my flask here."

"Oh. Whatcha drinkin' there?" said the first voice.

From the accents, Whitman knew both men were from

Michigan's Upper Peninsula, with the first man's accent quite a bit more noticeable than the second.

"JD. You know, my usual."

The tape whirled for several seconds as neither of the men spoke.

"Have a seat, have a seat," the first man said.

Whitman heard the second man sitting down close to the tape recorder.

"So, what have you been up to, John?" spoke the first man. Whitman could now identify the second voice as belonging to John Hanson.

"Not a whole lot," John said. "I'm headed down state to work next week."

Whitman pressed the pause button and got up to retrieve his case file on Beverly Deerfield. Among the documents was an old 1972 calendar. Whitman flipped to August and saw that August 18 was a Friday exactly one week before he turned up in Mulliken. Whitman began the tape again.

"Whatcha doing down there?" the first man asked.

"I gotta line on a job down there at Motor Wheel in Lansing," John said. "Workin' on the line. And I gotta little unfinished business to tend to."

"That's gotta be some good money."

Whitman listened as one of the men lit a cigarette.

"You leaving for the reason I think you're leaving?" said the first man.

"What? Because of what happened with Denise?" John replied arrogantly. "Shit, Jake. Nobody don't know nothing about what happened to Denise—anymore than the other two. Nobody except you, and I know you're not telling, right?"

"Right," Jake said loudly. "No way."

Whitman pressed pause and wrote down "Jake Redmond: first voice" on his page. "So, Jake must be taping all of what John is saying," he said aloud. Whitman then recorded Denise's name, followed by the notation "two others?"

Continuing on, Whitman began the tape again.

"That Denise bitch got what she deserved," John said. "And if you rat on me about all this, your ass is going to prison just as fast as mine is."

"I'm just worried they're gonna find her out there," Jake said from across the room.

"She was a fuckin' cunt," John said coldly. "Forget about it."

Whitman could hear another beer being opened.

"There's no way anybody will ever find her or the other two out there. I sunk the bitch to the bottom of that swamp, so the critters out there can clean up after me," John said with a laugh. "Just like they always do."

From the sound of John's voice, Whitman could tell he was wasted.

"How'd you ever meet her?" Jake asked.

"She knew Beth. Beth bought a pair of sunglasses at her daddy's store there in Newberry. God, she loved those fuckin' glasses. Hey—before I go, I have my old footlocker in the trunk of my car. Can I stow it here?"

Jake apparently agreed to take it, because the two went outside to carry it in the house together.

A few moments later, voices began again. "Seriously, Jake— don't let anybody near this. It's all my stuff. You're the only one who knows this about me, and we're brothers," John was slightly slurring. "You're the only one I trust."

Whitman could hear the heavy trunk being set down on the floor.

"Just keep it for me. I can't take it all downstate with me. I'm not even sure where I'm staying yet. I'll get it back from you when I come back up here."

Whitman listened as Jake reluctantly agreed, and John left the house. The tape kept whirling like Whitman's mind as he thought about the magnitude of this evidence. Suddenly the quest to solve one murder, maybe two, had multiplied into three, maybe four.

Whitman pressed stop on the tape recorder, then rewound the tape. As he picked up its plastic cover, a small note slid out from behind the cardboard backing. In the same handwriting that appeared on the tape, Whitman finally knew for sure that Jake Redmond was responsible for the recording.

Sept. 5, 1972

To whom it may concern:

I was planning on blackmailing John Hanson with this tape, but when he died last month, I decided to put it with his things. What he done to those girls wasn't right, and it ain't right that I kept his secret and played a part in the murder of Denise Daniels. If I came clean now, I'd go to prison for it. I'll pay for what I done when I meet my maker one day. Maybe somebody can make things right for the families of these girls, because I can't.

Jake Redmond

69

"Hello?"

"Julie, hi, this is Al Whitman. Am I catching you at a bad time?"

"No, of course not," Julie said, shutting her bedroom door. "Did you get the footlocker?"

"Sure did. And to be honest with you, it's gotten me really shaken up."

"Really?"

"Yeah. And having been a detective for all those years, I'm surprised that it's had this effect. But yeah, it's all pretty disturbing."

"What did you find?"

"Violet Swansen's artificial arm for one thing."

"No shit?" The color began draining from Julie's face.

"No shit," Whitman repeated. "There's a lot more in here, too. I'm not quite sure what we should do with it. I probably need to turn it over to the authorities in Newberry."

"For the arm? Just because the arm was in there?"

"No, not just that. Actually, it's a long story. You and I need to talk. Is there any way you can come out to my place in Okemos?"

"Damn, I'm home for the entire break," Julie said. "I don't have a car, and my mom would really think something was wrong if I asked to go back to the dorm."

"OK … OK," Whitman thought out loud. "Today is

Saturday …what if I come out to Potterville and pick you up tomorrow morning?"

"Yes, I can do that. My mom works at seven, and she's pulling a double shift, so she won't get off until nine or so."

"Perfect. I'll come by at ten and we'll drive out to Mulliken. We can talk in the car."

"Mulliken?" Julie gasped.

"Yeah. I'll explain everything in the car. It's way too much to go into over the phone."

"OK. We live in the West Cherry Street Apartments, near the railroad tracks."

"Yeah, I know exactly where that is. I'll see you tomorrow at ten."

With that, Whitman hung up and left Julie with a head full of questions, especially why Mulliken?

70

Julie woke up early the next morning when she heard the front door to their apartment close as her mother left for work. Pulling back the dusty curtain from her window, Julie watched her mother operate the windshield wipers to remove a light coating of snow on the windshield of her car. Julie nestled back into bed and drifted off to sleep, thinking about why Whitman wanted to drive to Mulliken.

By nine-thirty, Julie was showered, dressed, and halfway through a bowl of Cheerios when she heard the buzzer ring. Walking to the living room window, Julie peered down and saw Whitman standing on the front stoop of the apartment complex, briefcase in hand. She buzzed him in and opened the apartment door as he climbed the stairs.

"Sorry I'm early," a winded Whitman said as he reached the landing. "I couldn't sleep. Hope you don't mind."

"No, not at all. C'mon in. I'm just finishing a bowl of cereal. You want a cup of coffee?" she asked, heading to the small kitchen.

"That would be great," he said, taking off his jacket and following her to the kitchen table with his briefcase. "I brought all my notes and my file on your aunt's case."

"So, what's going on?"

"Oh, Julie ... it's really quite a story." He took the cassette tape and his wife's tape recorder out of his briefcase. "Do you have a place to plug this in?"

"Yeah, there's an outlet right here," she said, pulling the table from the wall. "Man, I haven't seen one of these since I was a kid at Grandma's house," she said, flashing a gorgeous smile and setting a cup of coffee down in front of Whitman. "What's on the tape?" she asked, taking her seat at the table.

Whitman paused and took a sip of his steaming coffee. "This, my dear, is a tape of John Hanson and Jake Redmond talking about the murders John Hanson committed."

Julie's mouth fell open and her hands began to shake. "Oh, my God."

Whitman touched her hand. "Are you up for this? Because I think we might actually have a chance to solve your aunt's murder once and for all. I was thinking the sound of John's voice might jog a memory or maybe you'll catch something I missed."

Tears rolled down Julie's cheeks. "Can you handle this?" he asked again, gently. A solid lump in Julie's throat prevented her from speaking, but she nodded in agreement.

Whitman turned to pop the tape into the player and pressed play. "It's just remarkable."

Like Whitman, Julie listened intently, trying to interpret the sounds. Referring to his notes, Whitman commentated as the tape played.

"I think this is Redmond setting the tape recorder down somewhere," he said. "He didn't want John to know it was there."

Julie heard the first voice. "C'mon in. Can I get you a beer or somethin'?"

"That's Jake Redmond, letting John Hanson into his house," Whitman said.

Julie's face turned white as she heard John's voice for the first time. "Sure," he said. "But I've been nippin' on my flask here."

Whitman pressed pause and locked eyes with Julie. "My God," Julie said. "It's him—me. This is so fucking weird."

"I know," Whitman assured her. "Just bear with it." He continued the tape.

"Oh. Whatcha drinkin' there?" Jake asked.

"JD. You know," John answered.

"My usual," Julie said in unison with John's voice on the tape.

"Pause it," Julie said abruptly. "I love Jack Daniels," she said. "I never knew I did until I went to MSU and tried it, but I immediately loved the taste of it," she said. "It makes me into a monster, though."

"Julie, I know how hard this must be for you. Do you still think you can continue?"

Julie nodded.

After a long pause, the men began speaking again.

"Have a seat, have a seat. So, what have you been up to, John?"

"Not a whole lot," John said. "I'm headed down state to work next week."

Whitman paused the tape. "I forgot to mention that this tape was made on August 18, 1972, a week before your aunt went missing."

Julie's mood had changed to one of rigidity and angst as she contemplated her indirect involvement with her aunt's death. Whitman began the tape again.

"Whatcha doing down there?" Jake asked.

"I gotta line on a job down there at Motor Wheel in Lansing. Workin' on the line. And I gotta little unfinished business to tend to."

"That's gotta be some good money." A pause. "You leaving for the reason I think you're leaving?"

"What? Because of what happened with Denise? Shit, Jake. Nobody don't know nothing about what happened to Denise—anymore than the other two. Nobody except you, and I know you're not telling, right?"

"Right. No way."

Whitman pressed pause again and looked at Julie, who appeared as though she was in a trance. "Daniel," Julie said, and then turned to Whitman. "Why did the name Daniel just pop into my head?"

Whitman looked stunned as he realized Julie had recalled the last name of the victim almost exactly. "It doesn't matter," Whitman said, jotting down a note. "Just go with what pops into your mind. Are you still OK?"

Julie nodded and wiped her nose with a napkin. Whitman continued the tape.

"That Denise bitch got what she deserved. And if you rat on me about all this, your ass is going to prison just as fast as mine is."

"I'm just worried they're gonna find her out there."

"She was a fuckin' cunt. Forget about it."

"Pause the tape!" Julie blurted. "He helped—Jake helped. In a cloth bag of some sort, with rocks."

Whitman scrawled notes furiously onto his notepad.

"Lots of rocks," Julie added. "She was a big girl, and it was too heavy..."

Whitman stopped writing and stared at the innocent young face of a woman he could hardly recognize anymore. "Maybe we've done enough," he said patting her hand.

"No!" Julie shouted. "Start the tape!"

Julie's sudden burst of anger startled Whitman and caused him to sit back in his chair. Reluctantly, Whitman began the tape again.

"There's no way anybody will ever find her or the other two

out there. I sunk the bitch to the bottom of that swamp, so the critters out there can clean up after me." Laughter. "Just like they always do."

"How'd you ever meet her?"

"She knew Beth. Beth bought a pair of sunglasses at her daddy's store there in Newberry. God, she loved those fuckin' glasses."

Without looking at Whitman, Julie pressed pause and said. "Dubois. The name 'Dubois' just popped into my mind for whatever reason."

Whitman didn't question Julie, but just made a note of it. He felt a different energy coming from the young woman whom he knew as Julie. Julie continued the tape.

"Hey—before I go, I have my old footlocker in the trunk of my car. Can I stow it here?" A long pause. "Seriously, Jake—don't let anybody near this. It's all my stuff. You're the only one who knows this about me, and we're brothers. You're the only one I trust."

Whitman turned off the tape. "Jake kept the footlocker for him," he told Julie. "When John died a week later, Jake put this tape into the trunk along with this note," he said, showing Julie the handwritten note from Jake.

"Fuckin' son of a bitch," she said after reading it. "I trusted him."

"What?" Whitman said.

Julie snapped back into reality. "What did I say?"

"You called Jake an f-ing SOB and said that you trusted him," Whitman said, writing all of her comments down.

"Am I going to get in trouble?" she said, tearing up again. "I mean, if I was—if I *am* John Hanson, could I go to jail for all of this?"

"Honey, you didn't do anything—John Hanson did."

"I know, but …but clearly I was John Hanson!"

"It's complicated for sure, but now you—Julie Deerfield—have the opportunity to do something extraordinary for your family, for your aunt, and for all those other folks who loved her," he said. "You can bring her home."

Julie rewound the tape, put it back into the plastic case with the note, and handed it to Whitman.

"I have an idea, and I don't want you to think I'm crazy," Julie said.

"No, anything. What?"

"My friend Sarah's aunt is a psychic. She used to help the police departments out in California find bodies," she said, with her eyes darting away from Whitman's.

"Yeah—Mike told me about her," Whitman said. "I'm familiar with the technique. I worked with a few psychics in my day."

"Really?" Julie said looking back into his kind face. "Well, she just lives in Grand Ledge. It's right on the way to Mulliken."

Whitman smiled. "I think I know where you're going with this."

"Well, what if I called her to see if she could take a drive out there with us this morning?" she asked.

"It's fine with me—might be worth a shot."

"I'll call her on the way," Julie said. "Let's go to Mulliken."

71

It was after eleven by the time Whitman and Julie stood on Shirley's doorstep in Grand Ledge.

"Good morning," Shirley said at the door, fully dressed for cold weather, boots and all. "I'm bringing along my notes from your regression, Julie," she said, locking the door behind her.

"This is Detective Alan Whitman— he was the detective on my aunt's case back in '72," Julie said. "Alan, this is Shirley Taylor—she's an aunt of a friend and helped regress me a while back."

"It's a pleasure to know you," Shirley said, turning to shake his hand. "It's remarkable how the universe works—truly remarkable."

"That it is," Whitman said as they all walked back to his car. "This whole thing with Julie has been extraordinary," he said. "I've never seen anything like it before."

"Sometimes the universe works in mysterious ways, but it always wins out in the end," Shirley said. "I'm happy you think enough of me to call and allow me to help, Julie."

"I do," Julie said earnestly. "And I really appreciate the assistance." Julie opened the back door and got in. "You can ride up front with Detective Whitman."

Whitman started the car and backed out of the narrow driveway. "I spent all of last night reviewing Julie's aunt's case," he said. "I went back through everything: the interviews with the Prestons, with the grandparents, even with Julie's mom. It brought back a lot of memories, some of them even good ones."

"Now, why are we going to Mulliken?" Shirley asked.

"It's a very long story," Whitman began. "But in a nutshell, Julie has led us to a whole chest full of evidence linking John Hanson to several murders that occurred in the Upper Peninsula in the 1960s."

"I see," Shirley said.

"And in doing so, we think we figured out what John Hanson's mode of body disposal was. Julie had a breakthrough this morning, and we think—Julie thinks—if she goes out there, she might be able to tell us more."

"Good for you," Shirley said, looking into the backseat at Julie. "Listen to your inner voice, listen to your gut. That's the way it's done."

Julie nodded and stared out the window.

"I also reviewed the map last night," Whitman said. "It basically shows where we looked for her, where we found John's car, that kind of thing."

"The property could have changed a lot over the years," Shirley said. "Houses could have been built, and so on."

"True, but I don't think that's the case here," Whitman said. "Shimnecon is on state land, and it's the site of an old Indian burial ground."

Shirley's eyes widened with interest.

"Even old Chief Okemos himself is buried out there somewhere along the banks of the Grand River," he said. "It was very swampy in 1972, but that might have changed over the years. That's just how ecosystems generally work."

Whitman slowed the car and pulled over. "See that old tree over there?" he said, pointing to the other side of the road. "That's the tree that took John's life."

"You mean it's the tree that the deer ran in front of," Julie said without expression.

"Was it a fiery crash?" Shirley asked, paging through Julie's regression notes.

Whitman nodded. "It was."

"I sense that," she said. "Julie, do you remember the last part of your regression?"

Julie thought back to the session. "Yes, I do. And it makes sense now, doesn't it?"

Shirley smiled. "Yes, it does. You said your legs were burning just before I counted you back."

"I remember. It makes perfect sense now."

Breaking several minutes of silence, Julie spoke up. "Something is different," she confessed. "That tape—it shifted something inside of me. It's like I have a direct line to John now."

Whitman glanced into the rearview mirror. "What do you mean?"

"I don't know," Julie said. "There's just something differ-ent ...before, I couldn't access any of it, but right now it's all here," she said, and then blushed. "I don't know what I'm talking about. Just ignore me."

"No, no, no," Whitman said. "You don't have to prove anything to me, Julie. I know you're on the up and up. I think we both agree that this is really out of the ordinary for both of us."

"What tape?" Shirley asked.

"Remember how I said Julie helped lead us to some evidence that connected John with several murders in the U.P.?" Shirley nodded. "Well, in that evidence was a cassette tape in which John Hanson discussed the murders with his best friend," Whitman said.

Shirley remained silent and stared at Whitman.

"It was John Hanson talking to Jake Redmond, a man he

trusted and who helped him dispose of at least one woman he killed. Redmond made the tape because he intended to blackmail Hanson after he returned from downstate."

"I see," Shirley said. "Have you shared this with any of the authorities yet?"

"Not yet. But based on how he got rid of those bodies, Julie and I think there's an excellent chance that he did the same thing with her Aunt Bev."

"Julie, dear," Shirley said, turning around and looking into her young face. "You need to listen to your inner voice now more than ever. I was wondering how you were suddenly able to tap into that energy, but now I understand. You're right—you do have a direct line to John right now," she said. "Take advantage of it—trust your intuition with this, and I'll do all that I can with mine."

Julie nodded.

"So, let's just go with it, huh?" Whitman said, smiling. "What do we have to lose?

"Exactly," Shirley said. "That's the spirit."

"This is where you turn," Julie said without thinking.

"Has your grandma taken you back here before?" Whitman asked, turning north onto the long, straight road.

"No, never. I've just heard my mom talk about it."

"It 'Ts' up here at this gravel road," Whitman said as he brought the car to a halt. "It's all state land from here. Which way do we go?"

"Turn left," Julie said. The three rode in silence until Julie spoke up again.

"It's here, isn't it?" she said pointing to a gravel parking lot. "I remember the parking lot."

Whitman pulled in and put the car in park. Grabbing his brief-case, Whitman popped it open and took out his notepad and pen.

Shirley leaned back in the passenger seat and breathed deeply. "She's here," she said quietly. "She's definitely here."

"I know that to be true, too," Julie said from the backseat, her eyes closed. "I'm seeing flashes of a white car in my head."

Shirley shuffled through her notes. "You mentioned that car in your regression, too."

Whitman referred to his records as well. "Hanson drove a 1968 Dodge Dart, white."

"I'm feeling conflict, like there was a fight or a struggle right here," Shirley said.

Several minutes passed before Julie would speak again. "My hand is hurting. My right hand."

Both Whitman and Shirley looked at Julie's hand, which had become quite swollen and red. "Jesus." Whitman returned to his old file on John Hanson and realized that the autopsy had revealed a slight fracture to John's right hand, assumed to have happened in the car accident.

"She's in the woods," Julie said. "She rests in the swamp back there."

"The swamp is huge, Julie," Whitman said. "At least it was thirty-five years ago. Shall we take a walk back there?"

"It's not far from here," Julie said, opening her eyes. "I can feel it."

Whitman looked at Shirley, who nodded and began putting on her gloves. "Let's go find her, shall we?" she said.

The cold December breeze blew as the trio exited Whitman's car. Julie led the way into the woods as Whitman assisted Shirley behind her. It was nearly 300 yards into the woods before Julie stopped in a thorny patch of brush.

"I don't know why I stopped here." Julie looked at Shirley with tears streaming down her face.

"You stopped because you know," Shirley said. "You know this is where she died. But she's back further."

Whitman took an orange plastic tie strip from his pocket and tied it off on a nearby tree.

"Can we go back further?" Julie asked as the winter wind and snow flurries whirled around them.

"Might as well— we've come this far," Whitman said. "It's easier to walk in the winter, when everything is frozen. This was pretty swampy back in the day. It's not so bad now."

Julie began negotiating thorny thickets, swales, and rugged terrain that would challenge even the best of outdoorsmen, before finally coming to the edge of a vast wetland.

"This is where she is."

"Yes," Shirley confirmed breathlessly. "Indeed she is here," she said, moving 30 yards further into the swamp.

"This used to all be water here," Whitman said. "All slimy green water, starting from way back there," he said, gesturing to the direction from which they came.

"All I know is it's this swamp," Julie said. "She's here."

"I'm going to tie another wrap right here, but we're going to have to go back and figure this out," Whitman said. "I'd like to compare the old map with a current map of what's here today."

"She's right here. I know it, too," Shirley repeated. "You won't need a map—you'll need a shovel."

72

Having dropped Shirley off in Grand Ledge, it was three-thirty by the time Whitman pulled up at Julie's apartment complex. Shawn was emerging from her own car.

"Oh no," Julie moaned. "What's she doing home so early?"

"It's too late," Whitman said. "She's already spotted us, and you're going to have to come clean with what's going on anyway. You might as well get it over with." Julie's panic-stricken eyes locked on Whitman's.

"Honey, if we find your Aunt Bev out there—and at this point, I think we probably will—they're going to find out about it anyway."

As Shawn curiously made her way toward Whitman's car, Julie struggled to come up with a plausible explanation. Julie climbed out of the car and slammed the door. "Hi Mom."

"Hi," Shawn said in a confused tone. "Where have you been? And who is this?"

"This is Detective Alan Whitman," Julie said reluctantly.

"Do I know you?" Shawn shook his hand.

"You do—or you did, I should say," Whitman stammered. "I was the detective on your sister's case in 1972."

"Well I'll be damned," Shawn said smiling "That's right. I remember you now. But how do you know Julie?"

"It's a long story, Mom. Why don't we go inside?"

Looking thoroughly confused, Shawn nodded her head in agreement. "Yeah, of course. It's freezing out here."

"Why are you home early?" Julie asked, attempting to change the subject.

"My coworker, Carrie, wanted the extra hours, and I'm tired. It was a win-win. C'mon up—it's probably a mess, but…" Shawn said as she unlocked the apartment door. "So how do you guys know each other?" she asked again.

"I teach a criminal justice class at MSU. I met Julie through a student of mine, Mike Griffin."

"He's my friend Sarah's boyfriend," Julie said.

"OK, but that still doesn't explain how you know each other," Shawn said, becoming fed up with their stall tactics.

"Sit down, Mom," Julie said, gesturing to the kitchen table and going to the fridge. "I think we're all going to need a beer when we talk about this one."

73

Two hours later, Shawn's head was reeling with Julie and Whitman's news.

"I wondered why you had been acting so weird about school this fall, but I still don't know if I buy into the whole reincarnation thing."

"And I don't blame you," Whitman said. "I didn't either, until Julie and I met that day at the coffee shop. Since then, everything she's told me has been consistent with the evidence that we've managed to find."

With the pangs from the past creeping back into the pit of her stomach, Shawn felt emotional. "But if it is true, that you're a re-incarnation of the guy who killed my sister, well, let's just say that would be a lot for me, Ma or Oscar to swallow."

"You don't think it's a lot for me to swallow?" Julie said standing up from her seat at the table. "You think all this shit I've gone through for the last six months or so has been fun?"

"Of course not. I'm just saying …it's all pretty fucking weird." Shawn reached for her pack of cigarettes.

"Ladies, ladies, let's take it down a notch here," Whitman responded. "There's no reason to get upset. The good news is that Julie is using this, this whatever it is, to try and make things right."

Julie sniffed and wiped her nose with a napkin.

"Maybe what you guys need to do is forget about the

reincarnation thing and concentrate on the good that can come out of this," Whitman suggested. "Wouldn't it benefit everyone if Julie ultimately brought Bev home, after thirty-five years?"

Shawn stifled her sobs in a dishtowel.

"It would bring a lot of peace to a lot of people—including Bev," Whitman said.

"So what's the plan?" Shawn said, wiping her eyes with the towel and reaching for her cigarette in the ashtray.

"Well, I've marked the spots that Julie and Shirley identified earlier today. Now I need to get in contact with the sheriff in Eaton County and get somebody to reopen the case, so I can go digging out there."

"That will take way too long!" Julie said. "We need closure on this now."

"I know you're anxious, Julie," Whitman said diplomatically. "But there's a right way of doing this. We can't just go out there and start messing with a crime scene."

"You and I both know it's going to take months to convince anybody that my story holds water," Julie countered. "You heard Shirley and me both say it! She's there, and she's not very deep. Shirley was right—we'll just need a shovel."

Shawn began to cry again. "Oh, God. I can only imagine what this is going to do to Ma. It's taken so long for her to get over Bev."

"She's *not* over Bev, for Christ's sake," Julie barked. "She never has been. Don't you know that?"

Julie's harsh words resonated for a minute before she spoke again. "I'm calling Junior to help me, and I'm finding Aunt Bev tomorrow—that's all there is to it."

"Julie, you can't be tampering with evidence!" Whitman said. "You simply cannot do that."

"What evidence? We haven't found a fucking thing out there,

Alan, *nothing*. I'm acting on a hunch, nothing more. How can I tamper with something that I haven't found?"

Whitman watched, silent, as Julie called Junior and set up a time to meet.

"I'll fill you in when I get there, Junior. Just meet me there at 10."

"This is wrong," Whitman said, as Julie clicked her phone shut.

"I'm tired of this whole thing," Julie declared. "John's not in control anymore—I am. And if either one of you wants to help Junior and me find her tomorrow, you're welcome to come," she said, leaving the kitchen and going to her bedroom.

"I'm sorry," Shawn said to Whitman. "She's just about had all she can take."

"Nah, it's nothing. She's had a rough time of it. She has every right to be mad." Whitman grabbed his jacket off the back of a kitchen chair and put it on. "Be ready at nine-fifteen tomorrow," he said heading for the door. "And I *will* bring a shovel."

74

If there was one positive thing that could be said about Chuck Preston Jr., it was that he was a reliable guy who operated on a need-to-know basis.

As promised, a bundled-up Junior was sitting in his car as Whitman pulled in to the gravely hunters' parking lot with Julie and Shawn.

With a skiff of snow on the ground, the early morning sunshine gleamed on the leafless branches of the trees.

"Junior, thanks so much for coming," Julie said, giving him a hug. "You remember my mom, Shawn."

"'Course I do," Junior said, shaking her hand. "It's great to see you."

Shovel in hand, Whitman slammed the trunk of his car and walked toward Junior.

"Al Whitman," he said, holding out his hand.

"Hey, I remember you! You're the policeman from…"

"From Bev Deerfield's case—yes, I am," Whitman said, finishing Junior's sentence.

"Why are we here?" Junior asked. "I'm sure it's a long story, so just the short version, if that's OK."

"We're here because I think I know where Aunt Bev is," Julie said. "You remember how freaked out I was that night at the Sportsman, right?"

Shawn raised her eyebrows and looked disapprovingly at her daughter.

"Hold on, Mom. I'll explain all that later. But you remember, right Junior?"

"Sure"

"Well, some stuff has happened since that time, and Detective Whitman and me—well, we've just put our heads together, and we think we know where to find Bev."

"It's been long enough," Junior said simply. "Lead the way."

Julie led the group back to the second marked spot in the woods and took time to tune in. After several minutes of silence, Julie said, "When we find rocks, we find Aunt Bev."

Walking several yards ahead, Julie began scuffing away the layers of leaves with her feet. Soon, the rest of the members of the group spread out and began to follow suit.

"We may find nothing," Whitman said. "I don't want anybody to be depressed when we don't find her."

"Always the optimist, eh, Alan?" Julie joked as she continued pawing at the ground.

After nearly an hour of scraping, Junior spoke up. "There are some rocks over here. Quite a few of 'em."

Whitman walked over to where Junior was working and used his shovel to begin removing the first large rock, about the size of a basketball. Whitman dug below it before he could finally roll it out. "There's another one right under it," he said.

Whitman used the shovel's blade to chisel away at the frozen earth around it. "It's not totally frozen, but it's not easy by any means," he said, handing the shovel to Junior. A considerably younger man, and of a husky and muscular build, Junior made relatively short work of the second boulder before finding another in the same general area.

"Do I just keep digging these out?"

"I think you need to go just a little deeper," Julie said. "She's here—I really think she's here." Three shovels of dirt later, the group spotted remnants of fabric.

"What the hell's that?" Junior said, squatting down and pulling at the cloth. Whitman snapped on a pair of latex gloves and fell to his knees. Using a small digging trowel, he managed to remove a two-inch strip of the material.

"It's in pretty sad shape, but it looks like a piece of cloth. May have been an article of clothing. Your Aunt Bev was wearing some blue jean shorts and some sort of a women's short-sleeved shirt—white, I think, if I'm remembering the report right," Whitman said. "Keep digging around that third rock."

Junior worked on it for a few minutes before rolling it outward. Below the third rock, the group got their first glimpse of Bev.

"Oh God," Julie said, backing away. "It looks like a skull."

"Be very careful around that," Whitman told Junior, as he continued to dig deeper. "Those are definitely human remains."

"There seems to be some more clothing here," Junior reported.

Whitman reached into the deeper portion of the hole and carefully removed a pair of blue jean shorts, delicate and tattered, but still intact. As Whitman brought them to the surface, a dirty and tattered driver's license fell from the pocket.

"It's Beverly," Shawn cried. "It's my big sister!"

Whitman sealed the shorts and driver's license in an evidence bag and instructed the group to back away from the hole. Clearly marking it with more orange tape, Whitman glanced at Julie, who appeared to be in shock.

Whitman put his arm around Julie's shoulder. "Are you OK, hon?" Julie nodded. "I know I should feel relieved, but I'm… just numb."

"That's normal, sweetie," he said. "You just need some time to work through this. We all do. What about you Shawn, you OK?"

"It's really her," Shawn said as tears streaked down her cheeks. "You were right, Julie! You were right."

76

Memorial Service for Local Teen Held
35 Years After Abduction

Lansing State Journal
Dec. 29, 2007

On Shawn Deerfield's arm just above her elbow is a tattoo that on first inspection looks like a mistake: "Allways Remembered," it reads.

The misspelling is no accident.

"That's how Bev spelled it in her diary," Deerfield said, speaking of her older sister Beverly, who was abducted and killed at the age of 18 in 1972—and whose disappearance remained a mystery until this year.

Beverly Deerfield's story is a long and complicated one that spans more than three decades and initially left 1972 investigators clueless. The case was officially re-opened earlier this month by retired Michigan State Police Detective Alan Whitman. Through what only can be described as "divine intervention," Whitman became acquainted with Beverly's niece, Julie Deerfield. Through her psychic abilities, Julie was able to lead Whitman to her aunt's body.

"These last few weeks have been surreal," Shawn,

48, said at Logan Funeral Home in Sunfield. "I woke up this morning and thought this doesn't seem possible. I never thought we'd see this day."

For Shawn and dozens of other mourners who milled quietly about the funeral home, Saturday's farewell was a mixture of devastation and relief.

With all the pieces of the puzzle in place, niece Julie managed to do what many others had failed to do in the past: bring closure to a mystery long unsolved, and bring her aunt home.

Beverly's decayed remains were found in a shallow grave in Eaton County, near the wooded Shimnecon region, an ancient burial ground for Michigan's early Native Americans. DNA testing positively identified the teen.

Beverly will be buried alongside her father and other relatives at Meadowbrook Cemetery in a quaint plot near the very place she first went missing.

"It still doesn't feel quite complete," Shawn said. "But at least now we know what happened."

Beverly's story is one of gut-wrenching mystery and perseverance. Investigators from Eaton, Ionia and Barry counties gathered to pay their respects to a girl they never met.

"It's odd. I've never seen something end like this," said Daniel Hoffmann, retired sheriff of Eaton County. "The miracle of Alan Whitman and Julie Deerfield connecting in the first place is truly remarkable, and the fact that Julie's gift has brought so much closure to so many—it's all a lot to take in."

Pictures of Beverly's childhood were posted around

the funeral home: Beverly eating in her highchair; playing goofy games with her sibling, Shawn; and posing with her father with a ribbon she had won at the 4-H fair.

Draped across her casket was a blanket that read, "When someone you love becomes a memory, the memory becomes a treasure."

Meryl Deerfield said laying her oldest daughter to rest around the holidays was a fitting time, as it was one of the hardest times of the year for her family to be without her.

"This is the first time she's been with us for the holidays in a very long time," she said, dabbing a tear. "Thanks to Julie, she's actually home."

Printed in the United States
By Bookmasters